Courthouse Rebel: A Former Prosecutor Strikes a Blow for Justice

P. A. Moore

This work is a book of fiction. Names, characters, places and incidents are either the product of the author's imagination or are used fictitiously. Any resemblance to actual persons, living or dead, business establishments, events or locales is entirely coincidental.

Publisher: P.A. Moore, Inc.

Published in the United States of America

ISBN-13: 978-1492973782

This novel celebrates the real Courthouse Rebel, who risked all by standing up as a witness to the truth.

The author thanks her family for their ongoing love and support while she writes about America's justice system, and further thanks those in her critique group – Jim Satterfield, Deb Burke, Kathy Dunnehoff, Karen Wills, Bev Zierow, Dan Vogel, Randy Bekkedahl, and Michelle Luke, who, during various phases of production, added invaluable insights to the plot and characters. Thanks also to members of Authors of the Flathead, a writers' organization who share their time and talents with local scribes. A special thanks to Tom and Betty Kuffel for their expert assistance in all things techy and to Becky Lomax, the best copy editor in the business.

Courthouse Rebel

Table of Contents

PART ONE..1

PROLOGUE 2

CHAPTER ONE 4

CHAPTER TWO..9

CHAPTER THREE.. 15

CHAPTER FOUR 24

CHAPTER FIVE 30

CHAPTER SIX.. 36

CHAPTER SEVEN 45

CHAPTER EIGHT... 53

CHAPTER NINE... 59

CHAPTER TEN... 65

PART TWO... 71

CHAPTER ELEVEN 72

CHAPTER TWELVE 80

CHAPTER THIRTEEN... 86

CHAPTER FOURTEEN.. 94

CHAPTER FIFTEEN 100

CHAPTER SIXTEEN.. 108

CHAPTER SEVENTEEN....................................... 115

CHAPTER EIGHTEEN 127

PART THREE 139

CHAPTER NINETEEN... 140

CHAPTER TWENTY 150

CHAPTER TWENTY-ONE 160

CHAPTER TWENTY-TWO................................... 169

CHAPTER TWENTY-THREE 171

CHAPTER TWENTY-FOUR..180

CHAPTER TWENTY-FIVE...190

CHAPTER TWENTY-SIX 201

CHAPTER TWENTY-SEVEN...209

CHAPTER TWENTY-EIGHT 219

CHAPTER TWENTY-NINE 229

CHAPTER THIRTY 239

CHAPTER THIRTY-ONE 244

EPILOGUE...251

ABOUT THE AUTHOR..256

BONUS PREVIEW 257

COURTHOUSE COWBOYS 257

CHAPTER ONE..269

CHAPTER TWO 276
_Toc369361278

PART ONE

1986 - 1988

In the fictional county of Fairfax, California,
before those in law enforcement surrendered to political
correctness.

PROLOGUE

Berkeley, California July 1986
The Gilman Street Saloon

VODKA ON THE ROCKS, A FAVORITE OF SERIOUS ALCOHOLICS, sat on a cocktail napkin before J.T. "Cowboy" Jeffers. He raised the dewy glass, took a gulp, and swiveled on his barstool to address a fellow patron to his left. Cigarette smoke clouded any view of the front door, reflected in the mirror behind a multitude of liquor bottles.

The bartender, a large tattooed fellow weighed down by cheap gold chains, placed the vodka bottle back in the well. He noted that Cowboy, like the other regulars at this hole-in-the-wall neighborhood bar, sat on the same stool every night, ordered the same drink, and repeated the same war stories from his days fighting in Vietnam.

Plying a large-breasted blonde in front of him with more booze, the bartender hoped he'd get lucky at the end of this shift. Only a few minutes past midnight, the remaining two hours until closing portended a slow crawl of the clock. Even then, given the customers' inebriated states, getting the dozen or so barflies to depart would be tough.

As the front door opened, he watched three newcomers enter. A man with a limp stood near the entrance, another walked to one end of the copper-clad bar, and the third, the smallest and oldest of the three, approached Cowboy at his seat by the cash register.

The bartender's sphincter tightened as the little man withdrew a .38 snub-nosed revolver, sticking it behind Cowboy's right ear.

He heard the gunman utter one simple command. "Give me your wallet."

Cowboy raised his glass as if in a toast and growled, "Fuck you."

Without hesitation, the robber pulled the trigger, blowing a crater in Cowboy's head.

The bartender's bladder released the beer he'd swallowed earlier, spreading a warm spot over the front of his jeans. As the small robber-now-killer moved down the line of customers, they forked over their wallets, watches, and jewelry. Before the three criminals fled with their loot, they snatched a bundle of cash from the register.

The entire event comprised no more than five minutes.

Yet the long-term consequences of Cowboy's death—from the cops' investigation to the District Attorney's strategy used in the killer's trial—knocked California's criminal justice system right on its ass.

CHAPTER ONE

Berkeley, California
July 1987

SHORTLY AFTER COWBOY DEPARTED THE PLANET, Berkeley police officers arrived on scene, led by Detective Kevin Dorrian and Sergeant Jane Moore. They helped the county coroner bag Cowboy's body in preparation for transport to the morgue. Since the entry hole in the dead man's skull had no corresponding exit path, they hoped an autopsy would provide ballistics information allowing them to trace a gun to the shooter.

The remaining bar patrons, each scared shitless, had done their best to recall anything that might help point to the killer's identity. Unfortunately, with their blood alcohol levels shooting far above the legal limit, none could describe a single feature of the three robbers—not their hair color, height, weight, clothing, presence of a beard or mustache, or even a vocal tone.

On the other hand, the bartender, who was slightly more lucid than his clientele, recollected enough details for a sketch artist to produce a composite drawing of each man. Yet as artistically accurate as the likenesses appeared, no suspects emerged.

Now, twelve months later, the solution to Cowboy's murder remained as elusive as it had on the day he died.

"Jesus, we need a break in this case." Kevin screeched to a halt as he slammed on the horn in his unmarked patrol car, scaring the crap out of a jaywalking gangbanger. Yelling "Asshole!" out the window, he added, "Just one decent clue that points us to Cowboy's killer."

Jane clutched the "Oh Shit" handle above her passenger window. "Yeah, well, could you slow down while we wait for that miracle?"

Kevin shot her his women-drivers-are-weenies look. "Listen, I got a tip yesterday that a Mexican babe may know something about the Gilman Street homicide, and she'll be at

Sonny B's funeral tomorrow." When Jane winced at his use of the word "babe," he laughed. "Her name is Carmen something. I think we should go undercover and see if we can ID her. Maybe even talk to her." He parked the car so he could grab some coffee at Peet's.

Jane, five months pregnant with her third child, unhooked her seatbelt. "Damn it!" Her holstered Glock tangled in the buckle. "You want me to go undercover as what? A beached whale?" She gingerly withdrew her loaded weapon. "Just get me a hot chocolate, Inspector Gadget, while I think up a disguise." Then she headed for the nearest ladies' room as Kevin got in line.

What they had after a year, Kevin mused, was exactly nothing, unless he counted the composite drawings of the three robbers. Yesterday's tipster, however, thought one of the sketches resembled Joey Hernandez, a local punk known for sloppy thefts. The woman who might attend Sonny B's funeral was reputedly Joey's lover. Kevin wanted to show her the sketch. He didn't expect her to rat out her boyfriend, but he'd watched enough lying witnesses to know when they recognized a suspect.

If Carmen recognized Hernandez, Kevin had his first lead. He could run surveillance on Joey and his known associates. With a little luck, he'd match up two more suspects with the faces in the other drawings. Then he'd get the Gilman Street bartender to pick out the three suspected perps from a lineup, dig up some physical evidence, maybe even the revolver, and take the whole mess to the DA for charges.

Yeah, that'll happen. Kevin carried the drinks outside where Jane waited for him under a shaded table.

The sergeant licked whipped cream from the top of her chocolate. "A gravedigger."

Kevin squinted at her. "Say what?"

"I'll go as a gravedigger tomorrow. They wear baggy overalls. I'll cover the burial site while you go to the church." She slurped her drink. "A Hells Angels' funeral. Haven't been to one of those in a while."

Kevin nodded. "Sounds like a plan. You know, Jane, maybe you should stay inside for the next few months, ride a desk until the little guy shows up."

"I appreciate your concern, partner." Jane stood, stretching her back. "Yet why do I suspect you want me out, so you can adopt the newest recruit? What's her name? Cupcake? Muffin?"

Kevin smirked. "Yeah, right. Like Meg wouldn't kick my skinny ass back to Ireland if I cheated on her." He tossed his cup in the trash. "C'mon. Let's roll through the projects and look for something fun to do this afternoon."

* * *

The next day, Kevin got more than a lucky break. He found Carmen, the Mexican babe, grieving over Sonny B's open coffin. Donning a straight face, Kevin offered Carmen his condolences even though he didn't give a shit that an ice cream truck had crushed the meth-dealing asshole on his Harley. However, as a fellow biker, Kevin managed a sad look for the loss of a great machine.

Before the service began, Kevin squeezed in next to Carmen. He charmed her with his Irish bullshit and offered her a ride to the cemetery. He chatted with her in the car before he parked near Sonny's burial plot, where he spotted a bulbous maintenance worker standing by with her gravedigger shovel. As people gathered, Kevin mentioned he was a cop who'd known Sonny B through mutual motorcycle connections.

When Carmen didn't recoil at his law enforcement job, he figured he'd go for it. "You said earlier you worked at a beauty parlor near El Cerrito. You remember that murder at the Gilman Street Saloon last year?"

The woman shifted away from him, just a few inches, as they stood in the crowd awaiting the arrival of the hearse. She nodded. "Yeah, so what?"

Kevin raised his aviator sunglasses, glanced around, and lowered his voice. "I'm just wondering, you being in business in the area and all, if maybe you've seen this guy." He offered her the artist's sketch of Joey Hernandez.

Carmen's eyes widened when she took the piece of paper. "Maybe. Why?"

"Nothing serious. I think he may have witnessed somebody coming out of the bar, that's all. I just want to talk to him. Pick his brain a little." He shrugged as if it were no big deal.

Hesitating, the woman sighed. "Maybe it looks like Joey Hernandez, but he isn't the one who killed that guy in the bar. Tom Seavers shot him."

Kevin nodded at her to continue. *This is way too easy.*

Carmen explained she'd been at a motel with Hernandez and Seavers a few hours after the homicide. The two men had argued because Seavers killed a guy earlier in a bar robbery, and Hernandez wanted nothing to with it. Then Seavers pulled out a "little gun" and shot at Hernandez, who ducked. Angered by the gunshot blast, the motel manager threw them out and called the police. Carmen gave the responding officers a statement the next morning. She'd forgotten about it until Kevin mentioned the murder.

"Carmen, if we arrest Seavers, I may need you to testify at the preliminary hearing." Kevin pressed on.

She looked at the motley group of pallbearers about to lower Sonny's casket into the ground. "I ain't sayin' nothin' about Joey, but I'll talk about Seavers if I have to."

Kevin thanked her, exchanged a slight nod with his gravedigger partner, and left the group of Hells Angels to smoke their joints at Sonny B's graveside.

Now he needed to get a recent photo of Seavers, compare it to the artist's sketch of the other two men, and arrange for the bartender to identify Seavers in a photo lineup. His heart raced as he picked up Jane at a pre-determined corner a few blocks south. "We've got him."

She stretched the seatbelt over her belly. "Maybe, but don't get all happy until the bartender makes a positive ID." Jane pulled a tissue from her pocket and wiped her brow, exhausted from walking the short distance to meet Kevin. "Does that lady have any clue that her loverboy goes down when Seavers goes down?" She shook her head. "Cripes, women are stupid around men."

Kevin pulled into the Berkeley PD lot. "I told her we only wanted Hernandez as a witness. I never said he was a suspect. Doesn't matter. Once the DA subpoenas her, we'll get her to court and make sure she repeats what she just told me."

Jane struggled out of the car. Over her shoulder she wheezed, "You got an address for Carmen whoever she is, right? And her last name?"

Kevin turned away, so Jane wouldn't notice him mouth the word, "Fuck!" As a matter of fact, he'd forgotten to get Carmen's address and last name. Unwilling to admit his mistake, Kevin entered the building to pull Seavers' old files.

CHAPTER TWO

Fairfax County District Attorney's Office
November 1987

JACK DEFALCO, A FAIRFAX COUNTY DEPUTY DISTRICT ATTORNEY, scratched out a trial memo at his government-issued metal desk. Heavy footsteps preceded his office mate, who plowed through their door, tossing a thick file on Jack's desk.

Bobby Erickson grinned. "You can thank me later with a bottle of Crown Royal, my man."

Jack glanced at the file labeled *People v. Thomas Seavers and Joey Hernandez*. "And I would do that because—?"

"Because I just talked the boss into assigning you your very first death penalty case, buddy. And it's a slam dunk out of Berkeley."

Jack blinked back at Bobby's smirk. "Are you shitting me? You actually got me a capital case?" Jack's own grin slashed across his face.

The DA's office recently had established the capital crimes unit, a group of elite trial lawyers known for winning tough convictions. Getting selected meant Jack had just hit the big time among the one hundred fifty attorneys in his office. Fifteen years into his career, Jack's ambitions reached no higher than death penalty trials. Sending killers to the gas chamber glimmered as his ultimate rush.

Squeezing behind his desk, Bobby grabbed a dummy hand grenade that served as a paperweight.

Jack cleared his throat. "So, when you say this case is a slam dunk, what aren't you telling me?"

Bobby pulled the pin on the grenade and tossed it at Jack, who caught it with one hand. "No such thing as a perfect case, D-man. There's an ID issue in that one. The usual. Three robbers. One shooter. Who's the killer? But you've got the bartender as an eyewitness and some beaner chick who can finger Seavers pulling the trigger." Bobby leaned back in his chair. "Don't worry. It's solid."

The two friends had divided the small office in half, desks facing the door, so each could sit with his back to the window and still see anyone coming down the hall. Situational awareness mattered to Bobby and Jack because the pair, through stunning political incorrectness, caused more management problems than the other 400 or so employees combined. Those in charge often commented that no one besides Jack could stand rooming with Bobby, and no one else in the office wanted to room with Jack.

Jack grimaced at Bobby's latest outrage hanging in a noose from the ceiling in the corner—a black, life-sized, three-year-old doll, dressed in gang clothes, and sporting an Afro. Bobby's racism raged far hotter than the prejudice held by most of his white colleagues. The doll symbolized Bobby's enmity toward criminals in Fairfax County, the majority being poverty-ridden African Americans. While he claimed to tolerate "negroes" in general, disparaging only those who raped, pillaged, and plundered, the word "nigger" flew from his lips as often as "fuck." Or "cunt" to describe uppity women.

Behind the doll he'd named "Boon," as his shorthand comparison of blacks to baboons, Bobby covered the wall in framed, colorful Gauguin prints depicting brown, bare-breasted island women. Jack knew that Bobby, an art lover since his days at the University of San Francisco, stared at the pictures whenever he needed a reminder that beauty existed somewhere in the world.

Jack gazed at the lynched latex child. "When are you taking down Boon, by the way? The boss ordered you to cut him loose last week."

Bobby held out his hand to receive Jack's grenade toss. "I'll cut him down when you remove the body of Christ hanging over our door. That crucifix offends my delicate sensibilities." He laughed as he reached for his coffee mug. "Just because you studied to be a priest for seven years, doesn't mean you get to play on my Catholic guilt."

Jack shook his head. His years at St. Joseph's seminary had taught him discipline, along with Latin and Greek. His side of the office stood in stark contrast to Bobby's vivid imagery.

Instead of art, Jack hung up the most important document in his life, his ticket to practice law. His desk held one framed photograph of his wife and daughter, a Waterford crystal pen set, his grandfather's French carriage clock, and an in-box stacked neatly with files.

Both men professed the same ingrained Catholic beliefs, wore similar dark suits over crisp white shirts sporting red ties, and swilled the same crappy institutional coffee. They loved their families, fanatically followed the Raiders and Niners, and commiserated over a lack of decent food in the vicinity of the courthouse. Their personalities, however, distinguished one from the other.

Since Bobby Erickson despised humanity and crooks in particular, vile comments shot out of his mouth unfiltered by his otherwise intelligent brain. A sharp wit, shit-eating grin, blond straw hair fringing a bald head, and vivid blue eyes each emphasized his Celtic heritage. His college basketball career had trained him to keep in shape, so he ran his big body over city streets every morning, regardless of the intensity of his hangover.

From early morning until lunch, Bobby labored without stopping. He finished each workday at noon, when he left for The Fat Lady to consume a bottle or two of cheap chardonnay and an order of grilled fish, no sauce.

Jack Defalco, like his Spartan desk and wall, epitomized the expression "anal-retentive tight-ass." He, too, detested bad guys, but not because of their ethnicity. Jack divided the world into good and evil, and since, by definition, scumbags fell in the latter category, they incurred his full wrath.

Rather than coasting after a booze-filled lunch, Jack ran the lake, drank diet cola, and spent the afternoons attacking his cases with the precision of a surgeon. Emotion never factored into his work, even while watching autopsies of murdered children. The priest factory, as he referred to St. Joseph's, had bled compassion from his veins. "Never get attached," the prelates had intoned, so he'd become a stoic observer.

At five feet seven, Jack's lean frame sported no body fat. His dark Mediterranean skin, inherited from his mother, contrasted with his own blue eyes and slightly crooked white teeth. Forty years of hard living hadn't added any gray to his thick, black hair.

Like Bobby, Jack avoided fat people like they spread bubonic plague. Three years earlier, when his wife, pregnant with their daughter, ballooned to the size of a rhino, Jack buried himself in baseball and beer to await the day she'd deflate.

Studying to be a Catholic priest, followed by two years at U.C. Berkeley during the height of Free Love, had left Jack with a flummoxed worldview. His Democratic Party affiliation interfered with his tough on crime, jail-criminals-for-life, or better yet, kill-them-all philosophy. His pot-smoking, cocaine-sniffing days stood long forgotten as he maligned addicts who shuffled daily through the Fairfax County courthouse.

Although Jack railed against the Church for its institutional refusal to modernize ancient rules, he nevertheless attended Mass every Sunday. He'd not only placed a crucifix above their office door, but over every entrance to his home. Like his parents, he hung photos of President Kennedy and Pope John XXIII on the wall in his den. Unlike his parents, he eschewed mounting a holy water font in his home's foyer.

Clothed in designer suits from The Tailored Man, Jack sipped, rather than swilled, fine wine from Lalique stemware. He polished his wingtips every night before retiring, had the laundry put extra starch in his shirts so they never wilted during trial, and kept his nails clipped and clean, especially after wrenching on his old Volkswagen's engine.

As he had during childhood, Jack spent his precious leisure time waterskiing at his family's vacation home, a shabby doublewide nestled in a rundown, lakeside trailer park two hours north of the city.

Known variously as the Poison Dwarf, the Gnat, or the Scorpion, Jack stayed true to his reputation as a mean-as-a-snake, go-for-the-jugular viper that kept people at bay with an invisible kryptonite field. Laughing with someone, he could switch, lightening-fast, to the person's worst critic.

To know Jack was to walk on eggshells. Except for his wife and a few close friends like Bobby, no one volunteered to be Jack's buddy. Yet everyone wanted to sit next to him at a dinner party since his most outstanding attribute, enhanced by his cynicism, was a rapier sense of humor that left people wheezing and teary-eyed. Accordingly, proving the adage that no one is all bad, he maintained a healthy fan base in his office and community.

Jack ran fingers through the top of his hair. "Listen, Bobby. The boss also ordered us to take down our homicide photos on Friday afternoons, so the janitor can clean. Apparently the guy took one look at them," he gestured to the front wall near the door, "and nearly heaved."

Bobby shrugged as he perused the pictures of burned corpses, blood spatter, and pathologists' headshots of dead people without brains. "That guy's a fuckin' pussy." He stood, grabbing the latest edition of *American Rifleman*. "Besides, we need those to prepare for trial. If he can't handle it, screw him."

With that pronouncement, Bobby left for his daily dump. Every morning around the same time, Jack watched him lumber out the door to park his ass on a mildewed porcelain pot, reading beneath a decapitated, plastic horse head. The horse head, a solitary remnant of little Claire Defalco's beloved Bob the Wonder Horse, fell off during Claire's last ride, so father Jack had retrieved it, securing it with molly-bolts to the bathroom wall.

Bobby turned back at the door. "Oh, by the way. Berkeley PD lost all the physical evidence in that case. Might be a hurdle." Another shrug. "And don't forget dinner at our house Friday at six. Bring Claire. She can play with The Lunker."

Only a guy like Bobby could nickname his little girl The Lunker.

Jack watched him leave, walked across the office, and closed the door. He noted the names of six other deputy DAs scrawled on the *Seavers-Hernandez* file, and that Bobby had orchestrated the homicide charges when he'd been assigned to the Berkeley office.

Jack now understood why he'd been gifted with his first capital trial. With an ID issue and no physical evidence, the case howled like the poisoned dog it was, a dying dog, a total loser. Bobby Erickson knew it and had passed it off, six other deputies caught on and pushed it away, and now this huge, steaming turd of a death penalty case sat in Jack Defalco's pocket.

Foisting it off, however, wasn't part of Jack's game plan.

CHAPTER THREE

Fairfax County Suburbia
That evening, November 1987

DONNING HIS FAMILY MAN PERSONA, Jack sauntered in from his garage whistling Jimmy Buffet's "Cheeseburgers in Paradise," briefcase in hand. He swept up a giggling, three-year-old Claire, planted kisses on her chubby cheeks, and sought out his wife in their bedroom. He found her folding laundry while she listened to audiotapes from her civil procedure class.

"Hello, sweet pea." He kissed her before he rolled out his big news. "Guess who got his first capital case assignment this afternoon?"

Paige Defalco stared at her spouse. "Really?" She grinned, raising her palm to return his high five.

Jack whirled in a circle, à la James Brown, and pumped his fist. "This is it, babe. My big chance to show those fuckers what I can really do in trial."

Ever the dutiful mom, Paige checked the hallway to make sure Claire now played out of earshot. "Language? We're trying not to swear, remember?"

As Jack removed his jacket and tie, Paige neatly tucked the towels into thirds. "So, tell me about the case."

The Defalcos had separate-but-equal closets in their 1970's suburban rancher, both small, with sliding doors, and room for only the most important hanging garments. Jack organized his closet by shirt type (dress or polo), sub-typed by color. Nary a wrinkle creased his suits, slacks, or ties, nor a speck of dust marred his neatly aligned, polished shoes. He stacked his old and tattered tee shirts, sweats, and workout clothes in their respective dresser drawers, a testament to his meticulous organization.

Paige preferred hooks to hangers and the closet shelf or floor for her tossed array of Levi's and sweatshirts. As an unemployed first-year law student, she often remarked that nobody gave a rat's ass what she wore. She was the oldest student by a decade and the only one with a small child accompanying her to class. After years working in suits, heels, and stockings, she gladly donned her hippie garb every morning before she and Claire went to school.

Jack glanced at his wife. At thirty-three, Paige wore little makeup, braided her red hair in a single plait down her back, and her lean frame rose several inches taller than her husband's. She deferred to him on some issues due to his age and legal experience. About housekeeping, not so much— hence the separate closets.

Paige had given up her obsessive cleaning habits after Claire's birth because she couldn't keep up with the vomit, spilled milk, scattered food, and mountain of toys filling the family room. Even the dog couldn't consume the edible portions of mess at a rate fast enough to stay ahead of the ants marching in regiments throughout the house.

Jack finished his brief dissertation of trial facts, gleaned from reading the case summary on a blue index card attached to the file. He slid a sweatshirt over his head, the sleeves long ago cut off to keep him cool while working in the yard.

He turned to her. "So, what do you think?"

After seven years of marriage, Jack wanted her to boost his excitement about the new trial.

She turned to him, frowning. "I think if Bobby dumped it, and six other guys dumped it, you're in deep shit, honeybun. No physical evidence and an ID issue, with an old, deaf guy as the supposed shooter?" She shook her braid. "I may only be a first-year law student, but it sounds like a piece of crap. Maybe you should push it on to the next guy in line."

Buttoning the fly on his faded jeans, Jack laughed. His eyes glittered like a heroin addict at a methadone clinic.

"Are you nuts? I want this case, Paige. It's my ticket to the top, to a promotion to Senior Deputy Two. Do you know how much more money we'd make with that?" He arranged his folded laundry into neat stacks in his drawers. "Besides, you know me. I love a challenge. So what if I don't have the evidence or a solid ID? I can still win it, and if I don't, there's no downside because nobody, including the boss, expects me to succeed." He ran a brush through his hair.

Both parents turned when Claire ran down the hall toward them, eyes huge. "Daddeee…up!" She jumped into thin air, only absolute trust separating daughter and father. Jack caught her around her tiny waist and hugged her to him.

"Daddy, you're smashing me!" Claire squirmed. "C'mon! Time to watch Big Bird."

The two trotted off to view, for the millionth time, a giant yellow avian travel through *Sesame Street*. Settling on the couch, Jack caught his shoulder angel whispering, "There's always a downside, bucko."

He ignored her.

* * *

The following morning Jack entered the DA's law library to gloat about his new capital case, not an easy brag since only Bobby and a few female deputies sat around the large conference table.

"D-man!" Bobby rattled the *San Francisco Chronicle* as he flipped through the front page. "What's up, buddy? What did your lovely wife think about your new death penalty assignment?"

Jack grabbed some coffee before he sat across the table from his office mate. "She thinks it's a piece of shit, actually. No physical evidence, shaky ID, pitiful old and deaf defendant." He grinned as Bobby looked up from his article.

"Well, what the fuck does she know? One, she's a woman—," Bobby glanced around at the women lawyers, who stopped chatting to glare at him. "Two, she's a first-year student at a second-rate law school, your alma mater, in that faggot-infested city across the bay." He swilled coffee from his own cup. "And three, yeah, the case has a few glitches, but so what? It's a capital case, D-man. Your ticket to the big times."

Jack held up his palm. "Got it. You asked me what Paige thought, and I told you. And she loves you, too, by the way. We'll be there Friday for dinner." Jack knew, despite Bobby's overt sexism, and every other ism, that Paige enjoyed the man's gallows humor—in limited doses. She also liked his wife and kids.

Jack cleared his throat. "Bobby, did you know when you gave me the *Seavers-Hernandez* case that it was assigned to

Solomon's court?"

"Yep, and that's another plus for you, pal. Solomon P, whiny little Hebrew that he is, may be opposed to the death penalty, but he seems to have no problem sending convicted killers to the gas chamber."

The two prosecutors loved Judge Solomon P. Green. They'd known him for years as both a criminal defense attorney to the rich and as a Superior Court jurist. That the old man attended high holidays at a local temple within hours of sentencing someone to death seemed not to bother his admirers—or him.

From the other end of the library table, a tall lesbian chimed in. "Bobby, explain to me again why neither I, nor any other woman, has been considered for a capital case, yet Jack gets one before me, even though I'm senior to him."

Jack lowered his head, awaiting Bobby's blowback.

Looking directly into the woman's eyes, Bobby answered, "Because, Ms. Mackinaw, Jack is a better trial lawyer than you'll ever dream of being. And just maybe, if you weren't so busy entertaining your fellow clit-lickers, you'd have time to learn a few things from the men around here who know how to deliver verdicts—along with real orgasms, unlike the ones you chicks offer with your snap-on tools."

Bobby returned to the *Chronicle* as Jack cringed. Deputy DA Janet Mackinaw huffed out of the law library, no doubt on her way to the boss' office to register a complaint.

Not that it would do any good.

The man in charge always excused Bobby's diatribes, and nobody, it seemed, had the guts to sue Fairfax County. Besides, Bobby had dirt on most of the senior lawyers, the boss included. They knew he'd expose them to the public, and to their wives, if ever they tried to discipline him. Bobby operated in a golden cloud, the owner of endless get-out-of-jail-free cards.

Another female deputy sighed as she shook her head. "Jesus, Erickson. Is there anything you won't say? A single topic that is off-limits for you?" Jack knew Bobby adored this woman because she was built like a pin-up girl, screwed like a bunny, kept her blonde locks long and flowing, and wore her skirts short.

"Maggie, darlin', for you, I'll try to hold back." He leaned over, grabbed a fat strand of her tresses, and sucked on it.

She batted him away and stood. "You're incorrigible, Bobby. Seriously, one of these days…" She sighed, shook her head, and left the library in disgust, but not before casting a pointed look at Jack.

Bobby grinned. "God, I love that broad. If the Bitch of Belfast wouldn't slice me up and cook me in a stew, I'd have my way with Maggie Tornow."

The Bitch of Belfast, a.k.a. Bobby's wife, managed to keep Bobby on the straight and narrow, despite his outrageous flirting with the girls. As far as Jack knew, Bobby had never strayed from his spouse.

The last woman at the table, a short, curly-haired brunette, gathered her legal pad and pen into her briefcase and watched Bobby resume reading the world news. "Don't you ever worry about Karma? I mean, this shit's gonna come back to haunt you in your next life." She rose from her chair, to her full five-foot height, and sunk herself with a final query. "Think about it, Bobby. If you could come back as anything in the world, what would you be?"

Without missing a beat, still reading his paper, Bobby replied, "A whale, with a forty-foot tongue and an air hole in the top of my head, so I never have to come up for air."

The brunette took a second to absorb Bobby's cunnilingus reference before she, too, stormed down the hall.

Jack rubbed his eyes. "Where do you come up with that crap? What happens in your brain before you talk, Erickson?"

Before Bobby could answer, Rick Peters, the Chief Assistant DA, walked in. Ichabod Crane had nothing on this guy for height, wispy hair, bony frame, or missing chin. As second-in-command, Peters often got the Bobby Erickson cleanup detail.

He stared through thick lenses at Bobby. "About Janet Mackinaw and the dyke comments—?"

Bobby rolled his eyes. "That snatch has no sense of humor. None of them do around here."

Peters leaned on the back of a chair. "Listen. I'm getting tired of covering your ass, Erickson. So is everyone else. Just tone it down around the women. How tough is that?"

Bobby's face colored as he stood. "Peters, you wimp-ass, Ninja Turtle-looking reprobate, you couldn't talk to a woman if she had her mouth wrapped around your dick. Now get the fuck out of my way."

After Bobby cleared the door into the hallway, Peters looked at Jack, but his perpetual bland expression didn't change. "Defalco, if you don't do something about Bobby, the boss will, and it won't be funny."

Jack grabbed more coffee and headed toward the library door. "Rick, if you want a keeper for Bobby, you're looking at the wrong guy. Besides, he has a point. You do kind of look like a Ninja Turtle."

Whistling, Jack sauntered toward his office, unaware of the red hue creeping up Rick Peters' possibly retractable neck.

* * *

Looking over the city of Fairfax from his eleventh floor window, Jack considered what sort of jurors would vote to fry Tom Seavers.

Men, yes. Drunks, definitely, and preferably ones who drank in bars instead of at home. He made a note to run criminal checks on the jury panel to ferret out which people had DUI convictions. Anyone who drank and drove most likely imbibed at his favorite neighborhood tavern and would avenge the murder of Cowboy Jeffers.

Jack's secretary buzzed the intercom. "Judge Green on line one."

"Thanks." He clicked the line to reach Solomon. "What's up, Your Honor?"

Solomon coughed before inhaling on a cigarette. "Jack, I know you've got the *Seavers* case, and it's your first capital jury. I'm sure Bobby's told you how it works, but I want to make sure you don't fuck it up. No fat people, lots of Asians, and no Jews. Come down here at four." The line went dead.

No Jews? Jack recalled Bobby saying no decent trial lawyer left a Jewish person on a death case since they'd never sentence anyone to the gas chamber, a reaction to the

Holocaust. But to have Solomon bring it up before trial? Private conversations between a judge and counsel were strictly forbidden by the ethics code. Collusion between them to select a conviction-prone jury could cost Jack his precious ticket to practice law.

His office door opened and closed. He watched as Maggie Tornow parked her luscious body in a wooden witness chair. She crossed her long legs, showing plenty of thigh below the hem of her short skirt. Jack's gaze moved from that patch of creamy skin to Maggie's cleavage, gaping from her too tight white blouse, and finally to her blue eyes.

The younger deputy raised her palm to him. "Save it. I'm not here to beg. You've made it clear you're not interested."

Jack eased back into his chair. "I'm married, Maggie, and I'm not losing Paige and Claire for a roll in the hay with you, no matter how tempting the offer."

Maggie smiled. "Ah ha! So you are tempted?"

The comely Ms. Tornow had dogged him for months, freely offering her wares. She'd brought him a homemade cake for his birthday, spent hours watching him in trial, dusted his office, and once followed him into the men's room as she begged him for help on one of her cases. He didn't know if she hounded him because she actually wanted to sleep with him, or whether she thought sleeping with him would advance her budding career.

Jack sighed. "What do you want? Bobby will never let it go if he finds us alone in here when he comes back from court."

"So, Bobby's your new watchdog? Keeping you safe from the evil clutches of Maggie Tornow?" She shook her blond tresses and inhaled, further enhancing her sizable bosom. "Okay, look. I only came in here to warn you that Rick Peters is watching you. After all the crap you've dished his way, he's waiting for any excuse to jettison you from the courthouse."

Jack steepled his fingers. "And you know this…how?"

Maggie uncrossed her legs, allowing Jack a small glimpse of her pink panties. She drummed her nails on his desk as she sat forward. "Because I just overheard him telling the boss that you weren't ready for the big cases, and that if you screw up the *Seavers* case, they should send you back to Family Support. He really hates your guts."

Jack sat forward. "Yeah, well, Peters can pound salt. He hasn't won a trial in years, and now he's too chickenshit to try another one. Besides, who is he anyway? Just another flunky. He's got no power over me or anyone else in this office."

Maggie stood, brushing imaginary dust motes from her lap. "Maybe not now, but one day he'll buy his way to the top of this organization, and then we're all in trouble. You know how much money he has. His family owns most of South County."

She turned to leave but paused, looking at Jack over her shoulder, her long hair cascading down her back. "Seriously, watch your back."

Jack listened to Maggie click her stilettos down the old linoleum hall. Packing up his briefcase before he extinguished his office light, Jack considered Maggie's warning. He knew Peters hated him. The feeling was mutual. But he also knew that as long as he continued to win convictions, Peters couldn't touch him. Still, he decided to pay more attention to Peters and his cronies. If they wanted to play hardball, he'd slam their pitches out of the ballpark.

* * *

Jack rode the elevator to the tunnel that led from the courthouse to the underground garage where he parked his '69 Porsche 911S. His other car was a '65 Porsche. Each was white with black leather interior. Paid for in full, both were babied with hand waxing and expert tune-ups. Jack didn't just own his cars—he wore them like his designer suits. He couldn't explain his addiction to the brand, so he simply caved into it, like a woman who loved diamonds.

He thought of Paige's affection for her old Volkswagen bus. She didn't understand his love affair with sports cars but never complained about it. On the other hand, she'd kill him if he had a love affair with Maggie Tornow or any other woman. Yep, better to keep Mr. Happy tucked in his pants.

Making his way to his assigned stall, Jack noticed steam covering the interior windows in Rick Peters' battered station wagon. Intrigued, he walked over and peered inside. What he saw made him laugh aloud, then howl even harder after he rapped his huge college ring on the windshield. Rick Peters' startled expression as he looked up from suckling his secretary's exposed breasts was priceless. Old Rick and the lovely Roberta were doing the wild thing, right there in the parking lot, in the front seat of Rick's family vehicle. Jack wondered what Rick's wife would say about that, or Roberta's hulking police officer husband.

Looking directly at Peters, Jack winked and gave him a thumb's up.

Slipping into his Porsche, Jack acknowledged that the Fairfax County District Attorney's Office was a hotbed of immoral and outrageous behavior, wrought by a bunch of arrogant assholes who had too much power and excess time on their hands. He counted himself in that group.

However, at least now he had dirt on Rick Peters. Pay dirt. Just the sort of insurance he needed to keep Peters from fucking with him down the road, especially if he lost the *Seavers* case.

Downshifting as he left the garage, laying rubber as he turned onto the freeway that would take him to the comfort of his suburban sanctuary, Jack Defalco decided life was sweet. Now if he could just keep old Solomon from ruining his career.

CHAPTER FOUR

Fairfax Superior Court, Judge's Chambers
Four Months Later, February 1988

"YOU DON'T LISTEN, HOWARD, DO YOU? Bears and bulls get rich, and pigs go broke." Judge Solomon P. Green gestured to the wall behind him, toward a plaque proclaiming that personal philosophy. He puffed on an unfiltered Camel, swilled yet another toxic cup of county-issued coffee, while he observed the multiple lawyers milling around his chambers, throwing darts, arguing possible plea bargains, or reading the sports page.

Howard Evans, a former prosecutor turned private defense attorney, tossed his file on the judge's desk. "I'm not trying to be greedy, Judge. But you can do better than two years in custody for my guy. All he did was diddle a fifteen-year-old, and she happily agreed."

The judge blew a smoke ring as he squinted back at Evans. "Number one, she's only a kid, and your client is twenty-five. Number two, he impregnated her, and now that baby is going to cost the taxpayers a bundle while she works her way through the welfare system." Solomon ground out his smoke and reached for another. "Two years in custody, credit for time served, your guy will be back on the streets, fucking his brains out, in less than six months."

Howard shook his head, grabbed his file, and stomped out of the judge's chambers.

Solomon P, as Jack and Bobby called him, presided over his citadel with grace, humor, and an iron fist. He took comfort in his chambers' dark-paneled, 1930's molding, long black leather couch, matching chairs, enormous windows overlooking the lake, and forty-cup coffee pot sitting by the windowsill.

His crowded quarters resembled an Arabian marketplace full of men haggling over the price of a rug, or in Solomon's arena, someone's life. Not surprisingly, those who earned their way inside Solomon's inner sanctum referred to the judge's domain as "The Casbah." The judge loved that analogy as much as he reveled in the attention the lawyers and staff lavished on him.

Solomon P smiled when local prosecutors swore his middle initial stood for "prison," convinced Solomon hammered defendants by incarcerating them for decades. Defense attorneys pegged Solomon for the lightweight liberal he was, thus claiming the *P* represented "probation." Neither side had figured out Solomon's pattern of sentencing, let alone his paradoxical code of ethics.

Solomon knew all about wheeling and dealing legal cases. Fifteen years earlier, before Governor Newton had appointed him to the Fairfax County Superior Court, he'd practiced as a defense attorney, representing those who were dumb enough to get caught but rich enough to line Solomon's pockets with substantial cash. Back then, he'd even maintained a bayside bargaining table at Trader Vic's, the iconic Polynesian restaurant known for serving Mai Tais the old fashioned way, using Bacardi 151 rum.

In those days, members of the criminal bar had known Solomon as a tough negotiator, a small man with a penguin gait, and as a lawyer whose personal connections to the elected District Attorney provided his clients with a sharp advantage. Solomon and the DA had served overseas in the Korean War together, and their wives were best friends who shared an apartment during that war. Old friendships bought access that allowed him the freedom to demand light sentences for those bad guys rich and savvy enough to hire him. That he was Jewish while the DA was Mormon never factored into their relationship.

A loud thump brought Solomon back to the present. Coughing, he lit another cigarette. "Defalco, goddamn it, put down that bat before you kill somebody." The judge grabbed for his personally autographed Reggie Jackson slugger, normally kept in the closet of his spacious den of iniquity.

"Ah, c'mon, Judge. You never let us have fun anymore." Jack laughed, handing it over.

Setting the bat in the corner, Solomon admonished, "We're picking a jury in a death penalty case, remember?

Show some class, Defalco." He took a long drag on his cigarette before pointing it at Jack. "And since this is your first capital trial, and Tom Seavers' life is on the line, maybe you could show the appropriate amount of decorum beforehand."

Solomon had known Jack for years, their professional contact stemming from Solomon's days trying cases in the very courtroom over which he now presided. Solomon's own sons proved a sad disappointment to their father, so the judge viewed Jack as the offspring he should have had.

Bobby, once a regular guest at the Trader Vic's table, also rated high in Solomon's book. As a defense attorney, Solomon used to meet weekly with Bobby to dispose of multiple cases at a time. After a sober Solomon liquored Bobby up on Crown Royal, he'd move in for the kill, convincing Bobby to dismiss cases or reduce felonies to misdemeanors.

Afterward, surprised young deputy DAs had found notes in their files that eviscerated their cases by allowing the defendant to plead guilty to offenses far less serious than those with which they'd been charged. Each of those entries, authorized by Bobby, had shown a checkmark followed by the initials BE.

Ah, yes, Solomon smiled, *the good old days*.

Now, however, after fifteen years on the bench, he could no longer afford a table at Trader Vic's, or even dinner there. Still, life rolled along more easily as a judge. His appointment as a jurist had occurred in the usual way, through nepotism. One night, while sipping scotch in his home library, Solomon received a call from the governor's close associate asking him to represent a political aide caught with a young boy. Immediately, Solomon drove to the mountain community where the alleged assault had taken place, brokered a confidential disposition, shipped the offender off to a clinic, and collected his fee. All without one word of publicity or backlash on the governor, who, it turned out, planned to run for President of the United States.

In appreciation, the governor rewarded Solomon with any appointment to any bench in the state. Solomon had debated for all of five minutes before opting to accept an appointment in Fairfax County. No fool, he'd known his private law practice bordered on lethal, especially after his latest homicide case in which his client, a local Mafioso, had threatened to snuff Solomon's wife and three kids. By the grace of God, or so Solomon figured, he'd won an acquittal for that killer, but still needed to get away from Mafia scrutiny. Only two acceptable excuses permitted such a departure from the mob: death or appointment to the bench, the latter providing surety only if Solomon stayed away from federal court where most Mafia cases were prosecuted.

Since Solomon dreamed of dying from natural causes, he notified the governor's office of his choice. *Voila.* To the bafflement of the local bar association, the very conservative Republican governor appointed the most liberal criminal defense attorney in northern California to the next available superior court judgeship.

Solomon interrupted his ruminations to admonish Bobby. "Erickson, get your feet off my table. That belonged to my mother, bless her black-hearted soul." The judge often told tales of the late Mama Green's terrifying temper tantrums.

Bobby peered over the top of the *San Francisco Chronicle's* "Green Sheet," so named because the sports news contained thereon once was printed on green newspaper. Alas, when the cost of color grew greater than the paper's profits, they'd switched to beige. Still, the term "Green Sheet" remained in every loyal reader's vocabulary. Bobby lowered his feet.

Jack, meanwhile, found a Nerf basketball and threw it at the hoop on the back door leading out of the judge's chambers. "Hey, Scummus Tongus, what was the score in the Niners' game last night?"

Bobby, a.k.a. Scummus Tongus, for reasons apparent to all, set down the sports page. "Listen, Dinky Dickus, what difference could it possibly make? You bet against them in the pool yesterday. You should know by now they're unbeatable this season."

Solomon interrupted. "Alright, you two. Don't start. There are ladies present, and I'm not in the mood."

The judge, Jack, and Bobby looked to the lone female

attorney sitting in a chair by the window, who sat with her legs crossed, her expensive suit hugging her tiny frame and her blonde hair coiffed into a French twist on the back of her head. Women lawyers were few and far between in 1988, although their ranks were growing. In the early '70s, during the Defalco and Erickson law school era, only three females graced the lecture halls. Bobby often remarked that even after multiple martinis, those women still couldn't rate a two on a scale of ten.

Mary Jane O'Malley, however, the stunning female defense lawyer near the coffee pot, stood far above her courtroom-weary female colleagues. Never mind that Mary Jane and her law school sisters broke through the proverbial glass ceiling, empowering many more women to aspire to legal careers. Solomon, along with most men, looked no further than her breasts.

She returned the men's stares. "It's okay, Judge. I'm quite used to Bobby's filthy mouth and Jack's nasty sense of humor. How could we function in here without them verbally jerking off?"

True to form, Bobby moved toward her. "You're just jealous because I have a pud to pull, and you don't. And it's a big damned pecker, if I say so myself." He leered at her. "And I do." He moved in closer so that the front of his fly inched within range of her face. "Want a peek?"

She rolled her eyes as she sat further back in her chair. "Only if the judge has a magnifying glass I can borrow."

Jack grabbed Erickson's arm and pulled on the larger man. "Come on, Bobby. You've got to be in Department Seven in two minutes."

Solomon scratched the top of his large, balding pate. He knew Jack liked the lady, even dated her before he married Paige, but the judge also recognized Mary Jane had an explosive temper. The last thing he needed at the moment was a fight between Ms. O'Malley, the midget advocate, and Mr. Erickson, the massive ex-basketball star.

Solomon shook his head at Mary Jane, a silent admonishment to keep quiet while Jack ridded Solomon's chambers of her tormentor. Bobby, for his part, had the decency to apologize to her before he grabbed his coffee cup and left.

The judge looked at his watch to confirm it was 9:45—show time. He clapped his hands together, brushed ashes from his shirtfront, and stood as he grabbed for his black judicial robe. "That's it. Everybody out." Solomon pointed to the back door rather than the one that led into the courtroom where the press and public waited. "Except you, Defalco."

When his chambers cleared, old Solomon looked at Jack. "You need to get Bobby under control. This is 1988, for godsakes! Some woman is going to file a sexual harassment claim, or worse, and take away his license to practice. I don't want any part of it, you hear me?"

Jack hefted his trial box, filled to the top with neatly color-coded manila folders, and sighed. "Right. So what am I supposed to do? Nobody's ever been able to control Bobby, including his own wife. But I'll talk to him—again."

Solomon held open the door to the courtroom, allowing Jack to enter from chambers. "That's all I can ask. Now, let's get jury selection finished so we can start the trial. This *Seavers* case has been going on for two months, and the jurors are getting pissed."

"Judge, you set the precedent on how to select death penalty juries. You're the one whose ruling in the *Hovey* case took normal jury selection from two weeks to...shit, six months." Jack stared at the old man.

Solomon snapped the top clasp of his robe. "Yeah, well, it makes it fairer that way. Now, let's go, Defalco, or I'm getting out my bat."

CHAPTER FIVE

Fairfax County Superior Court
Courtroom of Solomon P. Green

WHEN JACK DEFALCO EMERGED FROM SOLOMON'S CHAMBERS, he smiled at the court clerk, nodded at the bailiff, but ignored the accused men sitting with their defense teams.

Due to a weird glitch in California's death penalty history, his office could charge the actual shooter, Thomas Seavers, with capital murder, but not Joey Hernandez, who'd only acted as an accomplice. Thus, Hernandez faced life in prison instead of the gas chamber. Nevertheless, the two sat in court as co-defendants, Seavers represented by two attorneys, Hernandez by one.

Dropping his trial box onto a scarred wooden table, the one closest to the jury box, Jack pulled out a Rolodex full of index cards. He'd written the name of every potential juror on one of the cards, along with facts about them that he'd gleaned from their jury questionnaires.

That wasn't the only information on which he relied. He'd run everyone through the local and national criminal justice systems to discover any criminal records, in particular, prior DUI convictions. He'd also sent his investigator to their neighborhoods to spy on them and interview anyone remotely connected to them who might be able to add to his data.

Access to such personal information, a job perk for prosecutors, remained unavailable to defense attorneys. The latter had neither sufficient investigative funds nor technical means to ferret out possible criminal histories. Jack figured skirting the ethics code to surreptitiously intrude on potential jurors' privacy was well worth the risk. He needed to cull out the weak links, the wounded wildebeests that might vote "not guilty" or refuse to impose a death sentence.

Over the last two months, as he, Solomon, and the defense attorneys individually interviewed each prospective juror, Jack rated them on a scale of zero to ten. Zero indicated "No way in hell would I let this person sit on my jury," and ten meant "Please, God, just let me get this one past the defense attorneys' challenge."

As a veteran trial jockey, Jack had prosecuted hundreds of criminals in as many jury trials. After fifteen years working as a deputy DA, he'd seen it all, but *Seavers* was his first death penalty case, and death, as the U.S. Supreme Court famously noted, was different. Each case had to be handled with kid gloves, from the DA's decision to seek execution to individual voir dire of the jury pool. Moreover, killing U.S. citizens required a two-phase trial, one to determine guilt and the other to impose an appropriate sentence, either life without possibility of parole or death.

Jack reminded himself that of the top lawyers in his office who made it onto the capital crimes team, Bobby was the only one who'd actually sent a defendant to the gas chamber. The boss didn't pay his troops to lose these cases, so those who failed found themselves charging misdemeanors in some far-flung corner of Fairfax County.

He shook off a wave of insecurity as Maggie Tornow's warning danced across his brain, reminding him to watch his back. Nothing would stop him from convicting Tom Seavers and sending him to hell via the green room at San Quentin State Prison. Especially some nitwit juror who couldn't vote for execution.

He recalled the judge's advice to toss off Jewish jurors. Jack hadn't decided whether or not to follow Solomon's wisdom. He rose as the judge entered the courtroom.

Let the games begin.

From his black leather chair, Solomon settled his microphone. "Places everyone. This court is again in session in the matter of *The People v. Thomas Seavers and Joey Hernandez*. The defendants and their attorneys are present along with the prosecutor. Bailiff, please seat our next jury candidate."

The bailiff returned with an older matronly woman sporting frizzy silver hair, makeup-free wrinkles, and a longish, billowing skirt that exposed her unshaved legs.

"Mrs. Friedman," Solomon intoned as he peered at her over his reading glasses, "welcome to Department Eleven." He waved a hand in Jack's direction. "This is Mr. Defalco, a prosecutor for the Fairfax County District Attorney's Office, representing the People of the State of California. The accused, Mr. Seavers, sits next to his defense attorneys, Mr. Parker Brolin and Mr. Mikel Moore. Mr. Hernandez, the other defendant, sits next to his attorney, Mr. Pete Kennedy."

Ever the critic of Berkeley liberals, despite the fact that he'd married one, Jack Defalco took one look at Mrs. Friedman and placed a big fat zero at the top of her Rolodex card. Not only was she a pinko Commie, she couldn't pass the weight test.

Jack, like every trial lawyer, abided by certain unwritten rules of jury selection. He reminded himself of the first rule for prosecutors: No chubs. Fat people, experienced DAs theorized, received no attention because the Beautiful People either looked past them, as if invisible, or mocked them for their inability to stay fit. Thus, tubby people who sat on juries could, for the first time in their lives, become the center of attention if they voted contrary to the rest of the group. A beefy behemoth nearly always served as the lone holdout that created a hung jury, so DAs tossed off the rotund.

Other groups DAs routinely excluded from jury service included black women on a case in which the accused was a black male (prosecutors viewed them as maternally biased in favor of the bad guy), anyone working in a profession that started with the letter *P* (probation officer, priest, policeman, psychologist, philanthropist) either because they worked too closely with the criminal justice system or because they were too sympathetic to the downtrodden, and, finally, anyone whose career involved helping people (teachers, counselors, nurses, doctors, nuns). In other words, compassionate people, since they might sympathize with the accused and cut him loose.

Defense attorneys excluded Asians, Samoans, and Philippinos, deeming them conviction-prone.

Of course, an attorney who excluded any potential juror based on membership in an easily identified group committed misconduct. In fact, if caught, such conduct could doom a criminal proceeding and send the offending lawyer on a quick trip to the State Bar Office of Discipline. Nevertheless, that didn't stop most trial lawyers from clinging to those illegal stereotypes during jury selection, ethics be damned, and Jack Defalco was no exception.

Mrs. Friedman, along with her flowery skirt, hairy legs, and chubby arms, was history.

Jack stood to question her. "Good morning, Mrs. Friedman. At the end of this case, I'm going to ask you to vote to kill Mr. Seavers, to have him walk into the gas chamber at San Quentin, get strapped into a chair, and die by inhaling cyanide-infused fumes." He gestured toward the defendant. "Can you promise me that you will do so, if you and the other jurors decide that is the appropriate punishment?"

The lady blanched. "Uh…well, no actually. I don't think I could ever sentence someone to death."

Jack smiled at her, thanked her, and turned the questioning over to the defense attorneys. He had what he needed, a juror who said she could never vote to execute a convicted killer. He could exercise a *for cause* challenge, not wasting any of his precious *I just don't like you* challenges. After all, if a potential juror didn't believe in the death penalty, or refused to consider it as a possible punishment, why should that juror sit on a capital case?

Parker Brolin fumbled with a messy pile of papers before he stood up. He looked befuddled, as if he couldn't fathom where he was or why he was there. His rumpled brown suit and unpolished shoes highlighted his status as a poorly paid county public defender. He cleared his throat before sipping some water. "Mrs. Friedman, you're not saying, are you, that once all the evidence is in, and if you believe that Mr. Seavers deserves to be sentenced to death, you'd ignore the judge's instructions and your fellow jurors' opinions, and vote for a life sentence?"

Mrs. Friedman's brows furrowed. "I'm not following you."

Mr. Brolin sighed. "What I'm asking is this: Will you or will you not follow the law as Judge Green gives it to you?"

"Well," she shifted her girth in the wooden chair, "of course, I'd follow the law. I'm just not sure—"

Brolin raised an open palm at her to stop her from sinking herself as a possible member of the jury.

Jack knew Brolin needed the Mrs. Friedmans of the world, chunky, soft of heart and body, and likely opposed to the death penalty in all circumstances. After all, the defense attorney's end game was life in prison instead of death. He'd likely already conceded his client's guilt.

"Madam, if you would kindly wait until I ask the next question? Now, when my client is convicted, or I should say *if* my client is convicted, we will move on to phase two of this trial. Then Judge Green will instruct you that if the aggravating factors so outweigh the mitigating ones, making the death penalty appropriate, you may vote to execute Mr. Seavers."

He paused for a breath or possibly dramatic effect.

Mrs. Friedman frowned, obviously trying to track his words.

"So, if you, Madam, personally and individually, believe that the bad evidence outweighs the good, can you follow the law and impose the death penalty? Yes or no?"

At first shaking her head, Mrs. Friedman sat taller before shouting out an emphatic, "Yes, I can!"

Smirking, Mr. Brolin resumed his seat. He had just rehabilitated Jack Defalco's dreaded juror, allowing her to remain on the jury panel, for the moment, forcing Jack to waste one of his limited freebie challenges to get rid of her when they entered final jury selection the following week.

Solomon clapped his hands together to end the session, eschewing use of his gavel. "Thank you, Mrs. Friedman. We'll need you to return after lunch for some additional questions, and again next week if you survive the lawyers' scrutiny today. We thank you for your time and attention. This court is in recess until one o'clock."

With that, Solomon swept into his chambers as the defense attorneys left for coffee.

Before heading upstairs, Jack watched Thomas Seavers, the defendant on trial for his life, turn his shackled feet toward the bailiff, who escorted him toward the bathroom. Deaf, missing his hearing aid, and likely confused by what just happened in court, Seavers hung his head as he passed by a mural of Lady Justice.

Jack shrugged off the tightness in his chest.

Sorry, Seavers. You play, you pay.

CHAPTER SIX

Jack Defalco's office
Four o'clock the next day

JACK LEAPT FROM HIS CHAIR, striding toward the much taller Kevin Dorrian, who stood near the door at military parade rest stance.

"What do you mean, you can't find Carmen whoever-she-is? She's the key witness to this whole case. Without her, I don't have shit!"

Kevin stared over the top of Jack's head, avoiding eye contact. "We're doing the best we can. Jane and some other detectives are combing the area, tracking down every lead. I think we may be able to find Carmen through her sister."

Leaning toward Kevin, Jack struggled to remain calm. "How could you lose her? The Big Spin is in one week, Kevin. One. Fucking. Week. Then I have to tell the jury in my opening statement how I'm going to prove beyond a reasonable doubt that Thomas Seavers shot Cowboy Jeffers while Joey Hernandez watched. Carmen said she heard Seavers admit to being the shooter the night of the murder. Without her testimony, all I have is a bunch of drunks who can't remember crap, which means," Jack slammed his fist on the bookcase, "I'm screwed!"

The Big Spin signaled the end of months of jury selection in Seavers' capital trial. All jurors who passed the initial screening in voir dire—those not dumped for bias, prejudice, financial hardship, or their refusal to impose a death sentence—had to appear in court the following Wednesday. Much like in Bingo, Solomon's clerk would spin a large wire hopper containing two hundred slips of paper with the names of each eligible juror. After the clerk withdrew the names of twelve jurors and sat them in the jury box, Jack and the defense lawyers exercised their preemptory challenges.

A preemptory challenge, as opposed to a challenge for cause, meant the lawyers could dump whomever they pleased, provided they didn't get caught throwing off those in a cognizable group, such as women, blacks, or Jews.

Each side had twenty-six free challenges, and Jack intended to use all of his. In a case with excellent evidence, even an imperfect jury normally voted for guilt. In a case like *Seavers-Hernandez*, Jack needed to load the jury with conviction-prone citizens because his evidence against both defendants sucked.

Once all sides exhausted their preemptory challenges, the last twelve seated in the jury box constituted the final, sworn group to determine both defendants' fates. The clerk then selected more names, the attorneys issued more challenges, and finally three to six alternate jurors swore in, listening to the evidence in case something happened to someone on the main jury panel.

Running fingers through his shaggy hair, Jack reminded himself to visit the barber before next week. Solomon had declared a week's recess so the attorneys could prepare for final jury selection, and the judge could attend to other court matters.

Jack glared at the detective. "I'm not going to belabor the point, Kevin. I need Carmen. You lost her, never got her address, or even her last name, so you have to fix this. Christ, it's bad enough your department lost the physical evidence, which would be oh-so-helpful at the moment. Without Carmen, all I've got to identify the actual shooter is the bartender and those composite drawings."

Kevin had the decency to look sheepish. "I fucked up. I know that. But I promise you, Jack, whatever it takes, I'll find her and get her to testify."

After Kevin left, Jack returned to his desk. He took out his Rolodex filled with juror cards, checking for the hundredth time to make sure his numerical ratings lined up with each other.

His concentration ended as Bobby lumbered in carrying his own trial box. "Hey, D-man, how goes the battle?"

Sitting back in his chair, arms raised behind his head, Jack grimaced. "This great death penalty case you gave me? Berkeley PD lost the gun holster, the hat, the vest, and pretty much anything else that could prove Seavers pulled the trigger.

And now Dorrian's lost Carmen."

Instead of commiserating, Bobby stared at the wooden witness chair in front of Jack's desk. "Holy shit! That Seavers' witness you had sitting in here the other day left a muffin print on this chair. All that sweat of hers ate the varnish off the seat. Jesus, you can see an outline of her puss! I'll requisition a new set of chairs from the law library."

Frowning, Bobby dragged the chair toward a file cabinet.

Incredulous, Jack stood. "Erickson, I'm about to lose my first capital case, and you're worried about a fucking chair?"

Bobby glanced up. "You're not going to lose the case. Dorrian will find your witness, no matter how he has to do it. Besides, if you follow Solomon's advice on jury selection, you'll be fine."

Sighing, Jack recalled his earlier conversation that afternoon in the privacy of Solomon's chambers. The judge, snapping the ashes off the end of his cigarette, had proclaimed, "I'm a Jew. My wife's a Jew. We threw expensive goddamned bar mitzvahs for our three boys. And I'm telling you, Jack, no Jew is going to vote to gas someone."

Solomon had noted that when Nazi leader Adolph Eichmann faced execution in Israel, the citizens split on whether the government should kill him, even though he'd annihilated millions of their brethren. Jack had to give it to Solomon. His argument was persuasive.

Bobby tossed over his hand grenade, grabbing Jack's attention. "Buddy, you need to listen to Solomon. Every prosecutor worth his salt knows to kick off Jews in a capital case, not just in California, but in every state that has the death penalty. You hang this, and you'll be in worse shape than if you lost it. And if the juror fucking it up is Jewish, you'll be back at Family Support before you can shout 'penalty box.'"

Jack placed the grenade on Bobby's desk. "And if the defense figures out I colluded with Solomon to dump the Jews, my legal career is over anyway." He picked up a red duffel bag. "Fuck it. I'm going to the gym."

Entering the elevator on the eleventh floor, Jack wondered how he was supposed to distinguish Jewish jurors in the unlikely event he made that choice. By last name? Political persuasion? Neighborhood? Nose size?

With no great ideas, he decided to ignore Solomon's advice, Bobby's cautionary words to the contrary.

Too complicated.

Too risky.

* * *

The next morning, Jack's blood pressure spiked when Chief Assistant Rick Peters ordered him to cover the felony calendar in Judge Haugen's department. Right now the last thing Jack needed was wheeling and dealing cases with whiny defense attorneys and their smelly clients. He needed to prepare for the Big Spin, and he especially needed Dorrian to find Carmen, his key witness.

Nevertheless, he headed to Judge Haugen's courtroom carrying a box of blue index cards, each containing the case name, a summary of the facts of the crimes charged, and the proposed plea bargain as determined by whatever young deputy happened to be assigned to the case. Those prosecutors reluctant to go to trial gave away the case for little or no jail time. The ones who begged for courtroom experience refused to offer anything short of prison in even the most benign situation. It was up to Jack, as a senior deputy, to strike the best deal as circumstances played out in court.

Dropping the calendar box on the prosecutor's table, Jack smiled at the clerk, nodded at the bailiff, and perused the sea of mostly chocolate faces in the audience. Fairfax County's population was an eclectic majority of African Americans sharing space with a few Latinos, Asians, and Caucasians. A smattering of Vietnamese and Laotians had taken up residence near the local lake, an area once inundated with stray dogs. Since the latter group immigrated to the neighborhood, those critters had disappeared into their local cuisine. As a guy who ran around that lake every day, Jack rejoiced in the lack of dog shit on the bottom of his shoes, but felt a twinge of sadness for the poor animals wok-fried for dinner.

Defense attorneys milled about, as did a few of Jack's colleagues. He noted one public defender with a huge nose—about which Jack never failed to comment—speaking to a female DA who claimed to be a witch and hung out with her lesbian buddy, Janet Mackinaw. He glanced at another defense attorney who had just filed a motion in a death penalty case, requesting that his client be sentenced to live in a Hutterite Colony, under the theory that living amid such rigorous religious scrutiny would constitute a pain worse than death. Then there was Jack's buddy, Ted, a prosecutor who hated minorities even more than Bobby Erickson, and whose mind always seemed close to snapping. Jack figured old Ted might end up in a clock tower someday, shooting randomly at Fairfax citizens as he swilled on a bottle of bourbon.

If the public ever finds out what goes on in this courthouse, they'll raze it and sow salt where it stands.

Everyone rose when the bailiff announced the entrance of Judge Haugen.

"Be seated. This court is now in session. Mr. Defalco, I see you're substituting today, so please call the calendar."

Jack grabbed the first index card, loudly proclaimed the name of the case, and defense attorney Scott Kelly came forward with his client, standing at a wooden table to Jack's left.

"Scott Kelly appearing with the defendant, Your Honor. We've read the charges set forth in the Information. My client understands his rights. At this time, we plead not guilty, and time is not waived."

Judge Haugen leaned forward, peering at the attorneys through his glasses. "Is there a proposed disposition in this matter, Mr. Kelly?"

Kelly squirmed. "There is, Your Honor. However, my client wishes to proceed to trial as soon as possible, despite the prosecutor's generous offer of ten years state prison."

Jack read the charges on the index card, robbery of a clerk for a bottle of baby aspirin at a local discount store. The defendant had one prior theft conviction five years earlier. Jack looked up at the judge. "Could Mr. Kelly and I have a moment, Your Honor?"

At the judge's nod, the two attorneys met between the tables, heads together.

"Kelly, what the fuck did you do to piss off my junior DA?"

Kelly laughed. "I told him he could never win this trial given the equities of the case. My client stole the aspirin for his very sick little girl. He's got no job, no health insurance, and his wife left him for another guy."

Jack rolled his eyes. "Tell him I'll give him a misdemeanor, straight probation, six months."

Kelly smiled. "That'll do it."

Moments later, Scott Kelly announced, "Your Honor, my client would like to change his plea to guilty pursuant to the offer Mr. Defalco will outline to the Court."

After Kelly's client left grinning, Jack heard Bobby Erickson bellow from the back of the court, "Blackie!" The courtroom fell silent before Bobby added, "Is there an attorney here named Blackie Blackburn?"

Indeed, a resigned Blackie Blackburn stood amid the sea of dark-skinned faces, his rumpled suit matching the harried expression on his face. "Yes, Mr. Erickson, I'm here…as always."

Jack knew Bobby loved the pure theater of watching the startled faces of the audience every time he proclaimed the attorney's first name, which he did at least once a week during the calendar call.

The judge glared at both men, Jack smiled, and the bailiff smirked as he shook his head.

Jack slogged through the rest of the day, bad guy after bad guy, attorney after attorney, index card after index card. He knew every hour he spent running the calendar meant one less hour he could prepare for the *Seavers-Hernandez* case. Given Maggie's warning about Rick Peters' hatred for him, Jack wondered if Peters had assigned him this duty to screw up his chances of winning at trial.

At the end of the day, heading to the elevators, Jack commented to no one in particular, "Motherfucker!"

* * *

As Jack pulled into the garage, Claire raced from the house into his outstretched arms. "Daddy! Guess what? Papa's here!"

Papa, Jack's aging father, had suffered through major heart surgery the year before. The stress caused Jack's mother to suffer a debilitating stroke, all within forty-eight hours. After his release from the hospital, Papa had insisted on caring for his wife, who lay paralyzed and aphasic, only able to utter the words "No, no, no." Papa's heart issues couldn't heal, nor could his wife's speech or movement, so the two of them sat in their condo, staring at one another, a shitty situation after half a century of marriage.

Claire grabbed Jack's cheeks in her tiny hands. "Daddy, Papa's acting funny. He doesn't answer when Mommy talks to him, so Aunty Feebs is coming over."

Concerned, Jack carried Claire toward the house as his sister, Phoebe Defalco Tripp, pulled into the driveway. He paused while she got out of her car with her son who was the same age as Claire. He set his daughter down, and the cousins raced off to play.

Jack gave his sister a quick hug. "What's going on with the folks?"

Phoebe stared at him. "Didn't Paige call you? Mom fell off the bed and broke her hip. They're taking her into surgery in a couple of hours. Dad's a wreck."

At that moment, Paige opened the door, jaw taut. "Sorry. I tried to call, but your secretary said you'd already left. You two go to the hospital. I'll keep your dad busy and feed the kids. Feebs, the twins are with your nanny until Matt gets home, right?"

Phoebe nodded. Jack loosened his tie, grabbed his briefcase from the car, handed it to Paige as he kissed her, and left with his sister to face yet another Defalco family fiasco.

Driving to the hospital, Jack mumbled, "How much worse can this fucking year get?"

Besides the devastating health issues with his parents, Phoebe had prematurely delivered twins who'd barely survived, even after two months in intensive care. The neonatal specialist couldn't predict if any long-term brain damage might later create problems for the babies.

Lowering her window, inhaling crisp evening air, Phoebe glanced at her older brother. "It really has been shitty, hasn't it? Mom and Dad, the twins, Paige's miscarriages, and now Mom breaks her hip. Christ on a crutch."

Jack sped off the freeway exit. "The miscarriages, yeah. They're killing Paige. I'm not sure how she makes it to school every day." He hoped Phoebe didn't notice his eyes moisten as he thought of the siblings Claire would never know.

Phoebe, a nurse, interrupted his sorrow. "By the way, I told the hospital not to resuscitate Mom if her heart stops during surgery. The last thing we need is for some idiot to revive her and keep her alive in this hellish condition."

Jack maneuvered his Porsche into the hospital lot. "I'm with you, but Dad has her medical power of attorney, so you may get out-voted."

Two hours later, consistent with typical Defalco luck, some idiot indeed revived Jack's mother during surgery.

"Why in the hell did you code her?" Phoebe shot an accusing look at her medical colleague.

"Because your father, the one with the legal authority, insisted when we called him. What were we supposed to do, Feebs? Overdose her? I think your brother might call that murder."

The colleague walked away before Phoebe quietly asked Jack, "Could we overdose her when she gets to the rehab facility? If we use potassium chloride, no one will know, and at her age, as sick as she is, nobody will bother with an autopsy."

Jack jerked his head toward the exit. "Outside. We'll talk in the car."

Cruising back to the Fairfax suburbs, Jack shook his head. "Listen to me because I'm only going to say this once. If you overdose Mom, or help do it, it's murder. And if you get caught, you'll go to prison. I don't want any part of it although I wish to hell she'd died from the stroke last year. It's awful to see her like this." He turned into the driveway. "But you can't kill her. Got it?"

Phoebe sighed. "Got it."

As they approached the door into the house, Jack laughed, "Jesus, Feebs. The Gestapo could have used your help to eliminate the old, the weak, and the Jews. What happened to your Hippocratic oath?"

His sister slugged him in the arm, then donned her mom persona before entering the Defalco household.

Jack inhaled roast chicken and rosemary potatoes, wondering how he was supposed to concentrate on the *Seavers-Hernandez* case amid the endless chaos of his family life.

And speaking of Jews, what to do about Solomon's adamant insistence that he throw them off the jury panel?

CHAPTER SEVEN

The Big Spin
Wednesday, February 17, 1988

AT MORNING MASS ON ASH WEDNESDAY, Jack yawned as he kneeled next to Paige. Glancing at the crucifix above the tabernacle, he said a quick prayer for the continued safety and health of his family, then asked for guidance on how to select the best jury to win the conviction and execution of Tom Seavers. He winced at the irony of petitioning the Lord for advice on killing another human being. Sometimes his job took him into bizarre territory.

Yet he relished every gritty second of it.

At home, Jack grabbed coffee before turning to the *Chronicle's* sports section.

Paige shoved her heavy law books into a backpack. "So, honeybun, have you decided to follow your conscience and the ethics code, or cave in to Solomon and toss off Jewish jurors?"

Jack understood his wife was far more inclined to follow rules, especially ones proscribing lying, cheating, and stealing. He knew she worried for his soul, not to mention his possible disbarment, should he make the wrong choice and get caught. She poured her own coffee before sitting across from him.

"How the hell am I supposed to know somebody's Jewish? Even with an obvious name like Melvin Feinstein or Menachem Begin, you still don't know if the guy's a Jew. He could be adopted, for God's sake. And with the no-hat rule in court, I doubt anyone will show up wearing a Yamaha."

Paige smiled. "That's yamulke, if you're referring to skull caps. If you're talking motorcycles, I withdraw the correction."

Claire appeared in her pink bathrobe, crawled onto her dad's lap, and cuddled into his chest. Over her head, Jack bit into his toast. "Whatever. If Solomon can ferret them out and give me a heads up, I might toss them off, but probably I'll just pick the best jury I can with what I have on my Rolodex cards."

Paige noticed breadcrumbs in Claire's hair and brushed them away. "Since it's a holy day today, you might get more points in heaven without cheating."

Setting Claire in her own chair, Jack smiled at his wife. "Do not start with your aunt's platitudes about how cheaters never prosper or, my personal favorite, 'Oh, what a tangled web we weave.'"

"Hey, don't criticize my aunt, or we'll revisit your mother's opium rub on Claire's gums when she was teething."

Laughing, Jack headed to the bedroom. "I told you she was a witch."

After showering and changing into a navy blue designer suit, Jack polished a speck of dirt from his already shiny wingtips. He insured his buttons hid behind the starched placket on his white shirt, straightened his red striped tie, and poked an American flag pin through his lapel. The outfit, one of many he owned, constituted a trial lawyer's version of battle fatigues.

Entering the kitchen, his mind lost in the *Seavers-Hernandez* case, Jack absently kissed his wife and daughter goodbye, patted the dog, and left for the courthouse.

Driving through the Fairfax hills, Jack put the Porsche through its paces as he careened around curves on the winding back road. He pushed the speedometer far beyond the recommended thirty-five miles per hour while he reflected on jury selection, missing witnesses, and shitty evidence. He warred with his conscience, pricked by the priest's quick but pointed homily that morning reminding him to fearlessly defend the truth, regardless of personal cost.

Yeah, about that personal cost.

If he ignored Solomon's advice and lost his first death penalty case, he could taste his own failure. He envisioned demotion to Family Support, or worse, Consumer Fraud. He imagined his loss of status as a big deal prosecutor. Most significantly, he'd kiss goodbye any possible advancement and the money that accompanied it. His hands slipped on the steering wheel from sweat forming on his palms. He inhaled to quell the tightening in his chest.

As his Porsche's tires squealed around the last corner

before the freeway, Jack remembered Claire's non-existent college fund that begged for any cash accompanying a promotion. Their savings account had all but dried up after Paige quit her job to attend law school. With his parents vegged-out from their respective health issues, it was only a matter of time before the Defalcos had to assume part of the cost of their care.

Pulling into the underground parking garage, in a space reserved for the Porsche by an attendant whose felony Jack had dismissed, he thought of his sister's suggestion to snuff his paralyzed mother with a quick shot of potassium.

The Church definitely frowned on murder, unless it was committed in the name of God, of course. Yet cynic that he was, even Jack couldn't countenance homicide, despite the fact that his mother would welcome death.

In the men's room, before he left for court, Jack reconsidered the merits of rigging a homicide jury. He wetted a paper towel to wash away the last smudge of holy ashes from his forehead. If only his doubts would wash away so easily.

* * *

By mid-afternoon, Jack and the defense attorneys had exercised most of their challenges, signaling the end of the Big Spin. Solomon removed his glasses, clapped his hands together, and announced a recess in the proceedings. "Ladies and gentlemen, you are free to wander the courthouse, use the restrooms, or get some coffee. Do not, under any circumstances, discuss this case among yourselves or with anyone else. Be back in half an hour."

All counsel stood as the potential jurors left the courtroom.

Solomon stepped off the bench. "Jack. My chambers. Now." Looking at attorneys Brolin, Moore, and Kennedy, he added, "Gentlemen, I need to speak with Jack about an unrelated matter. Alone."

Since the entire Fairfax Bar Association knew Solomon engaged in *ex parte* confabs with both sides in a case, the attorneys smirked. The judge would advise Defalco just as he offered advice to them. While unethical, it exemplified the workings of the courthouse, especially in Solomon's chambers.

Everyone overlooked it, just as they overlooked the off-track bets placed to various bookies from Solomon's phone. The judge bet, his brethren bet, and the lawyers bet. Everyone knew. No one cared, or at least no one dared to snitch on the players.

Inside, door closed and locked, Solomon removed his robe as he gestured for Jack to sit. Knowing the judge had something serious on his mind, Jack restrained himself from grabbing the Reggie Jackson bat for some practice swings.

"What's up, Judge?"

Solomon sighed. "Mrs. Freidman is still sitting in the jury box, Jack. So are Mr. Edmonton, Mrs. Berman, and the fat lady in the back row. Not to mention the *schvartze* in front. You're running low on challenges. How do you intend to handle this?"

Jack tapped the chair's arms with his pen. "By schvartze, I assume you mean Mr. Jackson, the black guy in row one?"

Solomon nodded as he lit a cigarette. He held out his coffee mug, so Jack would fill it from the large pot by the window.

"Mr. Jackson is solid, Judge. I tracked down his brother in Washington, D.C., who, it turns out, is a Secret Service agent on the vice president's detail. He says his brother would vote to kill their mother if he thought she deserved it. So the black guy stays."

Sipping his coffee, Solomon sat back, cigarette near his lips. His eyes squinted against the smoke. "And the Jews, Jack? What have I told you about leaving Jews on this jury?"

Ignoring the fact that he'd already committed malpractice by discussing jury selection with Solomon outside the presence of the defense, Jack brought up the obvious. "Mrs. Friedman and the other fat lady are history with my next two challenges. As for the others, how do you even know they're Jewish? They said they could kill Seavers at the end of the case, so I don't see the point in kicking them. And coming up behind them are a couple of libs who the defense is dying to keep on."

The judge leaned toward Jack. "Mrs. Berman? With a name like 'Berman,' what do you think she is? Don't be stupid, Jack, and don't waste my time picking a jury that's going to hang or vote for life. Either do this right, or dump the death penalty against Seavers, so we can all go home a lot sooner."

Standing, Jack walked to the window. He paused, staring at the judge. "And Mr. Edmonton? How do you figure he's Jewish?"

Solomon smiled. "I see him at Temple on high holidays."

Nodding, Jack crossed his arms, resigned to his fate. "Anyone else? Somebody not yet in the jury box that might get seated before we exercise our final pre-emps?"

"Nope," Solomon replied. "That should do it. Now let's get out there before we waste more taxpayers' money."

As court resumed, Solomon shot Jack a pointed look. "I believe the challenge is with the People."

This is it. No guts, no glory. Jack stood to address those remaining in the jury box. "The People thank and excuse juror number eight, Mrs. Friedman. Thank you for your patience, Mrs. Friedman."

Looking miffed at her rejection, the lady shuffled toward the door, flowery skirt swishing around her hairy legs and Birkenstock-clad feet.

The defense tossed off a couple of great prosecution jurors, but not Mr. Jackson, and announced they were satisfied with the jury panel. Having dumped Mrs. Friedman, Mrs. Berman, and the fat lady, Jack had one more challenge. He looked at Mr. Edmonton's Rolodex card, scored with a high mark of eight out of ten points, and at the gold slash of color in the corner, indicating the guy was a keeper at all costs.

"The People thank and excuse juror number seven, Mr. Edmonton. Thank you, sir, for your time and patience."

When both sides passed on the next juror, Jack glanced at Solomon, who smiled. "Ladies and gentlemen, we have our jury. Would the twelve of you please rise and be sworn in by the bailiff?"

Looking bewildered now that they actually might have to vote to execute Thomas Seavers, the twelve left with the bailiff for a private jury room in the back.

Solomon addressed the remaining citizens in the audience. "Now we'll pick four alternate jurors who will hear the evidence and substitute in if one of the twelve can't fulfill his duties."

Weary, Jack again checked his cards. Same process. No Jews to dump. No fatties. They completed alternate juror selection in record time.

Several minutes later, Jack rolled his head to stretch the tension from his neck. He sat alone in court at the dark oak table that would serve as his home base for the next few weeks. As he repacked his trial box, he glanced at the jury roster the clerk had handed him minutes before.

He knew every juror by name, occupation, political persuasion, and criminal record, if one existed. Mrs. Madison, a Hawaiian of Philippine heritage, would vote his way. She'd withheld the fact that the purse snatch she'd endured a few years earlier actually involved a violent, bloody altercation with an ex-con who got away with a light sentence. Jack felt confident she'd execute Tom Seavers herself, if given the chance.

The only other woman on the panel, who Solomon dubbed "Dog Face" due to her unfortunate resemblance to his Rottweiler, never smiled, but her job as a prison guard put her solidly on the side of law enforcement. The lone black person, Mr. Jackson, remained, thank God, as did nine other men, four with multiple drunk driving convictions.

Yes, indeed. For his first death penalty jury, Jack hadn't done half bad. In the elevator heading up to the eleventh floor, he whistled a Jimmy Buffet tune. Not only had he stacked it with conviction-prone people, he'd rendered moot Solomon P's Jewish juror issue.

Or so he hoped.

* * *

Two days later, as Jack worked on his opening statement, Kevin Dorrian and Jane Moore rapped on his open office door. Earlier, Jack had mentioned to the detectives that while he was calm at the moment, come Monday morning when the trial began, if they hadn't delivered Carmen, he'd tear them new assholes.

Kevin grinned. "Jack, meet Carmen Velasquez. Carmen, have a seat."

A good-looking Hispanic woman entered but refused to sit down. Her dark eyes stabbed Jack. "I'm not sayin' a word, and I ain't testifyin' against Joey."

Jane pushed the woman into Jack's witness chair, requisitioned from the law library but showing no signs of any dreaded muffin prints. "This is Mr. Defalco, Carmen. He needs you to be in court Monday morning to talk about what happened at the motel with Tom Seavers and Joey Hernandez, when Seavers admitted he shot the guy in the bar."

Carmen squared her shoulders. "No."

Jack came around his desk, his hip leaning against its front edge, only a foot from his recalcitrant witness. "Ms. Velasquez, I don't need you to testify against Joey. What I need," he reached for a single page of a police report, "is for you to tell the jury what you told the cops in this four-line paragraph." He held it up for her to read.

Instead, she stared out the window.

The detectives exchanged a nod with Jack and left the office.

Jack crossed his left foot in front of his right. "Carmen, you have children. Two, I believe. You work. You're married to a new guy now, and your life is pretty good. It would be a shame if Child Protective Services launched an investigation into your parenting skills and found them lacking. They might take your kids from you."

As her mouth slackened, Jack knew he had her attention.

Carmen squinted at him. "Are you threatening to take away my kids if I don't show up for court on Monday?"

Jack walked back to his chair and sat. Shirtsleeves rolled back, tie loosened, he leaned his elbows on his desk. He clicked the pen in his right hand a few times before he answered. "Carmen, you are the key witness in a capital case. I don't need to threaten you. I can place a call right now, and the judge will issue a warrant for your immediate arrest as a material witness. You'll go into custody and stay there until you testify. It's your choice how you play this out."

She stood. "You motherfucker! You just gotta fuck up my life, right? Just when it's goin' good for me and my family? Well, fuck you, Mr. Hot Shot DA. I ain't doin' it, so go ahead and arrest me. You can't take my kids. I got rights."

At her raised voice, Kevin and Jane re-entered the office

and grabbed the now very pissed off woman before she took a swing at Jack.

He remained in his chair, unfazed. "See you first thing Monday morning, Ms. Velasquez. The detectives will pick you up. We'll make sure your employer knows you're performing your civic duty. And your kids, as we know, will carry on with their studies at Elrod Elementary while you're in court."

After Carmen and her armed escorts left, Jack rubbed his afternoon stubble. Whether or not Carmen showed up Monday morning was anyone's guess. He probably should have arrested her, but something about putting a young mother in custody bothered him. Besides, they knew where she lived, her place of employment, and, yeah, where to find her children.

If Jack had to play hardball to get her to testify, he'd do it. So would the detectives.

Confident Carmen would appear, he wrote in his opening statement that her testimony would prove Tom Seavers murdered Cowboy Jeffers. And if she didn't, well, he'd take her kids and make her fight like hell to get them back.

Grabbing his briefcase, Jack flicked off the pesky shoulder angel who whispered one word in his ear. "Ethics?"

CHAPTER EIGHT

Jack Defalco's Office
Two days later

SUNDAY MORNING SILENCE ECHOED THROUGH THE DISTRICT ATTORNEY'S OFFICE. Not even a janitor's cart squeaked in the halls. No other lawyer, and certainly no underpaid staff member, filled the empty space on the eleventh floor. Jack, on the other hand, had spent many weekends there nailing down his meager evidence to try to convict Seavers and Hernandez.

At ten o'clock sharp, Kevin Dorrian and Jane Moore arrived, prepared to go over their trial testimony.

His flannel shirtsleeves rolled up, Jack poured each detective a cup of coffee. "Okay, tell me more details about how you arrested Seavers."

Jane took the lead. "Over a year after the murder, we got a tip that Joey Hernandez lived in a house not far from the Center Street Projects. We stopped by for a knock and talk. When the door opened, who should greet us but Tom Seavers. We recognized him from the composite drawing, except he'd grown a beard since the murder."

Sipping his coffee, Kevin interrupted. "We told him we were cops looking for Joey in connection with a murder we thought he'd witnessed. Seavers didn't even blink. He told us Joey wasn't home. So, we asked him whether he'd be willing to come to Berkeley PD with us to pick Joey out of a photo lineup."

Jane smirked. "And the idiot said, 'Sure.' So we hauled his dumb ass over there, and he picked out Joey's picture. Then we told him that a witness had positively ID'd Joey as the shooter but couldn't identify anyone with him. We asked Seavers if he'd stand in a line-up with some guys who looked like Joey, and again, the moron agreed."

Kevin, animated like a six-year-old waiting for his dad to sit on whoopee cushion, chuckled as he rubbed his hands together. "Right away we sent a patrol car to pick up the bartender and bring him down to the PD. The bartender looked at the line up and mentioned Seavers might be the guy, but he couldn't tell for sure because of the beard.

"So I went to Seavers and said, 'Hey, Tom, man, you've been great, and we thank you for your cooperation in this. Just one more thing. The witness says Joey didn't have a beard, so we were wondering if you might be willing to, you know, shave off your beard and get back in the line up.'"

Jack rocked back in his chair. "Are you shitting me? Don't tell me he shaved!"

His Irish eyes sparkling, Kevin laughed. "Fuck, yeah, he shaved. Right there in the department bathroom. When he got back in the line up, our bartender positively identified him as the guy who shot Cowboy. And he also agreed the booking photo of Joey Hernandez looked like one of the accomplices." Kevin high fived Jane. "So we took old Tom into custody."

Suspicious of anything that sounded too good to be true, especially when it came to a cop's version of "positively identified," Jack pressed for specifics. "What exactly did the bartender say when he saw Seavers without the beard? Jane? Your version this time."

Jane averted her eyes, picking instead at her fingernail. "Well, maybe Kevin's overstating the witness' certainty a little. Maybe he said Seavers 'looked like' the guy, but he couldn't be sure."

Jack frowned. "That's kind of a big difference, don't you think?" His gaze travelled from Jane to Kevin. "Now do you see why Carmen's testimony is so critical? The day you arrested Seavers, you found her at that same house living with Joey, right?"

At Kevin's nod, Jack continued. "And at Sonny B's funeral, she told you the three of them had been at the Forty Flags Motel the night of the murder, and Seavers and Hernandez argued because Seavers shot some guy in a bar robbery, correct?"

Another nod, this one from Jane.

Jack clapped his hands in true Solomon-like fashion. "Alright then, folks. I need Carmen in court tomorrow morning with the two of you standing by in case I have to impeach her with her statement. No bullshit excuses. Just have her here by the time court starts at ten. Are we clear?"

Sensing Jack's frustration, neither detective argued. "Clear," they chimed, quickly escaping before Jack could do more than hurl a pen at their retreating backs.

* * *

As the bailiff called court into session the next morning, Jack peered around for any sign of Detectives Dorrian and Moore accompanying the elusive Carmen Velasquez. His sphincter tightened when he noticed the smug look on Joey Hernandez' face, as if the little fucker knew his ex-girlfriend wouldn't show.

"Mr. Defalco?" Solomon coughed. "Are the People ready to give an opening statement to the jury?"

Solomon's rhetorical question returned Jack's attention to the sixteen people anticipating some solid evidence that proved Seavers and Hernandez robbed and killed Jeffers.

"The People are ready, Your Honor."

Without Carmen's presence, Jack decided to hedge his bets. He explained the facts of the murder, dropped the bad news that Berkeley PD had lost most of the physical evidence, and portrayed the bartender's identification of the defendants as both sober and precise. He never mentioned Carmen.

Mr. Seavers' attorneys argued that their client wasn't at the bar that night, so the bartender, drunken sot that he was, had misidentified the killer.

Mr. Hernandez' attorney, whose client didn't face the death penalty, waived his opening statement, leaving both Jack and the jury clueless about his possible defense.

"Mr. Defalco, please call your first witness."

At Solomon's order, Jack glanced at the back of the courtroom, planning to introduce the pathologist who performed the autopsy. Since Carmen had failed to appear, Jack figured he'd get the jury's attention with gory photos of Cowboy's brain, removed from his skull, to show the .38 slug's bullet path. With weak evidence, Jack hoped to dazzle the jurors with collateral bullshit so they wouldn't notice the shaky nature of the bartender's ID.

"Your Honor, the People call—"

The courtroom door crashed as a breathless Kevin Dorrian bolted in, smiling while signaling Jack with a thumbs-up and vigorous nod. Then he mouthed, "Carmen's here."

Jack's knees softened with his deep exhale. "The People call Carmen Velasquez."

The comely Ms. Velasquez approached the clerk, raised her right hand, and swore to tell the truth, despite her clenched jaw. She rearranged her short skirt before sitting on the witness stand, sipped a bit of water from the paper cup in front of her, and glared at Jack.

"Good morning, Ms. Velasquez."

Silence.

Gesturing to the defense table where the bad guys sat with their lawyers, Jack noticed the group looked a little ashen. "Ms. Velasquez, two years ago, you were Joey Hernandez' girlfriend, correct?"

"Yes."

Pointing at Tom Seavers, Jack continued, "And you know Mr. Seavers here as a close friend of Joey's, correct?"

"Correct."

Parker Brolin, Seavers' lead attorney, could see his I-Wasn't-At-The-Bar-That-Night-So-It-Wasn't-Me   defense slithering into the sewer. "Objection, Your Honor!"

Solomon looked annoyed. "Grounds?"

"Surprise witness, Judge. The defense had no idea Ms. Velasquez would testify in this case."

Solomon grimaced, motioning all counsel to approach the bench. He turned away from the jury and lowered his voice.

"Parker," Solomon perused a sheet of paper in front of him, "this woman has been on the People's witness list for months."

"But, Judge," Brolin persisted, "we believed she'd refuse to cooperate with the prosecution, so we're not prepared. In fact, we move for a mistrial."

During this colloquy, although Jack remained silent, he wondered what the hell Carmen planned to say. She could torpedo his whole case if she lied about what happened at the motel, or worse, denied anything happened. Everything hinged on a witness who could go sideways and leave him standing there holding his dick.

"Jack!" Solomon hissed. "Are you paying attention? Parker just moved for a mistrial. What's the People's response?"

The court reporter's fingers paused, awaiting his answer. Jack felt nausea roil his stomach as his morning coffee burned its way back up his esophagus.

He swallowed bile. "Judge, they knew Carmen could testify, and they have copies of her statement. Just because they failed to hide her from us doesn't mean they get a mistrial. So, the People object."

Solomon sat back. "Motion denied, objection overruled. Back to your places, gentlemen."

At counsel table, Jack grabbed Carmen's statement. He knew as he approached her that he tiptoed into a minefield.

"Ms. Velasquez, on or about July 13, 1986, were you at the Forty Flags Motel when a verbal fight erupted between Mr. Seavers and Mr. Hernandez?"

After Carmen's curt "Yes," Jack continued. "Describe that argument, please."

Oh, shit. Here it comes. She's either going to make the case or kill me.

She huffed out a breath. "They'd just come back from pulling a robbery at a bar in Berkeley, off Gilman Street. Nobody was supposed to get hurt. Joey was pissed because Seavers shot and killed a guy sitting at the bar."

The perspiration collecting in Jack's armpits rolled down the inside of his highly starched shirt. "And then what happened? Did you hear Seavers admit to shooting the man?"

"Yes, I heard him say he shot him. But Joey didn't shoot nobody, you understand?" Another glare. "And then Seavers got really angry and pulled out a little gun and shot at Joey and me. Except he missed, and the bullet went into the wall."

The bullet in the wall was news to Jack. Despite the two years that had passed since the event, Jack made a mental note to get Dorrian to the motel in the unlikely event they could find the bullet.

"So what did you do next, Ms. Velasquez?"

Carmen frowned at him. "What the fuck do you think we

did, Mr. DA? We ran outta there like our assholes were on fire."

Some jurors snickered. Jack knew when he'd pushed far enough. He had what he needed from her: both men admitting to the robbery, Seavers confessing to the murder, and Seavers' possession of a small gun that arguably resembled the .38 used to kill Cowboy.

"Thank you, Ms. Velasquez. Nothing further."

Parker Brolin, who'd staked his entire defense on a theory of mistaken identity, shuffled some papers, asked a few inane questions, and sat down. Co-counsel Mikel Moore propped his head in one hand, doodling on his legal pad with the other.

Carmen Velasquez had just blown their case out of the water.

CHAPTER NINE

Berkeley, California
Later that evening

AT THE FORTY FLAGS MOTEL, Jack and Dorrian searched for the missing bullet. Although no ballistics expert could match it to the flattened slug removed from Cowboy's brain, if it proved to be from a .38, that fact corroborated the bartender's testimony the shooter used a .38, and the pathologist's testimony that the slug from the brain came from a .38 caliber weapon.

Most importantly, it added credibility to Carmen's testimony.

Convincing the motel owner to let them rummage through the room after so many years required mentioning an unwanted visit from the health department, but eventually he agreed. Without much effort, Kevin Dorrian located the bullet by digging it out of a small hole in the wall. Grinning, he held it up. "Ta da!"

Jack relaxed. "Excellent. Now if only a janitor at your agency hadn't thrown out Seavers' holster that fit the .38, along with the hat and vest he wore the night of the murder, I'd have a near-perfect case."

Kevin's face fell. "I know, I know. We fucked up. But you still have the photograph we found during the search warrant that shows Seavers wearing that vest and hat, and the bartender can ID Seavers in that photo, along with the clothing."

Jack nodded. "But think how much better it would be if I had the real items to show the jury." He knew he should let it go, but he couldn't help adding, "I still can't believe an officer in your department put all that shit in a garbage bag and left it out, instead of logging it into the evidence room after he served the warrant." Scratching his head he added, "Tell me again how you knew Seavers shot off a round in here, but never looked for the evidence before today?"

Kevin placed the bullet into a small plastic bag. "Shit

happens, Jack." He photographed the hole in the wall, took measurements of the room, and handed a subpoena to the motel manager to guarantee his appearance in court the next day.

Jack grimaced. "Indeed it does." He patted Dorrian on the shoulder. "Thanks for the overtime, buddy. I've got a hot date with my three-year-old and her teddy bear."

Outside the motel, Jack tossed his Brooks Brothers overcoat in the rear of the Porsche. Instead of the freeway, he took a twisting road from Berkeley to his Fairfax home. He gunned the accelerator and raced through the fading light, his mind focused like a laser on each turn. The *Seavers-Hernandez* case would have to take a back seat, at least for a few hours.

* * *

A week later, Jack rested his case. With Carmen's testimony, the bartender's ID, the pathologist's description of the bullet wound path, and Dorrian's testimony about finding a similar bullet at the motel, Jack felt confident he'd done his best. Now, it was time for the defense to present their version of the events.

Parker Brolin elected not to put his client on the stand. Instead, through cross-examining the bartender, Brolin raised the possibility that Seavers had accidentally discharged the gun. Thus, Brolin's theory of the case evolved from It-Wasn't-Me to It-Was-Me-But-I-Didn't-Mean-To-Shoot-Him, a classic cover-your-ass trick utilized by desperate defense attorneys throughout America.

One mystery remained unsolved: The identity of the third robber. During the bartender's testimony, he'd described a slender man who stood near the door but walked with a pronounced limp. The police never developed any leads on the man's identity, despite the precision of the suspect's features as sketched in the composite drawing.

Mr. Hernandez' attorney, Pete Kennedy, stood before the jury, announcing, "Your Honor, the defense asks the bailiff to bring in Scott McCall."

Jack turned to see a thin man enter the courtroom on crutches, his left leg missing from above the knee. Mr. McCall provided an alibi for Joey Hernandez, testifying to Mr.

Hernandez' presence at a family party the entire evening during the robbery and murder of Cowboy Jeffers. Mr. Kennedy sat down, satisfied that the alibi created reasonable doubt as to his client's guilt. Either the jury would believe Carmen Velasquez or Scott McCall.

Jack stood to cross-examine this new defense witness, a man about Seavers' age who bore an uncanny resemblance to the third robbery suspect depicted in the composite drawings. The "door man," as the bartender had labeled him.

God, I love this job. "Mr. McCall, do you have a twin brother?"

The witness adjusted his crutches next to his chair. "No, sir."

"Well, do you have a fake leg? A prosthetic limb?"

"Yes, sir. I do."

Again Jack looked at the composite drawing of the missing robber. "And when you walk with that fake leg, do you limp?"

The witness, face schooled into a bland expression, replied, "I do."

Showing the composite drawing to McCall, Jack asked, "Can you explain why you look exactly like the guy in this drawing who happens to be the third accomplice in this robbery, Mr. McCall?"

Silence from the witness, but explosion from Hernandez' defense attorney.

"Objection! No foundation. Arguing facts not in evidence!"

Solomon rubbed his eyes. "Objection sustained. Mr. Defalco, move on."

"I'd like to mark for identification this drawing as People's Exhibit Seventy-One. I'll lay a proper foundation when I recall the bartender."

Before the defense could utter a protest, Solomon accepted the drawing of Missing Suspect Three, who strongly resembled Scott McCall.

On a roll, Jack switched topics. "Mr. McCall, you say Mr. Hernandez attended this family party on the night of the murder, correct?"

McCall smiled at the jury. "Yes, sir."

Jack moved toward him. "So, was Mr. Seavers also at the party that night?"

"Yes, he was there, too."

Jack heard a strangled noise from the defense table. His mind flew to opposing counsels' extraordinary blunder. Seavers' attorneys first claimed mistaken identity, that their client wasn't present at the bar. After Carmen testified, they switched their defense to one of accidental discharge, admitting that Seavers was at the bar, but claiming the gun went off in error. Now, thanks to Hernandez' attorney, they faced an unwanted alibi defense. Obviously, the three lawyers hadn't coordinated their strategy before trial.

Glancing at Parker Brolin, Jack caught him rising from his chair as if to strike Pete Kennedy. Instead, Brolin shouted, "Your Honor, we object!"

No shit. Jack nearly rolled his eyes.

Solomon shook his head, fully aware of Brolin's dilemma. "The three of you can confer at the next recess. Objection overruled."

Jack, ever ready to kick the defense when they were down, turned back to McCall. "Sir, you and Mr. Seavers are old friends, so you'd easily recognize him at that party, correct?"

McCall's smile faded. "No, we're not old friends. I barely know him, but I remember he was there that night, along with Joey."

Jack paced to his table to grab an official-looking document. "Isn't it true, Mr. McCall, that you and Mr. Seavers committed a robbery together in 1962 and then shared a cell at state prison for six years?"

Attorneys Brolin and Moore exploded from their seats, shouting "Objection!" at the same time.

Solomon closed his eyes as if in pain. "Ladies and gentlemen, we will now take our morning recess. Please do not discuss this case among yourselves or with anyone else. I want to see all counsel in my chambers. Now!"

Jack knew he'd walked a legal tightrope when he dropped in the fact that Tom Seavers had a prior robbery conviction, but he rationalized it as proper impeachment. Or at least that was the story he'd offer Solomon.

In chambers, the three defense lawyers cannibalized each other before they turned on Jack. Jack kept quiet, knowing any response would fuel their outrage.

Without removing his robe, Solomon sat at his desk, lit a cigarette, and held out his coffee mug for Jack to fill. "Parker, you idiot!" Solomon glared at his former law partner. "What the fuck were you thinking telling the jury your guy wasn't there when you knew Carmen whoever-she-is could put him at the scene firing the murder weapon?"

Before Parker could defend himself, Solomon turned his wrath toward Pete Kennedy. "And you, Kennedy! Putting on a witness to alibi Seavers when you knew his defense was…what? First misidentification and then accidental discharge?" The judge shook his head. "Gentlemen, this case is a cluster fuck."

After handing Solomon his coffee, Jack waited by the closet, not daring to grab the bat. Sure enough, Solomon blasted him next. "And Defalco, why the fuck did you bring in Seavers' prior conviction? And don't give me some bullshit excuse that you did it for impeachment. You know that maneuver could get this case reversed on appeal."

Jack took in the old man's reddening complexion as the judge launched into a coughing spasm. Solomon rarely got this upset in trial.

Inhaling, Jack sought neutral ground. "Okay, maybe I got carried away when I mentioned the prior. But screw it. Judge, that guy not only lied about knowing Seavers, he's the fucking third person in this robbery! And he's up there testifying like a goddamn white knight here to spread truth and justice."

"Bah!" Solomon stood, entered his bathroom, and took a leak without bothering to close the door. He washed his hands, returned to his chair, and lit another smoke. "Alright, this is what we're going to do. Parker, Mikel, I'm not granting a mistrial, but you can put your objections on the record before the jury returns, to preserve them for appeal. If these goofballs are convicted, I see a huge issue of ineffective assistance of counsel coming up."

He turned to Jack. "How do you intend to prove the prior for Mr. McCall, Jack? And believe me, that's also going to be a huge issue on appeal."

Jack handed Solomon a certified copy of McCall's conviction, showing his photo and name, right next to Seavers' photo and name. Indeed, they'd spent six years together in state prison for a robbery they'd committed in 1962.

After reading the document, Solomon nodded. "Then prove it and move on. Kennedy, you'd be smart not to ask another question of your star witness. As far as you two clowns are concerned," he looked at Brolin and Moore, "I don't know what to advise you. Your client is in deep shit."

* * *

Three days later, after both sides delivered their closing arguments and the judge instructed the jurors on the law, the twelve left to deliberate the fates of Thomas Seavers and Joey Hernandez.

Including the time it took to consume their lunches, catered from a local restaurant so as not to disturb their deliberations, the ten men and two women spent precisely seventy-six minutes to reach verdicts for both defendants.

Guilty.

CHAPTER TEN

The Defalco Dining Room
Two days later, Saturday night

PAIGE PASSED PRIME RIB AS THEIR GUEST, Sam Leonard, poured expensive French burgundy for his wife. The foursome ate together at least once a week, the childless Leonards serving as little Claire's godparents. Each time they brought excellent vintages of wine for the adults and a new gizmo to delight their goddaughter.

Jack's friendship with Sam spanned years. The two shared season tickets to the Raiders and Niners and watched the A's during the summers. They enjoyed a passion for spirits and politics, entering into robust discussions on the merits of various proposed pieces of legislation pending before California's congress.

Now retired from teaching at U.C. Berkeley and employed as Chief Deputy Counsel to the Speaker of the House, Sam had special access to juicy insider information. He was a power player, more influential than the elected officials he served. He drew up the congressional districts and authored most of the legislation that mattered in the state. His name garnered both fear and respect. Jack often remarked that it was nice to have friends in high places.

Sipping his wine, Sam turned to Jack. "So are you going to get death on that killer you just convicted?"

Jack looked around to ensure Claire still played in the family room before he answered. "Not likely. He has a prior from 1962, but this robbery-murder is pretty run-of-the-mill. One bullet to the victim's head, everyone else fell in line and handed over their valuables. Nothing gory or horrific to inflame the jurors."

"Honeybun, why don't you tell Sam about the jury you picked?" Paige's eyes held a wicked gleam.

Chuckling, Sam ventured, "You kicked off all the blacks?"

Jack nudged his wife under the table. Even though Sam served as the best man at their wedding, Jack didn't want him to know about kicking off the Jews. "Actually, I left on a black guy, along with nine other men. There are two women who could vote to kill Seavers, if they had enough evidence in aggravation. But that's where I'm a little thin."

Paige ignored his hint. "You also sneaked on four guys with prior DUI convictions who normally drink in bars. They may have helped you get such a fast guilty verdict, so maybe they'll get you your coveted death verdict."

Sam turned to Paige, his former student at the university. "Ever the diehard liberal. Even you have to admit, some criminals deserve a good killing."

As she excused herself to check on Claire, Paige smiled. "Let's just say I have a tough time squaring the death penalty with that pesky commandment, 'Thou shall not kill.'"

Jack reached for his wine glass. "Sam, you're still tight with the president of the senate and the guy running for Attorney General, right?"

Sam swallowed his beef before answering, bliss evident in his sigh. "Yep. I've known them since we were kids growing up in Alameda. We're like the Three Musketeers."

"More like the Three Stooges," his wife piped in.

Patting her hand, Sam added, "You're just lucky you married me instead of Bill Hughes. Once he's the AG, who knows what kind of a jerk he'll become."

Yeah, Jack thought, because unfettered power can certainly corrupt otherwise ethical individuals.

* * *

Two weeks later, Solomon looked haggard after so many months of trial. "Ladies and gentlemen of the jury, in this sentencing portion of the trial, Mr. Defalco has presented the People's evidence in aggravation. Mr. Brolin and Mr. Moore have presented their client's evidence in mitigation and their argument. Now, the People will give you their closing statement."

Jack moved to the podium. He hadn't provided the jury much reason to gas Tom Seavers. He'd introduced the guy's prior robbery conviction and the facts surrounding it. He put on a few of the bar patrons who'd delivered their valuables to the robbers after witnessing Cowboy's murder. Predictably, they described their trauma. But since Dorrian couldn't unearth any of Cowboy's family, no weeping relatives testified to what a nice fellow he'd been, or what a hole his death had left in their lives.

Overall, Jack figured, that wasn't nearly enough evil to justify a death sentence.

The defense, on the other hand, introduced Seavers' wife and young daughters, who cried as they begged the jury to spare their father's life. The lawyers put on prison officials to testify to Seavers' perfect record as a prisoner. They'd even shown the jury various pictures Seavers had painted while in custody. Some of those, Jack decided, weren't half bad. The attorneys stressed Seavers' middle age and his inability to hear. They wheedled, whined, and cajoled each juror to show mercy for their client.

Regardless of who spoke to them, not a single juror reacted with even a slight change of expression. In over three hundred trials, Jack had never encountered such a stoic group of citizens. From the podium he looked into their faces, clearing his throat. He smoothed the front of his suit jacket before sipping water.

Fuck it. No pain, no gain.

Jack emphasized how quickly Seavers had plugged old Cowboy in the head, without a hint of conscience. What would stop him from killing in prison, he argued, possibly murdering an innocent guard? And what if some parole board down the road decided to let Seavers out? How could justice be served if that happened?

Ten men and two women stared at him, some with their arms crossed, a few frowning, all of them appearing skeptical.

Well, desperate times called for desperate measures.

"So, ladies and gentlemen, in closing I just want to add one thought. The defense attorneys paraded these two girls in front of you," Jack gestured to Seavers' children in the front row, their patent-leather Mary Janes swinging at the ends of their short legs, "and asked you to spare this killer's life for their sake. To instead send him to prison for life without parole."

Jack took a breath, turning away from the kids and their mother. "But what are they supposed to tell their friends and teachers as they grow up, when they're asked where their father is? Are they supposed to say, 'State prison, because he's a murderer?'"

Shaking his head as he slowly walked before the jury box on his way to counsel table, Jack paused. "I submit to you, folks, it would be kinder for them to have no father to discuss at all. So, instead of condemning them to a life filled with awkward explanations, do them a favor and vote to kill their dad. Send Tom Seavers to the gas chamber."

Silence sucked the oxygen from the courtroom.

Sitting down in his chair, Jack glanced up at Solomon. The judge had removed his glasses, leaned forward, and covered his mouth with his right hand. His brown eyes bulged in their sockets. Evidently, he wasn't impressed by Jack's final plea for death.

The jury filed out to deliberate whether or not to execute Seavers. Jack hefted his trial box before walking over to Paige, who'd ditched her law classes to watch her spouse deliver his first death penalty argument. Kissing her when she rose, he murmured, "So, what'd you think?"

Before she could answer, Solomon bellowed, "Defalco. My chambers. Now!"

Paige winced. "I'll hang around until you can talk. I brought homework."

As Jack entered Solomon's chambers, the judge slammed the door.

"What the fuck…" Spittle flew from the old man's lips as he tried to catch a breath. "… kind of argument was that? 'Do the kids a favor and kill their dad?'" His voice rose to a shout. "Are you out of your fucking mind, Defalco, or is your head so far up your ass, you can't think anymore?"

"Judge, I—"

"Don't! Don't even try to justify what you said. Sit down, Jack, and don't move because this case is over. I give that jury one hour, tops, before they return a verdict of life without."

Jack sat, chastised and miserable that he'd screwed up his

first big death case with a flippant, unnecessary comment during the final throes of trial.

The defense attorneys wandered in, along with various prosecutors and public defenders that relished the courtroom drama. All concurred with Solomon that Jack had torpedoed his case, wasting everyone's time and money at trial. On the other hand, as the minutes ticked by, plans blossomed for a huge victory party in honor of Brolin's and Moore's life verdict.

One hour later, as if Solomon were the omniscient bastard he claimed to be, the jury pushed the buzzer, indicating they had a verdict. The judge donned a smug expression as the parties returned to their places in court, waiting for the jurors to reassemble.

Jack looked at Paige and shook his head. Putting on his game face, he straightened his tie, brushed off some imaginary lint from his lapel, and prepared for his colleagues to shove failure up his ass.

"Has the jury reached a decision on whether or not Mr. Seavers should face execution?" Solomon addressed this question to the foreperson, the Hawaiian woman who'd had her purse snatched.

"We have, Your Honor."

"Please hand the verdict form to the bailiff."

The bailiff received the folded piece of paper and handed it to the clerk. She opened it, cleared her throat, and pronounced in a loud voice, "We the jury, in the case of *The People of the State of California versus Thomas Seavers*, fix his punishment," she looked toward the accused, "at death."

The courtroom erupted. Solomon shouted, "Quiet!" The defense attorneys hugged each other as they wept. Jack, shell-shocked, frowned at Paige, while members of the audience either sobbed or laughed, depending on their view of the verdict.

"I want order!" Solomon clapped his hands together. When silence reigned, he thanked and excused the jury before he swept into his chambers. Members of Jack's office swarmed around him, back slaps and high fives abounding. He told them he'd meet them for celebratory drinks at The Fat Lady, their favorite hang out, and watched as Seavers' attorneys accepted condolences from the defense bar.

Her backpack slung over her shoulder, Paige hugged him. As he held his wife, he noticed Tom Seavers sitting quietly at counsel table, ignored by everyone else in the courtroom. Jack moved Paige to one side and approached the man he'd just sent to San Quentin's gas chamber.

"Mr. Seavers?" He tapped on the deaf man's shoulders to get his attention.

The condemned prisoner looked up. "Yes?"

Jack spoke slowly, aware Seavers could read lips and hear some words with use of a hearing aide. "Do you understand what just happened here in court?"

Seavers shook his head.

Jack glanced at Seavers' lawyers, wallowing in their defeat. "The jury just sentenced you to death."

Without expression, the defendant responded, "Oh. Thank you for telling me."

Jack nodded at him, his stomach queasy. "I thought you should know."

And then Thomas Seavers asked a strange question, one that would haunt the Defalcos for decades. "Mr. Defalco, will you be there, at my execution? I'd appreciate that."

Jack glanced at his wife, only a foot away. "If you want me there, Tom, I promise I'll be there."

"Thank you, sir."

The bailiff cast Jack a curious look, shrugged, and led Seavers toward the exit where a van waited to transport him to San Quentin's death row.

Paige grabbed a tissue from her pocket to wipe away tears seeping down her cheek.

Jack threw an arm around his wife's shoulder as he watched Seavers shuffle away from Fairfax County and out of their lives. He ran a hand over the top of his hair, picked up his briefcase, and decided to spend a quiet evening at home with his family.

Something about death had extinguished his appetite for merrymaking.

PART TWO

Seventeen years later

2004

An imperfect man strikes a blow for justice.

CHAPTER ELEVEN

Law Offices of Defalco & Defalco
Beartooth, Montana
March 2004

JACK RUBBED HIS EYES AS HE LEANED INTO HIS BLACK LEATHER OFFICE CHAIR. No longer a government drone sitting amid scratched metal desks, he admired his wife's decorating—soft yellow walls, rosewood furniture, cream trim surrounding windows that showcased mountain views, and a Persian rug in red and blue hues covering the oak floor.

Without question, life as a private attorney in Beartooth, Montana had its perks.

He could hear Paige speaking on the phone in the second floor office adjacent to his. She'd designed their new building to provide them privacy upstairs, away from the daily chaos. From a well-equipped domain downstairs, Stormy, their steadfast legal assistant, ferociously screened the two attorneys from deadbeat clients and local press.

Jack sighed. Seven years ago, when they'd quit their careers as California prosecutors to move the family to the hinterlands of Montana, he called Paige bat-shit crazy. They'd abandoned their friends, family, and lucrative incomes to practice law in a more-cows-than-people county with two judges, a cranky prosecutor, poorly trained cops, and few hard-charging defense attorneys. Worse, they'd landed in a good old boy system that violated every tenet of the U.S. Constitution.

As experienced trial lawyers, coming from a jurisdiction that at least gave lip service to the Bill of Rights, Jack and Paige couldn't resist taking on the local Courthouse Cowboys. Indeed, after only four weeks appearing with various clients, the Defalcos managed to piss off pretty much everyone at the Kootenai County Justice Center.

In what seemed like a good idea at the time, Jack had talked Paige into applying as a public defender, and once hired, she'd represented several accused killers in high profile cases that netted national media coverage. When juries acquitted her young clients, the Cowboys sought her disbarment and slammed her reputation statewide. When their attempts failed to rid the valley of the pesky Defalcos, the Cowboys dumped Paige as a PD.

No loss there. The publicity from the fracas brought more clients to the law firm than either attorney could represent. Their business thrived, hence the need to build their own office. Not surprisingly, Paige's goal in moving to Montana, to slow their pace of life, fell by the wayside.

Glancing out at icy streets, Jack reminded himself he loved every stress-filled minute of the controversy that plagued them. Besides, he needed something to amuse himself in this godforsaken wasteland. For the last seven years, he'd craved their days in California, from wine tasting in Napa to the symphony in San Francisco. Most of all he missed professional sports. He still rued the day he kissed goodbye to his Raiders and Niners season tickets. He mourned the loss of his seats behind home plate, cheering on his beloved baseball team with Sam Leonard—traded for a state that had no professional sports teams.

Paige interrupted his pity party when she slumped into his visitor's chair, crossing her long, jean-clad legs. "Let me guess. Since it's March, you're thinking about baseball and how, once again, you'll miss the Athletics' games?"

He picked up a ballpoint pen and clicked it repeatedly, knowing it irritated her. "Pretty much. God, how I hate this place."

His wife raised her open palm. "Don't start. We agreed this was a better place to raise Claire and Sean. Besides, if we'd stayed in California, we'd be divorced by now." She snatched the pen out of his hand. "Why don't you fly down to visit your sister next month? Take in some games, visit Sam and your old buddies from the DA's office?"

Jack smiled at her. "What would you do without me, sweet pea? With Claire at college and Sean away at school, who will you talk to at night?"

She laughed. "I'll manage. Actually, it looks like we'll have company next month. That was Scott Kelly calling from

the Appellate Project. He's arriving here in a couple of weeks
to check out my work on the death penalty case."

Jack frowned. "Scott Kelly? The defense attorney I
worked with in Fairfax County?"

Paige nodded. "One and the same. He's my mentor buddy
for this case. I'm a few months late on the habeas corpus
petition, and he's planning to help me get it filed. Really, I
think he just wants an excuse to get away from his job."

Four years earlier, the California Supreme Court had
appointed Paige to represent a condemned prisoner on San
Quentin's death row. For the daunting task of re-investigating
his entire case, the Court paid her an hourly wage that most
lawyers would shun. Still, she loved the challenge of capital
litigation and the added income earned outside Kootenai
County. Adhering to policy, the Court had assigned a senior
attorney to supervise her work.

"Scott will be here for a few days. He's staying out at The
Lodge, but I invited him over for dinner. You can trade war
stories about your wild days practicing in front of Solomon
Green."

Closing his eyes, Jack murmured, "I still can't believe
Solomon's dead."

Cancer, from endless coffee and cigarettes, eventually
destroyed the judge's stomach and lungs. He'd refused
treatment and died two years ago. Even in death, he remained a
legendary figure in Fairfax County legal circles.

Paige stood. "I'm heading to the store. Sean called this
morning, begging for more food in his care packages. I'll see
you at home."

Listening to his wife's descending footsteps, Jack thought
of their son, the miracle baby. After Claire's birth, the doctors
swore she'd remain an only child. Paige entered law school
believing them. Then, at the end of her first year, they'd
discovered she was pregnant with Sean. His birth in the middle
of her second year complicated the chaos, but now, at sixteen,
Jack and Paige longed for their son's humor and adolescent
shenanigans.

Why had Sean, the child of two anti-war protesters,
followed a siren's song to a military academy? When he first

broached the idea, both parents rejected it. Yet when Sean made a case for a drug-free learning environment that would enable him to pursue his long-held dream of flying Navy jets, like his uncle and grandfather, they'd relented.

That was six long months ago. His absence left an aching chasm in his dad's heart.

Sighing, Jack shut down his computer. So, Scott Kelly was coming to Montana. Interesting. Long ago they'd shared many a courtroom moment in front of Solomon and other judges on the Fairfax County bench. Swapping stories over a fine cabernet seemed just the remedy Jack needed to salve his wanderlust.

If he couldn't entice his son home or move back to California, at least he could pretend he still worked as a DA.

* * *

Two nights later, Jack stared into the fire, warming a snifter of cognac between his palms. Paige had long ago retired, leaving him to ruminate about life in the wilderness. He loved the crackle and smell of lodgepole as it burned. The brandy, purchased for a small fortune at the state liquor store, removed the chill his down vest couldn't touch. Outside, a late March snow fell in fat, drippy flakes that would melt before morning. The family's two chocolate Labradors snoozed at his feet. Both cats curled together in Paige's soft leather chair.

To an outsider, Jack's life in Montana appeared perfect. He lived in a big-windowed house that sat in the middle of five parked-out acres. Across the road, trains rattled by at regular intervals, crossing below the ski mountain's many runs. Wildlife ran through the property, grass stayed green all summer, and the Fourth of July, with fireworks legal, fed a pyromaniac's dream. His kids were healthy and happy, and while his twenty-four year marriage to Paige had its ups and downs, overall it remained solid.

So what ate at him?

His job.

Switching sides of the courtroom to represent the very evildoers he'd once sent to prison or death row gnawed at his stomach lining every time he sat next to his clients. He'd relished accompanying cops on search warrant busts, watching autopsies, chasing down recalcitrant witnesses, collecting evidence to prove his case, and going to trial.

Of all he'd lost moving to Montana, Jack most missed prosecuting bad guys. Prosecutors started ahead of the game, with most jurors believing DAs waltzed into court wearing the white hat. DAs possessed instant credibility. Most citizens figured the defendant must be guilty of something if a DA brought him to trial.

As a defense attorney, however, Jack struggled with the disdain he received from judges and jurors alike. Every day brought a fight to get someone at least to listen to his client's version of the crime. Worse, the sentences handed down in Montana for minor infractions offended even Jack's tough-on-crime approach to the law. Every felony boded a possible hundred-year sentence. Instead of a three strikes law, Montana had the PFO, persistent felony offender, a designation that could add a hundred years onto any sentence, merely because the accused had a prior felony conviction.

Local judges wielded their power inconsistently, without any thought to the Constitution's requirement of uniform sentencing for similar crimes among defendants. One judge gave probation to pedophiles, but hammered bad check writers with state prison. None of it made logical sense to Jack, nor did it provide him with any peace at work.

Suddenly, the dogs alerted, racing to the glass doors leading to the field. Following them, Jack caught the shadow of deer bounding through snow. He sensed Paige's presence behind him before he felt her hand on his shoulder.

"Brooding again, honeybun?"

Jack turned to her, pulling her into a fierce hug. "Screw this place! I'm lost, Paige. I don't know what the fuck I'm doing in Montana, except making barely enough money to pay for Claire's college. She's gone, my Porsche's gone, and Sean's gone. I miss my old life and," he leaned away to look at his wife, "I miss being a prosecutor."

Paige sighed. "We've danced this dance before, Jack. It's too late to retreat to the Bay Area. Besides, you forget you hated your job by the time we moved. Every single morning, you left the house ranting that you detested your transfer to

Consumer Fraud."

That transfer, from death penalty prosecutor to civil division paper-pusher, had nailed the lid closed on Jack's career advancement. His old nemesis, Rick Peters, at last achieving his own dream of becoming The Boss, spared little time in sending Jack to the hinterlands of south Fairfax County.

Jack turned toward the darkness outside. "I know. And I know there's no going back, that Montana kept our marriage together and turned out to be a better place to raise the kids. I just can't feel any contentment here, any peace."

Paige ran her fingers through the top of her hair, a sure sign of frustration. "Then quit practicing criminal law and focus on your civil and business cases. If it bothers you so much to sit next to defendants in court, then don't do it."

Jack called the dogs before he set his empty brandy snifter on the counter. "Which sounds so easy, doesn't it? Except you and I both know that we're addicted to criminal trials and all they involve. No matter how we try to break away, we fly right back into the flame."

Addiction, that shoulder demon that whispers, "Just one more," whether referencing a trial, a cigarette, a drink, or a shot of heroin, haunted the Defalcos as it did most junkies. After thirty-some years in the arena, with over three hundred fifty jury trials behind him, Jack, like Paige, remained a slave to that addiction.

Turning out the lights, his heart constricted, a painful reminder of recent loss and future emptiness.

* * *

The following week, ensconced in her office with the door shut, Paige reviewed crime scene photos for the hundredth time. Her California death row client claimed he hadn't committed the robbery-murder that resulted in the death of a middle-aged store clerk who also happened to be a mom and grandmother. The gruesome pictures depicted the victim, face down, a portion of her skull blown away, lying in a large pool of blood. Whoever killed her had forced her into a janitor's closet, made her kneel, and then executed her. A large bruise to her upper forehead hinted the killer might have pistol-whipped her into unconsciousness before shooting her.

Since her defense for the case was eyewitness identification—someone other than Paige's client had committed the crime—she deemed the manner of death irrelevant. For the jury, this had been a clear question of who-done-it.

Unfortunately, those jurors had concluded Paige's guy not only killed and robbed the clerk, but that because he had a similar prior conviction, he deserved to die. Her job, via a four-hundred-plus-page habeas corpus petition, was to convince the California Supreme Court to grant a hearing, so she could present new evidence of her client's innocence, and of his prior counsels' incompetence.

The latter issue, Paige mused, appeared a sure-fire winner on appeal. Two public defenders had been assigned the case. The lead attorney had no prior capital crimes experience and happened to be on probation with the State Bar of California for borrowing client funds from their trust accounts. The other attorney, a fellow weighing in at nearly four hundred pounds, gave less than a shit about his client and played solitaire on his laptop throughout the trial. When Paige questioned him about his behavior, he'd claimed it was part of his trial strategy to distract the prosecutor.

Right.

For Paige's purposes, the best proof of incompetence had appeared during the penalty phase, after the client had been found guilty, but before the jury recommended death or life without parole. That second mini-trial had provided the defense team the opportunity to present evidence of the client's good side from his family, friends, psychological experts, probation officers, and jail guards.

Instead of allowing those folks to testify, the lead defense attorney had wandered into the hall outside court and asked a heavily tattooed white man, passing out leaflets advertising a drug rehab program, to tell the jurors about life in prison. This fellow qualified as an expert on the subject based on his twenty-seven years spent in custody for various felonies, including assault with a deadly weapon and rape.

The attorney hadn't pre-tried the witness, instead letting

the guy take the stand and wing it. With Swastika tattoos wrapping his exposed arms, the man told the jury precisely where and when he'd served time in California's penal system and for which crimes. He described with relish how easy it was to make a shiv—jail parlance for a knife—in the machine shop, then shove it up one's ass to escape its detection. It was critical, he told the jurors, to arm oneself and kill others when necessary to survive the rigors of prison life.

Paige closed her eyes as she remembered the key question her client's attorney had asked: "If, instead of sentencing this man to death, the jury recommends life without parole, what sort of danger does a life prisoner present?"

"Well," the convict on the stand had offered, "life prisoners are the most dangerous people on earth because they've got nothin' to lose. Hell, they'd just as soon kill you over a pack of cigarettes than borrow one. Nobody's worse than a lifer, that's for sure."

Not surprisingly, with that expert opinion and not another shred of mitigation evidence from the defense, the jury had no choice but to recommend execution.

After a mere twelve-year delay, Paige's client had jumped to the head of the line to have his appeal heard. Indeed, like the other seven hundred fifty-plus prisoners on California's death row, he'd neither been assigned nor spoken to an attorney in more than a decade.

So much for cleaning up the backlog at San Quentin.

For that matter, so much for justice.

Paige closed the case file, figuring she should grab groceries before heading home. As she left the office, she, too, wondered why she slaved to help the downtrodden, for little money, when the Defalcos needed serious cash to fund their kids and mortgage.

Sam Leonard had been right years ago. She truly was just another bleeding-heart.

CHAPTER TWELVE

Beartooth, Montana
Early April 2004

THE DEFALCOS WATCHED BLACK MAKEUP dribble down the fifteen-year-old's cheeks. She sat defiantly in their living room, alert despite the midnight hour.

"I hate him! Don't you understand? He hits me, for chrissakes!"

The three sat before the fire as a sheriff's deputy stood in parade stance a few feet away.

Paige glanced at the officer. "Did you arrest her father?"

Deputy Kimber shook his head. Jutting his chin at the sobbing teenager, he added, "She doesn't want to press charges. She wants to move in with you."

Jack winced. *That explains why Kimber appeared on our doorstep with this kid.* Jack and Paige had known the girl's family only a few months when her mother committed suicide a few weeks earlier. Afterward, the teen had bonded with Paige. Now, thanks to another blow up with her dad, the girl phoned 9-1-1 and begged the cops to take her to the Defalcos' home.

Glaring at his wife, Jack furiously shook his head "No!" The girl, her face buried in her hands, couldn't see his refusal. No fucking way were they taking in this messed up teenager. He might miss his own children, but common sense told him this girl's presence spelled disaster if they gave her a foot in their door.

Despite his vehement denial, Paige murmured, "Jack, maybe we should let her get some sleep in Claire's old room and take a fresh look at this in the morning."

The deputy smiled. "Great idea, Paige. I knew I could count on you to help out." He turned toward the front door. "The alternative, as you know, is foster care and—"

Jack jumped to his feet. "Wait!" He exhaled, rubbing a hand over his sleep-rumpled hair. "Just...wait a second, George. Legally we can't keep her here without her father's permission or a court order. We're not her parents."

The girl's large brown eyes widened as she begged, "Please, Mr. Defalco? My dad hates me. He told me he doesn't want me. And now with my mom dead…" Another torrent of tears washed her puffy face.

Jack absorbed the deputy's disapproval, his wife's furrowed brow, and the teen's terror. He felt his already chaotic world crumbling like a suspect folding under interrogation. This girl's father, a rigid Catholic and retired Army general, had abandoned his only daughter after beating the crap out of her for staying out past curfew. Worse, no longer able to cope with her husband's brutality, the child's mother died after swallowing vast quantities of sedatives and gin.

Stymied, Jack compromised. "Okay, here's the deal." He addressed the young girl's hope-filled face. "You can stay here tonight. Tomorrow, I'll talk to your father and a judge. We'll figure something out."

Leaping off the sofa, young Kayla Rider hugged her new savior. "Thank you! I promise I won't be any trouble if you let me stay here. I'll help around the house and take care of the dogs. And I'll go back to school and get good grades!"

Jack hesitated before patting Kayla on the back. He was no one's hero and had little interest in that role.

Deputy Kimber gave a mock salute at the front door. "Thanks, you two. Let me know what happens, so I can add it to my report."

While Paige settled Kayla in Claire's old room, Jack poured himself a couple of fingers of scotch, which he swallowed before Paige walked into the kitchen.

Pissed, he glared at his wife as she poured herself some milk.

She held up her palms in surrender. "So what was I supposed to do when the police showed up with her? She's not a dog they can drop off at the shelter."

He poured another shot of Glenfiddich into his Baccarat glass. Only the best in booze and crystal for Jack Defalco. "Do you know how fucked up that kid is? According to what we know, she's screwed half the high school, claims she's pregnant every other week, drops in and out of ninth grade whenever the mood strikes, and generally appears to be stoned. We cannot keep her, Paige."

"I know all that, honeybun. But it's like *The Ransom of Red Chief*. We've got her, and her dad won't take her back. He told me so when I called him earlier. She's right. He does not want to see her, ever again." Paige sipped from her mug.

"Well, fuck him! This is his child, for God's sake. He can't just give her away like a hamster. She's only fifteen, and she just lost her mother."

Paige nodded. "Exactly. And he beats her for the smallest infraction, then hauls her off to Mass, so she can confess her sins. Ergo, sending her home, even if he agreed, may not be an option. Which leaves her either here or in foster placement."

Swilling the last of his drink, Jack put his glass on the counter. "I'm too tired to deal with this shit right now. Let's sleep on it."

Paige rinsed her mug. "You know what Mother Teresa says? That God puts people in our path for a reason. Then it's our choice whether we step around the person or try to help him…or her."

"Then let's ship her to that convent in India, so the good sisters can figure out what to do with her." With that, Jack huffed off to their bedroom. Climbing into bed, he resolved to take a wide detour around troubled Kayla Rider. No way would he allow that kid's drama to consume their lives. Besides, they had their own kids to support, not to mention their clients, and each other.

He watched Paige don a filmy nightshirt. A good Catholic herself, his wife often quoted the wrinkled old holy woman who cared for Calcutta's poor. Well, screw Mother Teresa and the horse she rode in on.

And speaking of screwing, maybe he could salvage an otherwise shitty day.

* * *

The next day, General William "Billy" Rider refused to take his wayward daughter back into his home. He offered to sign a temporary custody agreement allowing the Defalcos to make crucial life decisions for Kayla, from where she attended school to whether or not she took birth control pills. The general, physically and emotionally battered from thirty years of military service and clueless why his wife took her own life, simply opted out of fatherhood. Worse, he refused to provide any money for his daughter's expenses, forcing the Defalcos to absorb another major financial hit by taking her in.

Jack sat at his desk as Paige slumped in the chair across from him. He thrummed his fingers as he glared at his spouse. "Foster care, Paige. That's where she needs to be right now. There's a system in place, good families who participate, and special counselors to deal with her emotional problems."

Paige sighed. "I know that. And I know you're right in a way, but crap, Jack. What if she isn't one of the lucky ones to get a nice family? Look at her body. She looks like she's twenty-five. How long before some asshole molests her?" She leaned forward. "What if this was Claire? Would foster placement be the answer, or would you want her to live with a family who at least kept her safe?"

Ouch. Thinking of his darling Claire studying at college in Seattle, Jack knew he'd just lost the battle. He'd never let Claire live in a foster home. Then again, he'd never abandon his own kids, for any reason. He used the pen in his hand to sign the custody agreement. "And that fucker calls himself a Christian? Besides, what kind of cheap bastard won't give his own kid money for food and clothes?"

Paige signed her name below his. "The kind who wants to punish her for being who she is, and who wants to control everyone in his life." As she rose to return to her own office, she added, "One day at a time, okay? This can all change in a week. You just have to trust that God's got our backs."

"Horseshit. God's not paying any attention to us, sweet pea. But we'll deal with this like we have everything else during the last twenty-five years together."

After Paige closed his door, Jack shut his eyes.

Kayla Rider. Truant, doper, liar, cheat, and a kid who desperately sought love from someone. Jack didn't love her. He didn't even like her. But he knew he couldn't throw her out the door. They'd keep her for as long as necessary, but no matter what, he'd insure her safety, just as he'd kept his own kids safe all these years. Kayla might be a little shit, but she'd be a safe little shit for as long as she lived in his house.

And didn't life just get better by the day?

* * *

Sunday morning, Jack listened as Paige, upstairs, tried to drag Kayla's reluctant carcass out of bed for Mass. "C'mon, Kayla. Up!"

He heard the teen groan. "Are you fucking kidding me? I might as well be home with my dad if I have to get up for church! Screw this, I'm not going."

Down in the kitchen, Jack yelled, "Kayla, either get your ass down here, now, or you can argue about church with your new foster parents."

Another groan, a "Fuck!" and a thud on the wooden floor preceded movement. Paige looked weary when she came down to grab a cup of coffee. A few minutes later, Kayla pranced before them wearing short-shorts, a halter-top, and four-inch platforms.

Jack pointed toward the stairs. "Nice try, honey. You look like a strumpet. Try long pants, tennis shoes, and a normal shirt. No cleavage. And brush your teeth."

Rolling her eyes, Kayla huffed, "They call this fashion, Jack. And what the hell is a strumpet?" Once she'd moved in, she'd cut the obsequious "Mr. Defalco" in favor of his first name.

"A strumpet, young lady, is a hooker. And fashion be damned, you're not leaving the house in that outfit, whether it's to go to church or a Halloween party. Now change, and do it fast. Paige hates to be late."

Ascending, Kayla stomped a foot on each step, but eventually returned in Jack's preferred outfit. "How's this? Christ, I look like a little kid. I think I'll get a tattoo across my back. Maybe my mom's name?" She grabbed a banana on the way out the door.

Jack muttered to Paige, "She should get a tattoo on her butt that says 'pain in the ass.'"

Kayla remained quiet on the short drive to St. Cecilia's. After they parked, she begged, "Couldn't I just wait here? I don't want to see my dad."

More likely she wanted to avoid the embarrassment of town folks pitying her. Opening her rear car door, Jack smiled. "I doubt he'd have the guts to show his face here, honey. Everyone in Beartooth knows he dumped you, so he's not real popular right now. Besides, attending Mass matters to Paige, so suck it up, buttercup. You can do it for her."

In the pew, Kayla sat stiff as a statue, obviously aware people stared at her. Jack admired her bravado. This kid hid her pain better than most adults, and she didn't take shit from anyone, including him. When they stood, Kayla rose at least two inches above him. At fifteen, she'd developed more than most girls her age, but still held on to some baby fat. Her tight brown curls, deep whiskey eyes, and latte complexion reflected her mother's African-American heritage, but her jawline replicated her father's stern Irish countenance. Neither parent nor child often smiled.

Jack watched Paige on the altar as she prepared to hand out communion. Her unflagging energy to volunteer in the community, in addition to full time trial work, amazed him. And now, she'd returned to bygone days packing lunches and chauffeuring a kid to dozens of activities.

They'd hoped to retire in a couple of years, even purchase some acreage in southern Arizona to escape Montana's brutal winters. That, Jack thought, won't happen now, not until Kayla graduates from high school.

During communion, his eye caught Kayla next to him, texting on her phone. He reached over, plucked it from her fingers, and pocketed it. Shaking her head, she laughed quietly.

Most likely, in ten minutes, all hell would break loose again. The winds would shift, pitting a crusty, aging lawyer against a street-smart, young girl. But for now, kneeling next to one another in the peace of St. Cecilia's, they enjoyed a quiet truce.

"Please God," Jack prodded, "if you're there—and I'm not so sure you are despite all my years studying in the seminary—help us do what's best for this kid."

Christ, however, neither winked nor gave Jack a thumbs-up.

CHAPTER THIRTEEN

Beartooth, Montana
One week later, mid-April 2004

SCOTT KELLY, THE DEATH PENALTY EXPERT FROM CALIFORNIA, yanked a single sheet of paper from the thick binder on Paige's desk. "Voila! The ubiquitous 'cover your ass' memo."

Paige glanced at the single paragraph written by her client's former trial lawyer, the one who'd played solitaire on his computer to psyche out the prosecutor, and rolled her eyes. "Right. Why is it every lawyer who loses at trial places one of these 'my client confessed' letters in his file? I've never done that."

"Yeah, but you haven't lost that many cases."

Paige sighed. "Not as a defense attorney, but I dumped some as a prosecutor."

Scott sat in Paige's office chair while she handed him various parts of the habeas corpus evidence: autopsy photos, crime scene photos, crime lab reports, police reports, and witness statements. As he read, Paige noticed the lines creasing his face. Twenty years in criminal law's fast lane had added gray to his hair and probably holes in his stomach lining.

Like me, she noted as she slumped into the chair across from him, her hiking boot jiggling over her knee. "The client swears he didn't do the murder, and the evidence shows his trial team should have mounted an identification defense. When you look at it, the cops had nothing but the woman who wandered into the 7-Eleven, saw the dead storekeeper, and ran out screaming. When she knocked into the killer on her way out, she peed her pants. How could she be a reliable ID witness?"

Scott gazed out the window to the ski mountain. "Nice digs, Defalco. I can see why you and Jack love Beartooth." He looked at her. "As to the witness, I'd agree, if that's all the prosecutors had. But didn't they find rolls of coins in your guy's apartment that were similar to the ones taken from the store's cash register? And some burned payroll checks bearing employees' names?"

Nodding, Paige added, "But he says his roommate did the crime."

"Yeah, right." Scott rose, arching his back. "I've had it for today. Are we still on for dinner at your house?"

Paige smiled. "You bet, for the famous Defalco flank steak, pesto pasta, and Caesar salad. And bonus, you get to meet our newest family member, the lovely and profane Kayla Rider."

When Scott's brow rose, Paige grimaced. "A wandering waif we took in. She's not a bad kid, just one who's had a screwed-up childhood full of unrelenting trauma and violence."

Scott grabbed his briefcase. "Sounds like every one of our clients."

Listening to him trudge downstairs, Paige put her boots on her desk. She stared out the window at snow melting on ski runs. Just enough green poked through to signal the end of the season. Besides, the mountain always closed in early April since grizzly bears awoke hungry about that time. To protect the bear's habitat, and to prevent munched-for-lunch tourists, those in charge wisely shut down the chair lifts.

Closing her eyes, she reflected on her life since The Waif's arrival. The Defalco's first week with Kayla could have been worse—only two days caught skipping school and a single phone call from a local merchant, promising if Kayla returned the stolen makeup, he wouldn't file charges. Paige sighed. Her own kids had put her through her paces, but now that they'd moved out, she thought she'd seen the end of teenage angst and sleepless nights waiting for a call from the local jail. Or worse, the local hospital.

Scott certainly had nailed the prototype of America's killers lined up for execution, with San Quentin harboring some of the worst. Guys who'd killed multiple victims, cops, or other prisoners. Ones who popped out their victims' eyes before slitting their throats, and still others who garroted little kids in rest stop bathrooms. Paige long ago had dubbed the high security prison housing her clients "The Land of the

Broken Toys."

In a few years, without serious therapeutic intervention, Kayla Rider might fit right in. More likely, she'd end up as some asshole's punching bag or sold in the sex slave trade to a sado-masochistic pervert. She might avoid execution through the court system, but could still die young from the horrors in her life.

Paige realized the question posed for the Defalcos was whether or not their particular broken toy, young Kayla, could be fixed. And, if so, were they the doll makers who could accomplish that task?

Just as crucial as saving Kayla, Paige needed to persuade the California Supreme Court to give her death row client a hearing on his bid for freedom. If she failed at either task, a life would end, literally in the case of the client, and maybe literally for the teenager.

But, hey, no pressure.

* * *

Jack passed Scott the bowl of tortellini pesto. "More flank steak?"

"I want more—" Kayla withdrew her grab for the last piece of meat when Jack kicked her under the table. "Uh, salad."

Scott smiled at the teenager. "Kayla, you look like you could use some more protein. Delicious dinner, Paige."

Nodding her head, Paige cleared plates, absently patting Kayla's shoulder.

Jack poured Scott more wine, enjoying their exchange of past war stories. Just hearing a smart Bay Area lawyer discuss legal issues made him relax. Not as great as Bay Area sports, but heck, Kelly's banter was better than nothing.

"How often did you appear in Solomon Green's court? Weren't you a Fairfax County public defender?"

"Yep, before I went into private practice, and long before I took this job working on death penalty appeals."

Young Kayla stood, picking up her plate. "This conversation is boring. Can I watch TV?"

Jack dismissed her with a wave. "By all means, leave us in peace. And no more eating upstairs or in your room. We'll get mice."

"But I like mice, Jack. They're cute." Kayla smiled sweetly at Scott as she turned for the back stairs. "Nice to meet you, Mr. Kelly."

Jack tossed his wadded napkin at her back, hitting her between the shoulders.

Whipping around, she giggled. "Geez, Jack, you're such a child. I'm appalled!" She threw the napkin back at him.

He caught it in midair. "Be appalled, sweetheart. Be anything. Just don't eat up there."

"Yeah, yeah." Her clomping steps echoed in the Defalco's kitchen.

Draining his wine glass, Jack laughed. "God, she's a wiseass. I kind of like that about her." He opened a second bottle of red, pouring himself another hefty refill. He felt buzzed from the alcohol, but rejuvenated by the conversation.

Scott nodded. "Good of you guys to take her in. My boys are easy compared to her." He, too, swallowed cabernet. "Jack, didn't you try your first death penalty case in Solomon's court? The *Seavers* case?"

"Yep, seventeen years ago. Do you know if he's been executed yet?" Jack had Seavers' mug shot attached to the death verdict in a frame on his office wall, along with those of his other convicted death row defendants. Paige called it his "Wall of Shame."

"Not even close. Tom Seavers is still going through his federal appeal. A friend of mine is handling that."

Jack leaned his chair back, so the front legs hung inches above the floor, while the back legs supported his slight weight. "That's the problem with capital punishment. Once a guy's convicted, it takes years to kill him and a ton of money. And for what? So the victim's family can have closure?"

Scott nodded. "Agreed. How in the hell did you ever win that case?"

Paige coughed.

Jack glanced at her, but with so much booze on board, ignored her slight headshake and widened eyes. "Well, mainly because the defense attorneys were incompetent. I've never seen such a cluster fuck, like watching the Three Stooges in trial."

Excited to regale Kelly with a blow-by-blow of his first capital trial, Jack let his chair land on all four legs as he leaned forward. Describing defense witness Scott McCall, the never-arrested accomplice with the missing leg, his voice rose.

"You should have seen the look on the lawyers' faces when that gimpy guy alibied Seavers, saying he was at the family get-together with Joey Hernandez. Not to mention when Carmen Velasquez fingered Seavers as the shooter."

Instead of laughing, Scott stared at him. "You know, Jack, it's funny, but then again, it's not. Seavers had the right to competent counsel, especially in a death penalty case. I'm surprised Judge Green didn't declare a mistrial."

Jack snorted. "Are you kidding me? Solomon would never allow that. Shit, he even called me into chambers and told me to kick off Jewish jurors. He said he didn't want to waste his time for a life verdict since Jews would never vote for death."

At the sound of metal clanging off the tile, Jack watched Paige kneel beside a stainless steel bowl, its contents of fresh strawberries strewn across the floor.

"Hey, honeybun, you want to help me here?" She jerked her head at him, giving him a get-over-here-and-shut-up look.

He leaned down to grab some fruit, nearly falling out of his chair. "Whoa. Maybe not." His attention again directed at Kelly, Jack added, "I loved Solomon, kind of like a second father, you know? But he sure interfered at trial."

Scott paused, his wineglass near his lips. "Yeah, everyone knew he gave advice to both sides." He gulped some red, handing his glass to Jack for a refill. "But, fuck! Colluding with the prosecutor to rig a capital jury, insuring a death verdict? Even Solomon must have blanched when the jury voted to kill Seavers."

Far into a wine-induced stupor, Jack smiled. "First off, I'd hardly call that collusion, and second, Solomon didn't care about Tom Seavers or any other defendant. He cared about wasting the taxpayers' shekels. Besides, Seavers murdered a guy. It's not like he's innocent."

Paige slipped behind him and ran her palm down the back

of his head. Then she circled her fingers around his neck, squeezing, as she smiled at Scott. "Dessert?"

Again, Jack felt her pressure. Instead of pausing to consider her hints, he slurred out, "Makes you fat, buddy. Don't eat it."

Scott accepted Paige's offer of apple pie. "So, Jack, what else happened in *Seavers*? You know Solomon's been accused of misconduct in a bunch of criminal cases. The appeals courts have written several opinions excoriating him for unethical crap he did in trial."

Having resumed her place next to him, Paige nudged his leg with the toe of her boot. "Can you check on Kayla, sweetie?" She turned a smile toward Scott. "Not to change the subject, but how much longer will it take you to review my death row case?"

Rising a bit unsteadily, Jack excused himself. Holding onto the stair rail for balance, Jack wondered whether he'd said too much. If perhaps he'd given up his favorite judge to a defense attorney who'd likely attack the jurist's good reputation, albeit posthumously. On the top step, Jack let out a low, "Fuck!"

Entering the TV room, he found Kayla parked on the couch wearing bunny pajamas and slippers with ears. She wagged a finger at him. "Language, young man! And are you drunk?"

He turned off the television. "Bedtime, bonzo. You've got school, and since you're serving detention, you have to be there at 7:30. Nice move, by the way, smoking in the alley behind the police station."

Kayla stuck out her tongue before she entered her room, slamming the door.

Running his fingers through his hair, Jack looked at the ceiling, as if God hovered there laughing at him. In that moment, he prayed for two miracles: First, that Kayla's father would straighten up and take her back. Second, that Scott Kelly's wine consumption would erase all memories of tonight's discussion about the *Seavers* case.

Yet after seven years studying to be a priest, Jack pretty much knew those kinds of miracles never happened, at least not in his life.

* * *

At her vanity, Paige brushed out her red hair, much shorter now than during her law school days. In her mirror, she watched Jack struggle out of his jeans, hopping on one foot to extract the other from his pant leg. He fell against the wall, barely maintaining his balance. Paige frowned at his reflection, but kept brushing. "Still think you and Scott needed that second bottle of wine?"

Jack belched. "Not the wine that's the problem. It's the two martinis before dinner…" His voice trailed off as he pulled his sweater over his head.

When she could see his face, Paige turned to her inebriated spouse. "Jack, when I drove Scott back to his hotel, he mentioned he was going to call Seavers' federal appellate attorney. He figures they can raise the jury rigging claim to reverse Seavers' conviction." At her husband's blank look, she raised her voice. "That means you'll have to testify, Jack, and admit you colluded with a Superior Court judge. I know you're shit-faced, but do you have even a tiny clue how this could affect your career?"

Without stopping to brush his teeth, still wearing his polo shirt, Jack wove his way to the bed and collapsed against his pillow. "Fuck it, sweet pea. Kelly can do whatever he wants. I'm not testifying for that little prick, Seavers, and I'm sure as hell not ratting out Solomon." He shut his eyes. "Kelly'll forget the whole thing by tomorrow. Trust me."

Paige returned her gaze to her own reflection, swiping off her mascara. "I hate to say I told you so, but I did. Seventeen years ago, I said there'd be backlash when you kicked off the Jews. I even begged you not to do it. I asked you to follow your conscience, to be ethical. But you didn't listen, as usual." She stood before offering one last comment. "Mark my words, dear heart. This is going to bite you in the ass, big time."

Turning toward their cherry sleigh bed, Paige at last heard her husband's slack-jawed, open-mouthed snoring. He'd missed her wisdom, yet again. She threw back the covers on her side and bounced on the mattress as she got in.

No reaction.

Except for his drunken snorts, Jack Defalco laid beside her like a corpse in a coffin.

As she turned on her reading light before settling in with a new novel, Paige sent up a silent prayer that her spouse's drunken confession wouldn't kill his legal career.

Or him.

CHAPTER FOURTEEN

Defalco home
The next morning

JACK WATCHED FROM THE DOORWAY as Paige braided Kayla's now burgundy-striped hair. He shook his head. "I don't get why you keep changing your hair color. You look like a tie-dyed poodle."

Kayla rolled her eyes. "Because brown is boring." She nodded at Jack's brunette locks. "Really boring, like this conversation. And FYI? Poodles are cute." She smiled at Paige, "Plus highly intelligent."

Jack narrowed his eyes at his young charge. "Yeah? Well if they toss you out of school again for screwing up your hair, you'll be the first dumb member of the breed. Now, let's hustle. I need to drop you off in five minutes."

Following the teen to the car, he realized that with very little effort, this girl could piss off the pope. His hangover didn't add to his patience. Way too much wine, on top of gin, never played out well the next day, but he felt particularly sick to his stomach this morning. Something about his conversation with Scott Kelly the night before bothered him. *Yeah, you idiot, maybe the part where you confessed to tossing off Jews, with Solomon's help?*

After dropping Kayla at the junior high, Jack headed into work. He found Kelly perusing Paige's death penalty file in her office, sipping Stormy's acidic swill.

Scott grimaced. "Good morning. Does your secretary really think this passes for coffee?"

Jack smiled as he sat across the desk in Paige's chair. "It's Folger's crystals. She loves it, and since the espresso machine lives at our house, you're stuck with it."

Clearing his throat, Jack considered whether to approach the attorney about last evening's discussion. He decided to forego any reminder of it.

Scott gazed at him. "You know I have to tell Seavers' federal attorney that his trial lawyers screwed up the case. That behind-the-scenes stuff isn't in the official record, so he can use it in the habeas corpus petition."

"Right," Jack leaned back in his chair, returning Scott's stare. "Except Seavers' case went down seventeen years ago. I'm not testifying against the idiots who represented him or ratting out my old office for its jury selection practices."

As Scott opened his mouth to reply, Jack added, "And I'm definitely not burning Solomon. He was a good judge and one of my closest friends. He attended my wedding, for chrissakes. Let him rest in peace." Abruptly, Jack sat forward. "You push this, Scott, and I'll deny our conversation ever took place."

"What the fuck?" Scott's complexion reddened as he stood. "Whose side are you on? Do you want Seavers executed?"

Jack also rose. "I don't give a shit if he's drawn and quartered. He's guilty. The Supreme Court upheld the conviction. And since no judge on the Ninth Circuit has the balls to change that outcome, there's no reason to dredge up crap best left in the dark." He crossed his arms. "Drop it."

"Or what?" Scott stepped toward him.

A familiar voice from the doorway arrested Jack's response. "You two look like you're about to duke it out. What's going on?" Paige leaned against the jam.

Jack smirked at her. "Scott's about to leave for the airport." He turned to the California attorney. "You don't want to miss your flight to San Francisco. It's supposed to freeze here tonight."

Frowning, Scott collected his suitcase. "Jack, I'm talking to Seavers' federal lawyer when I get back. I'll give him your number." He walked toward the stairs. "You could save a man's life. If not, you'll have to live with it." Descending, he called out, "Paige, I'll expect you to file your legal work by the end of the month."

Paige inhaled a long breath, then released it, gazing at Jack. "Just so I'm clear here, Scott Kelly plans to expose your trial tactics to Seavers' federal lawyer, correct?"

Nodding, Jack rubbed between his eyes. "Yeah. I told him I'd deny all of it. Shit! That'll teach me to drink with old enemies."

Ceding Paige's chair to her, Jack moved toward the door. "No fucking way will I repeat that story, especially under oath, to benefit some asshole who deserves a needle full of poison." He turned toward her. "Too bad California abandoned the gas chamber. It's a much better way to snuff out killers like Tom Seavers."

* * *

Mid-afternoon, as Paige took a break from composing her client's legal plea to avoid lethal injection, she shook her head at the irony of her husband's pro-death penalty stance. More times than she could recall, he'd labeled her a bleeding-heart liberal, too sympathetic to her clients, especially the ones on death row.

True enough. She took a there-but-for-the-grace-of-God approach to criminal defense that left her far too emotionally involved with those incarcerated or facing death. Ditto for their families and friends, some of whom stopped by her office just to chat, even when their loved ones' cases had resolved. So far, she'd been lucky, and no clients had died. She planned on maintaining that record.

Still, what would become of her job if Jack testified to cheating seventeen years ago in a capital case? How would the California Supreme Court regard their law firm after such an admission? Would they fire her under a guilt-by-association theory? More importantly, could they somehow come after Jack, or even her, for their licenses to practice law?

In her fourteen-year career, Paige had never committed an ethical breach. She'd zealously prosecuted the bad guys in her day, pursuing extreme sentences for minor felons, especially in the frenzy following Three Strikes legislation. But lie, cheat, and steal? No.

And what about the systemic corruption in the Fairfax County District Attorney's Office that would surface in Jack's testimony? Not only was excluding Jewish people from capital juries a common practice, the boss had sent Jack statewide to teach prosecutors how to get away with it. Hell, at the Top Gun Prosecutors' College, they'd even videotaped his presentation. So, it wasn't as if Scott Kelly or Seavers' federal lawyer lacked proof of a pattern and practice of illegal exclusion. Besides, Paige had read numerous statistical studies supporting the premise that district attorneys, nationwide, stacked the legal deck against the accused.

Glancing at her watch, Paige realized she had to pick up Kayla from school. Thank God they could go home instead of racing off to some extra-curricular activity.

Paige's chest tightened, as it often did from stress. Before grabbing her coat, she swallowed half an Atavan to stop her racing heartbeat. She hated taking the prescription meds, especially for something so stupid as panic attacks, but quitting work wasn't an option.

She waived goodbye to Stormy and loaded her bulging briefcase into her Tahoe. While Kayla did homework, Paige could hammer out a few more pages on her client's habeas corpus petition. Then dinner, more work, and sleep. God, how she looked forward to going to bed every night.

And wasn't that a sad state of affairs, that she'd moved her family to the hinterlands of Montana, escaping the stress of their former life in California, only to find a different, but equally chaotic life in Beartooth?

At least the pace had slowed a little since the kids left for college and prep school.

"Hey, Paige!" Kayla wrenched open the car door as she dumped her backpack onto the seat. "You'll be happy to know I'm in love. He's twenty-two and has a job and everything. I can leave now and get out of your hair!"

Paige pulled away from the curb, weaving the SUV through students and teachers. She'd gone on high alert at the mention of a twenty-two-year-old male anywhere near her fifteen-year-old charge. "So, how did you meet...what's his name again?"

"Ryan something. He's gorgeous." Kayla withdrew a fruit chewy and stuffed it into her mouth.

"And where does Ryan work, honey?" Paige cross-examined the girl without shame, determined to string up old Ryan, the almost-pedophile, by his gonads.

"At the burrito place where we have lunch. He doesn't know I exist...yet. But he will."

Take a deep breath, you idiot. She hasn't even met the guy.

As they pulled into the garage, Paige put her hand on Kayla's arm. "Listen, kiddo. You're what's known in the trade as 'jail bait.' Since you're under sixteen, any guy you sleep with automatically gets a felony on his record. There's no defense, even if he claims he didn't know your age." At Kayla's frown, she finished. "Give Ryan whoever-he-is a break, sweetie. Leave him, and every other guy, alone until after your next birthday. Clear?"

Kayla laughed. "Whatever. Like I'm not going to date until I'm sixteen?"

Paige nodded. "Yep. Just like that. Our house, our rules."

Before she slammed the car door, Kayla yelled, "That's so unfair!"

Paige heard her own mother's voice whisper from the grave. "Remember what I told you? Whoever said life was fair?"

Geez, thanks Mom.

* * *

Alone in his office near closing time, Jack stared at the wall where his old badge, the one that identified him as a Fairfax County Deputy District Attorney, hung in a black frame. The gold star, etched with the seal of California, represented twenty-five years of his legal career, during a time when he'd worn the white hat. When he'd been one of the good guys.

Reflecting on his numerous *ex parte* talks with Judge Solomon Green, Jack questioned, for the first time, whether prosecutors who cheated deserved that exalted status. He felt a little nauseated thinking about Scott Kelly publicizing his admissions from the night before. In law, as in every profession, an attorney's reputation for honesty, integrity, and talent translated to income. And he needed income, a lot of it, to pay for his kids' educations in their private schools. Not to mention the new expense of young Kayla Rider.

No, if Scott Kelly or Seavers' federal attorney questioned him again, he'd disavow everything he'd blurted out.

Fuck those guys.

Tom Seavers could rot in hell.

CHAPTER FIFTEEN

Beartooth, Montana
August 2004 – January 2005

JACK'S   INTERCOM   BUZZED,   interrupting   his
concentration. "What's up, Stormy?"

His legal assistant's voice floated into his office. "Jack,
there's a lawyer from California on line one, Harry Bowers.
Claims he needs to talk to you about an old death penalty case
of yours. Shall I put him through?"

So Scott Kelly followed through after all.

Jack had hoped Scott would drop the *Seavers* matter
when he left in April. During the ensuing four months, the
California lawyer hadn't contacted him, not even after Paige
filed the habeas corpus petition in her death penalty case.

Partly from missing lunch, but mostly due to dread,
Jack's stomach clenched. "No, don't put him through. Just take
a message."

He disconnected as he rubbed the stubble on his chin.
After a few minutes he walked the few feet to Paige's office
and found her looking at crime scene photos depicting the
burned body of a teenage murder victim lying in a snowy
ravine.

"The Glendive case?" He sat down across from his wife.

"Yep." She took off her reading glasses. "Do you know
how sick I am of looking at mangled corpses? And what really
gets to me with this one?"

At Jack's head shake, she held up a picture of the body,
curled in a fetal position, naked where the kid's clothes had
burned off, the fire leaving his skin singed, black, and
blistered. "This." She pointed to the boy's buttocks, her eyes
misting. "Can you imagine if his mom saw this? I mean, it's
her little boy's bottom, the one she wiped and diapered and
probably kissed when he was a baby."

She threw the photo on a stack of similar pictures. "And
now she has no child, or even a decent memory of him before
he died. Instead, she has to live every day for the rest of her

life knowing my client and his friends shot her son to death and tried to burn up his body."

His wife's rant caught Jack off guard. "Maybe you need to take a break for the day, sweet pea. This shit gets to everybody sooner or later."

She looked out the window, dodging his concern. "Not you. You just chug along like the Energizer Bunny, body after body, case after case, and you never let your emotions get involved." She swiveled her chair forward. "You're right. I'm burned out on this job—again—but I need all the prep time I can get for this trial." She looked closely at him for the first time. "What's wrong?"

How does she always know when something's wrong?

"It appears your buddy, Scott Kelly, contacted the federal attorney on the *Seavers* case. Harry Bowers just phoned to talk to me. I told Stormy to take a message."

His wife, who'd sworn off cursing to set a good example for young Kayla, slapped her hand on her desktop. "Well, fuck."

Jack smiled. "Exactly. Don't worry, I'm not phoning the guy back, and I'm not testifying under any circumstances."

Paige looked at the ceiling. "They can issue an out-of-state subpoena and force you to testify if there's a hearing, Jack. For that matter, they could put you in custody on a material witness warrant if they think you won't cooperate."

Jack shrugged. "Maybe, but there's no evidentiary hearing set, so they can't issue a subpoena or a warrant. The case is sitting in federal court. Even if I talked to Bowers, he's not going to convince a judge to grant a hearing based on my conduct with Solomon, or on the crappy job those idiot defense attorneys did for Seavers."

"So you think this will just go away if you don't respond?"

Nodding, Jack stood. "I do. I've got to go down to Aberdeen to file some papers at the courthouse. Why don't you come with me? Take a short break?"

Paige glanced at her watch. "I can't. I have to get Kayla to soccer practice by four. Just wait until you see her hair color today—green and gold for Bulldog Booster Day. And the coach can't say a word because school hasn't started."

Jack laughed. "Well, at least she hasn't shoplifted anything lately. Is she smoking cigarettes?"

Paige paused. "Maybe. I kind of smell it on her sometimes. Why do you ask?"

"I found about a million Marlboro filters in our field. They could be from the neighbor's kid, although Kayla's my primary suspect."

Paige grabbed her purse. "I'll ask her."

Jack planted a kiss on her mouth. "Like she'll admit it. By the way, having her in the house all the time is cramping our sex life. We need to find her a hobby, so we can be alone once in a while."

Paige hugged him. "Maybe she can volunteer at the beauty school as a guinea pig. Can't get much worse."

Jack watched her depart. *Oh, it can always get worse, sweetheart.*

Back at his own desk, Jack considered returning Harry Bowers' phone call. Maybe if he downplayed the conversation with Scott Kelly, claiming the alcohol caused him to embellish details, the federal lawyer would leave him alone.

Hell, it was worth a try. On the other hand, maybe he'd go home early and think about it over a martini or two.

Yep. That was a much better idea.

* * *

Christmas morning, Claire, Sean, and Kayla sat near the tree waiting for Jack to pass out their presents. Kayla, especially, seemed excited to be part of the Defalco family's celebration.

While Jack waited for Paige to bring everyone orange juice, he realized Kayla's former holidays differed from this one in enormous ways. Her mom had been alive, albeit a little intoxicated and depressed. Her father still put up with Kayla, although he beat the crap out of her on a regular basis. She'd had her dog, her cat, and her bunny.

Now she sat among this group of well-meaning people who tried their best to understand her past trauma, along with her present, often bizarre, conduct. She'd taken to wearing prim, long-sleeved, button-down collared shirts, knee-length pleated skirts, and sweaters. She deemed it her Fifties retro look, and would have pulled it off, but for her heavy Goth makeup and strangely colored hair. And the Army boots, or Doc Martens, or whatever she called them.

Jack adjusted his red felt elf hat. The girl was too weird to figure out at the moment.

"Hey, Santa! Let's get to the goodies!" Kayla clapped her hands like an anxious first grader.

Sean, sixteen with beard stubble, laughed. "She's right, pops. You're slowing down on the job here."

Jack smiled at his son. God, how he missed this kid's intelligent commentaries, his acerbic sense of humor, and his male presence in the house. He hated the thought of Sean spending high school at a military academy. He dreaded the idea of Sean realizing his dream to pilot Black Hawk helicopters in combat, although he understood his son's passion for flying. He consoled himself with the belief that by the time Sean earned his wings, the wars in Iraq and Afghanistan would long be over.

Watching Claire silently drink coffee on the couch, Jack marveled that his beautiful little girl was now twenty and a junior in college. Sitting before him, with her light red hair cinched in a lop-sided ponytail and face free of make-up, she more resembled the five-year-old he'd taken to Fairyland and the merry-go-round in Tilden Park. Before Sean's birth, when Paige seemed to work or study hundreds of hours each week, Jack and Claire had been inseparable. Now they spoke only on the rare occasions when she freed herself from academia long enough to call home.

Shaking off sudden melancholy, Jack reached for the first gift. "To Kayla, from Santa," he announced. "Maybe Santa brought you a gag, so you can't talk so much. Oh no, wait. That would be called a miracle."

Kayla grabbed her gift, sticking out her tongue at him. "You're so immature, Jack. How old are you again? Oh yeah, ancient. I forgot."

Everyone waited while she gently pulled the tape away from the shiny paper, never marring or tearing it. Carefully, she set the paper next to her instead of in the proffered garbage bag. "Who knows? I might need it later," she explained.

She opened the oversized box, paused, and pulled aside the tissue paper. She withdrew a zebra-striped fur blanket, big enough for her bed, but soft enough to comfort her in times of sadness. She held it to her face and rubbed it slowly across her mocha skin. Unable to stop her tears, she jumped up from the floor and ran to hug Paige.

"You made me a furry blanket, just like the ones you made for Claire and Sean!" She wiped her nose with her pajama sleeve. "I love it so much, Paige. When I saw theirs, I wanted one so badly." Her whiskey eyes grew large. "Does this mean I can stay…in your family?"

Uh oh. Jack's attention snapped to his wife. He dreaded her answer, but recognized defeat. It appeared Kayla Rider, this traumatized, damaged, pain-in-the-ass child, would torment his life for all eternity. Silently, he cursed her father, the piece of shit Army general who'd dumped her like a cur at a kennel. Looking at his own kids, also staring at Paige for an answer, he again wondered how any parent could abandon his child.

Paige held Kayla against her, patting her back. She looked to the Defalco children, as if seeking their permission before she committed. First Sean, and then Claire, nodded at their mom, giving her their personal green light.

Jack held Paige's gaze several seconds before he, too, slowly nodded. "Merry Christmas, Kayla. Welcome to the family."

The adolescent turned to Jack with a smile that made his heart constrict.

Damn! Okay, so she'd grown on him, more like a carbuncle on his ass than a rose in his garden, but still, he had to admit she was kind of fun to have around.

Besides, how much trouble could one kid create?

* * *

A week later, on the first workday in 2005, Jack shook hands with federal public defender Harry Bowers, Tom Seavers' rumpled, wrinkly attorney from San Francisco. Despite Jack's insistence on the phone that he remembered nothing of the events in Seavers' 1987 death penalty trial,

Bowers landed in Montana, during an arctic freeze, to convince Jack to come clean.

Teeth chattering, Harry moved toward the blazing fire in the Defalco's office conference room. He refused to remove his coat, hat, and gloves. "Good God! How do you people survive in this cold?"

Jack sat in a leather armchair, his hiking-booted foot resting on a jean-clad knee. "I can take the weather. It's the lack of professional sports I hate most about Montana. Can I get you some coffee?"

Harry cast Jack a shrewd glance. "I heard about your coffee from Scott Kelly, so thanks, but I'll pass. What you can get me, Jack, is an affidavit outlining exactly what happened in Tom Seavers' murder trial."

Jack Defalco merely smiled.

For the next two hours, Harry Bowers inveigled, manipulated, begged, whined, sniveled, and nearly bribed Jack so he'd agree to tell the truth about the events in 1987.

At Bowers' every pause, Jack shook his head, replying, "No, Harry."

At the end of two hours, Jack leaned forward, averring, "Hell no, Harry."

When Paige entered the discussion after introducing herself to the California lawyer, Jack relaxed as he watched his wife cross-examine poor Harry on the benefits and drawbacks of her spouse ruining his career over a guilty killer's future.

At the end of another forty minutes, Paige announced she represented Jack as his counsel of record and added, "My client won't testify or talk to you about Seavers' case anymore, Harry." She clapped her hands together, stood, and invited the now thawed out lawyer to dinner at a local Cajun restaurant.

Harry accepted, zipped his far-too-lightweight coat, and left in a funk for his hotel.

Score one for the Defalcos, zero for the federal public defender.

At dinner, however, Jack watched in a panic as Harry, recognizing a bleeding heart liberal when he saw one, prevailed upon Paige's conscience.

"Paige, you guys have switched sides of the courtroom.

You're no longer prosecutors. Besides, you've promised to uphold the Constitution, regardless of the client's guilt or innocence. Seavers had a Sixth Amendment right to a fair trial. If what Scott told me is true, he didn't get one. Not only were his lawyers the shits, the judge skewed the jury, so they'd be more prone to sentence him to death. In your soul, you know that's not justice."

Paige sipped her tea, not meeting the lawyer's gaze.

Oh, for crapssake! Jack could feel her crumble under the guilt she'd learned as a convert to Catholicism. He cleared his throat. "I think we should order dessert. Bread pudding anyone?"

Predictably, Paige glanced at him with her what-the-hell-are-you-doing look. "Not for me, thanks. Harry?"

Harry smiled. "No, thanks. Gotta watch the weight."

Paige excused herself to use the restroom. Jack signaled their waitperson, paid for dinner, and stood. "Nice try with Paige, Harry. I think you almost had her. But seriously, it's not happening. Good luck," he held out his hand, "and safe travels back to the Bay Area."

Harry Bowers shook Jack's hand. "To paraphrase Yogi Berra, the case ain't over till the fat lady sings. Thanks for your time, Jack, and please tell Paige I'll be in touch." He left the restaurant whistling.

Jack gazed after him. Had he missed something? Both he and Paige had made it clear he wouldn't blab the facts. Why, now, was Bowers so confident the Defalcos would change that decision?

Moments later, he took one look at his wife's reddened eyes when she met him at the front door and knew the answer. Paige Defalco, his beloved battle buddy for twenty-five years, wanted him to tell the truth, to throw himself on the sword of justice, and take one for the bad guys.

They walked in silence to their car, snowflakes swirling around them. Jack handed the keys to Paige before getting into the passenger seat. Since he'd had wine and she hadn't, it made sense for her to take the wheel. No reason to give the local cops a bona fide reason to arrest him.

In the five minutes it took to reach their home, Jack

reconsidered Harry Bower's request to testify, to rat out his old office and its jury selection strategies, and burn Solomon Green to the ground. When Paige parked, closing the garage doors against howling snow and wind. Jack remained in his seat, too lost in his thoughts to bother getting out of the car. After a few seconds, he decided.

Act the snitch?

Not now, not ever.

.

CHAPTER SIXTEEN

Beartooth, Montana
Winter 2005

JACK STARED AT THE DOCUMENT, *Affidavit of Jack Defalco*, that he'd just received via email from Harry Bowers. In it, Harry detailed facts—more like a defense attorney's Christmas wish list—that he hoped Jack would sign under penalty of perjury.

Alone in his office, Jack smirked as he read the first part aloud. "In 1987, I, Jack Defalco, worked as a Fairfax County deputy district attorney and prosecuted Petitioner Thomas Seavers for capital murder stemming from a bar robbery in Berkeley, California. During jury selection, presiding Judge Solomon P. Green called me into his chambers, without notifying Mr. Seavers' attorneys, and advised me to exclude Jewish jurors because they would not vote for death in the event Mr. Seavers was convicted of murder. I agreed, and in fact dismissed any jurors who I believed were Jewish."

True, but do I really want to admit it?

In addition to that legal bombshell, the affidavit detailed Jack's assertion that the practice of throwing off Jewish people in death cases was widespread in the Fairfax County District Attorney's Office, that he personally taught the practice statewide at the Top Gun Prosecutors' College, and that any DA worth his trial reputation throughout the U.S. employed the same tactic.

Oh, yeah, that'll light up Rick Peters and my old colleagues.

Rick Peters now worked as the elected District Attorney of the most respected prosecuting agency in California. Given their troubled history, Jack figured Peters would fight those accusations and Harry Bowers' efforts to overturn Seavers' conviction with every resource at his disposal. And that, Jack realized, meant Peters and his cronies would make his life hell.

Jack grabbed a printed copy of the affidavit, entered Paige's office as she typed, and dropped it on her desk. "Have a look at how they want me to commit professional suicide, sweet pea."

Paige whirled in her chair, glanced at him, then read the document. "Well," she hesitated, "these are Harry's proposed facts, not necessarily what you have to include. If you do this...and I'm not saying you should...except..." She looked away.

Jack marveled at his wife's black and white conscience, noting his own remained slush puddle gray.

"Think about this, Paige." Jack leaned on her desk. "I know you believe I have a duty to tell the truth and testify to this crap," he pointed at the affidavit. "And in theory, I agree I probably should try to right this wrong and maybe save Tom Seavers' life." He ran his hands over his thick salt and pepper hair. "But they could disbar me for admitting to it, and there's no way I can claim ignorance that it was unethical. Besides, as I told Scott Kelly, the real problem with that case wasn't the jury I picked. It was the fucking total incompetence of Seavers' defense team."

Leaning back in her chair, his wife checked out her fingernails before looking at him. "I've researched the statute of limitations on California State Bar prosecutions. It's five years, so what you did is way outside that range. They can't touch you, legally. Not to mention, how would it look for the State Bar to punish a guy who comes forward after so many years to right a wrong on death row?"

Jack nodded. "Okay, let's assume you're correct and the State Bar ignores this. Rick Peters won't. At the very least, the reputation of his DA's office will come under very public scrutiny. If I were him, I'd pull out all the stops and fight like a bastard to make me look like a liar."

Paige sat forward, both hands on her desktop. "Lying? Jack, how can he allege you're lying now, when you didn't breathe a word about this in over seventeen years? What possible motive would he show for you going to bat for a guy you condemned to death?"

"I don't know, but he'll have to do something to undermine my credibility." Stretching, Jack stood. "If he loses, and Harry Bowers wins, dozens of death penalty verdicts in

Fairfax County could be overturned. And if they believe that my jury selection advice at the prosecutors' college infected all the DAs in the state, then literally hundreds of capital case convictions will be reversed."

Jack stared at his wife. "Which means, Paige, the stakes in this are huge. Don't kid yourself. They'll marshal their law enforcement troops, statewide, to excoriate me on the stand and preserve those verdicts."

Jack returned to his office, ignoring his wife's gaze, the one that lectured: *Sometimes, honeybun, you just have to stand up and do what's right, even when you know it'll hurt.*

He knew Paige walked her talk, defending her clients with passion he could only envy. That walk had cost her a fair amount of public vitriol and personal stress. The local legal community, who Paige long ago dubbed the Courthouse Cowboys, shunned her because of her successful work and her challenges to the good old boy network controlling the Kootenai County justice system.

Recently he'd seen her health deteriorate from the fight, exacerbated by her work on California's death row. Even when she'd been hospitalized for a possible heart attack, which turned out to be stress-induced panic attacks, she'd soldiered on, chin up, ready for the next legal punch.

With anxiety medication always at the ready.

Jack didn't share his wife's do-gooder philosophy. That was her thing. He loved her for it, but a boy scout he wasn't. Even though he billed his hours as a defense attorney these days, his heart remained in law enforcement. He still believed in the death penalty, didn't give a rat's ass about convicted killers, and cared even less for child molesters.

He opened a carton of yogurt and clicked onto his email. Harry Bowers' proposed affidavit lighted up the screen, so Jack tabbed over to sports news. As he spooned the creamy, fruit-filled acidophilus into his mouth, he thought about Tom Seavers. He remembered the day Tom had sat in his chair while the clerk read the jury's recommendation for a death sentence. Tom's attorneys had wept as they comforted each other, the bailiff had shaken his head, and the jurors had quietly filed out of the courtroom. Mostly, Jack recalled Tom's bewildered look. That confused expression, plus the guy's age and deafness, had bothered Jack, as had Paige's tears. The scene had prompted him to approach Tom, to ask him if he understood what had just happened in court.

When Tom replied, "No," Jack had felt a little nauseated when he explained to the man that he'd just been sentenced to die in the gas chamber. Even now, remembering that day, just-swallowed yogurt curdled in his stomach. He tossed the half empty container in the trash.

"Fine," he muttered aloud. He clicked open a new document, cut and pasted in Harry Bower's proposed affidavit, and modified it so it told a more accurate account of the truth.

* * *

In the middle of February, Jack glared at his wife over lunch at the Buffalo Café. "When I rewrote that affidavit, signed it, and sent it off to Bowers, he assured me the federal court would ignore it and move the case up the ladder. He all but promised there wouldn't be an evidentiary hearing."

Paige picked at her salad, too nauseated to swallow. "Look, I know I urged you to do this, but now that Seavers' case is back in California, I'm not sure you should testify. Rick Peters will label you a disgruntled ex-employee because he banished you for—"

"Using the C-word." Jack winced at the mention of his transfer from Superior Court.

In 1991, assigned to head up the felony trial team, he'd supervised deputy DAs as they picked juries, procured evidence, and presented testimony. One day, furious because a female underling failed to show up for a murder trial, Jack, in the privacy of his office, with only Bobby Erickson present, referred to the woman as "a lazy fucking cunt."

Rick Peters, always looking for a reason to eradicate Jack from his life, overheard the comment as he passed by their open door. Peters made a very public display of Jack's sexism, forced him to go to sensitivity training, and then transferred him to the Consumer Fraud Unit, every prosecutor's equivalent of a Siberian gulag.

Sighing at the memory, Jack shook his head. "All Bowers needs is a local judge to issue a subpoena forcing me to testify in California." Jack poked a French fry in her direction. "That wouldn't be tough given how they feel about us down at the courthouse."

Nodding, Paige pushed her plate away. "I've read through the discovery Bowers' sent me, over a thousand pages so far, including statements about you from your old office mates. Out of nearly two hundred lawyers, only six came forward with nasty stories. And those, frankly, are ridiculous."

Fear crawled up Jack's neck. He knew one particular lawyer who could torpedo his life: Maggie Tornow.

While his relationship with the young, blonde prosecutor had never blossomed into an ongoing affair, one drunken night in his Porsche, they'd done their best to make Bill Clinton and Monica Lewinski look like rookies.

At work the next day, he'd regretted the encounter and vowed not to repeat it. When he'd informed Maggie, she begged him to reconsider. He'd wiped away her tears, assured her he cared for her, but explained again that he loved his wife and child too much to risk losing them. Maggie's silence as she left his office had chilled him, and while she remained cordial, she no longer smiled at him or laughed at his jokes.

He'd never confessed his indiscretion to Paige. Now, so many years later, would Maggie play the woman scorned and burn him on the witness stand?

Jack decided to fish for more facts before he succumbed to paranoia. "So, who besmirched my sterling character, and what did they say?"

"Six guys, some I thought were your friends. Stupid allegations, like you had crack cocaine in your desk drawer, you told a lawyer to destroy exculpatory evidence, and you advised another lawyer to ignore ethical rules in his closing argument." Paige waived to a local teacher they knew. "They even interviewed Charles Jefferson, some convicted killer you once used as your star witness."

Jack laughed. "You remember Charles, don't you? Killed a guy on the prison bus when they transported him up to testify. He was the guy with the fucked up hair—"

"Oh, yeah! He scared the crap out of me when I walked into your office. Chained to the chair, looked like he'd been electrocuted, with his dreds all mushroomed out." She splayed her fingers around her head.

"That's the guy. Remember Bobby Erickson tossing that fake hand grenade in Charles' lap?" Jack's shoulders shook with laughter.

"Oh, God, the look on his face!" Paige wiped away tears beneath her eyes. "I thought Charles was going to shit his pants."

"And what did Mr. Jefferson have to say about me?"

"He called you a twitchy meth addict. He swore you had spies everywhere to listen in on people." Smiling, Paige added, "I've always said you were hyper, but twitchy on meth? Charles sounds so crazy, even Peters' investigator doesn't believe him."

Jack reached for the check. "Anything else you've read that concerns you? Something that might nail me at the hearing?"

A dumb-ass doper calling him a meth head didn't bother him. Paige mentioning statements from his former colleagues did, especially any comments about Maggie and their little peccadillo.

Paige put her napkin on the table. "Crazy stuff aside, there's nothing so far that hurts you. But I get a new pile of paper every day." As they stood to leave, she snaked her arm through his. "I've got your back on this, Jack. We're in it together."

Jack could barely meet his wife's green eyes, so full of trust and optimism. Instead of replying, he squeezed her hand to reassure her that…what? He was without past sins? Above rigging a death penalty jury in cahoots with the trial judge?

Jack Defalco was no fool.

In that deepest, darkest corner of his soul, he knew, very soon, light would shine on his entire, ugly past. The only question was whether that exposure would destroy his marriage, his family, and his career.

Heading across the street with his spouse, Jack stumbled, righting himself before he fell. Looking up, he silently vowed to come out the winner in this fiasco, using whatever means necessary to secure victory.

After all, that's what Fairfax County had trained him to do, when he was one of the good guys wearing the white hat.

CHAPTER SEVENTEEN

Beartooth, Montana
Spring 2005

AT THE BEGINNING OF MAY, Paige read Maggie Tornow's statement aloud in her empty office.

> "The Jack Defalco I knew in 1987 was honest, full of integrity, and never would have committed an unethical act. He trained me and the other prosecutors in my class to turn over all discovery to the defense, never to lie about evidence, and to speak to judges only in the presence of opposing counsel. I remember Jack for his honesty, his loyalty to this office and law enforcement, in general, and for his amazing trial skills. Without his expertise and advice, I would not have been promoted to my current position as supervisor of the death penalty team, nor would I have won so many murder trials. In truth, I owe my career at the Fairfax County District Attorney's Office to Jack Defalco."

Removing her glasses, Paige tried to imagine what Maggie would look like in middle age. Back in the Eighties, the large-breasted, young blonde had been a stunner, her looks a stark contrast to Paige's girth during her pregnancy with Claire. Even after Paige had slimmed down again, she envied how Maggie's sex appeal radiated through any room she entered. Rumor had it she'd slept her way through Fairfax County's fire and police departments and a good part of the local bar association.

Searching Maggie's name under images on the Internet, Paige found a picture showing Maggie in court, thinner but still gorgeous.

Yep, jealousy is a terrible thing.

For years, Paige had fed her insecurities wondering if Maggie counted Jack as one of her many conquests. Once, after a few glasses of wine, she'd confronted her spouse, but Jack denied it, swearing he'd never strayed. Paige had believed him and let it go, especially once they moved to Montana.

Now, perusing Maggie's statement, she realized Maggie cared about Jack. In fact, Maggie's statement was one of the few from his former colleagues to extol Jack's virtues instead of lambasting some fabricated vice. But why would Maggie, after so many years, and under obvious pressure from Rick Peters to burn Jack in her affidavit, stand as his champion?

Footsteps pounded up the stairs, causing Paige to turn. Kayla appeared, dressed in ripped up jeans, a furry, leopard-print vest over a hot pink, long-sleeved turtleneck, and leather boots up to her knees. She slowed her pace before she entered Paige's office. She'd styled her purple-tipped hair in a huge Afro. Plopping onto the chair across from Paige, she asked through her wad of bubble gum, "What's up, pickle?"

Smiling at Kayla's latest nickname for her, Paige tapped her pen. "Not much, my little munchkin. What's up with you?"

Kayla laughed. "Pickle, I am so not a munchkin! Face it. I'm huge like my dad. Big hands, big feet—"

"Big mouth."

Whiskey eyes widened as the fifteen-year-old gasped, "Pickle! I'm appalled! You sound like your husband."

Paige quit tapping, her eyes twinkling. "Yeah? Well, be appalled, toots. In case you haven't noticed, I don't look much like a pickle, so why don't you think of some other term of endearment?"

Kayla shook her head. "Nope. Pickle fits with Paige. Two *P*s together. And it's better than piggy."

"When two words begin with the same consonant and are used together, it's called alliteration," Paige noted. "Very popular in poetry, fiction, and comedy writing." She stared at her young charge. "Just so you know…in case it comes up at school." *Geez, I'm such a nerd.*

Shaking her head, Kayla stretched her arms. "You're hopeless. You know that, right? Always the mom, always the teacher, always the—"

"Nag," Paige supplied. "It goes with the territory. Claire and Sean survived, and so will you. Now how about homework? We set up a little area for you…" Paige pointed with her pen toward a desk and chair, just outside her office.

Kayla looked at her designated homework station. "Nice. Thanks, poppy."

Sighing, Paige gazed at the teen. "Poppy?"

"Yep. I've reconsidered. You're definitely a poppy from now on."

Rising, Paige nodded toward the door. "I can live with that. Now, about your homework?"

Kayla grabbed her backpack and eased toward her new desk. "I'm going already. Lordy! Can't a kid get a break here? I need food, poppy, like Bulldog fries."

Paige put her arm around Kayla's shoulders, squeezed, but pulled back in alarm. "Hey, you feel thin under all these clothes. Are you losing weight?"

Kayla stiffened. "I'm fine." She pulled away. "Forget the fries. I've got math to finish." She sat at the desk, pulled out her iPod, shoved in earbuds, and swayed to whatever tune might help her solve equations.

Or block out my voice.

Paige watched her for a few seconds before returning to her desk to brood.

Well, shit. She'd been down this road before, not that long ago, with Claire. Bulimia and anorexia.

Common addictions for young girls, especially vulnerable girls like Kayla, who'd just lost their mothers to suicide. Whose fathers abused and abandoned them. Girls who thought of themselves as huge, when the mirror told a different story.

Even Claire, family intact, spoiled with all life could offer, resorted to binging and purging when she turned fourteen. At five feet nothing, in Claire's eyes, her well-developed, curvy body didn't fit the image projected by the stick figure models in *Seventeen, Vogue,* and *In Style.* Six years later, when she'd finally come to Paige for help, she'd reached the stage where she vomited blood, along with her meals.

It took Jack and Paige over $10,000 of medical, psychological, and nutritional therapy to pull Claire back from the edge of death. During the course of her daughter's treatment, Paige wept so many tears, she figured the dark, swollen pockets under her eyes were as permanent as tattoos.

Those memories still caused Paige's heart to race, like it did right now when she looked at another messed-up teenager. Panic threatened to choke her with a repeat of the chaos. Paige buried her eyes in her palms.

I. Cannot. Do. This. Again.

* * *

An hour later, the intercom buzzed, shattering Paige's misery.

"What?" she snapped at Stormy, glaring at Kayla's back as the kid hip-hopped her way through algebra.

A pause. "Paige, there's a Detective Paul here to see you from the Northwest Drug Task Force. He says he needs to talk to you…now."

Huffing out a frustrated breath, Paige stood. "I'll be right down." To Kayla, seemingly oblivious in her tune-filled world, Paige cast a sad glance. *I won't abandon you, sweet girl. I may kick your ass from here to Texas, but I won't let you go.*

As she entered the conference room, Paige shook hands with the detective, closed the double doors, and sat across from him at the long, granite conference table. She loved this room, having designed and decorated it. Its green and gold slate floors, caramel leather couches, antique wooden chairs, and stone fireplace lent a cozy feel to a space all too often filled with tears and anger from clients suffering the worst that life could dole out.

Plastering on her professional lawyer mask, Paige smiled. "So, Detective, what can I do for you?"

The young officer, dressed in undercover jeans, boots, and a hoodie, leaned back in his chair, his gaze turning to his fingernails instead of Paige's face. When he looked up, his eyes softened in apology.

"Mrs. Defalco," he sighed, "look, I don't know how to tell you this, so I'm just going to say it."

Paige sat forward. *Oh crap! Which one of my clients has killed somebody?*

"Kayla Rider, the girl you have custody of? I know you

and Jack have been doing your best and all...but, well, we have evidence that she's using and selling meth and prostituting herself when she needs a fix." He eased away from Paige, as if he expected her to fly into a defensive rage, or maybe cry.

Paige did neither. Instead, she froze, her countenance a rigid, stiff-backed, stiff upper-lipped vision of numb. As she returned the detective's uneasy stare, years of muscle memory kicked in for the impassive lawyer whose clients faced life in prison or death.

"I see. And your evidence, Detective?"

Detective Paul claimed he had surveillance videos, recorded phone conversations, text messages retrieved from Kayla's cell phone, statements from witnesses—some fellow users and buyers, others Kayla's sex customers—detailing her activities selling and buying methamphetamine over several months. He finished by warning Paige that the county prosecutor, her old nemesis, Frank McShane, had prepared both a warrant for Kayla's arrest and a search warrant for the Defalco home, to be executed within the hour.

Paige's face reflected none of her inner turmoil, neither her roiling gut, pounding heart, nor inability to catch more than a shallow breath. Her quiet but deadly tone quelled any possible argument. "I want to see the search warrant affidavit you wrote that McShane's relying on to search my home." She held out her hand.

The detective's eyes widened, but he gave her several sheets of paper. After she read them, she opened the conference room doors, told the detective she'd be back in a moment, and walked to Stormy's counter. Looking at her longtime legal assistant and friend, Paige murmured, "Get me Frank McShane on the line, and don't take any bullshit excuse that he's busy." Before she returned to Detective Paul, she added quietly, "Then go upstairs and tell Kayla to stay put. She is NOT to come down here, got it?"

Less than a minute passed before Stormy announced McShane was on line one.

Back in the conference room, Paige took a breath as the detective squirmed in his seat. She clicked on line one. "Frank?

You're on speakerphone. I'm sitting here with Detective Paul. I've listened to his evidence, and I've read the affidavit for your search and arrest warrants."

She could hear the smirk in McShane's voice when he answered, "Then you know we'll be at your house this afternoon. Anything stashed in your underwear drawer you don't want me to know about, Mrs. Defalco?"

"Frank, Frank, Frank. You need to get your wild fantasies about me under control, or I'll have to go for another restraining order." Paige tapped the table as she looked at the ceiling.

"Funny, Defalco. Will you be laughing after our search, I wonder?"

Paige sat forward. "See, that's the thing, Frank. There isn't going to be a search or an arrest. This affidavit is shit, and you know it. You might have been able to get Hank Winston to sign off on it, senile old judge that he is, but I'll have it quashed by the Montana Supreme Court before you can get your fingerprint powder packed."

Silence.

If this bluff works, I deserve an Academy Award. While there was plenty of evidence against Kayla Rider, all of it had been obtained illegally. The state would never be able to use it in court to prove its case.

The detective stood, staring out the window at roads muddied by the spring thaw. Paige also looked outside as she waited for Frank's response. She figured he and the detective knew their evidence collection was flawed. Only an idiot like Judge Winston would sign warrants so lacking in probable cause.

Still, ever since Paige thwarted their practice of sending everyone to prison without due process, Winston and McShane had gunned for her, taking shots whenever they could. After all, the two were old friends who still shared a common enemy—Paige.

Frank cleared his throat. "Let's assume for the sake of argument that Detective Paul and I agree not to execute either warrant. The fact remains your little charge is up to her ass in crimes ranging from petty theft to drug dealing, not to mention the STDs she's spread screwing all these guys."

Bingo. Here it comes, what Frank really wants.

"I'm listening, Frank."

"What if we agree that little Kayla goes to rehab for thirty days, or however long it takes her to get clean. Then, after she's back, she agrees to give over the big dealers up the chain, in exchange for a deferred prosecution. She cooperates, we get the bad guys we're really after, she sobers up, and if she stays out of trouble, we don't file any charges."

Paige exchanged a glance with the detective, who nodded at her. "And if she screws up, you throw the book at her as a juvenile, and she goes off to Pine Hills until she turns eighteen, right?"

"Correct. I think it's a pretty fair deal, Paige. Our evidence may not be perfect, but we've got enough to make some of it stick. Besides," Frank sighed, "She's just a kid. She needs help. She needs to get some therapy to deal with her mom's death, and her dad's…assholeness, if that's a word, and try for a real future in your family."

For once in their fifteen-year professional relationship, Paige agreed with Frank McShane. "Okay, it's a deal."

She heard skepticism drip from Frank's voice. "Just like that? No fight? No threats to take me before the State Bar?"

"Nope, for the first time in history, we're on the same side." Before she hung up, she added, "Thanks, Frank, for the heads up…and the offer. Jack and I will do our best to make this work."

After she broke the connection and showed Detective Paul to the door, Paige paused before heading upstairs. Jack, still tied up in court, would flip out at this latest Kayla debacle.

Adding to the stress, they'd received notice from Harry Bowers that the evidentiary hearing in Tom Seavers' case was set for late June. That meant somehow Paige had to get Kayla through at least a month of rehab, arrange counseling and possibly medical treatment, all while she handled her own cases and prepared to go to California when Jack testified.

Meth? Shit! And what if Kayla really has contracted AIDS or Hepatitis C?

Suddenly her worry over a possible, long-ago affair

between Jack and Maggie Tornow moved to the back burner.

* * *

After Jack returned from court, he noted the absence of Stormy's car in the parking lot, but figured she'd gone home sick. When he entered the building and heard his wife and Kayla shouting upstairs, he realized their legal assistant had fled an inferno. Once he heard about Paige's visit from Detective Paul, he wished he, too, could flee.

Upstairs, he sat in his leather chair, too angry to speak. He stared at the teen as she wiped at snot with the sleeve of her turtleneck. Without a word he shoved a box of tissue across his desk. Paige stood in the doorway, arms crossed, foot tapping, anger simmering in her green eyes.

"I'm so sorry," Kayla wailed.

Jack slapped his palm on the rosewood surface. "Don't say that again! Listen to me. You are in a world of hurt here, little girl, and apologies are not what we need to hear." He stood and moved next to Paige. "What we need, Kayla, is the truth—all of it, right now."

Sniffing, Kayla squared her shoulders. "I told you, I can't give you any names because they'll kill me if I tell. I'm not gonna be a snitch, especially if I'm going to juvie."

Clenching his fists in frustration, Jack lowered his voice, not wanting to be accused of yelling, God forbid. "While you may think you're a big time drug dealer, honey, you're not. You're only a minor user caught in a very dangerous drug war, and not just in this valley. The people you've talked to, maybe bought drugs from or slept with…" he cringed at the idea of this child having sex for money, "are dangerous men bringing drugs into this state from other countries—"

Paige cut in. "You're making her point. If they're that violent, then not only is Kayla's life in danger, but so is ours. They could take us out in a drive-by or firebomb our house, for God's sake!"

Jack stared at Kayla. Nodding toward his wife, following her lead, he added. "She's right, Kayla. You've risked the lives of our entire family and—"

Paige cleared her throat so he stopped talking. Time for his wife, the good cop to his bad cop, to finish persuading

Kayla to give up her suppliers and johns.

Paige kneeled next to Kayla's chair and placed a maternal arm around her shoulder. The teen sniffled, but wouldn't make eye contact.

"Listen to me, honey," Paige crooned, in what Jack called her "understanding mom" voice. "You can fix all of this. Tell us, as your lawyers, not your guardians, the names of your dealers. Agree to go to rehab and stay clean. Then, this whole thing goes away. You won't go to jail, the bad guys will never know who gave them up, and we'll be safe. It'll be like getting a do-over, okay?"

Stroking the girl's wild Afro mane, Paige grabbed a tissue and wiped tears from Kayla's cheeks.

Finally, after a huge sigh, the teen relented. "You're sure no one will ever know I'm the snitch?"

Jack knelt next to her, so the Defalcos flanked her. "I talked to Frank McShane a few minutes ago. They'll use the information you give them, but only to get admissible evidence for court. You'll never have to testify. They won't write any reports. Your name will never be mentioned. Tell us what you know, we tell the cops, and then we get you to rehab and therapy."

He grabbed Kayla's hand. "Look at me, sweetheart." Her brown eyes reluctantly met his blue ones. "You trust Paige and me, right?"

She nodded. "You're about the only people on the planet I trust."

"Okay, then. Trust us one more time on this. I'm going to take notes, so I can meet with Detective Paul later and tell him names, places, everything. You just talk to us."

And so she did.

Over the next few hours, with only a couple of bathroom breaks, fueled on canned chili and chips borrowed from Stormy's lunch staples, the fifteen-year-old-going-on-thirty spilled her guts. How she started with a little pot, then a few meth-laced marijuana cigarettes, then to snorting meth powder, and finally to cooking and shooting the drug straight into her veins.

She explained she always wore long-sleeved shirts or

sweaters to hide the needle tracks. The meth also caused her rapid, nonsensical speech, her constant dry mouth, and her hysterical swings from laughter to tears to rage.

Meth also explained her rapid weight loss, a side effect that kept her using, even when she wanted to quit. "I have to be honest with you guys," Kayla admitted, "I love being skinny, and using meth is the only thing that's ever worked to help me lose weight."

Paige broke in. "Are you also binging and purging, or is the weight loss just from meth?"

Kayla looked at her hands, clasped tightly in her lap. "Yeah, sometimes I force myself to throw up, but not that often." She looked up at Paige. "I hate to do that. Meth is so much easier."

Jack winced as he wrote down the details.

How did they not see this, especially after Claire? And after representing so many drug-addicted clients? Were they so wrapped up in this California crap they overlooked such obvious signs?

After Paige took Kayla home, Jack phoned in every piece of relevant information to Detective Paul and Frank McShane. He left out some of Kayla's personal, self-destructive information.

McShane sounded grateful. "We've learned more about these dealers tonight from Kayla than we have during the last six months of our investigation. Based on what you've told us, I think we can get the feds involved and really nail these fuckers. Thanks, Jack, and pass that along to your wife. Just don't let it go to her head."

Tidying up his desk before heading home himself, Jack picked up the out-of-state subpoena Harry Bowers had faxed over that morning. The evidentiary hearing in Tom Seavers' case was set for June 25th, his wife's birthday.

And won't that be a joyous event?

Assuming they could get Kayla in and out of a juvenile rehab facility, hopefully the one Detective Paul recommended in Washington, and keep her clean until the hearing, the only thing the Defalcos had to sweat was the hearing itself. During the past two months, Rick Peters had launched a media frenzy attacking Jack's honesty, integrity, and loyalty, claiming he lied about Judge Green to get back at Peters for exiling him to Consumer Fraud.

Jack smirked. *Yeah, that'll be a walk in the park.*

Entering Paige's office to turn off her computer, he wiggled the mouse to reach the screen, and sucked in his breath at an image of Maggie Tornow. There she was, looking far younger than her forty-five years, wrapped in a clingy, black, low-cut dress that enhanced her ample cleavage. Her long, blonde locks cascaded over her shoulders, lingering above lithe arms crossed under her breasts. She rested her curvy ass on a wooden rail inside a Fairfax County courtroom. The caption had something to do with a death penalty case she'd just won.

What the hell? Why had Paige checked up on Maggie? He tossed aside documents on Paige's desk and found Maggie's statement. After reading it, he sighed with relief that she hadn't mentioned their less-than-professional liaison. For a second, he felt flattered that she attributed her career success to him.

But only for a second.

Paige wouldn't have pursued details about Maggie unless she suspected something after reading Maggie's statement. Yet based on Maggie's benign words, what could Paige conclude other than Maggie respected him?

After he extinguished the office lights and locked the doors, Jack eased into his Jeep for the quick drive home. Rain poured down the windshield from a blackened May sky, as two-inch-deep puddles splashed the sides of his freshly washed car. The grim weather added an exclamation point to his dark mood.

Maybe, given the situation with Kayla, he'd just fail to appear at Tom Seavers' hearing. The subpoena wasn't really legal, just a courtesy since he was a cooperative witness. The document merely afforded him an excuse to testify against his old office, and Solomon Green's memory, without looking like he did so voluntarily.

Yep. Time for reliable, old Jack Defalco to develop selective amnesia, specifically about events occurring in

Fairfax County between 1986 through 1987. He turned down his long driveway, to a house full of warmth and a wife he adored. No good could come from testifying for Tom Seavers, especially if it might expose his less than stellar conduct with the sexy Ms. Tornow.

If nothing else went wrong, he and Paige could get through this.

And after donating seven years of his life to a Catholic seminary, God owed him a break, right?

CHAPTER EIGHTEEN

Yakima, Washington
June 2005

IN EARLY JUNE, JACK SAT WITH PAIGE and Kayla in a small room at the juvenile rehab facility. This was the third weekend they'd spent here, after driving seven hours, each way, from their home in Montana. Paige, Jack knew, was a rock on the outside and a jellied mess on the inside. She'd lost pounds, gained gray in her hair, which her colorist carefully hid, and grew increasingly silent with every mile and day that passed.

For the first time in their twenty-five-year marriage, Jack couldn't read his spouse, and it scared the shit out of him. He sensed her withdrawal had something to do with Maggie Tornow, but then again, that could be guilt haunting him. She'd never mentioned Maggie since the night they'd confronted Kayla.

When he'd later informed Paige he wouldn't testify for Tom Seavers, she'd stared at him like he'd grown horns. Then, in a tone so quiet he had to lean forward to catch her words, she'd asked, "You can save a guy's life, but you're too…what? Scared? Selfish?" So, he'd called Harry Bowers and promised to show up. And wasn't that the dumbest decision he'd made lately? Now, with Seavers' hearing only two weeks away, Jack found sleep elusive and food unappetizing.

A clap of hands interrupted his dreary musings.

"Mr. Defalco?" The drug therapist glared at him. "We need you to participate in this discussion. To be present, as it were, in the here and now. Do you think you can do that?"

Jack bristled at the man's sarcastic edge. "Look, pal, I'm here, I'm paying for this program, and I'll talk when I have something to say."

That earned him a glare from both his wife and Kayla.

The therapist sniffed, his nose rising slightly as if a foul odor permeated his nostrils. "Very well." From a three ring binder, he recited, "The assignment for this weekend is to write down every instance in your life where you've been deceptive, dishonest, or downright lying. You will bring your list to our fire ceremony tomorrow and burn it. After that, you're never to discuss those mistakes again. You must give them over to your higher power, forgive yourself and each other, and move forward." Looking at Jack, he added, "Is that clear?"

Jack inwardly smirked. *Yeah, like that's gonna happen.* Still, he nodded his agreement, as did Kayla and Paige.

After they kissed Kayla goodbye, ignoring her wistful gaze as she retreated into the rehab's dorm, Jack drove Paige to the Holiday Inn, Yakima's finest. After a quick dinner, one Jack barely touched, they returned to their room to complete their homework. Jack sat at the desk while Paige lay on the bed. Each opened a small notebook provided by the rehab facility.

Jack gnawed on his pen as his wife wrote line after line.

"This is bullshit," he announced after a few minutes. "I've spent my whole life confessing my sins to a priest. I'm not doing it anymore."

He scowled at Paige, inexplicably angry at her lengthy list of transgressions. "Are you making stuff up? Because the Paige Defalco I know rivals Mother Teresa in saintliness. Perfect Paige, right? Or is it Perfect Poppy now?"

Jack realized he was trying to pick a fight with his wife. He wanted to end her silence. Having her scream and shout sounded so much better than nothing. He waited until she stopped writing, removed her readers, and laid them on the nightstand.

Her forehead smooth, hands in her lap, she asked him, "What is it that you don't want to confess, Jack? You've been edgy ever since Kayla started this program and downright nasty to that poor man trying to help our family figure out how to handle her addictions."

Standing, he loomed over his wife as she stared up at him from the bed. "I'm edgy because you've barely spoken to me in three weeks, Paige. I'm edgy because we've just shelled out thousands of dollars on this program for a kid who isn't ours and whose father won't contribute a dime." He paced away and then turned back, his pitch rising with every step. "And I'm edgy because in two weeks my legal reputation is going down the crapper after somebody talked me into testifying for some murdering scumbag and against my old office."

His wife rose, crossing her arms. "Is that it? This hearing and your testimony is my fault? Aren't you the one who cheated in the first place?"

Jack stepped back as if she'd slapped him, his brain wrapping around one word.

Cheated.

Perhaps the drug counselor's admonishment to tell the truth overrode his common sense. Maybe years of aggregated angst over his misdeeds finally came to a head and popped like a carbuncle. Whatever just happened inside his cerebral cortex, for years to come, Jack Defalco would regret his response to his wife's question.

Seemingly without volition and against his usual advice to clients that they should never, ever confess, Jack's mouth opened, his lips moved, and his words raced out ahead of his logic. "I only slept with her once, and it was over fifteen years ago."

His wife recoiled from him.

What had he just said? Done? Shit!

Paige inhaled as she uncrossed her arms. For a moment she looked confused, as if he'd spoken to her in Swahili. "You slept with someone else?" Slowly she raised her fists over her chest, right where her heart likely had stopped beating. "Who, Jack? When?"

Jack panicked. Paige had told him more than once she'd leave him if he ever had an affair. "I...it wasn't exactly sex, like intercourse, more just messing around in a drunken stupor—"

He ducked as Paige heaved her notebook at him.

"You asshole! You miserable, lying, son-of-a-bitch asshole!" Tears rolled down her cheeks. "Who? Tell me who it was!"

When he sat on the edge of the bed without answering, Paige spat, "Maggie Tornow?"

Jack's silence condemned him. "Christ, Paige, I'm sorry. I—"

"Don't! Don't say another word you...fucking liar!" She whirled and reached for her suitcase. As she ripped her clothes off their hangers, she muttered, "I should have known...no...I knew...I just didn't want to believe it." She turned. "It was when I was in law school, right?"

More silence.

Jack watched his world explode like a Roman candle, sparks flying through space, his marriage and life shattering before his eyes. His eyes met his wife's. "Yes, it was during law school. It only happened once and never with anyone else besides Maggie. I know that doesn't—"

Paige threw a Gideon's Bible against the wall. "Shut up! Just shut up! I don't want to hear your voice again—ever. I'm getting my own room for tonight. You're not telling Kayla about this because it could screw up her recovery. When we get home tomorrow, you're moving out. I don't care where you go or who you're with anymore."

Jack reached for her across the bed as she closed her suitcase. Tears clouded his vision, his voice cracking. "Paige...sweetheart, please don't—"

She wrenched her arm away before he could touch her. "We're done."

Jack watched the door slam after her. As it closed, he knew he'd just lost the most important trial of his life: The one in which a single juror, Paige, had to decide if, as Rick Peters alleged, Jack truly lacked honesty, integrity, and loyalty.

He buried his face in his hands.

She'd reached the correct verdict.

Guilty as charged.

* * *

Two weeks later, as Jack waited outside the courtroom to testify in Thomas Seavers' hearing, ice flowed through his veins, despite California's mild Bay Area temperatures. He sat across from Paige, who leafed through a magazine as if she could care less that her spouse faced imminent crucifixion. Earlier, they'd plowed their way through a sea of reporters, refused to answer any questions, and ignored the shouted taunts from protesters accusing Jack of anti-Semitism.

They both shared the same thought: "Such a perfect way

to celebrate Paige's birthday."

Not that either of them was in a mood to party.

Since he'd inadvertently confessed his one-night-stand with Maggie Tornow, his marriage, like his reputation in the legal community, had slithered down the toilet, landing in a cesspool of murky silence and self-recrimination. He and Paige managed to get Kayla through rehab and into regular therapy sessions back in Beartooth, without letting on that they'd parted ways. Jack slept in the apartment above their garage, Paige explaining to Kayla that his snoring kept her from getting the sleep she needed to cope with the upcoming evidentiary hearing. Phone calls with both Defalco children never hinted at their parent's schism. Jack ate meals with the family, then faked his way through the evenings until Kayla went to bed.

That's when he crawled upstairs like the low-life rat he resembled, to a cold bed in which only his heartbeat broke the quiet. In his most morose moments, the little bedroom reminded him of his cell, as the priests had called it, back in his seminary days. He recalled that era as halcyon times, when clergy in long cassocks told him when to wake, how to pray, what to wear, eat, study, and even what sports to play. Other than struggling to learn Latin, Jack remembered those seven years like a kind of Nirvana. No one attacking him, accusing him, or hating him, as his wife now did.

And no shit storm of bad press maligning me from San Francisco to goddamn Istanbul.

Jack watched Paige select another magazine from the stack. He cleared his throat, hoping to get her attention, maybe glimpse one of her lost smiles, or hear a few words of encouragement.

Nothing.

Okay, he deserved her silence. He accepted his exile to the apartment. He'd even stayed quiet when Paige blasted him again for trying to weasel out of this court appearance. "Don't you think, Jack, for once in your life, you should think about somebody other than yourself?"

That hit home, just as her other barbs pierced his steel exterior. "Jack, you made a promise to Harry Bowers, and even though you're not big on keeping promises, don't you think that when a man's life is at stake, you should step up?"

Jack cringed at the memories of his once loving spouse excoriating him, her words slicing through his heart with a cardiologist's precision. And in a few minutes, it would be the attorney general's turn to chew his ass, with Paige sitting in the audience, her stand-by-your-man mask firmly in place. Harry Bowers and his minions would sit at counsel table, supposedly there to protect their star witness, but Jack suspected Harry would soon hang him out to dry.

Paige had agreed to stick with him through the hearing because "Some of us know the meaning of loyalty, Jack." She'd arranged for her best friend to stay with Kayla and alerted everyone she knew in town to be on the lookout for any trouble from their young charge. She'd packed their bags, arranged for their flights, and booked their hotel accommodations, in separate rooms.

Sighing, Jack stood to pace the hallway. He nearly knocked over a tiny woman in a dark suit emerging from the courtroom.

"Sorry," he mumbled. She looked vaguely familiar, but he couldn't place her among the many people in his past.

The woman stared at him, then looked toward Paige. Jack saw Paige return her gaze and then smile in recognition. She stood and extended her hand. "Hello, Carin. What brings you here?"

Carin shook her proffered hand. "Paige, nice to see you again. Making progress on the habeas corpus petition for your latest death row client?"

Jack moved next to his wife, forcing the ever-so-polite Paige to introduce him.

Paige edged away from her spouse. "Carin, this is my husband. Jack, this is Carin Cross, head of the California Supreme Court's capital appeals team." As the two shook hands, she added, "Essentially, Carin's my boss. She's the gatekeeper and money person who makes sure I get paid."

Jack smiled. "Really? Any way you could convince the Court to pay Paige the back money they owe her? I think it's over a hundred thousand bucks." Okay, that probably wasn't the most tactful way to broach the massive debt the Court owed his wife, but that payment would defray Kayla's rehab costs and the Defalco kids' school expenses.

Before Paige could respond, Carin backed away from the couple. "I really must return to San Francisco. Mr. Defalco." She nodded at him before she turned on her highly polished, three-inch stilettos, and walked off.

Jack looked at his wife. "Kind of bitchy, isn't she?"

"Like me?" Paige crossed her arms. "I doubt she's a fan of yours. As you recall, there are certain justices on the Court who used to work with you in the DA's office. They're just waiting for a chance to shoot you down when Tom Seavers appeals this hearing." Then she, too, pivoted on her stiletto heels, returning to her magazines and silence.

Faces of Jack's former colleagues rose before his eyes. Justice Janet Mackinaw, a.k.a. the Amazon lesbian, and the inscrutable Justice Stephen Ong.

Those two former DAs hated Jack as much as they hated his old office mate, Bobby Erickson, and Bobby's incessant jokes about bull dykes and Orientals who couldn't drive. Each justice surely remembered Jack's and Bobby's laughter ringing through the hallways at their expense. Now that both Mackinaw and Ong had reached the exalted positions of California Supreme Court justices, they held Jack's reputation and Tom Seavers' life in their hands.

Yeah. He and Seavers were screwed.

* * *

Proving the axiom that no good deed goes unpunished, Jack sat on the witness stand as Attorney General Bill Hughes, acting as the state's prosecutor, tried to rip him a new asshole.

Cameras rolled as Jack testified about Judge Solomon P. Green's *ex parte* advice to him to toss off Jewish jurors, the Fairfax County DA's unwritten policy to do so in all capital cases, and the ineptitude of Tom Seavers' trial counsel. Hughes, red-faced and sweating, hefted his huge weight around the courtroom in a tenacious effort to malign Jack's character.

A couple of hours into this debacle, Jack relaxed in the witness chair. *Where do they find these morons?* He'd known

Hughes for years, from their political days with Sam Leonard, but never liked the guy. Hughes had wormed his way through the county's Democratic machine, finally reaching elected office as the head law enforcement official in America's most populous state.

Hughes' third wife worked for the Fairfax County District Attorney's Office, as did his daughter. Judge Green's son also worked for Jack's old office, as did Justice Stephen Ong's son. Yet none of these employment situations presented a conflict of interest for Bill Hughes, or for the hearing judge, despite Harry Bowers' strenuous objections to the contrary.

As some attorneys had predicted, the deck was stacked, and not in Tom Seavers' favor. If, by some miracle, the hearing judge tossed out Seavers' conviction, the ruling could reverse every death penalty case in California, since Jack had disseminated his jury selection strategy to prosecutors statewide, thereby spreading the taint of illegal juror exclusion.

Jack managed to smile at Hughes, fully expecting the fat fuck to keel over from a heart attack. He'd always known Hughes was a heavy boozer. Nobody got a face that red from drinking tea. Given the pressure Hughes was under to win at this hearing and uphold Seavers' death sentence, Jack guessed the man's dinner last night consisted of olives, ice, and a bottle of gin.

So far, he didn't think Hughes had made any headway. Jack emphasized how much he cared for the now-deceased Solomon Green. He explained why Solomon's advice that Jewish jurors' sensitivity toward execution by poison gas made logical sense in light of the Holocaust. He carefully danced around the common practice of discriminatory jury selection in the Fairfax DA's office, but couldn't sidestep the fact that he'd taught those very methods, statewide, at California's Top Gun Prosecutors' College.

When it came to the seemingly absurd accusations brought by six deputy DAs—that he'd tossed away drug evidence, advised underlings to hide discovery, or insulted other lawyers in the Fairfax bar association—Jack denied everything but the insults.

In fact, he *had* mentioned the size of one guy's nose

during a heated confrontation. And, yes, he *had* hidden another lawyer's shoes in the oven at a party where said fellow was in the bedroom screwing his secretary, who bore little resemblance to his wife. Admittedly, it was a churlish prank, but unethical behavior? Jack thought not.

Suddenly, Bill Hughes, in a grand gesture, tossed his notes onto the counsel table, removed his glasses, and held out both arms toward the judge. "One last question, Your Honor." He sneered at Jack. "Mr. Defalco, is it your testimony that you colluded with Judge Solomon Green to rig a death penalty jury by throwing off people you thought might be Jewish?"

Silence fell over the courtroom. Reporter's pens paused above notepads, more tech-savvy fingers hovered over laptops, and television cameras whirred.

Either admit it, or live with a lie that may kill a killer.

Jack leaned forward, pulling the microphone within an inch of his lips. He locked his eyes on Bill Hughes. Then, in a loud, clear voice, Jack Defalco sealed his fate.

"It is."

He turned in the witness chair to face the judge. "And because of that, Your Honor, and because Mr. Seavers received an inadequate defense due to obvious lack of preparation by his attorneys, it is my opinion, based on over thirty years as an attorney, that this court should reverse Mr. Seavers' conviction and order a new trial on the merits of his case."

The courtroom erupted in groans, clicking keyboards, and a smattering of applause from members of various Bay Area defense attorney associations. The judge yelled for silence and warned against any further outbursts.

Jack sat back, expecting Harry Bowers to come out punching. A week ago, Bowers had returned to Beartooth with his minions to prepare Jack for his testimony, assuring Jack and Paige that he had volumes of statistics and witnesses to support the truth of Jack's statements. Not to worry. All would be well.

However, Bowers conceded he walked a fine line between portraying Jack as a lying, cheating rat, which would assist Seavers' claim of prosecutorial misconduct, or bolstering

Jack's reputation as an honest, ethical prosecutor whose testimony about judicial misconduct was true. Nor could Paige assist Bowers in court. She represented Jack on the issue of whether or not to testify, so she could only observe the proceedings from the audience.

Given the shaky state of their marriage, Jack figured it was better if Paige stayed in the crowd, although he'd appreciated her hanging in as his advisory counsel.

Standing, Bowers made a show of shuffling papers, perusing them, and moving toward the witness stand. Jack crossed one leg over the other and again leaned toward the microphone.

"Mr. Defalco, you'd practiced law for fifteen years at the time you prosecuted Mr. Seavers, is that correct?"

"Correct."

"And the three jurors you excluded because you thought they were Jewish, did you actually know whether or not they were Jewish?"

"No, except for the man who went to temple with Judge Green."

Bowers nodded. "And it was the pattern and practice of your office to exclude Jews from all death penalty juries, is that correct?"

Jack looked in the audience, at members of his old office emanating hatred. A prosecutor or cop could screw up and be forgiven, but never if he broke rank by snitching off his brethren.

Too late now. "That's correct."

"Thank you, Mr. Defalco, that's all I have."

Stunned at the brevity of Bowers' examination, Jack looked at Paige. Her furrowed brow and head shake confirmed what he knew. Tom Seavers' lawyer had just left Jack's reputation in tatters, to protect Seavers' other legal claim of prosecutorial misconduct.

Double-crossed by a defense attorney. Go figure.

As Jack left the witness stand, furious, head high, shoulders back, a smile pasted on his face, he breezed by Paige and slammed the exit door's fire bar loud enough to send a *crack* reverberating through the courtroom.

Striding back to the hotel, his chest exploding with rage, Jack blamed Paige, the sainted bleeding heart, for badgering him into signing that fucking affidavit and testifying for Seavers.

Maybe she was right. Maybe it was time to divorce.

* * *

After court adjourned at five, Paige keyed the door to Jack's hotel room. She threw her suit jacket on the bed, watching her spouse gulp amber liquid from a highball glass as he stared at her over the rim, his eyebrows raised in question.

She nodded at him. "It got worse. Your former colleagues, the six who signed affidavits against you, testified to all manner of misdeeds you supposedly committed during your years at the DA's office."

Another huge swallow of booze.

She sat in the chair across from him, uncertain how to read him, even after two decades of marriage. She wished she still drank or smoked. "I tried to watch the judge's reaction, but he's pretty stoic. Mostly he looked down and took notes. Harry thinks it's going well, and that you came off credibly."

Jack set his glass on the table next to a half empty bottle of Jack Daniels.

Annoyed by his refusal to speak, Paige stood. "Why the silent treatment? I've spent hours in court covering your ass and hundreds more preparing for this hearing." She dragged a hand over her hair, "And I did that despite your little affair with that slut, Maggie Tornow." Snatching a pillow from the bed, she added, "Although why I bothered when I couldn't even sit at counsel table or object, I'll never understand."

Jack rose. "Why?" He wobbled as his icy blue eyes skewered her. "Because you're a fucking Joan of Arc who never should have involved me in this farce of a legal hearing. And who never seems to know when to shut the hell up!"

Paige backed away from his fury, stung by the venom in his accusations. Her eyes teared, but her chin jutted forward with stubborn determination. She hugged the pillow over her broken heart, defensive, although in their many years together, never once had Jack shown any violence toward her or their kids.

Her spouse fell into his chair, shouting "Fuck!" as he reached for more whiskey.

Hurt, even though she hated him for his treachery with Maggie Tornow, sad that their marriage was over, and worried about her spouse, despite him being a lying weasel, Paige murmured, "I'll see you downstairs. The flight leaves at seven."

Jack gave her a mock salute, along with a sneer, and tossed down the rest of his drink. Just before Paige left, her once-beloved spouse released his final arrow.

"What makes you think I'm going home?"

PART THREE

Fall

2005

There's always a downside.

CHAPTER NINETEEN

San Francisco
August 2005

CARIN CROSS EASED INTO HER LARGE LEATHER DESK CHAIR, one she'd inherited from a former Chief Justice of the California Supreme Court. She'd worked at the Court for nearly fifteen years now, ever since she fled her job as a deputy DA in Fairfax County.

God, how she'd hated working there. When her dear friend, Janet Mackinaw, newly appointed to the Court of Appeals, had offered her an appellate attorney position, Carin jumped at it. After Janet became the first female African-American state Supreme Court justice, she'd taken Carin with her to head the Capital Appeals division.

Carin refilled her champagne flute from one of several bottles she stocked in her personal refrigerator. Dom Perignon, only the best for her these days. She smiled as she raised a silent toast to Fairfax County, visible across the bay through her tenth story window.

That asshole, Jack Defalco, didn't even remember me when he ran into me outside the Seavers' hearing in June.

Neither, apparently, had he connected her to the petite brunette who'd stormed from the law library years ago, disgusted by Bobby Erickson's sexist humor and disparagement of Janet Mackinaw. Nor was it likely Defalco remembered Carin's later threat to sue Rick Peters if he didn't shut Erickson up.

In defense of Defalco's failed memory of her, she acknowledged she'd had a few nips and tucks since those days, changed her hair color from brown to blonde, divorced her worthless husband, and readopted her maiden name. Besides, why would Jack ever remember mousy little Carin, when he'd been panting after Maggie Tornow?

Carin swallowed the last bit of bubbly and poured another glass.

Well, it might have taken a few years for karma to catch up with Defalco, but he was about to get his just desserts. Thomas Seavers was screwed, and Jack Defalco's legal credentials would be in tatters when the Court published its final opinion.

Jack should have known not to piss off Justices Janet Mackinaw and Stephen Ong, especially by dragging Fairfax County's stellar reputation through the mud. District Attorney Rick Peters happened to be a regular lunch guest of those justices. As soon as Harry Bowers had filed Defalco's affidavit, the phones between Peters and Mackinaw had lit up like a nuclear flash.

It didn't take long for Mackinaw and Peters to arrange for a close-to-the-bosom judge to preside over Seavers' hearing, nor encourage Jack's former colleagues to conjure up dirt on him.

Talk about a perfect set-up.

Carin felt no remorse at the conspiracy. Tom Seavers was guilty of murder and deserved death, the sooner the better, in Carin's opinion. And, while every attorney knew Judge Solomon Green made a practice of giving *ex parte* advice to lawyers, there was no need to smear the man's reputation posthumously. Better lawyers than Harry Bowers had made that same claim in the past and failed to get any traction on appeal.

Likewise, every DA worth his salt knew to throw Jewish jurors off a death penalty case, and not solely because Jack Defalco and Bobby Erickson had trained half the state on that practice. Even Rick Peters had handed down the same advice to his troops while Carin had worked for him. Why spend a million bucks and six months in trial, trying to get a bad guy into the gas chamber, if you weren't going to get twelve people to vote for execution?

So, while everyone understood Bowers' argument, and likely agreed he was right both legally and morally, they'd never let him prevail in Seavers' case. To do so would open a proverbially floodgate of litigation, forcing the courts to throw out hundreds of capital convictions across the State of California. In many of those cases, decades had passed, so witnesses and evidence were lost, making re-trials impossible. That meant lower courts would have to let a bunch of killers out of prison.

Simply put, that was not going to happen.

Period.

Carin heard her door open and stood as Justice Janet Mackinaw entered, dressed in a smart but conservative suit. Janet hadn't changed much since their days together in the Fairfax DA's office. She stood as tall as ever, towering over Carin. Her black curly hair, cut an even half-inch thick over her skull, had silver streaks throughout. Janet wore no makeup, but her normally cheerful smile more than compensated for her plain, mocha features.

As the justice drew closer, Carin noticed her boss' frown, so she walked out from behind her desk. "What's wrong?"

Janet bent slightly to look in Carin's eyes. "Now that my buddy just ruled Jack Defalco's a lying sack of shit, I'm a little nervous. Are you sure Jack didn't recognize you at Seavers' hearing?"

Carin laughed. "Are you serious? With this facelift and blonde hair?" She shook her head. "Even the great Jack Defalco isn't that astute, especially after all these years."

"True enough, I guess, but if he ever makes the connection…" Janet's voice trailed off as she poured herself a glass of champagne and appropriated Carin's chair.

"Janet, he won't. Besides, you and Justice Ong are right to protect our old office, not to mention safeguarding hundreds of death penalty verdicts across the state."

"I lied under oath at that hearing, Carin, and Bowers impeached me with my own testimony from years ago. If he realizes how closely we're all involved in this..." Janet rubbed her forehead. "I really should recuse myself."

"No!" Carin's heart raced. "Jesus, Janet! After all we've done to stop Jack Defalco and his insane effort to free a murderer?"

"Calm down. I said 'I should,' not 'I would.' I know without my vote on the Court, Defalco and Bowers might win this fight." She took a gulp of bubbly then held out her flute for a refill. "Stephen Ong is old and weak. Besides, he's developed an annoying penchant for fairness lately." She sniffed. "Rather worrisome, really."

"He might not like it, but he'll vote against Seavers."

Carin poured herself half a glass. "At least he'd better. What's the use of having him around, if he's not on your side?"

Janet stood. "The old goat should retire, shouldn't he?" She walked toward Carin. "Now, let's move on to more important matters." She unbuttoned Carin's blouse. Her fingers found Carin's nipple and rubbed it through her bra.

Standing on tiptoe, the petite Ms. Cross put her arms around the justice's neck and kissed her lightly on the lips. "God, Janet, this is all I've thought about since you left this morning..."

* * *

Near the end of summer, Jack soaked up Beartooth's rare sun on the deck of his family's home, wherein Paige still ignored him. His dreary mood sank into grim as he read the latest media headlines from Tom Seavers' case: "Defalco: A 'Bad Apple' Who Lied to Get Revenge!" He tossed away the local newspaper, even more pissed that he'd stepped forward for Seavers and disgusted at the California justice system for rigging the outcome of a death penalty appeal.

Yeah, like he and Solomon P. Green hadn't done the same thing.

The case now would go before the California Supreme Court for a final ruling. Harry Bowers believed that the Court would rule in Tom Seavers' favor. Harry had introduced plenty of statistical and testimonial evidence that Solomon Green had interfered with several death penalty trials, and that Fairfax County and other prosecutors' offices routinely dumped Jewish people in capital cases. Harry relied on a recent investigation in Texas that disclosed the same pattern and practice in that state's district attorney offices. The discovery only came to light because a Dallas office was dumb enough to immortalize their jury selection policy in a written trial manual that someone mysteriously leaked to the press.

Despite such great evidence, Jack lacked Harry Bowers' confidence in a fair outcome.

All too well, Jack remembered his run-ins with Justice Janet Mackinaw, and while he'd never personally had a problem with Justice Stephen Ong, he knew Ong and DA Rick Peters were close friends. Jack also wondered if the hearing judge had any ties to Peters. He hoped Harry Bowers had looked into that possibility, since such a relationship should have disqualified the judge from presiding at Seavers' evidentiary proceeding.

Given the language that very hearing judge used to vilify Jack's character and testimony, Jack suspected Peters had fixed the case, probably with Janet Mackinaw's help. That didn't bode well for Harry's prayed-for resurrection of Seavers' claims at the Supreme Court.

So be it.

Jack's role was over, and nothing he did now could alter the condemned man's future. He'd done his best to help Seavers. He'd told the truth, sullied his personal and legal reputation in the process, and ruined his marriage.

In short, he'd done enough.

More than enough.

Gazing at the mountain views in front of him, at Montana's clear blue skies, Jack listened to the whinny of a neighbor's horse. Every half hour or so, a freight train a few fields away lumbered down the tracks. Flies buzzed, geese honked overhead, and the family's two chocolate labs, Fred and Molly, lay near his feet, their aging bones absorbing the heat.

Jack had lived upstairs in the apartment for four months now. He and Paige maintained silence unless they had to discuss the kids, Kayla, or a pressing legal matter. He continued to eat with the family and attend Mass with them every Sunday.

Still, he couldn't recall a time in his life when he felt, as he did now, like he'd lost everything. He had his health, yeah, but his wife? No. His stellar reputation as a lawyer? Not anymore.

Worse, he wondered if his kids would abandon him when they learned the reason behind his all-but-certain divorce. That he couldn't handle. His wife still hadn't filed the paperwork to end their twenty-five-year marriage, but he knew it was coming.

Home for the summer from his military academy, son Sean had entered into an uneasy truce with Kayla. Sean didn't trust the younger teen, so he cut her a wide berth whenever the two came into contact. He'd found a job as a waiter on the ski mountain and spent little time at home.

To her credit, young Kayla really seemed to embrace her new-found sobriety and family. She studied online to make up for the classes she'd missed and responded gratefully to Paige's tutoring. Jack insisted she join the local swim team, and with Jack volunteering as a lane timer, just as he'd done for his own kids years before, the two of them kept busy with meets and practices.

Claire had her own apartment in Seattle and found a job at Nordstrom for the summer before her last year at college. She'd come home one weekend, caught Jack sneaking up to the apartment, and immediately questioned her parents' sleeping arrangement. Jack, always the happy warrior, stuck to the snoring story, but he suspected his daughter sensed marital discord.

Hell, she'd unmasked her parents as Santa Claus at the age of three when she realized Santa used the same gift-wrapping paper as Paige. Jack smiled as he remembered her little arms crossed over her chest, brow creased, chin up, as she accused her parents. "You are fibbin' me. You are not tellun me de truth!"

That memory caused his eyes to tear, so he swilled a beer, his third of the day.

Maggie Tornow. What the fuck was I thinking?

And then to confess to Paige? No wonder his wife wanted to leave him.

Or did she?

Jack sat up straighter. He'd known Paige most of his adult life. She was his best friend, lover, confidant, legal partner, and the only person with whom he shared his soul. They'd never been a very social couple, instead relying on each other for entertainment, intelligent conversation, laughter, and strength. They had few close friends in Montana or California. Neither was especially close to their siblings.

And Paige? Yeah, while he kidded her about sainthood, she was far from sin-free. She'd been through a lot growing up, falling down a rabbit hole of drugs, sex, and crazy capers during her teens. Eventually she'd cobbled together enough education to gain entry to law school.

Ten years ago, Paige wrote her father a letter of forgiveness for beating and molesting her, even though the bastard hadn't asked for it. If Paige could forgive that asshole, could she forgive a husband who'd once strayed into Maggie Tornow's arms?

Maybe.

With that razor-thin slice of hope, Jack dumped out his remaining beer and headed for the lawnmower.

* * *

Near the end of August, Jack's intercom buzzed with what he expected to be the announcement of yet another client. While the adverse publicity surrounding his testimony in the Seavers' case had hurt him personally, it actually enhanced his reputation in Kootenai County. The office phone rang continuously for people seeking his legal counsel in all types of cases. Apparently, some folks admired him for breaking rank with his old office and testifying on behalf of a convicted killer.

Business was booming.

Over the intercom, Stormy's voice rang with impatience. "There's a woman on line one. Name is Mary Jane O'Malley. She claims she's a former colleague of yours, but now works for the California State Bar." Jack heard a tense huff. "You want to talk to her or should I giver her the bum's rush?"

Mary Jane O'Malley? Now there's a voice from the past.

Jack stared at the phone. "You can put her through. I know her."

Seconds later, Jack heard the familiar voice of another old flame. He and Mary Jane had only dated a few times, well before he met Paige.

"Hey, Jack, it's MJ. I know it's been a while, but I thought you'd want a heads up, so I'm giving you one for old time's sake. Off the record, by the way."

Yep, that was MJ. No preliminary chit-chat, no catching up with the family. After fifteen plus years, Jack thought she could at least ask about his wife and kids. Then again, maybe that wasn't the best subject to discuss at the moment. And did

Stormy mention something about the California State Bar?

Jack put her on speaker-phone as Paige walked into his office. "Hey, MJ, it's been a few years. Did I hear something about you giving up your defense practice to work for the State Bar? And what's the heads up about?" He shrugged at Paige, his I-have-no-idea-why-she's-calling-me gesture. She sat across from him, frowning at the phone.

"Yeah, I needed a steady income and most criminals commit crimes because they're broke, meaning they don't pay their attorneys. The State Bar offered me a job prosecuting smarmy lawyers, so I grabbed it. Which brings me to the point of this call." Jack heard MJ inhale as he and Paige exchanged wide-eyed looks. His wife might hate him and want a divorce, but he could always count on her having his back when trouble hit.

"Jack, the State Bar has launched an investigation into your conduct surrounding the Seavers' case. The word is, the Cal Supremes want you taken out…as in disbarred."

Paige hunkered forward in her chair, elbows to knees. Jack sat back in his, his hand rubbing over beard stubble. "Well, fuck if that isn't great news, MJ. Are you the prosecutor on this?"

"Of course not! Jesus! I'm calling you from my private cell number because I wanted to let you know so you could start preparing your defense." After an exasperated sigh, she added, "I'm trying to do you a favor, you moron. They are seriously out to get you."

Paige mouthed, "For what?"

Jack nodded at his wife. "MJ, what are the charges? The statute of limitations ran out a long time ago on my rigging the jury with Solomon. They can't come after me now for telling the truth."

MJ sniffed. "Yeah, well, the judge ruled you lied on the stand under oath, applying some bullshit theory that you were trying to get revenge against Rick Peters. So, think perjury, my friend."

Jack and Paige leapt to their feet as Jack shouted, "Perjury!" at the same moment Paige yelled, "Bullshit!"

MJ paused for just a moment. "Well…hi, Paige. I didn't

realize you were in on the conversation."

Paige moved toward the phone. "Hi, MJ. No deception intended. I walked in after it started. But explain to me how they get to charge perjury. What proof do they have that Jack lied?"

Jack sat down again as the two women took over the discussion, lawyer to lawyer, Paige morphing from her cheated-on-wife role to attorney.

"Paige, they have no proof. Everybody, and I mean everybody, including Solomon's own kids, knows he talked privately to lawyers in cases and gave them advice. He cheated so much, it's become part of his legacy in the legal community."

"So how can you guys proceed against Jack?"

"We have all the money, Paige, all the power, and the Supreme Court justices, at least two of them anyway, want Jack punished for attacking the reputation of their dear friend Rick Peters and the Fairfax County DA's office."

Paige paced off two steps and then turned back. "So your office files charges, and we have to fight our way out of them, at a cost of thousands of dollars, with no way to win? Is that what you're saying?"

Jack heard MJ sip on something, probably her millionth cup of coffee that day. "Pretty much. This place is as incestuous as Fairfax County, even though we're supposed to operate independently from the Court. But the Court appoints the State Bar officials and their judges, so it's a closed box. Even if you want to appeal, it's to a board—"

Paige cut in, "Appointed by the Supreme Court?"

"You got it. And the two justices who've taken such a personal interest in Jack's case? Janet Mackinaw and Stephen Ong, his two former colleagues in Fairfax County. And between Jack and Bobby Erickson and their incessant sexist, racist rants, those justices have a big bone to pick with your spouse."

"Geez, that crap happened ages ago." Paige queried, "Are you sure they're still pissed off?"

"I'm just repeating what I've heard. Unless you have some friends in high places who can quash this investigation before it gets off the ground, I'm afraid you guys are in for another firefight."

Jack shook his head at Paige then added, "MJ, thank you doesn't begin to cover what we owe you for warning us. You know we'll never burn you, so will you keep us updated?"

"You bet. Just don't try to call me or connect me to this mess, okay?" She suddenly lowered her voice. "I gotta go before somebody catches on that I'm talking to you. Take care, you two."

After she hung up, Jack stared at Paige for a second. "This just gets better and better, doesn't it?"

Holding up her palm, likely to ward off getting blamed for his involvement in all things Seavers, Paige answered, "I know you think this is my fault—"

"Stop, Paige." Jack came around his desk and cupped his hands around her upper arms, the first physical contact they'd had in five months. She didn't pull away, but she wouldn't meet his gaze. "This whole mess is my fault, from my betrayal with Maggie Tornow to this fiasco with the State Bar. I did it, Paige, and I'll face whatever happens on my own."

Finally, she looked up, her green eyes teary, staring into his moist blue ones. "No. Not alone. Not now." She swiped a lone tear as it started down her cheek. "What is it you always tell me? Don't let these fuckers get you down?"

Jack nodded.

She smiled. "So, we won't. I think I know exactly the right friend in a high place who can help us."

Stunned that she wanted to assist him, Jack paused. "And that would be…?"

Paige headed toward his door. "Sam Leonard. I need to make some calls."

Watching his wife walk away in combat mode, a purpose in her step he hadn't seen in a while, Jack closed his eyes.

If she comes back to me, I don't give a rat's ass what the California Supreme Court does.

CHAPTER TWENTY

Beartooth to San Francisco
September 2005

SITTING IN THE KOOTENAI COUNTY SHERIFF'S OFFICE WITH JACK, Paige stared at Kayla as the teen smiled from her intoxicated stupor. Deputy Dave Carman, an old friend and sometimes client, held out a portable breathalyzer machine and urged, "If you blow into this, Kayla, and the number is zero-point-zero, then I'll let you go. Otherwise, I'm holding you at juvenile hall until you're sober."

Kayla turned pleading whiskey eyes at Paige. "Really, poppy, I promise I haven't been drinking. You know I've tested clean from drugs since I left rehab."

Paige, ever the hard-ass when she was pissed, looked directly at her young charge. "Fine. Then blow into the machine, Kayla." At the girl's startled look, Paige added, "Do it."

Everyone watched as the machine registered 0.16 percent alcohol, twice Montana's legal limit, and an automatic guilty, especially for any kid under the age of twenty-one.

Kayla slid sideways in her chair and leaned on the table holding the machine. "Well...I guess I'm fucked. Go ahead and take me to jail, Dave." With a dramatic sigh, she held out her wrists.

At five in the morning, Jack showed less patience than Paige when he jumped to his feet, shouting, "Oh, for crapsakes, Kayla! How stupid are you, anyway? We get you out of a bunch of felony charges, stick with you through weeks of rehab, give you a great home, tutor you through school, and you sneak out to a party and get shitfaced?"

Paige winced as his pitch spiked to Yes-I-am-yelling-so-fucking-what?

Deputy Carman also stood, beckoning both Defalcos to step outside with him. He turned back to Kayla. "Young lady, don't you dare puke on the desk. Use the garbage can next to you, alright?" At Kayla's mumbled promise, the three adults conferred in the hallway.

Dave held up his index finger at Jack before he could rant. "Calm down for a second, Jack. You know better than anybody what the success rate is for teenage drug recovery, so let's look on the bright side and be glad she's drunk instead of high on meth."

Paige rolled her eyes at that bit of spin. Jack thumped the wall with his fist.

Undaunted by the lawyers' shows of frustration, the deputy continued, "The real question is what you want to do with her. Normally, we don't take kids to juvie for drinking, especially when their parents show up to take them home." He looked around and lowered his voice. "And for you guys, as a professional courtesy, I don't even need to submit paper on this. I can just let her go with a warning and leave the prosecutor out of it."

"No!" Paige faced the cop. "If nothing happens, she'll just do it again. Write the ticket, and we'll take her home and put her to bed. But she's going to court, and she's going to plead guilty."

She saw Jack shake his head before he disagreed. "We don't want to saddle her with a record, Paige. What if I work a deal for a deferred prosecution, so it won't show up? She appears before the judge, he dumps a ton of community service on her, and if she fucks up again, he can hammer her."

Before Paige could respond, the deputy jumped in. "Paige, that seems pretty reasonable. She's a good kid who's had a tough time. The fact that drugs were available, and she turned them down, says something, I think."

Crossing her arms, Paige asked, "What does it say, Dave? And besides, how do we know she didn't use drugs?"

"She voluntarily took a urine test and offered her arm up for a blood test if we wanted one. Her urine tested negative. Besides, all the kids at the party swore she didn't touch the pot that was there, and that was the only drug we found."

Paige paced a few steps, looked up at the ceiling, and relented. "Okay, but damn it, she's going to hear more about this when she sobers up!"

The Defalcos took home a belching but sleepy Kayla, watching her fall into bed where she curled under her furry

Christmas blanket and passed out.

Minutes later in the kitchen, Paige poured two cups of strong coffee and sat across the table from her spouse. Between the dubious state of her marriage, her addicted and drunken teenage charge, and the stress of handling Jack's disbarment proceedings, Paige's abiding Catholic faith threatened to crumble.

She set her mug on the table and rubbed her temples. "I don't know how much more I can take. I feel like the threads holding me together are unraveling." She looked at her husband of twenty-five years and felt hot tears run down her cheeks. "I don't want to be alone anymore, Jack. I'm tired of facing every day without you. I'm sick of the silence and never being held. I just…"

In one fluid movement, she rose and walked into Jack's proffered embrace. She listened to his murmurs of hope, of loyalty, his promise never again to deceive her, and felt warmth melt the ice shrouding her heart.

Jack leaned away from her, staring into her green eyes. "Can you really forgive me?"

She sniffed as she nodded. "I've forgiven everyone else, haven't I? How could I not forgive the guy I've loved forever?"

In the middle of their first kiss in six months, another voice piped in. "Lordy! This is enough to make me puke. You two need to get a room."

Paige almost laughed as Kayla entered the kitchen and poured herself a glass of milk. When Jack wrapped an arm around her shoulder, she absorbed his touch like a desiccated Bedouin sucked up water. Crossing her arms, Paige squinted at the girl. "You know you're in a world of hurt here, right?"

Kayla swallowed.

As Paige glanced at Jack, she noted his perpetual scowl had relaxed since their reunion. Still, he added, "Don't think this will go away, little girl. You're going to court, and the judge won't find you nearly as charming as we do." He paused. "Or did."

To her credit, Kayla's watery gaze and small head shake showed her remorse. Her words did more than that. "I let you guys down. I know that. And I failed…again. But I'm really going to try harder, I promise. So, could you please forgive me just one more time?" She put her glass in the sink. "Look, I know I'm a pain in the ass. And Paige, I heard you say you can't take anymore. And I'll leave if you want me to, but…" The tears flowed. "I'm just asking you for another chance."

Paige sighed and held out her arms. Kayla quickly leaned into Paige's hug. "Poppy, please let me stay in your family."

Brushing a hand over the teen's wild curls, Paige whispered, "It's your family, too, sweetie." Paige knew the bonds of trust would take time to mend, with both her husband and Kayla, but she also knew that she didn't want to live her life without them in it

Louder, Paige declared, "We may be a crazy bunch, but we're together. And since we all screw up, we need to forgive each other, right?"

"Right." Kayla chorused with Jack.

So, it appeared to Paige that peace reigned in the Defalco household, and all seemed right with the world.

At least for the next couple of hours.

* * *

At the office later that morning, Paige opened a registered letter from the California State Bar. She felt her breakfast revolt when she read the words:

"Dear Mr. Defalco, We have opened an investigation into allegations that you committed perjury in April 2005 when you testified in the matter of *The People of the State of California v. Thomas Seavers*…"

Without hesitating, she hit the speed dial on her cell. Sam Leonard, Jack's best man at their wedding, godfather to their children, still Chief Deputy Counsel to the Speaker of California's House of Representatives, and close friend to both the Attorney General and the president of the California Senate, picked up on the first ring. Before Paige could utter "Hello," Sam stated, "I heard they started an investigation."

Paige sat at her desk, relieved he'd answered. Some friendships survived decades, divorces, and thousand-mile distances. The close relationship between the Defalcos and Sam Leonard exemplified that truth.

"Sam, this scares the shit out of me. We don't have the money to defend this, even with me representing Jack. And if they take away his license to practice law in California, reciprocity with Montana will mean forfeiture of his license here as well."

She heard Sam light a cigarette and inhale before he answered. "Not gonna happen, Paige. I've talked to Bill Hughes, the AG, and to Don Dooley, the president of the senate. I told Hughes in clear terms that if he doesn't drop this immediately," Sam paused for another drag, "Don and I will swear in affidavits that we personally know that everything Jack said about Solomon P. Green is true, and we have evidence to back it up." Another drag. "And we do."

"You do? Why didn't you tell Harry Bowers that before the hearing, Sam?"

He laughed, but the sound turned into a gravelly cough. "Because unlike your husband, I'm not an idiot. Why offer up the truth if you don't have to? And don't give me that crap about him being subpoenaed. Jack could have kept his mouth shut, and none of this ever would have happened."

More guilt heaped onto Paige's mental pile of rubble. "I know. My fault for insisting he come forward." She wished she hadn't quit smoking years ago because a cigarette sounded like the perfect crutch at the moment. That or booze, another drug she'd eschewed to set a good example for her kids.

More coughing before Sam added, "Aw, don't beat yourself up, honey. You've always been a bleeding heart, so saving a killer's life falls right in line with your liberal, commie beliefs. Besides, I've got Jack's back. I promise you, this will go away."

Smiling because Sam had pegged her views so succinctly, she thanked him before she added, "When, Sam?"

"Within the week. Count on it." Paige heard another flick of a match, followed by another inhale. "Gotta go, sweetheart. People to see and all that. Give the old man a kick in the ass for me."

Of all the power players in California, Paige knew Sam Leonard got whatever he wanted. Always. She opened her office window and breathed in fresh Montana air but jumped at

Jack's voice. Turning, she saw him reading the State Bar letter.

"So, they're really coming after me, just like MJ predicted." Jack shook his head as he stared at his wife, frowning.

Paige nodded. "Except we have a secret weapon. The fix, as they say, is in."

At Jack's raised eyebrows, she explained, "Sam Leonard. I just got off the phone with him. He's talked to Don Dooley and Bill Hughes. He said the investigation will go away within the week."

Jack laughed as he high fived her. "Genius, sweet pea! If Sam says it's a done deal, we're free and clear!"

"Yep." As they hugged each other, she murmured, "God, what a mess this whole Seavers fiasco turned into. I just hope this is the end of it."

Jack grabbed her sweater and held it out to her. "It will be. What else can they do to me? Let's get some lunch before I go to court."

Slowly putting her arms through the sleeves, Paige wondered aloud, "I guess you're right. But I still work for the Court on my death row cases." She frowned at her spouse. "You don't think they'll screw with my clients do you?"

Walking toward the door, Jack paused. "No, but I guess they could screw with your money. Don't they still owe you a shit load of back pay on your first case?"

Paige nodded. "Yeah, about $70,000, as a matter of fact. Carin Cross, the woman you met at court during the *Seavers* hearing, promised me she'd get the state clerk to pay me soon. Right now, I'm working for free on that case, and I've only received one paycheck for the new case."

"Then maybe it's time to quit. You hate commuting to San Quentin anyway."

Paige shrugged as she picked up her purse. "I can't quit without the Court's permission. It's like indentured servitude. Although if they don't pay me soon, I may have to make a motion to get out of both cases. Except I really don't want to do that to my clients."

Relieved that at least Jack's State Bar problems were solved, Paige joined him at The Buffalo Café, inhaling the best burgers on the planet. Life didn't get much better than that.

Now, if only the Court paid her instead of punishing her for the sins of her husband.

* * *

Carin Cross sat beside Janet Mackinaw on the justice's deck, enjoying a view of the Bay Area from Janet's hillside El Cerrito home. They sipped chardonnay as they awaited the arrival of Janet's fellow justice, Stephen Ong, who lived a couple of houses down the block.

"I still can't believe the State Bar closed their investigation on Jack Defalco without taking any action." Bitterness tinged Janet's comment. Setting her wineglass on the table, she rose to answer the doorbell. "The man tormented both of us in the Fairfax DA's office and had the audacity to call me," she paused at the patio door, "a sitting Supreme Court justice, to testify at that damned *Seavers* hearing."

Carin knew Janet's anger toward Defalco had swelled into rage when Harry Bowers subpoenaed Janet as a witness at Tom Seavers' hearing. Then he'd made a fool of her in front of the world. He'd asked Janet if she, too, had engaged in back-door deals with Judge Solomon Green. When Janet denied it, under oath, Harry Bowers whipped out a decades-old trial transcript and used Janet's own words to impeach her, making her look like a liar. The media had run the story around the globe.

Still, Bowers hadn't done anything unethical. Janet had conferred privately with Solomon on many occasions, as had Carin. So had every lawyer who'd ever appeared in front of him. Neither she nor Janet disputed Defalco's claim that the judge told him to toss off Jewish jurors. Solomon advised every lawyer in each death penalty case how to pick a jury.

The two women, along with everyone at the California Supreme Court, knew Jack had told the truth about the judge and about those jury selection practices being part of the teaching lore of the Fairfax County DA's Office. Hell, they comprised a part of every district attorney's trial tactics in California and other states.

But for years, everyone in America's justice system had simply looked the other way.

Until Jack Defalco opened his big mouth and told.

Just like the cops' thin blue line, district attorneys had their own code of loyalty, and it included never ratting out the illegal shenanigans of one's fellow prosecutors—and certainly not under oath, to the world, to save the life of some reprobate killer. By breaking rank, Jack Defalco rightfully incurred the venom of law enforcement.

Carin watched Janet return with another wine glass, a fresh bottle of chilled white, and Chief Justice Stephen Ong. Carin stood to greet him, shaking the senior justice's liver-spotted hand. He signed her paycheck, so she'd never felt comfortable with hugs or air kisses. Besides, Ong was as warm as lizard skin. She suppressed a shudder as she smiled at him.

"Ladies, how are we this fine evening?" Ong sat in a proffered deck chair and gazed at the sunset.

Janet poured him a finger of chardonnay. "We've been better, Stephen. We received word today that the State Bar dropped the Defalco perjury investigation. So, while we still get to rule on the *Seavers* appeal and trash Jack's reputation, no charges will be brought against him."

"Ah." Ong continued staring at the San Francisco Bay.

Carin wasn't sure if he sighed over the wine or the news Janet imparted. *Damned inscrutable Asian.*

Finally, finishing his wine, Ong held out his glass for a refill. "Best pour yourself another one, Janet. You're not going to like what I have to say."

Carin sat forward, alert for whatever comment Ong next made.

"I had a call from the governor's office today. It seems the president had you down as his first choice to fill the vacant seat on the U.S. Supreme Court."

Janet choked on the remnants in her glass. "Had?"

Both women knew Janet was the front-runner for the vacancy, which would make her only the second female justice, and the first lesbian, albeit an in-the-closet lesbian, in the history of that exalted court. Her African-American heritage made her even more unique.

Ong turned toward them and shrugged. "The president doesn't want any problems in the confirmation process. Your testimony in the *Seavers* matter concerns him. He's already received hundreds of letters from various defense organizations calling you a liar and perjurer. They've threatened to do everything possible to block your appointment."

Janet's mocha complexion darkened. "But that's outrageous! I didn't lie on the stand! I simply didn't remember talking *ex parte* to Judge Green in that case!" She stood, pacing the small area of her deck. She whirled on her colleague. "So, it's over? Is that what you're saying? My whole career goal to reach that Court is just…up in smoke?"

Ong nodded as he helped himself to more wine. "I'm afraid so, Janet. You can blame Jack Defalco and Harry Bowers. They're the ones who called you to testify and found that old trial record."

Carin stood, moving to console her lover, who backed away with her palms raised.

Janet's voice lowered, belying her towering six feet of suppressed hatred. "This isn't fair, Stephen. First, Defalco gets off a State Bar prosecution because he has friends in high places, and now he ruins my chance at an appointment that I've worked my entire career to achieve?" She marched toward him. "No! You have to do something!"

Ong removed his glasses and rubbed them with a handkerchief taken from his back pocket. "Janet, my dear, there is nothing I can do. The president plans to announce tomorrow his appointment of Karla Black, the Chief Justice of Montana's Supreme Court. His call was merely a heads up, if you will, since he and I go way back to our days at Stanford. I'm sure his office left a message for you, but you two skipped out early today." He sighed.

Carin watched as Janet collapsed in a chair. Like a balloon with a slow leak, her lover seemed to shrink into a smaller version of herself, allowing only a squeaky hiccup to escape her pursed lips.

Fighting back her own anger, Carin reached for Janet's hand, but Janet quickly withdrew it as if she hated the idea of Carin touching her. *What the hell is this about?*

Ong stood. "Ladies, I must take my leave. Time for my medicine, or Harriet will have my hide. After that last heart episode, she tracks me like an old hound chasing a fox." As he donned his little beret, his signature chapeaux, he added, "There was something else I was supposed to tell you." He shook his balding head. After a second, he chuckled. "CRS, you know? Can't remember shit these days."

Carin stood as well. "Let me see you to the door, Your Honor."

Away from Janet's seething wrath, Stephen Ong turned to the petite Carin and lowered his voice to a whisper. "I made that up about not remembering. I want you to tell Janet…when she's calmed down, that is…that I'm not going to sign off on her majority opinion agreeing that Jack Defalco lied on the stand. We all know he told the truth in that hearing. It wouldn't be ethical for me to go along with her plan to ruin his legal reputation. You understand, don't you?"

Carin lowered her own voice to control her outrage. "Judge, if you don't sign on with Janet, there most likely won't be a majority opinion exposing Jack Defalco as the unethical cheat that he is!"

The jurist patted her arm. "I know that, dear. I'm afraid I can't bring myself to commit that ultimate sin, skewing our legal opinion to vent our anger at a renegade prosecutor."

Stephen Ong tipped his hat at her, latched onto his walking stick, and headed off down the street to his own home. She waited until he reached his front door, then slammed the one she held with shaking hands.

How much more bad news could her lover take? Jack Defalco had ruined Janet's career, made her an international laughing stock, and robbed her of any chance at revenge.

Carin cringed at the thought of telling Janet about Stephen Ong's betrayal. At over six feet tall, Janet was a force to be reckoned with when overcome by anger. In those rare moments, her calm judicial demeanor fled, replaced by violent object hurtling, cursing, and wall punching. In all their years together, Janet had never unleashed her temper on Carin, but Carin was no fool.

Let Stephen Ong do his own dirty work.

She planned to say exactly nothing about the old justice's refusal to crucify Jack Defalco.

CHAPTER TWENTY-ONE

Beartooth to San Francisco
October 2005

"THE CALIFORNIA SUPREME COURT DID WHAT?" Jack yelled as he dragged his fingers through the top of his thick hair, staring at the letter Stormy held in her hand. A month had passed since the California State Bar dropped their investigation of him, thanks to the back door machinations of Sam Leonard.

After a decade putting up with Jack's tirades, Stormy stood her ground, albeit from behind her desk. "They've ordered Paige to repay all the money she's earned in her current death penalty case because she wants to quit before she files the petition."

Throwing up his hands, Jack shouted, "That's ridiculous! She earned every cent of that money. We've spent it on tuition and a dozen other things, and they still owe her thousands she's just leaving on the table."

Stormy frowned at him. "Look, Jack, I'm no legal expert, but even I can see the justices are still mad at you. You might have dodged their effort to kill your reputation in the *Seavers* case, but they're not going to back down anytime soon."

Jack paced the area behind the front counter. "They said I testified to get back at Rick Peters and my old office." He wasn't surprised the Court had voted against Seavers, but found curious Justice Ong's dissenting opinion, recommending the Court toss out the condemned man's conviction in favor of a new trial. He figured Ong and Mackinaw would have marched lockstep to support their old district attorney's office.

Stormy shuffled some files before she added, "Right, but they didn't take it any further than that, which they could have, and the State Bar dumped its investigation. So Mackinaw, and maybe even Ong, are still mad." She stared at Jack. "It's like…if they can't get you, they'll go after Paige."

The office door opened. "Talking about me?"

His wife looked wind-blown from the fall weather. Her

turtleneck, tweed skirt, and boots emphasized the auburn shades in her hair. Jack thought she looked more beautiful now than when he'd first met her, despite the signs of stress creasing the area around her eyes. Reconciled for several weeks now, and without further intoxicated episodes involving Kayla, Jack believed he and Paige had turned a corner in their marriage. They'd been through some of the worst experiences any couple could face, yet had come out of it stronger and more in love.

She looked up from perusing her incoming mail. "What?"

Stormy showed Paige the signed order from the Court as Jack waited for her reaction.

Paige tossed it on the counter. "Well, that's pretty stupid. I have a right to keep money I've already earned. I advised them that health and finances prevented me from continuing to work on death row cases. How can they demand I repay money for work they've already approved?"

Jack placed his hands on Paige's upper arms and gave a little squeeze. "Because they're the California Supreme Court. And look who signed the order."

Paige glanced at the letter and murmured, "Chief Justice Stephen Ong."

"Exactly. My old buddy from Fairfax County. And just below his signature?"

"Justice Janet Mackinaw." Paige gnawed on her lower lip. "So you're saying the justices are taking out their failure to get revenge against you...on me?"

"Looks that way, sweet pea. The question is what do we do about it?" Jack already knew his wife wouldn't back down from a fight, even against an exalted nemesis like the California Supreme Court.

"Well, I'm sure as hell not returning money I've already earned." She looked out the window and paused before turning toward him. "You know, I made a third point in my motion, that certain members of the Court had a conflict of interest with our law firm based on the *Seavers* case and as a result, were biased against my clients. I specifically named Janet Mackinaw and Stephen Ong, and I referred to several comments they'd made about you."

Jack's mouth opened, but words escaped him for a moment. "Really."

Paige nodded. "Yeah, I thought I showed it to you before I filed it." At Jack's head shake, she added, "I found all kinds of stuff on the Internet about Mackinaw's and Ong's connections to the people in your old office, along with the Attorney General's office, and the guy who prosecuted you. I threw in those facts to support the claim they were biased against our law firm, you in particular, and me through guilt by association."

Jack motioned for her to follow him upstairs to his office. After she sat across from him, he lowered his voice. "I didn't know you'd included that in the motion, sweetheart. Did you run the claims by your buddies at the California Appellate Project before you filed it?"

Paige shrugged. "Scott Kelly approved it. I also talked to several lawyers in California who specialize in legal ethics. I explained to them that the Court made a bogus ruling in my first client's case—an outrageous and unfair one, as you recall—and that I thought they'd done that because they were furious with you."

Jack thrummed his fingers on his desk blotter. "You're talking about the ruling they made in your first case, right after they issued their opinion that I testified to get back at Rick Peters?"

Again Paige nodded. "Every lawyer I talked to agreed that the ruling was crazy because the Court had never ruled that way in similar cases. Mine was the first and only time they invoked a timeliness bar in a death row case, so the legal eagles agreed the Court was biased against me. Each felt I needed to withdraw from all death row work, so I filed the paperwork to do that."

Jack sighed. "For health and money reasons, but you also accused two justices of bias and prejudice, saying they couldn't be fair in your cases?"

"Yep. That pretty well sums it up. In today's order, the Court wants me to show good cause why I shouldn't repay the money. I'll send in an explanation, and then we'll be done with that whole viper's nest of assholes in California—the Supreme

Court, Rick Peters, Fairfax County, and the State Bar." With that proclamation, Paige rose, returning to her own office.

Jack sat back in his desk chair. Turning toward the window, he gazed at several leafless aspens on the office lawn. As the days grew shorter, darkness enveloped Beartooth by late afternoon. The weather matched his mood.

He knew his wife suffered stress-related health issues that made her decision to give up capital casework a necessity. He also acknowledged that the meager money she made in California wasn't worth her time to travel there, except that she cared deeply for her San Quentin clients.

However, Paige accusing Janet Mackinaw and Stephen Ong of bias and prejudice against her clients put a whole new spin on her motion to withdraw. Judges, whether of the small town-Kootenai County variety, or heavy hitters like the California Supremes, hated that accusation. Their exalted personas rejected any hint they might be human, show anger, or lean toward or against a particular cause or lawyer. They wouldn't accept Paige's very public claims without pushback. Their professional reputations were at stake.

Then again, what could they really do if the Defalcos refused to return the earned income?

Jack wasn't sure, but his gut told him the fight was on.

* * *

At the end of October, Jack smiled in Montana as his wife and sister laughed from a speaker-phone in California. The two women had been close friends even before Paige and Jack married. Since his sister, Phoebe, lived in the Bay Area, she provided both Defalcos with a mooch stop whenever they made a trip there for work or pleasure. At the moment, Phoebe was hosting Paige while she paid her clients a final visit at San Quentin and attempted to smooth over her problems with the California Supreme Court.

"Okay, guys," Phoebe sighed, "I'm going to bed so you can talk alone, and I can get some sleep. I have to be at the hospital at the butt crack of dawn." Phoebe's nursing career had spanned nearly thirty years, but she always showed up at Fairfax Medical Center, on time and alert.

"'Night, Feebs," Paige and Jack echoed. After Jack heard

a click on the line, he asked. "So, how did it go at the prison?"

He heard his wife sip something, probably tea, before she answered. "My clients are upset that I'm quitting, but they sort of get the conflict of interest problem. After that hideous ruling against my first client, both he and the second one seem to understand that the Court isn't playing fair with my cases. And they definitely get the health and money issues." She hesitated. "Do you think I'm making the right decision, Jack? I feel so guilty, even though Scott Kelly, Harry Bowers, and the other lawyers I've talked to down here tell me it's absolutely the right thing to do."

Thinking of Paige's recent hospital stay, he knew it was the smart decision. When the doctors thought she showed symptoms of a heart attack, Jack panicked. But later, the doctors modified the diagnosis to stress-related arrhythmia. "Your medical issues in the last few years, at least according to your doctor, are due to stress. You're not making any money, you're fighting with the Court or that idiot, Carin Cross, for every dime, and now you're in a pitched battle over whether or not you should repay those fuckers." He took a breath. "So, hell yes! It's the only thing to do."

"Okay, okay. Geez, calm down before you have a heart attack. You're the one with high blood pressure."

Opening a beer, Jack changed the subject. "So how are things with my sister? What's the weather like?"

"Your sister's great, as always. We have so much fun together, but I think she's sort of lonely rattling around in this big house by herself. She's making noises like she wants Hermes and Eris to move in."

Shuddering, Jack coughed. "She wants my two other sisters to live with her? Is she out of her mind?" Thinking of his siblings' names, Jack winced at his father's obsession with Greek mythology, thankful the old man hadn't named him Zeus. Still, none of his sisters seemed to mind their monikers.

Jack loved his siblings, but Hermes and Eris had resented him since childhood, the result of Mama Defalco doting on her only son to the exclusion of her daughters. He also found Hermes and Eris boring, their quiet lives no match for his fast-paced existence.

"She's lonely, Jack. She works in a cardiac ward all day, comes home to an empty house, yet she's too tired to go out and enjoy a social life. At least having Hermes and Eris around would give her some company."

Jack grimaced but said nothing.

Paige's voice perked up. "Hey, here's an interesting fact for you. Guess who lives just down the hill from Phoebe and goes to church with her?"

"No clue."

"The Honorable Janet Mackinaw. Can you believe it? They're actually former classmates from eighth grade in San Jose. They graduated from Mother Butlers' Catholic School for Girls."

Jack choked on his Budweiser. "Get out! From Ma Butt's?"

"Yep. They've kept in touch ever since. When Phoebe started back to Mass here in El Cerrito, she reconnected with Mackinaw. She even likes her. Phoebe told me she has a tough time believing Janet would retaliate against either one of us for your testimony in the *Seavers* case."

"Well, excuse me if I disagree. Janet Mackinaw has been a snatch...uh...bitch, since she worked in the DA's office with me. Besides," he lowered his voice, "she's a lesbian. Has Phoebe switched teams or—"

Exasperated, Paige cut him off. "Don't be a Neanderthal. Who cares if Janet Mackinaw is gay? Why can't your sister be friends with a lesbian without you hooking them up in some romantic drama?" Her voice dripped with sarcasm. "And snatch? Really?"

Chastised, Jack apologized. "So, just how social are they outside of church?"

"I guess they've met for coffee a few times, had drinks at each other's houses occasionally. Why?"

Jack paused. "I don't know. I was just down at Phoebe's, when, last month?"

"Right, in September, when she set you up with the heart specialist at her hospital."

The stress of forty years in criminal law had taken its toll on his cardiovascular system. Now, he had to take medication just to keep everything working.

"Paige, it's odd that Feebs didn't mention their friendship, since the shit had hit the fan long before my visit when the media broadcast Mackinaw's lies at the *Seavers* hearing." Jack paused as another thought struck him. "It's also strange that Mackinaw hasn't made the connection between Phoebe and me, since we have the same last name and look enough alike to be twins."

Paige agreed. "Phoebe knows how much you and Mackinaw dislike each other. You know what? I'll ask her about it tomorrow when she gets home from work."

"You do that. What time does your flight arrive Tuesday night?"

"Sadly, the red eye at midnight. Just leave me a car. I can drive myself home."

Jack laughed. "With your night vision? I'll pick you up in front of baggage. Love you."

Disconnecting, Jack sat by the fire, listening to Kayla upstairs singing along with Beyonce. He pondered the newly discovered relationship between his favorite sister and his nemesis, the less-than-Honorable Janet Mackinaw.

Did it mean anything important that his sibling never mentioned Janet's friendship? Or was his decades-old paranoia getting the best of him?

Just before he dozed off in the chair, he heard his shoulder angel whisper, "Just because you're paranoid, doesn't mean they aren't after you."

* * *

The next afternoon, Jack answered a tearful call from Paige. "Sam Leonard died yesterday!"

Stunned, Jack sucked in a deep breath.

"He had colon cancer and never told anybody. He refused treatment and just let it kill him."

Jack had known Sam longer than he'd known Paige. Even after the Defalcos moved to Montana, he and Sam had remained close. Sam had stood up for him at his wedding, shared innumerable bottles of wine over fine food and football, and just saved his ass from the State Bar's effort to take him out.

Although apparently they weren't that close or Sam would have confided in him.

"I don't know what to say, Paige. How did you hear?"

"It's all over the press down here. I heard it on the radio driving back from the city." She sniffed. "I almost ran off the Bay Bridge I was so shocked. Why wouldn't he tell us?"

Jack rubbed his chest, feeling pain he attributed to grief or shock. "That's Sam, sweet pea. He lived for his work and nothing else. He was matter-of-fact about life, death, and politics. When the game was over, that was it. He'd never try to prolong his own life with cancer therapy. Knowing Sam, he probably went out shit-faced from several bottles of exquisite French burgundy."

He heard his wife blow her nose. "Yeah, that was Sam. There's not even going to be a funeral or any kind of memorial service. Phoebe's pretty broken up about this, too. She knew Sam before I did."

"Do you want to stay down there for a while?

"No, I want to come home. You know how I hate California crowds."

Jack relaxed his shoulders, the pain in his chest abating. "I know this isn't the best time to ask, but did you find out anymore about my sister and Janet Mackinaw?"

Silence spanned the distance for a minute. "I did. She said they both acknowledged you two were siblings, that Phoebe supported you and Janet didn't, and made a decision never to discuss any of it again. And they're just friends, by the way. Your sister is as straight and lustful for men as ever, and Janet's been with the same woman for years. Phoebe's met her, but couldn't remember her name. Not that it matters."

"Got it." Jack filed away the information. "I'll see you tomorrow night, sweet pea. Happy anniversary in advance."

"Back at you, honeybun." The line went silent.

The reminder of their wedding, and Sam's steadfast support standing next to him on the altar, left Jack with a gaping hole in his soul.

Sam Leonard dead. Hard to believe.

Another thought struck Jack, generating guilt for even thinking it. If anything else happened in California causing he or Paige to need help from friends in high places, they'd just lost their cover.

Grabbing a jacket against the chill autumn air, he decided to fit in a quick workout at the gym before he went home to make dinner for Kayla. His mom had a stroke when she'd been just a few years older than him, and his dad had died from heart disease. Thank God for the ACE inhibitors that lowered his blood pressure. He popped one of the pills for good measure.

No sense taking any chances.

CHAPTER TWENTY-TWO

Fairfax, California
October 31, 2005

ON THE EVENING OF ALL SOUL'S DAY, or Halloween as most folks knew it, Chief Justice Stephen Ong lay in his hospital bed reading the latest appellate brief on yet another capital case. He shook his head, disgusted by the sheer volume of death penalty cases that clogged the high court's calendar every year. If only the California legislature would put an end to executions, his workload would lighten considerably.

His mind wandered to the *Seavers* case and his refusal to support Janet Mackinaw in branding Jack Defalco a disgruntled employee who'd only sought revenge against his former boss, Rick Peters. He'd nearly caved into Janet's incessant pressure because he was…what? Old? Tired?

For whatever reason, he'd finally found his balls. Yesterday he'd told Janet he intended to grant the defense motion for a re-hearing on the case. He'd convinced a majority of justices to change their minds, thereby preventing Seavers' execution by lethal injection and salvaging Jack Defalco's reputation. Janet had been beyond furious at his change of heart, but so be it. At seventy-two, it was high time he did the right thing instead of succumbing to politics or revenge.

Ong adjusted his reading glasses and glanced at the IV tube dripping glucose and sedatives into his left arm. Last evening, poor Harriet thought he'd died when she'd found him unconscious in his favorite leather chair. The EMTs revived him, pumped him full of heart-starter medicine, and whisked him to Fairfax Medical Center where his cardiologist prevented a potentially fatal heart attack. "A close call," the doctor had declared, but with the right medication and some rest, Stephen would be as good as new in a few days.

Feeling his limbs relax from the medication, the old jurist removed his glasses, lowered the bed, and pulled the blanket over his torso. As he drifted off, he hoped the nurse would leave him in peace for longer than a couple of hours.

His wish was granted.

But rather than his longed-for hours of rest, Chief Justice Stephen Ong instead sailed into eternity, at peace forever.

CHAPTER TWENTY-THREE

Fairfax, California
November 1, 2005, All Saint's Day

THE MORNING AFTER THE CHIEF JUSTICE HEADED
TO WHEREVER judges and lawyers go when they die, Paige
Defalco drank her coffee as she watched her sister-in-law's
expression turn from annoyance to shock. Phoebe's words to
the caller sliced through the morning calm. "What the hell are
you implying? I checked Ong's meds before I left yesterday
evening and wrote down strict instructions on how and when
he should be dosed. I talked to him, and he was fine!"

At the mention of the name *Ong*, Paige set her cup on the
table. She waited until Phoebe slammed down the receiver
before raising her eyebrows in a "what's up?" question.

Phoebe shook her head before she looked at Paige. "I
can't believe it. Chief Justice Stephen Ong died in his sleep
last night, not long after I left my shift. They're doing an
autopsy, but the head nurse claims there were two empty
bottles of liquid potassium in the wastebasket next to his bed.
And they think I might have overdosed him." Phoebe's eyes
watered. "I've lost patients before, but I've never been accused
of making a mistake with their meds and killing them."

The defense attorney in Paige took over. "Whoa, Feebs.
Slow down. Why was Ong in the hospital, and what does
potassium have to do with this?"

Phoebe stood, pacing off the short distance in her kitchen.
"Ong had a heart condition and passed out in his reading chair
a couple of days ago. He took potassium for his heart. He also
took several other meds for his blood pressure and prostate."
Turning, she added, "Most patients take their potassium in pill
form. But in the hospital, we drip potassium chloride into their
IVs to replenish any potassium they lose through diuretics."

"Okay, but what's the problem then with the presence of
the potassium bottles in the trash?"

Phoebe reached for her now-cold coffee. "First, two
bottles is way too much potassium for a patient unless it's

diluted and delivered over several hours. Second, the doc hadn't prescribed any potassium chloride for Justice Ong. His levels were fine just by taking his pills every day. And third," Phoebe heaped on the final coup, "if someone injected two bottles into his IV, the guy would experience a quick death from heart failure. The head nurse is implying that's what happened to Ong."

"When you say 'quick death,' how fast are we talking about? Your supervisor's saying Ong died an hour after you left the hospital."

Phoebe looked out the front door, open save for the securely locked screen. "It would be very fast, as soon as the potassium hit his heart, so a matter of seconds. Besides, the pain from an undiluted dose would have made him scream, so someone should have heard him. My supervisor said they caught onto his death only because the monitors flat-lined. That was an hour after I left the hospital." Shaking her head, she added, "I was the primary nurse on his case and the last one to check on him. I made sure everything was fine before I left my shift, but somehow, in the next hour, he died."

Paige rubbed the back of her neck. "Then he either died naturally or someone diluted the potassium chloride, so he wouldn't feel any pain, right?"

"Right. But who would do that? I mean, that's way beyond negligence."

Paige stared at her. "Oh, c'mon. The guy was old with a bad ticker. He probably just croaked in his sleep." She cleared her throat and quietly murmured, "But if somebody deliberately overdosed him, it's murder."

Phoebe jumped up. "Murder?"

Standing, Paige grabbed her sister-in-law's shoulders. "Look at me. That's ridiculous. In fact, this whole thing is crazy. Most likely your hysterical colleague jumped to conclusions. But I don't want you talking to anybody until we get more facts, okay?" Paige felt Phoebe crumple, so she held her close, rubbing her back. "It's gonna be fine."

After a minute, Paige eased away. "There's nothing distinctive about a bottle of potassium, is there? Why would they connect the bottle in Ong's room to you?"

"I guess because I have access to it, and he was my patient. Not just anyone can get prescription levels of potassium chloride. Only medical people and veterinarians."

Dropping her hands, Paige ran her fingers through her hair. "And executioners at San Quentin. Potassium chloride is one of the drugs they use for lethal injection in this state. Vets have it to put animals down, right?"

Phoebe nodded. "But because it's so lethal, it's highly regulated. I don't know how those bottles got into Ong's trash bin, but I sure as hell didn't put them there."

Before Paige could answer, a voice piped in through the open front screen door, so close it made both women jump. "That, ladies, is what I'm here to find out."

Paige squinted at the man silhouetted in the doorway, his face vaguely familiar. She walked closer and recognized Kevin Dorrian, Berkeley Police Department, Detectives Division. She hadn't seen him in over seventeen years, not since Jack had used Kevin's investigation and testimony to convict Tom Seavers back in 1987.

Kevin had the decency to look sheepish at his obvious eavesdropping. "Hey, Paige." He scuffed his loafers on the welcome mat. "Long time and all that. What are you doing at Ms. Tripp's place?"

Through the closed screen, Paige smiled. "Like you didn't know she and I are related, Kevin? That Phoebe is Jack's sister?" Paige gave a small laugh. "Or is it just coincidence that Fairfax County's finest comes to interrogate the Evil One's sibling?" Crossing her arms, she stiffened her spine. "Do you honestly think Phoebe killed the Chief Justice of the Supreme Court?"

Kevin held up both palms, the move exposing a semi-automatic holstered to his chest. "Don't jump to any crazy conclusions. Ong dies in my jurisdiction, from an apparent overdose of potassium, I gotta check out all the possibilities. You get that."

"And you know that's how he died because…?"

Kevin crossed his arms, as if they were in some weird game of copycat. "The crime lab rushed the blood analysis and autopsy this morning and found a ton of potassium chloride in his system. Coroner ruled that's the cause of death. The drugs stopped his heart." He looked past Paige, presumably at Phoebe. "Obviously Ong didn't self-administer the overdose, but Jack's sister happens to be the lead nurse on Ong's case. I'm not saying she did anything on purpose—"

"She didn't do anything, period, Kevin! This is bullshit, and you know it. Those bottles could have been dumped in the trash by anyone. And anyone with access could have administered the stuff through his IV. Besides, Phoebe wasn't even there when he died. I should know. I picked her up at the hospital a little after seven."

Kevin uncrossed his arms. "Paige, open the door and let me in, so we can talk about this. For old times' sake."

Paige noticed the much shorter Phoebe standing next to her. Paige looked down at the smaller woman, now red-eyed, and put a protective arm around her shoulder. "Not a chance, old buddy. You get enough probable cause for a search warrant, or an arrest, we'll see you downtown. You stay safe, Kevin."

She slammed the door in his face, shut the open windows, closed the drapes, and told Phoebe to move to the living room. After flipping on a lamp, Paige lit a fire, even though it was mid-morning.

Phoebe shrank into the couch, her legs curled beneath her. "This can't be happening. It could mean the end of my medical career."

Picking up her cell, Paige hit the speed dial. "I'm calling Jack to tell him what's going on, and that I'll be staying here for a while." She didn't add that murder charges could spell the end of Phoebe's freedom.

Phoebe wiped at a stray tear. "I can't imagine how those drugs got into Ong's room, let alone into his system." She paused. "Hey, at least my prints won't be on the bottles. That's one good thing, right?"

Hearing Jack's phone go to voice mail, Paige nodded, smiling at Phoebe before she left a message. "Hey, honeybun. Change of plans. I'm staying here a few more days and…you need to call me. As in *now*. Love you."

After two decades practicing criminal law, Paige

shuddered as dread prickled her neck. If Phoebe's prints were on the bottles, the shit storm had only begun.

* * *

That afternoon in Beartooth, Jack again thanked his friends for agreeing to let Kayla stay with them while he flew down to California. "You guys are the best, seriously. I hope I'll be back by the weekend, but no guarantees."

He hugged Kayla, then held her out from him at arm's length. He saw a tear slide down her cheek. "Hey, kiddo, where's that tough-cookie wise ass I know so well?"

Kayla sniffed and tried to pull away. "Right. So, just go ahead and dump me for God knows how long, okay? No problem. Say 'hi' to Paige for me." She swiped away another tear. "Bring me a tee shirt, why don't you?"

Jack smiled at the teen's martyr routine, but he held her closer. "I promise you, Kayla, I'll be back with Paige before you know it. In the meantime, don't give the police chief and his wife any shit, alright?"

Kayla hugged Jack hard as she whispered, "About that? You couldn't find anybody besides the chief of police to babysit me while you're gone? I call bullshit, Defalco!"

Overlooking the teen's language, because, what the fuck, his was much worse, Jack stared into Kayla's whiskey eyes as he took in her hair's more or less normal shade of red. "Don't give him any crap, Kayla, or I'll let him house you in the jail."

Kayla laughed as she backed off. "Yeah, like you'd do that. Happy anniversary, by the way, and seriously, have a good trip. Promise me you guys will call me every night, okay?"

As Jack climbed into the passenger side of Chief Bill Hileman's pickup to head to the airport, he nodded at her. "Promise." He paused before he closed the door. "We love you, Kayla. Remember that."

He ignored her tears as Bill hit the accelerator. They drove in silence until Jack let out a "Christ Almighty!" followed by, "What a cluster fuck! Between my wife and my sister getting into this mess with the now-deceased Chief Justice of the California Supreme Court, Claire's homesickness at college, Sean's determination to join the military instead of going to college, and keeping Kayla sober so she can get through her freshman year, I feel like I'm in the middle of a shitty reality show."

Bill laughed. "Your life's never dull, pal. That's for sure. Kayla will be fine with us. Ever since our son moved away, Jo Ann's been dying for something to mother besides the dogs. She and Kayla will have a great time." He turned into the airport and drove up to the Delta doors.

Jack grabbed his carry-on, thanked Bill again, and went inside Kootenai International Airport, international only because there were flights to Canada, fifty miles to the north. Otherwise, the little airport was high on security and low on amenities.

Grabbing a cup of coffee after he cleared security, Jack texted Paige. "Through security. Flight's on time. Kayla's in good hands with Bill and Jo Ann."

As he checked his emails, Jack saw his wife's return message. "Excellent. Kevin Dorrian just called. Found Phoebe's fingerprint on one of the potassium bottles."

Cognizant of his fellow passengers, Jack withheld an expletive. He typed back, "On my way. Meanwhile, don't let her talk to ANYBODY. What an anniversary!"

The coffee soured in his stomach, so Jack tossed the rest out. He knew it was only a matter of time before the cops arrested his favorite sister. His only consolation was that Paige appeared safe from whoever seemed to be setting up Phoebe on a murder charge.

He hoped.

* * *

That evening in San Francisco, Acting Chief Justice Janet Mackinaw sipped bourbon on the rocks as she stared out the window in her chambers. She loved this view of the city, especially at sunset. Across from her, Carin poured herself another glass of chardonnay. Turning her gaze to her lover, Janet clinked her glass to Carin's in a toast to Stephen Ong.

"To a dear friend and colleague," Janet offered. "May he rest in peace, even though the little shit betrayed me in the *Seavers* case."

Carin smiled and took a sip of her wine. "And don't

forget his refusal to go to bat for you on the U.S. Supreme Court appointment."

"Careful, my love, or you'll provide me with a motive in his murder."

Carin sat back. "The only one with a motive to kill Stephen Ong is Jack Defalco. Rick Peters wants to charge him with first degree murder."

Janet perked up at that news. "You've talked to Rick?"

At the other woman's nod, Janet relaxed. If the elected District Attorney of Fairfax County, who hated Jack Defalco as much as she did, wanted to nail the bastard's ass, so much the better. "Excellent news. What about his wife and Phoebe? I heard from a source inside the Berkeley PD that they'd found a print on one of the potassium bottles." She took a large swallow of bourbon. "I hate to see Phoebe roped into this, actually. She's such a nice person. Besides, I find it hard to believe she'd whack a Supreme Court justice merely to avenge her brother's sullied legal reputation."

Carin set her glass on the coffee table. "Actually, with such an obvious conflict of interest, Rick won't do the charging. He has the attorney general's office handling the case, but Rick's running the investigation from the sidelines. He's not sure yet how they'll word the criminal complaint, or whether they'll charge the three with conspiracy or as individual defendants."

She patted Janet on the thigh, resting her hand there. "Don't fret over this, sweetie. Whether one or all of the Defalcos lands in prison isn't your concern. You just stay above the fray and let Rick Peters take care of this."

Right, Janet thought, as if I can smile and act like my world isn't a fucking debacle.

To Carin, she raised her glass. "Once more, to Stephen Ong, for inadvertently taking out the two people I most despise, himself and Jack Defalco." She laughed as her lover joined her in the toast. Sometimes, life just seemed to work out.

At Carin's frown, Janet refocused. "What?"

"About Paige Defalco? She hasn't repaid the money we demanded from her in that death penalty case. Instead, she sent in a rather sarcastic response, explaining she'd earned and spent the money, after you and Ong approved her work and the payments."

Janet thought about that for all of two seconds. "Hmmm. In point of fact, she did earn the money. We have no grounds to force her to pay it back."

Carin's eyes narrowed. "But why let her get away with the allegations she made in her motion to withdraw as counsel? Jesus, she accused you of rigging the ruling in her case after collaborating with Rick Peters and the attorney general's office. And why? To retaliate against the Defalco law firm for impeaching your testimony in the *Seavers* case! Are you just going to ignore her calling you an unethical bitch and ruining your chances for that U.S. Supreme Court appointment?"

Janet felt heat rise to her cheeks. "She hardly called me an unethical bitch, Carin. You know I hate when you exaggerate." She held out her glass. "Get me another, will you?'

Still, Janet conceded, Carin had a point. In addition to the lack of respect Paige Defalco had shown toward her, Jack's spouse also had supported the California Defense Attorneys Association in destroying her chances for a higher judicial appointment. Hell, after the havoc CDAA had wreaked on her career, she probably couldn't get appointed as a justice of the peace.

She accepted her refill from Carin, crossed her legs, and smiled. "On second thought, refer Paige Defalco to the State Bar. Tell them we'll settle for nothing less than her disbarment. That will take care of her impudence…in two states."

She could see Carin's brain hitting overdrive contemplating such sweet revenge. "And while you're at it, contact the authorities in Montana and find out if the Defalcos have provided…adequate care for their young charge. What's her name? Kayla something?"

Carin stood, gave Janet a quick kiss, and announced as she left Janet's chambers, "I'm on it!"

Janet returned her gaze to the now darkened horizon west of San Francisco. The city's lights twinkled as brightly as Janet's grin.

Two can play this game, Jack Defalco.

CHAPTER TWENTY-FOUR

Fairfax, California
November 2, 2005

JACK TOOK IN KEVIN DORRIAN'S GAUNT FRAME before he shook the detective's outstretched hand. While Dorrian had never been huge, he looked skinny and pale, not the man he'd been so many years earlier. Then again, neither was Jack.

"Hey, Kevin, it's been—"

Smiling, Dorrian interrupted. "Cancer. Liver, pancreas, you name it, I've got it."

Stunned, Jack inhaled. "Man, I'm sorry to hear that. You're only what, mid-forties?"

Dorrian pointed Jack to the metal visitors' chair next to his department-issued fake wood desk. "Forty-four. The docs tell me I've got maybe six months. I'm trying to hang on long enough to get disability payments settled for Meg and the kids."

He poured coffee into a battered mug for Jack and took a sip of water. "A bunch of us who worked narcotics have weird cancers. We've filed a lawsuit to force our departments to agree the cancers are work-related, from disassembling meth labs without any protection. In those days, we just used our hands, inhaled all the toxic chemicals, let it seep into our skin, and never gave it a second thought. Now, they know those chemicals are carcinogenic." He sighed. "But that's not why you're here."

Jack remembered many cops back in the day who'd done the same thing. It didn't seem fair to deny them workers' disability, but Dorrian was right. That wasn't the purpose of his visit. "Obviously, I'm here about my sister. I want to see the evidence you have. The potassium bottles, in particular."

Dorrian reached for his phone and requested someone bring the evidence to his office. "First off, I didn't know Phoebe Tripp was your sister until I got to her house and talked to Paige. Second, nobody's saying she killed the guy on purpose. Maybe it was an accident. Maybe she was tired or—"

"Kevin, Phoebe didn't overdose Stephen Ong, intentionally or otherwise."

Dorrian shrugged. "Somebody did. The old guy didn't put that shit in his own IV, and your sister was the last nurse with him before he died. Not to mention her prints are on one of the bottles."

Jack had debriefed Phoebe after arriving yesterday, so he eased into his response. "Ong was on an IV to rehydrate him. He took potassium anyway, for his heart and blood pressure, so what makes the coroner think he died of an overdose, or that he didn't take too much on his own? Christ, the guy nearly had a heart attack a couple of days ago."

Leaning forward, Dorrian rested his elbows on the desk. "Granted, the report is preliminary, but the blood work shows more potassium than somebody could ingest orally." A clerk entered the small office and handed Dorrian a large manila envelope sealed with evidence tape that he slit open with a pocketknife. "And there's also the presence of these." He pulled out a sealed plastic bag.

Jack looked at the clear plastic baggie containing one brown bottle with a squeeze dropper next to it and another with no top. On the outside of the baggie, a chain of custody label showed where and when the items had been collected, the initials of the finder, and the contents.

Aware of Dorrian's shrewd scrutiny, Jack schooled his features to stoic. He turned the baggie over a couple of times to better view the bottles, then took a couple of photos with his cell phone before setting it back on Dorrian's desk.

"Do you really think, if my sister planned on murdering Ong, for which she has no motive, by the way, she'd be dumb enough to leave evidence like this in the guy's trash can?"

Dorrian scratched his chin as he looked out the window. "You know, I actually agree with you. I doubt a killer would leave that kind of damning evidence behind. As to motive, now that we know she's your sister, the DA could argue she sought revenge for the Court's nasty opinion calling you an unethical cheat."

Jack stood, leaning his hands on Kevin's desk, so he

could hover over him. "For chrissakes, Kevin! Seriously? She's been a nurse saving people's lives for thirty years. She loves me, yeah, but enough to kill the Chief Justice of the Supreme Court? C'mon!"

Dorrian held up a palm. "Simmer down, buddy. Geez, we haven't even taken this to the DA yet."

Jack backed off but noted Dorrian's frown. Then it hit him. "Do not tell me Rick Peters knows about Phoebe and her connection to me." As the detective nodded at him, Jack hissed out, "Fuck!" He paced the small area by his chair. "You know he'll turn this into a witch hunt. He'll probably try to include me in the plot, maybe say I coaxed Phoebe into it, or paid her, or he'll conjure up some other dumb-ass theory."

Before Kevin could respond, another clerk entered and handed him a sheet of paper, saying, "You'll want to see these. Further preliminary results from the prints lifted off the bottle with the dropper. Second one's clean."

Watching Kevin's expression change from a frown to raised eyebrows, Jack ventured, "More of Phoebe's prints?"

Dorrian stared at him. "Her right index finger already showed up." He threw the sheet of paper at Jack. "And now they've found a partial of your wife's right thumb."

Jack's gut clenched as he reached for the report. Sure enough, the lab had run the latent prints found on the bottle against his prints, his wife's, and Phoebe's, all on file with various state agencies. He held the sheet closer, as if that would put the contents into better focus, then looked at Dorrian. "Not possible, Kevin. Seriously, you've gotta know this is wrong."

Dorrian stood. "I don't know what to think. Now we've got Paige's thumbprint on the same bottle with Phoebe's? It smells…either like a Defalco family plot to take out the Chief Justice or a pretty clever set-up by an unknown perp."

Jack grabbed his jacket off the back of his chair. "Yeah, well stick with that last theory, will you? And don't take this to Rick Peters until I have a chance to do some independent investigation."

If Kevin Dorrian could look any paler, he managed it. "Whoa, pal. You're on the suspect list as of right now, which means I don't want you messing in this case. Let me track down some more leads before you really fuck things up."

Jack turned at the door. "Like you fucked up the *Seavers* case when you lost the evidence?" At Dorrian's wince, Jack sighed. "Sorry. That was a cheap shot. But, Kevin, after all we've been through over the years, you owe me. Just don't take anything to Peters until I've had some time to dig." He slumped against the jamb. "Please, for Paige's sake. Even if you think I killed Ong, which I didn't, you know Paige wouldn't harm anyone. Neither would my sister." Jack straightened. "Two days, Kevin. Just give me forty-eight hours."

Jutting out his chin, Dorrian narrowed his eyes then slowly nodded. "Deal. Forty-eight hours. But meanwhile, here's a heads up," he paused for effect, "we're watching…all of you."

* * *

His heart slamming against his breastbone, Jack settled behind the wheel of Phoebe's aging BMW convertible. November rain thrummed against the canvas top as he searched for the keys with shaking hands. Finding them in his jacket pocket, he started the car and cranked up the heat. Bay Area mist seeped into his bones, causing him to shiver even more than the evidence he'd just viewed in Dorrian's office.

He phoned Paige. Without preamble, he blurted, "I just looked at the evidence. We are in deep shit, sweet pea, so hang tight with Phoebe. I'll be there in a few minutes." Before his wife could pump him with questions, he disconnected and headed the BMW toward El Cerrito.

A crowd of media people surrounded Phoebe's hillside home. Jack parked, lowered the bill on his SF Giants ball cap, and pushed past throngs of reporters pressing him for comments.

Once inside, he kissed an anxious Paige before he hugged his teary-eyed sister. After settling in the living room, drapes drawn against curious binoculars, Jack cleared his throat. "Okay, it's worse than we thought. They collected two small brown bottles from Ong's trash can." Jack showed each woman the pictures he'd taken with his cell phone camera.

"This one," he pointed to the bottle next to the dropper, "we're going to call 'Bottle One.' It came back with a print of your right index finger, Phoebe, which we knew." Jack swilled some coffee before he looked at his wife. "No prints of mine showed up, but, Paige, the lab found what they claim is a partial print of your right thumb on this same bottle."

Instead of a dramatic gasp or tears, Paige crossed her arms as she nodded. "Okay, that's bullshit, but I get it. Phoebe and I have been set up. What about the second bottle?"

"The second bottle, which we'll call 'Bottle Two,' is clean. No prints, no lid, nothing of evidentiary value except the report that shows the presence of potassium chloride on the inside. So, we have two bottles in the trash, one with prints incriminating both of you, and the other significant only by its presence since no doctor ordered liquid potassium for the late, great Stephen Ong."

From their raised brows, Jack deduced both women expected a theory explaining how their prints ended up on Bottle One and how that bottle landed in Justice Ong's wastebasket.

Jack plugged his phone into Paige's laptop to enlarge the photos from his cell. "Here's an answer and also a bigger problem. See this?" He pointed at Bottle One, to a small piece of what appeared to be clear tape covering a tiny scrap of white paper. With further enlargement, they read on the paper, *STE. # 4*, and below that, three numbers, *609.*

At the women's puzzled expressions, he continued, "What I think we're looking at is a prescription bottle with most of the label torn off. Whoever tore it off left just enough for a detective like Dorrian to trace it to the pharmacy that issued it." He stood up, paced to the fireplace and back, then stared at Phoebe. "Feebs, the last time I visited, you got me a prescription for liquid potassium, remember? Because I whined about taking so many different pills every day?"

His sister nodded. "Right. You tried it, hated the taste and," she turned a startled look at him, "you left it here!" She jumped up and raced toward the guest bathroom adjacent to the bedroom in which Paige and Jack stayed during their visits. She shouted over her shoulder, "I left it in the medicine chest."

Jack and Paige followed Phoebe, but he had a strong suspicion the bottle had disappeared, a premonition Phoebe soon confirmed. "It's gone! What the fuck? Who would have taken it?"

Jack put his arm around Paige's shoulder. "If we can figure that out, ladies, we have ourselves a killer."

Paige stiffened. "Look, I've been here for ten days. It was in there when I arrived because I remember moving it to get to the Advil. And the label was on it because I thought about bringing it home with me, so you'd have it as a back up to your pills."

His sister added, "Which explains both of our fingerprints on the bottle, but why wouldn't yours be on there?"

Jack shook his head. "Don't know, but television leads people to think prints on objects are commonplace. In fact, they're not. Who knows? Maybe my hands were wet, or I smudged them somehow." He shrugged. "What matters is that scrap of paper. I'm guessing the suite number and partial zip code will come back to the pharmacy at your hospital, Feebs. Right?"

"Suite four, 609…yeah. Suite four is the pharmacy where I picked up the scrip, and 94609 is our zip. Shit!" Phoebe turned toward her sister-in-law. "So, we need to recall every person who's visited this house since you got here, Paige. That shouldn't be too tough."

Jack dropped his arm. "That is, if they took the bottle during a visit. But since you tend to leave your doors unlocked, somebody could have taken it while you were gone." He strode to the bed and sat. "The bigger question is, who do we know who'd want to kill Stephen Ong and frame you and Paige for the murder?"

He saw his wife frown before she sat next to him. "Not just frame us, Jack. The prescription was in your name. Just because your prints didn't show up doesn't mean you're in the clear. It seems to me that whoever did this is really after you."

After a pause, Jack agreed. "And that leaves a pretty broad range of suspects, because in this part of the world, there are plenty of folks who'd like to see me in prison…or dead."

* * *

At five that evening, Jack drove his wife and sister to Phoebe's local parish to attend Mass. The trio had decided that praying for an end to their legal traumas couldn't hurt. Jack knelt next to Paige, listening to the priest intone the magic words that mysteriously turned table wine into the blood of Christ. Phoebe sat on Paige's right, fumbling with an ancient set of rosary beads.

He watched as his sister made eye contact with an African American woman two pews ahead, who returned Phoebe's smile. Recognition jarred Jack.

Well, if it isn't my old buddy, Janet Mackinaw.

From what he could observe, the woman hadn't changed much in the fifteen plus years since he'd last seen her. While she'd appeared in court several months ago to testify against him in the *Seavers* case, Jack hadn't seen her that day, encountering only her minion, Carin Cross, outside the courtroom. He noticed gray hair peppered Janet's short, curly locks, and more wrinkles creased her cocoa skin.

Jack watched Janet's smile turn to a frown as she shifted her gaze from Phoebe to him. His first impulse was to flip her off—give her the old table-for-one sign—but refrained, only because he was in church. Instead, he smirked at her as he elbowed his wife.

"Check out the cow-faced judge two rows up," he murmured.

Paige looked at him before turning in the direction he nodded. She grabbed his arm in a vise grip, whispering, "Shit! Don't say a word! I mean it, Jack!"

He suppressed a laugh and then stood to get into the communion line. He let Paige and Phoebe leave the pew first, following them up the aisle as he kept an eye on Janet Mackinaw. How furious at him was she? He'd testified against their old office, made Rick Peters look like an out-of-control, smarmy asshole, and subpoenaed her to take the stand where she lied under oath. That last deception unraveled Janet's chances for career advancement and ruined her pristine image as a fair and unbiased judge. Yeah, she probably was pretty pissed at him.

After Mass, the Defalco trio moved through the few

stalwart Catholics dedicated enough to attend daily services, shook hands with the priest, and pushed toward fresh autumn air outside. Before he could grab his sister, Phoebe sauntered over to Janet Mackinaw who stood, at over six feet, high above the *hoi polloi*, chatting it up with several women. Jack noted the justice's body stiffen as Phoebe approached. Still, Janet hugged Phoebe, brushed an air kiss on her cheek, and murmured words he couldn't hear.

Phoebe returned to Jack and Paige, pointing at her BMW parked nearby. "Home. Let's get the hell out of here."

Jack drove with Paige riding shotgun, Phoebe in the back seat. She'd insisted on driving with the top down, so he turned on the heater for warmth in the early evening chill. He saw no reason to attempt conversation since he couldn't hear over the din of traffic. They arrived at Phoebe's home just as the sun set. That's what he loved about Catholic services. There was always one he could catch on any given day, regardless of geographic location.

Once inside, Jack opened a bottle of cabernet and poured two glasses, one for Phoebe, the other for him. Paige, still eschewing alcohol to set an example for their kids, boiled water for her tea.

Swirling his wine, Jack asked, "So what did the Amazon justice have to say, Feebs?"

After a large swallow of wine, Phoebe looked at him. "She's praying for me." She took another gulp and held her glass out to her brother. "Oh, and she hopes this will all get sorted out, so I can go back to work."

Jack refilled her glass. "That's it?" At Phoebe's nod, he added, "Not helpful. I always hated that—"

"Don't!" Phoebe set her glass on the table. "She's not like that, and besides, she's a friend. I get that she can't intervene in this mess."

"Nobody's asking her to intervene, Feebs. Christ, she's got as much motive to frame me for murder as Rick Peters." Jack looked at Paige as she settled next to Phoebe on the couch. "Okay, I admit, that's a stretch for both of them, that they'd kill off Stephen Ong to get back at me. Besides, fingering them as the perpetrators doesn't explain how those bottles landed in Ong's bedside trash. They'd have no access to them, right?"

Paige sipped tea. "Phoebe, didn't you say Janet Mackinaw had been a guest for dinner here?"

Phoebe nodded. "But that was over a month ago, before you arrived, and you saw the bottle in the medicine chest last week." She stood and paced to the large windows overlooking San Francisco Bay.

From his chair, Jack admired the lights from the Bay Bridge glittering off the water. He never tired of Phoebe's view. On a clear day, he could see the Golden Gate, with waves from the Pacific Ocean crashing into San Francisco Bay.

Phoebe turned. "I've wracked my brain to remember who's been in this house since last week. Besides you, Paige, there was the insect guy spraying for ants, but that's it. I hired a gardener to clean up lawn debris and trim stuff back for winter. He wouldn't have been in the house though."

Jack stood, moving in front of the fireplace to warm himself on the fake gas logs. "Great. The bug man did it in the library with a candlestick. Now it all makes sense." Sighing, he blurted, "Fuck this! Somebody wanted Stephen Ong dead. It wasn't any of us, so who the hell was it? Think outside the box, people! His wife? A relative? A criminal recently released from prison?"

Paige joined him at the fire. "Eyes on the crisis, sweetie. Whoever it is wanted to frame you and maybe Phoebe and me, although that's kind of unlikely. All I've done is piss off the entire Court by quitting and refusing to repay money I earned. That's not a reason to kill Ong. If I had a choice, I'd murder that little shrew, Carin Cross, for starting this whole payment drama in the first place." She rubbed her arms. "And Phoebe's a saint who has no motive to kill anyone."

Nodding, Jack again took in the breadth of the Bay Area below. "God, I wish Sam Leonard were here. He'd know what to do, or at least he'd be able to find out some inside information. But, that's not how my life works, is it?" He slapped his hand on the mantle. "And from colon cancer?"

The threesome looked at each other just as Phoebe

announced, "I've got a friend in pathology. Let me see what Sam's toxicology results showed."

Despite the gorgeous view, Jack Defalco closed the drapes and locked the sliding glass door to the deck.

In the words of someone somewhere, just because you're paranoid doesn't mean they aren't after you.

CHAPTER TWENTY-FIVE

El Cerrito, California
November 3, 2005

WHEN THE PHONE RANG JUST AFTER MIDNIGHT, Jack muttered, "Shit!" He tried to orient himself in Phoebe's guest room. Locating his cell, he mumbled, "Jack Defalco."

"It's me," a voice whispered. "MJ."

Shaking the sleep from his brain, Jack sat up in bed as his wife's eyes opened. "MJ? Are you okay?"

"No, I'm not okay, you moron! Why would I call you this late if life was great?"

Jack rolled his eyes. "So, what's wrong? And speak up because I can barely hear you."

MJ O'Malley, California State Bar prosecutor and self-appointed inside source to the Defalcos, raised her pitch slightly. "I'm on a disposable cell, Jack, but I'm still at the office. I'm just being careful."

"Paige is next to me. Is it okay if I put you on speaker, so she can hear whatever bad news you're about to tell me?"

"No problem." She hesitated a second before continuing. "Another heads up. The California Supreme Court, courtesy of our buddy Janet Mackinaw, issued an order for the State Bar to prosecute Paige for failure to repay the money she earned in her last death penalty case." She inhaled. "And we're doing it. The prosecutor in L.A. plans to file formal charges first thing Friday morning."

"Prosecute her? What have you guys become, a collection agency for the Court? And how about due process? A hearing on whether or not she actually owes the money?"

Paige leaned over and spoke at the phone. "MJ, how can the Court refer me to your agency without at least issuing an order to show cause? I mean, I sent them a letter, at their request, explaining that I'd earned the money, they'd approved both my work and the payments, and there was no statutory or legal basis to make me return it."

"Technically, they can't, but when you filed that motion

to withdraw as counsel? It was like you threw a hand grenade into the Court. You bombed two sitting justices, the attorney general, and Rick Peters. Shit, I think you even blasted a state senator!"

Jack frowned as Paige flung herself onto her back, staring at the ceiling.

He clicked off the speaker and held the phone to his ear. "Hey, thanks again for clueing us in. Any advice on how we should handle this? I know you told us before that the State Bar Court is different—no jury, only a judge who hears the facts and makes a decision, right? And an appellate process if we lose?"

Jack thought MJ's end of the conversation sounded muffled, as if she had her hand over her mouth. "No! I mean, yes, but remember? They're all appointed by the Supreme Court." She huffed. "The Chief Justice appoints the State Bar judges, the prosecutors, and the appellate panel who reviews the State Bar judges' decision. If all that fails, your only option is to appeal—"

"To the Supreme Court." Jack ran a hand over his beard stubble. "What a circle jerk."

"Yeah, hence the heads up. You should probably get a lawyer who specializes in this stuff, but most of them are worthless. You'll be notified Friday when the prosecutor files the complaint." After another deep sigh, MJ continued, "I'm sorry, Jack. Obviously, when they couldn't get to you on the *Seavers* case, they decided to go after Paige. And with Sam Leonard's death, Paige lost the big gun who could make this go away."

"True." Jack swallowed a yawn. "And we don't have any other friends in high places. Listen, I've got to think about this. Be safe, okay?"

"Trying."

Shutting off his phone, Jack lay down and pulled his wife to his chest. "Hey, sweet pea, we'll deal with this, alright? Like we do everything else."

Paige sniffed, clearly fighting back tears. "What the hell is going on? My motion to withdraw was a little harsh, yeah, but every word of it was true. And a referral for what?

Ethically I was obligated to file the motion. I talked to a bunch of expert lawyers before I mailed it, and all of them said I needed to withdraw."

Jack brushed a stray lock of hair off her forehead. "I'd like to re-read it. Do you have a copy of it on your laptop?"

Nodding, Paige left his embrace, opened her computer, and found the nineteen-page document. "Here. I'm going to make some tea."

As Jack scrolled down, absorbing his wife's logical but excoriating rendition of the facts leading to her withdrawal, his gut filled with acid. What MJ O'Malley had described as a hand grenade read more like a nuclear bomb.

Watching his wife set two steaming mugs of tea on the bedside table, he smiled. "Not to be a wise ass, but you might as well have accused Mackinaw and Ong of committing weird sexual acts with badgers. It's no wonder the justices are so pissed."

Reading along as he re-scrolled through the document, Paige groaned at certain barbs she'd written. "Okay, maybe I came on a little strong, but I still stand by the allegations in this document. What the court did in Tom Seavers' case when they called you a lying cheat was bullshit. And then taking it out on my death row client by blocking his chance for appeal? More bullshit. With this effort to disbar me, those fuckers are just piling it on."

Jack wrapped an arm around her shoulder. "Easy, Saint Joan. I get it. I also agree with everything you wrote." He kissed her forehead. "The problem is that this 'hand grenade,' as MJ calls it, may get you disbarred unless we fight like bastards at the State Bar Court."

His wife, chin out, looked at him. "Isn't that what we always do for our clients? If we can do it for them, we can do it for ourselves…again."

Sipping their tea, knowing sleep would elude them, the couple fell into their own thoughts. Jack's veered to one fact. Paige's hand grenade opened the door to a myriad of murder suspects, each with a motive to frame either of them for Stephen Ong's homicide. One of the people Paige had impugned killed the old chief justice, of that he was sure. He only had to figure out which one.

Yeah, and how hard will that be when I'm the prime suspect?

* * *

Sun burned away the fog the next morning, leaving only a few clouds to mar the view of the Golden Gate Bridge from Phoebe's deck. In the chilly November air, Jack swallowed strong coffee while he waited for a return call. As if on cue, his cell rang. He cleared his throat. "Yes or no?"

Kevin Dorrian clipped out, "Yes, Tilden Park carousel, one hour. I'll find you." Then, he disconnected.

Jack went to the kitchen and announced he needed supplies for some home repairs Phoebe had mentioned. He donned a baseball cap, hoodie, and sunglasses. "Ladies, I need you to go out front and distract the reporters. There aren't many here. Then I'll go out the downstairs' door and take the path to the rental car."

Phoebe glanced out a crack in the blinds over the sink. "I only see two guys from KABC. The rest are probably nursing hangovers." She looked at her brother. "You don't have to do this. I can hire someone to fix what's broken."

Jack smiled. "Save your money, Feebs. You might need it for legal fees." At her misty eyes, he softened his tone. "Sorry, sis, bad joke. Actually, I need to get out of here, so I can think straight. I'll only be gone a couple of hours. Meanwhile, you and Paige hold down the fort."

He wrapped an arm around each woman, kissed one then the other, and sprinted down the stairs. He made his way past Phoebe's lush rose garden, through a wrought iron gate, and down a path leading to the street below. Every house sitting west of Phoebe's El Cerrito hillside street faced the bay, and each had been built in tiers, usually three, with lots of glass and decking to take advantage of the area's views and weather.

At the rental car, Jack looked around to make sure no reporters or cops lurked nearby, keyed the door, and started the car. He glanced up at a reflection from a deck several houses down from Phoebe's. A woman stood in her bathrobe, shiny aluminum mug in hand, apparently drinking in the Sunday peace and quiet.

A big woman, tall, chocolate skinned, her graying curls blown gently by the breeze.

Well, if it isn't the less-than-Honorable Janet Mackinaw.

Jack knew she lived nearby, as had Stephen Ong, but he didn't realize she lived quite so close to his sister. Instinct told him that was a fact that might matter. Holding his foot on the brake, he opened his cell and clicked on the camera. As he snapped Janet's picture, trusting his intuition instead of his logic, another figure emerged from the house. Janet put her arm around the smaller person, also dressed in a robe, and the two kissed as the shorter woman slid a hand into Janet's robe. Jack hit the zoom button on the camera and zeroed in on the couple, snapping two more shots. At the end of the kiss, the smaller female turned to the view.

Jack sucked in a breath.

Carin Cross?

He pulled his ball cap lower, so he wouldn't attract their attention and eased down the street. In June, when he'd run into Carin in the hallway outside the *Seavers* hearing, she'd looked familiar, but he couldn't recall meeting her before. Of course, he'd been a little distracted that day, between testifying for Seavers and nearly destroying his marriage.

He remembered the black roots underlying her blonde hair and figured the color wasn't natural. Now, imagining Carin as a brunette, the truth hit him. Carin Cross was none other than his former colleague at the Fairfax District Attorney Office, back in the day when he and Bobby Erickson pissed off most females within hearing distance. He'd lost track of her after she left for the Court of Appeals and divorced her husband. Obviously, she'd changed her last name. Probably had a few nips and tucks, too.

She'd hated Jack back then. She must really hate him now, after he'd messed up Janet Mackinaw's judicial career.

Correction. Her *lover's* judicial career.

But did she hate him enough to kill Stephen Ong and set him up for the murder? And if Janet Mackinaw had access to Phoebe's house as a friend who'd eaten dinners there, did Carin as well? No question, this was a new twist worth pursuing.

He hit the rental car's accelerator, resulting in a painfully sluggish response. He thought back to the incident in the law library with Bobby, Janet Mackinaw, Carin Cross, and a cunnilingus joke. He regretted egging Bobby on, not only because it hurt the women in his old office, but also set him up for their current wrath. Or so it seemed.

More than regretting his past misconduct, however, Jack Defalco missed his damned Porsche.

* * *

Using back roads to make his way to Tilden Park, Jack found a parking place in the vicinity of the carousel. As he approached the historic amusement ride, his thoughts drifted from the two women on the deck to his days spent on this carousel, halcyon times with young Claire and toddler Sean.

He stopped near a tree, remembering his daughter's crossed arms and stubborn head shake, refusing to leave the ride, even when she'd finished round sixteen on her favorite purple pony. He'd had to bribe her with the petting zoo and ice cream more times than not to get her to relinquish the reins and dismount.

Sean, on the other hand, could have cared less about the carousel, dutifully taking a spin on a stationary coach. After that one ride, he'd zoom to the steam trains, miniature cars that he rode as many times as Claire lost herself on her fantasy horse.

A lump formed in his throat at the memory of his children when they were so young and happy. Now, Claire was at college, dating a guy Jack labeled *The Asshole*, and Sean proudly wore the uniform of his high school military academy.

He thought of Kayla, with her never-predictable hair color and mood, braving it out in Beartooth, as a guest of the police chief and his wife. He and Paige called her every night, as promised, but they could tell the teen missed them. Tough cookie on the outside, mush on the inside, Kayla told Jack she loved Paige and him more than she'd ever loved her own folks. Her unconditional trust in them to make her world safe squeezed his chest.

Hmmm. Had he taken his heart meds this morning? Yeah. Good old potassium, the drug that saved him but killed

Stephen Ong.

A touch on his shoulder caused him to whirl around, his fists raised to defend himself.

Kevin Dorrian held up both hands. "Whoa, buddy. A little jumpy, are we?"

Jack relaxed. "Jesus Christ, Kevin! Next time try 'Hello, Jack.'"

The two men moved to a picnic table tucked into eucalyptus trees that defined Tilden Park. Kevin's jeans, tee shirt, and jacket hung on him like they covered a broomstick. The thought of cancer eating away Kevin's flesh saddened Jack. What an unnecessary and avoidable death. Ditto for all the officers affected by the dismantling of meth labs without protective gear.

Sighing, Jack withdrew a copy of Paige's hand grenade motion. He waited until Kevin read all nineteen pages.

Dorrian, no slouch investigator, quickly caught on. "So you think Mackinaw had a motive to set you and Paige up by overdosing Ong?"

Jack nodded. "Not only Mackinaw. Any one of the players mentioned in this motion had a motive. Look at what Paige accused them of." He flipped to page four and read aloud:

"Bill Hughes, Attorney General for the State of California, represented the People at the *Seavers* hearing. When Justice Janet Mackinaw took the stand in an effort to attack Mr. Defalco's credibility. Seavers' attorney impeached her with her prior testimony from an unrelated capital case. Mr. Hughes' daughter, Lori, was, at the time and still is, a deputy district attorney in Fairfax County, hired by District Attorney Rick Peters. Mr. Hughes' wife, Nadine, also was hired by Rick Peters and now is employed by his office as the executive director of the Fairfax County Family Law Center. When Mr. Hughes was sworn in as the former California State Auditor, Justice Janet Mackinaw performed that duty. Rick Peters also hired Judge Solomon P. Green's son, Adam, as a deputy district attorney, and Justice Stephen Ong's son, Joshua, as a deputy district attorney, and both were so employed at the time of the *Seavers* hearing. Also, Chief Justice Ong and Justice Mackinaw are former prosecutors in Fairfax County and both were, and likely still are, colleagues and friends of Rick Peters."

Jack looked up at Dorrian, who smiled and shook his head. "Your wife's got balls, buddy. Gotta give her that."
Smirking, Jack read on.

"In short, all of these associations, viewed in light of this Court's scathing opinion of Mr. Defalco's integrity (as set forth in the *Seavers* opinion), appear to an impartial public observer as—"

Jack interjected, "this is my personal favorite," before continuing,

"...a solidified effort by the members of this Court to support Mr. Peters and the reputation of his office by punishing anything and anyone associated with the Defalco law firm. Such a serious appearance of adverse bias can only jeopardize my capital clients' efforts to receive a fair and impartial review of their habeas corpus petitions."

He folded the document and shoved it in the pocket of his hoodie. He took off his ball cap and ran his fingers through the top of his hair. "This is a public document, Kevin, although the Court's buried it, and the press has stayed away from publishing it...if they even know about it."

"So you think this gives us possible perps and their motives?" Dorrian replied. At Jack's nod, he added, "Maybe. But which one actually killed Ong? Who has the most to gain by setting up you and Paige, not to mention your sister, and letting you take the fall for the guy's murder?"

Jack shrugged. "Mackinaw is the most obvious because she lost a lot from testifying against me at the hearing. And get this. Last night, we got a call warning us that Mackinaw referred Paige to the State Bar for prosecution and disbarment for failing to repay money she'd earned and received from the Court. It seems a little odd that Mackinaw would do that just after the shit hit the fan with Ong's death, don't you think?"

"Jack, I've got chemo brain, and it's giving me a headache trying to sort this out right now. Let me have the hand grenade and check out Mackinaw's access to Ong when he was at the hospital. By the way, how would she get the potassium bottle with your sister's and Paige's prints on it?"

Jack debated for a moment whether he should disclose his theory, then decided he had nothing to lose. "You know the partial label on that bottle?"

Dorrian nodded. "We're chasing it down. Should have an answer soon on what pharmacy compounded it and for what patient."

"Let me save you some time." Jack then explained the bottle was his and disappeared from Phoebe's medicine chest. At Dorrian's slack-jawed reaction, he hurried on. "Kevin, Janet Mackinaw has been to Phoebe's house for dinner as recently as last month when that bottle was in the guest bathroom. If Janet saw it there, she could have returned last week, taken it wearing gloves, and used it to snuff Ong, setting up Paige and me. I think that's likely and also that Phoebe was just collateral damage. They're friends, so I don't think Mackinaw would intentionally rope her in."

Kevin scratched his chin stubble. "Kind of a long shot, but maybe. She'd know from the name on the bottle that it was your prescription, and that your prints, and maybe Paige's, would be on it. She could tear just enough off the label to make it look like the perp tried to hide his identity, but leave enough for us to track down. Nobody would suspect her if she went to visit Ong that night at the hospital, and any moron with an Internet connection can figure out how to inject crap into an IV."

Kevin stood, pacing between the picnic table and a tree before completing his thoughts. "Mackinaw would know it's Fairfax County's jurisdiction, but also that Rick Peters would have a conflict in handling the prosecution. That forces him to turn the case over to the attorney general, who happens to be in bed with both Peters and Mackinaw." He snapped his fingers. "Very slick, but how do we prove this?"

Jack also rose. "Especially with the legal eagles rigging the game. Can you stall a little longer? Not send the AG your reports yet? If I can find out Mackinaw's whereabouts the night Ong was killed, or you can, we might be in a better position to nail her."

Dorrian turned toward the carousel, children's laughter mixing with their parents' warnings to hold on. "And if it's not Mackinaw? What about Peters as a suspect? Or Carin Cross?

Jack shook his head. "Neither had access to the potassium bottle at Phoebe's house. Except..." He weighed his earlier sighting of Cross and Mackinaw on the justice's deck. "Cross might have had access. I saw her on Mackinaw's deck this morning, kissing my former colleague, so maybe both of them came to Feeb's house for dinner. Cross hates Paige, obviously, after Paige bombed her in the hand grenade for withholding her pay for three years." He handed Dorrian the document.

"Maybe she hates Paige, but why go after you?"

Jack smiled. "Because I hurt Mackinaw? Killed Janet's career advancement and helped make her a laughing stock across the legal community and the world?" He paused. "Besides, as it turns out, Carin Cross used to work with me in the DAs office, as a brunette using her married name. She hated me then, and I'm guessing she still does. I didn't recognize her until I saw her earlier with Janet."

Dorrian looked hopeful. "And since they're lovers, she wants revenge." A smile emerged from under his police academy-issued moustache. "That, sports fans, is what we call motive."

"The question is, how do we find out where Cross and Mackinaw were the night Ong was murdered? Have you checked the hospital's security cameras yet?"

Kevin nodded. "We're on it, but no results yet, other than your sister entering and leaving the room just before seven. Tell you what. I'll give our tech guy a call while you go home and find out if Phoebe ever had Carin over for dinner, along with Mackinaw. Also, ask her if she hides a key outside, like under a flowerpot—anything that can help us get the perp into her house to steal that potassium bottle."

Jack reached out to shake Dorrian's hand. "On it." Before he turned away, Jack added, "Thanks for believing I didn't snuff the Chief Justice. And for giving me a chance to clear Paige and Feebs."

When Dorrian turned the handshake into a buddy-hug, Jack felt the man's skeletal frame beneath his clothes.

Would Kevin live long enough to solve this one last homicide?

CHAPTER TWENTY-SIX

El Cerrito, California
November 3, 2005

RETURNING TO PHOEBE'S DECK THE SAME WAY HE'D LEFT, Jack checked the back of Janet Mackinaw's house. Neither she nor Carin graced the outside area. He heard someone unlock Phoebe's sliding door and, after twenty-five years of marriage, knew his wife stood behind him. He felt her arms circle his waist.

"How'd it go with Kevin?"

He turned to her with a squint. "What makes you think I met with Dorrian?"

Paige smiled. "Been at this game a long time, honeybun, and I know you pretty well." She nodded at his empty hands. "Besides, genius, you've never been to a hardware store and returned with nothing."

The two settled in Phoebe's bright red Adirondack chairs, inhaling the moist Bay Area breeze. Jack told her about his conversation with Dorrian, the game plan, and his sighting of Carin and Janet kissing. He showed her the photos on his cell.

"And you took these because you're suddenly into girls-gone-wild sex?"

"Suddenly?" He laughed. "Seriously, I don't know why I took them, except it seemed like they might have some evidentiary value at some point. I don't think it's well-known the two ladies are an item," he clicked off his phone, "and the fact that Carin is Janet's lover gives her a motive to come after me—defending her beloved's honor."

Nodding, Paige echoed Kevin's earlier comments. "Maybe, but how does Carin access the potassium bottle?"

Before Jack could explain, Phoebe joined them, carrying a tray of sandwiches, a pitcher of iced tea, and three glasses. "I thought about a pitcher of margaritas, but figured we might need to stay sober with all this shit hitting the fan."

Jack reached for a sandwich. "Feebs, a question? When you had Janet Mackinaw here for dinner, did she bring a guest?"

Phoebe paused. "Yeah, actually. I forgot. She brought her friend, Carin."

Jack looked at Paige. "Bingo!" Turning back to his sister, he added, "Second question. Do you keep a spare key anywhere around the outside of the house? And please, God, don't tell me you leave one under the front mat."

His sister frowned at him. "I'm not stupid, Jack. It's under that cute little garden gnome near the front porch. And no, I don't tell people where it is."

"Right," Jack pointed out, "but an astute person, perhaps a nearby neighbor or her snoopy girlfriend, might have observed you retrieving it at some point."

Like a goldfish, Phoebe opened then closed her mouth, before listening to Jack's theory that Justice Janet Mackinaw and Carin Cross were possible killers. When he finished, he added, "Of course, there are other potential perps, like Rick Peters or the attorney general, or maybe even one of Solomon Green's sons. But Mackinaw and Cross top my short list, especially after they've turned their wrath against Paige."

Swallowing a bit of sandwich, Phoebe shook her head. "Kind of hard to believe those two would come in here, steal the potassium bottle, and kill Ong, just to get back at you and Paige. Still, somebody came in my house, took the bottle, and set us up." She paused. "By the way, my pathology buddy looked up the tox report for Sam Leonard. Nothing weird. No sign of excess potassium, just a ton of cancer throughout his body."

Paige raised her sunglasses. "If we'd found evidence Sam had been murdered, how would that have helped us?"

Jack thrummed his fingers on the chair. "It would have mucked up the case against us since we clearly had no motive to kill him. It could have created reasonable doubt, assuming we could connect the two murders through potassium." He rose, stretching. "The bigger problem with Sam's death is that he can't intervene for you at the State Bar." He moved to the patio door. "I'm calling Dorrian with the intel about the dynamic lesbian duo having access to this house. I'll see if he's got anything more from the hospital security tapes."

Paige raised her glass to him. "Good job, Jack. And after that you can get on Phoebe's home repairs, right?"

Jack threw his wife a raised eyebrow stare. "Tell me again why I married such a wise ass?"

"Obviously you needed company."

Yeah, and I always will, sweet pea, so I need to keep us out of prison.

* * *

Inside the house, Jack's cell rang before he could dial Kevin. "Defalco."

"Jack, Bill Hileman."

Uh oh.

A call from Beartooth's chief of police didn't bode well. "Is Kayla okay?"

"Yeah, she's fine. But we've got some serious shit going down. Child Protective Services just gave me a call. Says they received an anonymous tip that Kayla's been abused under your care."

"Bullshit!"

"I know, and that's what Kayla said…actually used the same word, so I suppose they could get you for being a bad language influence." He chuckled.

"Is that a joke, Bill? Because this is so not funny, especially with everything we're facing here in California."

The chief coughed. "Sorry. Bad timing. Listen, I told them I'm very familiar with the whole situation and wouldn't have helped you out if I suspected even a hint of abuse."

Mollified, Jack lowered his pitch. "Who would call them with that crap? Kayla's dad?"

"Doubtful, since he wants nothing to do with her. I'm putting out some feelers, see if I can find the source, but this stuff is confidential." He sighed. "As much as we're enjoying having her with us, Kayla really misses you guys. Given that, plus this investigation, it might be a good idea for one of you to come home."

Jack closed his eyes. He wanted to punch his fist through Phoebe's wall, but checked himself. If either he or Paige left the Bay Area, Rick Peters and the attorney general would scream, "Murder suspects flee, showing consciousness of guilt!" On the other hand, neither had been charged with a crime, nor ordered to stick around. He rubbed his chin, pondering which of them should return to Montana.

"Okay, I'll send Paige home. It'll get her away from this mess, and I know Kayla would prefer her to me." He forced himself to stay calm. "Besides, if I come back there and have to deal with those zealots at CPS, I'm likely to kill one of them."

The chief groused, "Careful what you say, Defalco. You never know who's listening. I'll tell Kayla that Paige is on her way. I can grab her when her flight lands if you want."

"Perfect. Thanks, buddy. I'm really sorry we got you and Jo Ann involved in this crap with Kayla."

"Not a problem. She's a great kid, despite all the traumas she's faced."

Jack smiled. "Yeah. She kinda grows on you after a while, like a pimple on your ass. Talk to you when I know Paige's flight information."

Disconnecting, he again started punching in Dorrian's number, but heard Paige ask behind him, "My flight information? What's going on?"

He explained, watching Paige slowly sink into a nearby chair before burying her face in her hands. He knelt in front of her. "Listen, this is going to be okay. You and I know it's a bullshit accusation, so does Kayla, and we have Bill and Jo Ann on our side."

Paige looked up, her cheeks stained with tears. "Right, because our life runs so smoothly lately. And what about the publicity? Kayla's under enough stress as it is. The last thing she needs is media attention…" She held up a palm as Jack tried to interrupt. "And, yes, I get that the investigation is confidential. But once I'm home, you know someone will leak it to the press. Kootenai County is too small for this to remain secret."

Jack knew his wife refrained from mentioning her real fear—that the authorities would place Kayla in foster care during the pendency of an investigation.

"Look, we don't have much room here. Right now, if you go back, no one can stop you. If you wait, who knows what will happen tomorrow? We know for sure, at least according to MJ, that the State Bar is filing charges against you. Unless Dorrian and I can stop Rick Peters, it won't take much for him, or his lackey at the AG's office, to get an indictment naming you in Stephen Ong's murder." He rubbed her upper arms. "I think you should get out of here now, babe. It'll make it harder to arrest you, and you'll be with Kayla, at least for a while. Besides, you'll be more patient with CPS than me."

She grabbed his hands and squeezed. "What about you and Phoebe? Peters can indict you two as easily as me. If he goes for all three of us, obviously we'll need our own lawyers. But what if he only goes after you? Or just you and Feebs? I'll be in Montana, so I can't appear in court with you, to get bail set…or anything else. Who will have your back?"

As renewed tears leaked from his wife's eyes, Jack brushed them away with his fingers before he cupped her face with his hands. "I've thought of that, but we'll just have to deal with it when, or if, it happens. Meanwhile, we have a teenager in Montana who needs us. I'm going to book you on the next flight into Kootenai County. Bill said he'd pick you up." He kissed her. "Don't worry. I'm going to fix this shit. I promise."

She nodded, but after so many years together, he could read her thoughts. He knew doubt crowded out her logic, just as it ate at his own.

Well, screw it. They might go down, but they'd take these fuckers with them.

* * *

Shaking late afternoon rain from his overcoat, Jack watched Paige's plane lift off, removing her from Fairfax County's cesspool of legal drama. He knew more stress awaited her in Montana, but at least she'd be among friends like Bill and Jo Ann, and sleeping in her own bed. He sat behind the wheel of his rental car and punched in Kevin Dorrian's personal cell number.

After one ring, the detective answered. "Is she gone?"

"Yep. Safely on her way, and the press seems none the wiser…at least for now. You got anything from the hospital security tapes?"

Kevin's tone rose slightly. "Actually, yes, and I think it

may be good news. Besides Phoebe entering and leaving Ong's room just before seven that evening, we see another person enter his room at 7:13. He's wearing a long black coat with the hood up, kind of like the Grim Reaper. The person exits at 7:19."

Jack felt his chest cavity expand with relief. "Christ, Kevin, that's huge. Now we have another perp and reasonable doubt. Can you get a height or weight from the video?"

"Not really, although I'd say medium to tall. The coat is floor length, made from thin, billowing material, with a huge hood that covers the person's face entirely—seriously, like those creepy guys in *Harry Potter* who sucked out peoples' souls." Jack heard Kevin drink something before he added, "And the sleeves are rolled back in a cuff, exposing a raised, flowery pattern, so it looks like a woman's coat. Still, there could be a guy wearing it."

Jack's mind clicked into trial lawyer mode in an instant. "Was the person carrying anything? What about the hands? Are they hairy? What about hair or skin color? And can you see shoes?"

He heard Kevin cough for a few seconds then gulp and swallow.

"Negative. The person's wearing gloves, not holding anything, and there's no view of the shoes, except they appear to be black, like the coat. Can't tell if they're high heels or Army boots. Whoever it is seemed to know where the security cameras were located and avoided facing them, plus made sure there was nothing identifiable except the coat. I've got my guys looking into that."

"Well, shit, Kevin. With that little information, anybody could have been inside it...me, Phoebe, Paige, Rick Peters, Janet Mackinaw, even that shrimpy Carin Cross, if she wore shoes with heels."

"Hang on, pal, there's more. The security camera in the parking lot clearly shows Phoebe getting into the passenger side of her BMW, and Paige driving the two of them off at precisely 7:08. It would be a stretch to say they managed to return, in that coat, enter the building and get to Ong's room by 7:13 when the Grim Reaper guy enters. I think that might clear them or at least postpone an indictment. And you, my friend, weren't even in the state of California when Ong's murder went down. So while Peters and his boys may have some theory you hired a hit man to take out Ong, they're going to have a tough time proving it."

On his end of the line, Jack nodded. "Except we still have the potassium bottle in Ong's trash can, with both Phoebe's and Paige's prints on it, and my name on the prescription. How do you explain that?"

"I don't, Jack. That's a problem. We did trace that bottle to the hospital pharmacy and you, via your sister, so there's no question it's the same prescription from Phoebe's medicine chest. Listen, I'm going to email you the security tape video. Watch it and let me know if you see something I missed. I could get fired for this, but fuck it, what can they do to me, right? I'm dying anyway."

Jack winced. "Don't send it, Kevin. You could lose your pension for your family. Just show it to me tomorrow. We can meet somewhere, maybe in Tilden Park again."

Seconds passed. Then, Dorrian agreed. "Roger that. And thanks for the common sense. My give-a-shit-factor is pretty small these days, so I don't always think about long-term consequences. Which reminds me, we keep tying this murder into Tom Seavers' case. Why? What if they're unrelated?"

Jack thought about it for a few seconds. "The key to the case is that potassium bottle with my name on it and the fact that Ong died from a potassium overdose. We've ruled out suicide because of the presence of that particular bottle, so it has to be murder. Whoever killed him had to both want him dead and want me convicted for it. Or Phoebe and me. Or Paige, Phoebe, and me. There's also the conspiracy angle, that we were all in it together, or that it was Phoebe or Paige, acting alone to avenge me, which is pretty thin."

At Kevin's silence, Jack continued. "The security tape sort of shoots holes in that angle. But the bottom line is, the only connection between Chief Justice Stephen Ong and me, besides the fact that we worked together twenty years ago, is the Court's published opinion in the *Seavers* case that ruined my reputation by accusing me of lying. And while Ong dissented, his reasons didn't help me, only Seavers. Plus, Janet Mackinaw, who hates me for a myriad of reasons, authored that opinion along with several other justices."

Good cop that he was, Kevin asked, "But where does killing Ong get you, Jack, assuming you had a motive based on that legal ruling? It just doesn't make sense that you'd kill somebody over that."

"You're preaching to the choir, Kevin. So, around we go, my friend, circling back to other suspects. Maybe Janet Mackinaw because I helped wreck her future career plans, although that doesn't explain why she'd go after Ong. Or Carin Cross, who might be insane enough to avenge her lover Janet by setting me up, again without explaining why either would kill the old guy."

"Crap!" Kevin vented frustration, before adding, "Those two as killers also seem, as you put it, a little thin. Statistically, women are far less likely to commit murder than men. So, thinking outside the box here, are there any men who might want Stephen Ong dead, who also would want you to take the fall?"

Jack started the car. "Let me think about it. I gotta get back to Phoebe's. She's holding dinner for me. Where and what time tomorrow for our meeting?"

"Carousel tomorrow morning at eight. Make sure you don't have a tail."

Jack clicked off his phone and sped onto the freeway toward El Cerrito. Who indeed had a motive to both kill Ong and set him up for the murder? Other than Rick Peters or Solomon Green's sons, no males came to mind. Besides, what would they have against Ong, unless he was just a convenient victim murdered to set Jack up? And how would they have accessed the potassium bottle from Phoebe's house?

Still, somebody was out there, no doubt laughing his or her ass off, as he or she waited for Jack's imminent arrest and incarceration, or worse, Phoebe's and Paige's.

But who?

And, more importantly, why?

CHAPTER TWENTY-SEVEN

El Cerrito, California
November 4, 2005

MORNING FOG HUNG OVER PHOEBE'S BACK DECK, blocking Jack's view of the San Francisco Bay. Chilled, he walked upstairs to grab a sweatshirt from the front hall closet. He opened the door, reached in, and then stared at a long, black, hooded coat, sleeves rolled back to expose a flowery raised pattern on the inside. He backed up a few steps, refusing to touch it. He whirled when his sister's voice tugged at him from the kitchen.

"While you're in there, you mind grabbing my parka? I'm going over to the city and plan on having the top down in the Beemer."

In a rare instance, Jack lost his voice. He gazed at his beloved Feebs, nausea roiling through his stomach.

"Jesus, Jack! What's wrong? Is there a body in there?" She smiled at him.

Instead of answering, he pointed at the black Grim Reaper coat. Phoebe came closer, looked at the garment, and said, "Yeah, it's your wife's. What's the problem? She bought it when she was down here a few months ago, on sale at Nordstrom, and left it so she'd have a raincoat when she needed it for work." Phoebe grabbed it off the hook and threw it on. "Isn't this great?" she enthused as she twirled, the thin fabric billowing out around her. "I want one, but I just borrow hers whenever I need it."

Jack's silence weighed heavier than concrete.

"Look," his sister added, "it wasn't expensive, if that's the issue."

Jack shook his head. "Uh...I've got to leave."

He zipped up his hoodie, left his sister standing draped in his wife's damning wrap, crammed his Giant's cap on his head, and left through the downstairs door. His hands trembled as he unlocked the rental car.

He had to meet Kevin at Tilden Park in just a few

minutes to watch a video of Ong's likely killer entering and leaving Ong's room, wearing a coat possibly identical to the one he'd found in Phoebe's closet.

His wife's coat that happened to fit his sister.

What was he supposed to do with that fact? A very bad fact, as most lawyers would agree. If he told Kevin about it, the detective would be duty-bound to seize the coat as further evidence pointing to one or more Defalcos as Ong's murderer. Rick Peters, via the attorney general, would have the final puzzle piece to nail them for Ong's death.

He turned on the heat, but left the transmission in park. Fear froze his hands to the steering wheel. Logic forced him to consider the remote chance that his own wife and sister actually had conspired to kill Chief Justice Stephen Ong. Could they actually be playing him? Had they set up the murder, counting on Jack to get them off? Suspicion slithered down his throat. Worse, what if Paige hadn't really forgiven him for his fling with Maggie Tornow and decided to execute him via the court system?

No. Not Paige. She wasn't a vindictive asshole like he was.

Inhaling, Jack dismissed that possibility and discarded Phoebe's involvement at the same time. He knew these two women better than anyone else in his life. Neither had it in them to take a human life, unless somebody threatened their kids.

As he pulled out to meet Dorrian, Jack again faced the same question: Who had access to Phoebe's house, would take the potassium and kill Ong, knowing that the evidence would lead right back to the Defalco clan? Weirder still, who would borrow Paige's coat to wear during the murder and return it? Or was it simply a coincidence that the killer wore a coat similar to Paige's, as Dorrian had described?

Maybe.

But like most of law enforcement, Jack didn't believe in coincidence, and as his wife noted before she left, their life didn't run that smoothly. Then again, maybe he would look at the hospital security tape and see the coats weren't the same, just similar, which would relieve him of his ethical duty to turn over Paige's coat to Dorrian.

Or not.

* * *

Jack made it to the carousel in record time and found Kevin sipping coffee at a picnic table. Other than the two of them, the park was deserted at this early hour. After nodding at one another, each apparently too tired or preoccupied to exchange pleasantries, Kevin opened his laptop and clicked on the DVD of the hospital security tape.

Sure enough, the unidentified perp wore a coat exactly like the one Jack had left draping Phoebe's shoulders. Good thing he hadn't eaten breakfast because he could barely hold down the coffee making its way up his esophagus. Poker face on, however, he smiled at Dorrian as Kevin clicked onto the next video.

Jack closely watched that second tape of the hospital parking lot, the one showing Phoebe getting into her car and Paige driving away. Then, he had Kevin replay it several times.

Dorrian leaned in. "What do you see that I missed?"

"Not sure but…yeah, there." Jack pointed at a spot on the tape occurring a minute or so after the two women drove off. "Doesn't that look like Phoebe's Beemer driving down the access road to the freeway entrance?"

Kevin squinted at the tape as it replayed, pausing it for a better view of the black vehicle Jack tapped with the tip of his pen. "Sure does. Of course, there are dozens of black Beemers like your sister's in the area. Maybe there's a traffic camera near there that picked up the license plate number." He looked at Jack. "That would be a nice piece of exculpatory evidence."

Again Jack merely smiled. An understatement, especially if somebody served a search warrant at Phoebe's house and found that fucking black raincoat.

Should he tell Kevin about the coat? Ethically, yes.

Probably.

Then again, it wasn't like anyone knew for sure it was the same coat worn by the person on the video, right? And if he 'fessed up, Kevin would be all over it, and his sister and Paige, because really, what other choice would a cop have? Right now, the evidence all pointed in one direction—at him, or at least at his family.

Dorrian faced the morning sun burning through the fog, Ray Bans hiding his eyes. "It's times like this I wish Jane Moore still worked for us. She left for the FBI a few years back. I really miss her." He sighed before adding, "Let's go through this, buddy. Can the DA prove this case? We know he's got the manner of death from the medical examiner's conclusion—murder by poisoning, rather than from suicide or natural causes. He's also got the method—an overdose of potassium chloride."

Jack stared at the carousel. "He's got a shitload of physical evidence to support that theory. Two potassium bottles in Ong's hospital trashcan, plus the toxicology results showing Ong had enough of the drug in his system to quickly end his life."

Kevin nodded. "And the identity of the killer or killers?"

"Easy. Suspect One, me, proved through circumstantial evidence that counts just as much as direct evidence. My name's on the prescription label for one of the potassium bottles, and although I was in Montana at the time of death, the prosecutor will argue that I conspired with my sister and wife to take Ong out."

"And your motive?"

"Which the AG doesn't have to prove, is retaliation for Chief Justice Ong's comments impugning my honesty and integrity. Weak but sufficient."

Jack rolled on. "Then there's Suspect Two, my wife. Again, circumstantial evidence shows her print on my potassium bottle, her access to that bottle by staying at Phoebe's before and during the time of the murder, and her presence at the hospital, per the security video, at or near the time of the murder, albeit in a car outside."

Although let's not forget the presently-undiscovered-by-the-cops black raincoat in Phoebe's front closet identical to the one worn by the killer on the videotape.

"Paige's motive?" Kevin tossed in, "To avenge her husband's public humiliation at the hands of the California Supreme Court, either acting alone or in concert with you and Phoebe."

"Right. And Suspect Three, applying the same circumstantial evidence and motive, is my darling sister, who also happened to be the lead nurse on Ong's case, and entered and left his room not long before Ong died."

Not to mention, that goddamn raincoat fits her.

Neither man said a word for a few minutes.

Dorrian's wheezing cough cut the silence. "Fucking cancer. Looks like it's spread to my lungs. At this rate, I'm not sure I'll be around to finish this investigation."

Jack again weighed whether to disclose to Kevin the existence of Paige's raincoat. He knew neither he nor his family had anything to do with Ong's death. He just needed some time to figure out who did. By withholding the raincoat, he could buy himself more time.

Fuck it. Why help the State of California put us in prison?

"Kevin, Rick Peters and the attorney general don't know about the Grim Reaper guy yet, correct?"

"Nope. We're meeting at nine to go over the evidence. Once they see the hospital tapes, it should delay their move to indict…at least for now."

"Who's going to be at the meeting?"

Dorrian shrugged. "Peters, obviously. The AG. Me." Another cough. "Some other lawyers and cops. Even your old office mate, Bobby Erickson. He's on loan to the AG's office to help with the case."

Jack stared at Kevin. "Bobby? I thought he'd retired a few years back."

"He did, but like a booger, they can't shake him loose. He volunteered to come back as a special prosecutor. Between us, I think his wife drives him crazy."

Jack laughed. "The Bitch of Belfast! If I recall, she was a real ball buster. I wonder how Bobby's daughter's doing. The Lunker, he used to call her. Geez, she must be just a couple of years older than my Claire."

"Bobby hasn't changed much. Still as politically incorrect as ever. Personally, I love the guy."

Standing, Jack agreed. "Maybe, just maybe, Bobby will add a little common sense to Rick Peter's vendetta against me. He always was a brilliant lawyer. You think he'll talk to me?"

Dorrian also rose, tossing his empty coffee cup in the trash. "Possible, except at the moment, you're still the prime suspect in this investigation, even though you and I both know that's bullshit. But Bobby loved you like a brother, man. If anyone can save your bacon, he can."

Jack smiled as he remembered his days sharing an office with Bobby Erickson, at how close he and Paige had been to Bobby and his wife. Until a few years ago, they'd exchanged Christmas cards. For the first time since Stephen Ong's murder, Jack felt a glimmer of hope.

Then a picture of Phoebe twirling in his wife's billowing, black coat swam into his head. "Gotta go."

He raised the hood on his sweatshirt, patted Kevin on the shoulder, and walked away.

Time to destroy some evidence.

* * *

In Beartooth, Paige sat across from Kayla at their battered kitchen table, relieved to be home from California. After arguing with Child Protective Services on the phone, she felt she was a little closer to keeping Kayla than she'd had been last night on her flight home.

She sipped her tea as she tried to calm both of them. "Honey, I have no idea who called the authorities. That's the problem with anonymous reporters. But Bill and Jo Ann told them there was no truth to the allegations, and so did you. They've been to this house, spoken with your teachers and counselors at school, interviewed your probation officer and some of your friends." She reached for Kayla's hand, partly to stop its nervous tapping on the wood surface. "Nothing, Kayla. That's what they've found. Believe me, this is going to be okay."

If anyone other than a Defalco was involved, Paige might even believe her own bullshit. But since she and Jack had defended so many high-profile clients in the Kootenai Valley, and pissed off nearly everyone at the courthouse, she doubted things would go smoothly. CPS could cause big problems for them if they insisted Kayla move to temporary foster care pending the outcome of the investigation. And of course, being one step away from a murder indictment in California didn't exactly burnish Paige's credentials as Kayla's guardian. The investigator had made a few snide comments about it, based on what he'd read in the press.

Kayla squeezed her hand, causing Paige to look into the girl's whiskey eyes. "Poppy, you know I love you and everything, but you look like shit. Maybe you should, like, go take a nap or something? Besides, I don't care what these fuckers say. I'm fifteen, and I can live where I want."

Paige smiled at the girl's bravado, wishing Kayla could legally make that decision. "There's also the California thing, sweetie. If for some reason this mess with the Supreme Court justice gets worse," *like we're arrested,* "then you might have to live with Bill and Jo Ann for a while. They said they'd take you if," *I'm put in jail and have to go to trial for murder,* "I need to go back, you know, to help out Jack." *And we won't even talk about the State Bar prosecution, and me losing my license to practice law in two states.*

Kayla stood behind Paige, putting her arms around her. The girl set her chin on top of Paige's head as she sighed, "I really do love you, pops. I'm not gonna leave you all alone to face this crap." As quickly as she'd given the hug, she headed for the stairs. "I've got homework. Can we have pizza for dinner?"

Still with her back turned away from Kayla, Paige wiped a tear from the corner of her eye and took a breath. "You bet. And Kayla?"

"Yeah?"

Paige turned in her chair. "I love you, too, and I'm not letting anyone take you from me."

As Kayla clumped up the tiled staircase, Paige's phone vibrated in her pocket. She looked at the caller and answered. "Hey, MJ. Thanks for calling me back."

"Of course. I'm afraid it's not with happy news, though."

Paige closed her eyes. "What?"

"The State Bar prosecutor in L.A. returned my call, on the down low, right? He says he has direct orders from Janet Mackinaw to seek nothing less than your disbarment. No deals, no mitigation. Just basically, fuck your eyes out, ruin your legal career."

Paige's tea turned to acid in her stomach. "Why? Because of my motion to withdraw as counsel? C'mon, MJ! There has to be a defense to this! I have a right to a hearing, to present evidence, and they have to prove...what? What exactly is the charge against me?"

"Failure to comply with an order of the Court, to wit, to repay the money they paid you for your death penalty cases."

Paige stood, gazing out the window at the first snow of the year, large flakes softly covering their lawn. "The money I earned." At MJ's silence, Paige added, "I'm not going to let them do this. Not my style. So how do I fight the State Bar and the California Supreme Court?"

MJ snorted. "Not easily, girlfriend. I'd quick-set it for trial. That forces the prosecutor to show you whatever evidence and witnesses he has right away."

"The only witness he could call is Carin Cross. She's the one I yelled at over the Court's failure to pay me. Maybe I should subpoena Acting Chief Justice Mackinaw for the trial. That would piss them off."

MJ sighed. "Paige, like I said before, you might want to hire a lawyer. You're already up to your ass in legal problems with the murder investigation, at least according to the media. And now with the State Bar."

Not to mention the local Child Protective Services people. "You have anyone in mind?"

"I do, but she's expensive. Probably will run you at least $20,000."

Paige gave a short laugh. "Yeah, right! Like we have that kind of money to spend." *Plus what it will cost if the attorney general charges us with murder.* Ending the call before threatened tears started to roll, Paige murmured, "Thanks, MJ. Gotta go."

Walking into her bedroom, she slumped into an over-stuffed leather chair, kicked off her boots, and put her feet on the ottoman. She flipped the switch on the fireplace, letting flames contrast the snow slanting sideways out the window. She loved this room, with its two-hundred-year-old barnwood floors, the cherry sleigh bed and armoire, even the low-end tile in the master bathroom.

She picked up a set of rosary beads Jack had left on the small table to her right, but her ability to pray fled in the face of so much disaster. Jack's testimony on behalf of Tom Seavers had plummeted her family into a morass of crap.

Why?

What was the connection between the recent events, if one existed?

They knew Mackinaw and Cross were responsible for her fiasco with the State Bar, and the women's involvement in Ong's murder seemed possible as well, since they'd had access to the potassium. Yet why would they snuff out the old man? Just to screw with Jack? Had Kevin Dorrian even ascertained where either woman was the night Ong died?

What about Kayla? Would those two bitches have called in the abuse complaint to CPS just to retaliate against Paige? If true, and she could prove it, Paige could cost both women their legal careers because filing a false report, especially involving a kid, was a felony. Which meant, Paige realized, she had to discover the identity of that anonymous reporter.

Her mind clicked into linear lawyer-think. Mackinaw and Cross appeared to be the source of every problem the Defalcos now faced.

Then again, if Rick Peters, through his lackey at the attorney general's office, indicted her for murder, her State Bar issues and Kayla's guardianship would be moot. The Bar would convict her *in absentia*, and CPS would snatch Kayla from the Defalcos, placing her God-knew-where.

And what of Sean and Claire? How could either of them afford to stay in school when their parents had no way to earn money for their tuition? Claire could take out loans, but Sean? He'd just turned seventeen. Maybe scholarships?

During her daily calls with the kids, she'd explained the potential perils that lay ahead for their parents, begging them to tell her if they were getting harassed at school for those alleged misdeeds. They'd both denied it, but she knew they were trying to protect her. She'd also touched on the State Bar charges and CPS investigation, even though neither situation had yet been leaked to the press. If their parents' lives went further into the crapper, the kids needed to be prepared.

Paige rubbed her temples. No matter the final outcome, the mere allegation of murder had changed the Defalcos' lives irrevocably. Paige knew they'd never rid themselves of the stench surrounding the accusations. *Killer, murderer, conspirator.* Even if the real culprit confessed, the name *Defalco* would always come up in an Internet search attached to the homicide of Chief Justice Stephen Ong. People would forever look at them differently, even as they did now, whenever they went out to dinner or to the grocery store.

Curling her feet onto the chair, Paige let the fire warm her. She missed Jack, wished he were there with her, the two of them laying together in bed, sleepy after making love—cozy and safe, their problems behind them.

Shaking that image from her head, Paige admitted that solving Stephen Ong's murder sat first on their list of priorities.

So, if not a Defalco, nor Mackinaw and Cross, then who killed the Chief Justice, leaving evidence taken from Phoebe's house that pointed right at Feebs, Jack, and her? Solomon Green's two sons might hate Jack that much, but they must have loved Ong for defending their dad's honor in the *Seavers* opinion. Ditto for Rick Peters. He definitely hated Jack for breaking rank by exposing his office's illegal jury selection practices, but Ong was his close friend.

Frustrated, Paige closed her eyes. Prayer, that elusive comfort she rarely sought these days, swept her into restless sleep.

CHAPTER TWENTY-EIGHT

El Cerrito, California
November 4, 2005

DRIVING BACK FROM THE LOCAL MARKET, Jack saw a 9-1-1 text come over his cell. He pulled into a spot on the street below his sister's house and checked the sender.

Dorrian. Shit!

He took a breath. There was no way Kevin could have learned about Paige's raincoat, so what new crisis could have arisen since Dorrian's meeting with Peters and the AG earlier that morning? An indictment? A search warrant for Phoebe's house?

Rather than immediately seeking out more bad news from the detective, Jack made his way to Phoebe's back door, went inside, and opened the coat closet. The fucking Grim Reaper outfit still hung there, next to the hanger on which he now slung his hoodie. He'd thought about taking the evidence and throwing it in a dumpster somewhere, but he wasn't sure how to explain its absence to Phoebe.

When he'd mentioned the coat to Paige on the phone an hour ago, in an oh-by-the-way comment, she'd readily admitted it was hers. She'd even enthused over its practicality when her hands were full, explaining the huge hood obviated the need for an umbrella. Both women, it appeared, were clueless to the coat's use by whoever killed Stephen Ong.

And wasn't that the weirdest piece of evidence yet? Who would come into Phoebe's house, take the potassium bottle and the coat, and then have the balls to return the coat to the closet?

He removed the coat, wadded it up, and stuck it into a now-empty grocery bag. It definitely was time to shit-can that evidence, even though it might prove useful down the road. Right now, it burned holes through his brain. He put it in the guest bedroom, so Feebs wouldn't see it when she came home.

Returning to the hall closet, Jack's eye caught a leather sport coat he hadn't noticed before, crammed in the far right corner. He pulled it out. Black and a bit worn in spots, its label sized it as a men's forty-two. Judging by the lapel width, he figured its age at fifteen to twenty years old. Clearly it wasn't his, since he wore a thirty-eight small.

Puzzled, he turned when he heard Phoebe enter the front door a few feet away. Instead of greeting her, he held out the mystery jacket. "Was this Dad's?"

His sister, a master at secrecy when she wanted to keep him out of her personal life, shook her head. "Nope, just a friend's."

He tipped his head at her. "Don't tell me you've been holding out on me, and you're seeing a new guy?"

She looked sheepish. "Past tense, but not such old history. Turns out the asshole was married and lied to me about it. I really know how to pick 'em, don't I? Maybe I'll just give it to Goodwill." She grabbed the sport coat off the hanger. As she did so, something fell from the pocket.

Jack picked it up. He examined a large gold college ring, its blue stone overlaid by a University of San Francisco insignia. Inscribed on the inside, he saw initials too worn to read, next to the year 1967.

"A college man, I take it?"

Phoebe grabbed the ring. "I should mail this to his wife, tell her what her dear hubby's been up to. I threatened to do just that before I dumped him, but I don't think he believed me."

"Well, if he missed it, he would have contacted you by now. Hang on to it, Feebs. Guys tend to cherish their class rings." He replaced the empty hanger in the closet. "And don't tell his wife about your affair. Trust me, no good will come of it, especially for his loyal but betrayed wife." Grimacing, he thought of Paige's gut-wrenching reaction to Maggie Tornow.

He accepted Phoebe's offer of a sandwich, briefly considered filling her in on the Grim Reaper outfit, decided against it, and headed to the deck to return Kevin's call.

Dorrian picked up on the first ring. "Where the fuck have you been? Didn't you get my 9-1-1?"

The urgency in Kevin's tone made Jack pause. "What's the emergency?"

"For starters, it's like murder central here in gangland.

The head of the Project Trojans, the head of the Nortenos, and the head of the Devils Guard are all dead, man! Shot with what looks like the same gun, an older model Uzi. On top of that, courthouse security found a pipe bomb under Rick Peters' county car a few minutes ago."

Jack jumped up from his deck chair. He walked to the front of Phoebe's house and, sure enough, there wasn't a reporter in sight.

"Well, fuck. They can't nail me for any of that shit. I was with you until a couple of hours ago, and then at the market. The turbaned guy on lane three can alibi me."

"Jesus, of course nobody thinks you did these. We're not even sure the gang killings are related, except it's pretty fucking odd that the heads of each group got whacked one after the other early this morning—with what looks like the same weapon."

On his end, Jack nodded. "Too bad they found the bomb before Peters blew up." At Dorrian's silence, Jack laughed. "C'mon, I'm kidding. I may dislike the guy, but I don't want him dead. He's got kids, for chrissakes."

"Then do me a favor and don't say crap like that, okay?"

Jack's tone switched to hopeful. "Any chance the bomb under Peters' car is connected to the chief justice's murder? Sure would be sweet if somebody diverted the heat off my family and me."

Over the line, he heard scattered radio chatter as Dorrian let loose a string of expletives. "Jack, I'm outta here. We just got a call from SFPD. Sounds like something happened over there at the state building, also with an older model Uzi. Fuck!"

Jack stared at his silent phone before returning to the back deck. His brain felt like an over-inflated balloon about to pop. He knew something—or someone—connected the pieces of this bloodbath, but the answer hovered just beyond his thoughts.

When Phoebe emerged with two beers, he logged the time at 11:45, figured it was close enough to noon to justify alcohol, and joined her. He explained what had just transpired, how the gang leaders had eaten shit from an old-style automatic weapon, and the fact that Rick Peters barely missed his own demise. And now there'd been a shooting at the state building that housed, among other entities, the attorney general's office.

Phoebe shook her head. "Sounds like somebody with nothing to lose decided to take out a few bad guys. You know, I hear that from patients all the time, that if they ever received a terminal diagnosis, they'd blow away a few people on their bucket list before they go."

Jack swilled his beer. "I've said that. Dorrian's said it. Practically everybody I know in law enforcement has s—" He paused, sitting forward. "That's it, Phoebe! The connection! Somebody who's dying is taking out people he hates. Or she hates."

His sister raised her eyebrows. "An ancient Supreme Court justice, Rick Peters, and three gang leaders?" She looked toward the bay, now visible since the fog burned off. "That's a pretty diverse group, don't you think? And then you figure this mass murderer also had access to my house?"

Jack's head throbbed. "Yeah, that is kind of stupid." He finished off his beer before he stood up and stretched. "I need some aspirin. I'm going to call Paige again to get an update on how horrible life is in Beartooth."

As he left the deck, he turned back to ask Phoebe about her dinner plans. He stopped when he saw her retrieve the gold class ring from her pocket, absently rubbing it between her thumb and forefinger. A tear slid down her cheek.

Quietly, Jack slipped inside, leaving his sister to her sadness.

* * *

As couples do who have spent over half their lives together, Jack unloaded on Paige, right after she filled him in on the CPS and State Bar fiascos. He didn't mention her black raincoat again, it's likely connection to Ong's murder, nor that he intended to dump it in the middle of nowhere as soon as he got off the phone. He had no qualms about destroying potential evidence since it implicated his wife and sister, and indirectly, him, because he knew none of them was involved with Ong's death. Of course, he also knew he'd lose his license to practice and land in jail if anyone discovered his actions.

So be it. Protecting his family was worth the risk.

"Honeybun," Paige concluded, "I've got to agree with Phoebe on any connection between the homicides. The victims just seem too diverse. Why gang bangers and a prosecutor lumped in with Stephen Ong?"

"I know. It's thin. And remember, Peters is fine, sad to say. I haven't heard anything about what went down at the state building yet, other than a report of a drive-by shooting out in front. Nothing about injuries." He lay down on the bed, kicking off his shoes. The beer he'd had at lunch forced his eyes closed. "This whole month, in fact, this entire year, has been an absolute goat and pony show. All I know is we're innocent."

Paige said something to Kayla about pizza, then added, "If there is a single killer responsible for all this stuff, it would have to be someone with nothing to lose, right? Like someone with cancer or who's suicidal and intends to take himself out after he nails the last person on his list."

"So goes my theory, but why do we assume it's a guy? Let's not forget Carin Cross and Janet Mackinaw." He conjured an image of the two women embracing on their deck. "They both look pretty healthy to me, but that might not prove anything. Then there's Dorrian, who we know is going down for the count any time now."

"For all his bravado, Kevin would never do something like this, Jack. And he'd never set you up, let alone Phoebe and me. Plus, what's his beef with Peters? I get his hatred for the gang guys, but even then, it's pretty indiscriminate to shoot three of them when they haven't even been charged or convicted of a crime."

Eyes still closed, Jack smiled. "Spoken like the bleeding heart you are. Those three scumbags probably have a record a mile long. I'm sure we'll find out." He heard his sister in the kitchen. "Hey, babe, before we go, did Phoebe ever tell you about a guy she's been seeing who turned out to be married?"

Silence.

"Well, who is it?" His eyes snapped open as he sat up.

"I promised her I wouldn't mention it to you. Besides, I

don't know the guy's name or anything, just somebody from her past. She said she loved him for his brains and sense of humor. Plus, he was a great lay."

Jack winced. "You think it was a doctor from the hospital?"

Paige sighed, murmured something to the dogs. "Maybe. Look, who cares? We have far more important shit to worry about than your sister's sex life. Besides, I got the impression the affair ended months ago." More background noise that sounded like Kayla laughing and then Paige joining in. "I need to get off the phone. Love you."

Sitting on the edge of the guest bed, Jack considered whether or not to pursue the identity of Phoebe's former lover. What if the person had a key to the house and a grudge against gang bangers? Granted, that was a remote possibility, but not impossible.

Or maybe it had nothing to do with the gang victims, and the guy only wanted to shut Phoebe up, so she didn't tell his wife about their affair. But why wouldn't he just kill Feebs instead of resorting to such an elaborate murder set-up with Justice Ong? Still, a doctor at Phoebe's hospital would have the means, expertise, and access to kill him. But if the shootings were related to Ong's death, what doctor would also have a hard-on for three gang members and a prosecutor?

Forcing himself from the bed, he grabbed the plastic shopping bag containing Paige's raincoat and slipped out the downstairs door. After revving the rental car, he drove north on the freeway toward Vallejo. He'd dispose of the evidence near the closed naval shipyard. And while he drove the thirty minutes it would take to get up there, he'd think of possible dying or suicidal suspects desperate enough to launch a murder spree in the Bay Area.

The idea made him laugh. *Yeah, right.*

* * *

Before he'd made it to the Carquinez Bridge, Jack's cell chimed. He glanced at it and hit the hands-free button. "Kevin, what's up?"

He heard Dorrian pause amid background voices. "Jack, you're on speaker. I'm at the Fairfax Police Department with

Rick Peters and some other people. We'd like you to come in and talk to us."

Jack slowed for traffic, pulled to the farthest right lane, and got off I-80 at the Highway Four exit. "I don't think so, buddy. And Rick, you're way off base if you think anyone in my family—or me—had anything to do with Ong's murder."

A jumble of voices caucused unintelligibly before Jack heard his old nemesis, Rick Peters. "Defalco, we've had some…events…that changed my mind about your involvement in the Ong matter." His sigh sounded heavy, even credible. "What I need from you is your memory. We have a situation going down that…can you just come talk to me? I don't want this conversation on record or on the phone."

Jack gave Peters' proposal five seconds' thought. "Tell you what. You put it in writing that Paige, Phoebe, and I are no longer suspects in Ong's murder—give the three of us complete immunity, both use and transactional, and I'll talk to you. But not at the PD. I'll meet you and Dorrian at the Tilden Park carousel in…," he looked at his watch, "forty-five minutes."

That should still give him enough time to lose the raincoat, an act he intended to finish with or without immunity from prosecution.

From their silence, Jack could envision Peters' dilemma. He hated Jack for turning against the office. Worse, Peters just might be setting a killer free if the situation going down wasn't what he thought it was. If Peters were wrong, he'd have given Jack, Paige, and Phoebe a free ride. To make it worse, he had to meet Jack on neutral turf instead of surrounded by his law enforcement buddies.

"Alright," Peters capitulated, "Full immunity for the three of you. I'll see you at the carousel, but make it twenty minutes. We need to get a handle on this before the killer goes after another victim." The connection went dead.

If Jack planned to be on time for the meeting with Peters, he had no time to stop. If he was late, Peters might leave before Jack had the signed immunity agreement in hand. He needed that document to protect his wife and sister a hell of a lot more than he needed to shit-can the coat. He'd stuck the shopping bag in the rental car's trunk in case a cop pulled him over. It would just have to remain there while he met with Peters and Dorrian.

Eighteen minutes later, Jack pulled into the Tilden parking lot and spotted Dorrian, Peters, and two other people standing under a tree. Several yards away, laughing children circled on their magic ponies. Nearing the group, Jack recognized Bobby Erickson, several years older but still trim, chatting with a skeletal version of...Maggie Tornow.

Well, fuck me.

Jack stopped, and so did conversation between the prosecutors and Dorrian. As a single entity, they turned in his direction, staring as if Jack was a deranged serial killer. Then Kevin walked toward him, grabbed him in a bear hug, and muttered, "Keep calm, pal. This is a peace process. We're the good guys."

"Right. Somehow, I'm not reassured." Nodding at Peters, Jack shook Bobby's outstretched hand.

Bobby spoke first, a grin slashing his face, his blue eyes twinkling. "D-man, it's been too long. You remember Maggie Tornow, right?"

His old office mate had known of their one-night-stand, so Jack wondered at Bobby's comment. He glanced at her, uncomfortable at the memory, but shook her bony hand. "Of course."

"You haven't changed, Jack," Maggie smiled, multiple stress lines ringing her eyes. "You're still the same fit guy you were twenty years ago. Me? Nothing like a divorce and a son with cancer to help a gal lose weight."

Jack winced. "I'm sorry about your boy, Mags. Is he—"

"In remission for seven years now. Fingers crossed."

Peters held up his hand. "Enough chitchat, folks. Defalco, here's what's happening. We have a killer in a black face mask shooting people with an older model Uzi, out of the driver's side window of a black Cadillac Escalade. The killer wears gloves, so we aren't sure of race, but one witness today swears the perp has blue eyes. No height, or weight, not even gender. But here's the thing." He nodded toward his two minions. "Both Bobby and Maggie remember that our office prosecuted the three dead gang bangers a few years ago and sent them to prison. Today, Bill Hughes, the AG who handled the *Seavers* matter, but who also once prosecuted the dead gang bangers, took a hit while he was getting into his car in San Francisco in front of the State Building."

Jack shrugged. "Sounds like a family member or gang member hell-bent on revenge against law enforcement. What has this got to do with Ong's murder? And speaking of that…" He held out his hand.

Peters withdrew a folded document from his inside jacket pocket and motioned for everyone to sit at a picnic table away from the crowd. "Hughes is going to survive, by the way, which I'm sure was your next question." He smirked, likely believing Jack felt no affection for the AG who'd cross-examined him during the *Seavers* hearing and slammed his reputation in a legal brief to the Supreme Court. Peters handed over the folded papers. "This is a boilerplate immunity agreement, all we had time to prepare, but it covers everything, I think. I've signed it, so if you're okay with it, I need to ask you some questions."

Jack read the papers and nodded, relief flooding through him. Exhaling slowly, he answered, "This'll work." He signed next to Peter's scrawl. "So what do you want to know?"

Before Peters could answer, Dorrian interrupted. "As far as the Ong murder, I checked that traffic tape to see if your sister's car was the Beemer on the freeway access road that night. It was, so she and Paige are cleared, especially with the hospital tape showing the Grim Reaper person going in and out of Ong's room. But what's interesting—" he coughed for a few seconds, his eyes watering. "That same traffic tape shows a black Cadillac Escalade leaving the hospital parking lot a few minutes after your sister, following the same route to the freeway. It has the same license plate number from the one in today's shooting and those involving the gang bangers."

Erickson jumped in. "The plate was stolen from a pickup in Danville, not far from my house. And Maggie and I both had our hands in the gangsters' cases a few years ago."

Jack turned to Dorrian. "Did you ever figure out where Cross and Mackinaw were the night of Ong's murder?"

Dorrian slid his eyes to Peters who answered, "They were at an awards dinner put on by the local bar association. I sat with them, so they're also cleared. But it's odd because Janet wrote the opinion supporting the drug conviction for the dead Devils Guard leader."

"And Ong?" Jack asked. "Did he concur in that opinion? Is that how these victims are connected?"

Hacking into a handkerchief soon spattered with blood, Dorrian nodded. Taking a strangled breath he whispered, "We've warned both women they may be targets. What's missing, obviously, is why this killer would set you, Paige, and Phoebe up for Ong's murder. Or how the person accessed the potassium bottle in Phoebe's house."

Maggie shifted on the wooden bench. "Jack, we think the killer must be someone either you or Phoebe knows—a person who'd also have a reason to go after these other people. That's why we're here. Is there anyone you can think of who'd do this?"

Jack pondered, fast-forwarding through decades of past acquaintances. "Nobody, but fuck, I haven't been a player in the Bay Area for nearly twenty years. If someone's after me, they'd have to be from the era when I worked for you." His look pinned Rick Peters.

Silence fell on the group as November shadows covered the area, the looming darkness sending a chill through Jack's body. He realized Thanksgiving approached in a few weeks, and he ached to spend that holiday with his wife and kids. He stood quickly, patted his jacket to insure the safety of Peters' immunity agreement, and announced, "I've gotta go. Some murdering cocksucker has access to Phoebe's house, and she's home alone. If I think of anyone, I'll call Kevin."

Walking away, Jack heard Bobby and Maggie chorus, "Bye, Jack! Good to see you!" Their words rang hollow. He knew they both considered him a traitor and for a moment, his chest hurt from that betrayal.

Well, fuck 'em. He had his ticket to freedom, along with his wife's and sister's. Right now, that was all that mattered.

That, and keeping the three of them alive.

CHAPTER TWENTY-NINE

El Cerrito, California
November 4, 2005

SPEEDING BACK TO HIS SISTER'S HILLSIDE HOME, Jack didn't bother hiding the rental car on the street below. Instead he pulled into Phoebe's driveway, pressed the garage door opener, and parked the sedan next to her Beemer. No reporters stood in front of Phoebe's house. Listening to the news on his return from Tilden Park, Jack deduced that Rick Peters, or someone, had notified the local media the Defalcos were no longer suspects in Stephen Ong's murder. The rash of news people must have swarmed to the gang murder locations or the state building in San Francisco.

Phoebe stood at her gas range sautéing chicken breasts, her back to him. A half empty bottle of chardonnay stood on the counter next to her empty wine glass, the clear crystal marred by a red lipstick print. Unsure if she'd heard him enter, Jack coughed before he announced, "We've been cleared of the murder charges, Feebs."

She whirled, wooden spoon raised like a cudgel. "What?"

His sister stared at him, seemingly incredulous. From her red eyes and mottled skin, Jack knew she'd been crying.

She swiped under her eyes with the back of her hand. "How?"

He walked to her, took the spoon from her hand, drew her into his best big brother embrace, and explained the immunity agreement, the Grim Reaper person - omitting a description of the coat - and the security tapes. He mentioned the possible connection between Ong's death and the recent gang murders, the bomb under Peters' car, and the attempted assassination of the attorney general.

When he'd finished, he sat Phoebe on a counter stool, poured her more wine, and grabbed a beer. The chicken began to smoke, so he turned off the range. He tolerated Phoebe's weeping for a few seconds before holding up his palm. "Okay, Feebs, enough with the tears. We need to call Paige."

He cuffed his sister under her chin before he rang his wife with the good news. Phoebe stood, blew her nose, washed her hands, and resumed her place at the stove while Jack talked to Paige.

Jack rolled his eyes when his wife's sniffles turned to quiet sobs. "Hey, I know this is a huge relief, but we need to stay focused. There's a killer out there, targeting us. Besides, we still have to deal with the State Bar and Child Protective Services."

Phoebe nodded as she removed the chicken to a platter. He imagined Paige pulling herself together as well, dabbing away tears before she answered. "Yeah, you're right." A last sniff. "About CPS, Bill got the phone number for the anonymous caller. He's tracing it right now and said he'll get back to me." A pause. "About the State Bar? I talked to MJ. I think my legal career is pretty much screwed."

Jack listened to the details of his wife's conversation with MJ O'Malley. "Well, don't take your name off our letterhead just yet. Now that we're free from this murder investigation, I'll represent you. I don't trust anyone else, even if we had the money to spend on a lawyer. They'd either try to deal the case or be so afraid of trial, they'd screw it up."

Paige's sigh floated over the line. "Thanks, Jack. I knew you'd have my back on this." Her voice perked up a bit. "On a happier note, I talked to Claire and Sean, and they'll both be home for Thanksgiving. And the chief thinks CPS will back off since they haven't found a single piece of evidence to verify the abuse allegation. You should grab Feebs and bring her to Montana for the holiday."

Jack let his shoulders relax. "That's a great idea. God, I can't wait to see the kids, especially Sean. I need some testosterone to balance all this weeping and gnashing of teeth."

Both Paige and Phoebe laughed, a sound he hadn't heard in far too long. "Hey, I have to hang up so I can enjoy this dinner my sister's prepared. I'll call you when I have more news."

"Okay, but don't forget to tell her we're expecting her here for Thanksgiving. We need to celebrate every moment we can, right?"

God, is that ever true. "I'll tell her." He pictured his family gathered around the ancient mahogany table he'd inherited from his folks, decorated with fall leaves, tiny pumpkins, harvest colors, and candles, the way his wife always set it for Thanksgiving. "I love you, Paige."

"Love you back more. Be safe."

He sat next to Phoebe at the counter, picking at his chicken and rice. A killer on the loose crowded his thoughts. "Who wants us gone, Feebs?"

Phoebe swallowed a bite then sipped her wine. "If we go on the premise that the same person committed all these crimes, and whoever it is has a terminal illness or is just fucking crazy, that should limit the pool, right?"

"True. Plus, it has to be someone who also had access to your house or broke into it without you knowing about it. But there was no sign of forced entry anywhere, was there?"

"Nope. Not that I really looked." She lowered her fork, frowning at her brother. "Jack, why do you call the person on the hospital security tape the Grim Reaper? You threw that out earlier, but I didn't get it."

Crap! The raincoat's still in the trunk! Jack sat back in his chair, food forgotten. That goddamned black coat was the key to Ong's murder case and probably the others as well.

Briefly, he panicked, thinking he'd destroyed the killer's fingerprint evidence, but calmed when he remembered prints weren't left on cloth. There might be a latent, or at least a partial, on one of the buttons, however. And what about fiber evidence or a hair that might link the perp through DNA? What if the person was a pervert who'd left semen behind, or a drooler who dripped some saliva?

Obviously, it was time to turn the raincoat over to Dorrian. Hell, he could claim he'd just discovered it in Phoebe's closet that afternoon. Besides, it might not even be the same coat.

Yeah, right.

He smiled at Phoebe. "Interesting fact, Feebs. The Grim Reaper guy happens to be wearing a coat exactly like Paige's black raincoat. I…uh…have it in a shopping bag in my car, ready to turn over to Kevin Dorrian as possible evidence."

Phoebe's knife clattered on her plate. "What? Are you saying someone came into my house, took the potassium bottle, took Paige's coat, killed Ong, and then...came back here? And put the coat back in my closet?" Her calm nurse's tone ratcheted to a shriek.

Jack looked into his sibling's blue eyes, so like his own. "Yeah, pretty much. We need to change the locks on all the doors first thing tomorrow."

Phoebe rubbed her upper arms. "Jesus H Christ, that's so fucking...creepy!" She jumped up and flew out the front door. Seconds later, she returned with the house key she kept under her garden gnome, ruining another possible source for fingerprint collection. Then, she checked every window and door to make sure they were locked. Without a word, Jack washed the dishes. He didn't want to freak her out even more by mentioning the killer most likely had copied the outdoor key.

As his sister returned from her inspection, Jack draped the dishtowel on a wooden duck head next to the sink. "Feebs, where's the nine-millimeter I gave you last year?"

Nodding, she opened a large ceramic cookie jar on her counter. It bore the likeness of a gorilla eating a banana with one paw, its other arm looped over its head, forming a handle on the top. She reached inside and extracted the pistol. Holding it by the grip, barrel pointed at the floor, she gave it to him. "It's loaded, bullet in the chamber, and hot."

Jack nodded his approval. "Good. Let me keep it in my room tonight, just in case."

"Fine by me. I'm sleeping on the living room couch close to your room, where maybe I'll feel just a tiny bit safe in my own house." She sat on her stool and sipped more wine. "What kind of a gun did the guy use in the gang killings?"

Jack checked Phoebe's weapon for the chambered round, then made sure the safety was on. As he headed toward the guest room, he spoke over his shoulder, "An old model Uzi. Pretty unusual choice."

His sister's wine glass shattered on the tile floor.

Turning to her, Jack shook his head as he reached for a dustpan. "Crap, Phoebe. Maybe you've had enough vino tonight. Go to bed, and I'll clean up this mess." He noticed her pale complexion and frozen focus. "Unless there's something else that's upsetting you?"

"No!" Her answer shot out too quickly. She rose, shooing him away with her hands. "Listen, I'll clean this up. Get some sleep."

Puzzled, Jack went into the guest room. Later, as he lay in bed missing Paige, he wondered at Phoebe's spooked expression.

Tomorrow. Everything can wait until then.

* * *

Early Saturday morning, sitting with Phoebe on her deck, Jack realized he'd forgotten to share Paige's Thanksgiving invitation. He set his coffee mug on the side table and broached the subject. "You could get a cheap flight into Missoula, and I'll pick you up."

Phoebe nodded, but said nothing.

"Feebs? Something wrong?"

She nodded, took a breath, and started. "About the Uzi–"

A massive *boom* shook the deck, showering brother and sister in a scatter of glass and leaves. Knocked from their chairs, the two huddled, hands over their heads, for several seconds. Jack's first thought was that Phoebe's house had blown up. A leaking gas line. That had happened recently in the Bay Area, thanks to the power company's failure to maintain the lines.

Shaking debris from his back and head, careful not to let anything get in his eyes, Jack reached for his sister and brushed her off with a cloth napkin. She moved, thank God, so the two cautiously stood. They checked each other for tiny glass bits, realized they'd dislodged most of them, and hugged for a second before surveying their surroundings.

The first thing Jack noticed was the absence of Phoebe's windows at the rear of her house, hence the glass. The second was the eucalyptus tree overhanging the deck that once provided shade from the western sun. Cracked in half, the top of the tree hung by a few limbs tangled in the deck rails.

He smelled burning wood mixed with smoke. Turning north, the two saw the source. Janet Mackinaw's home, previously perched on the hillside a few houses from Phoebe's, lay in a tatter of steel and glass, flattened, and flaming.

Jack reached in his pocket for his cell, quickly dialing 9-1-1. Before the call connected, he swore softly, "Holy fuck!"

Phoebe's nursing skills kicked in. "We need to get over there. See if anyone's alive or injured."

She raced inside for her medical stash, while Jack walked gingerly to the front of the house, worried the rest of the deck might collapse under the effects of the explosion. Other than shattered windows, Jack saw no damage to Phoebe's home or deck. He joined his sister as she came out the front door, bag of medical supplies in hand, and the two ran toward Mackinaw's house. They arrived just as the ambulance and fire trucks rolled up, accompanied by multiple police cruisers. Neighbors stood nearby, staring helplessly at the destruction.

Jack looked at Phoebe. "Nobody survived this."

Expressionless, she lowered the bag of bandages to the sidewalk. The homes on either side of Janet's also suffered damage, but mostly to their windows, siding, and landscaping. It looked as if the justice's house had imploded rather than blowing apart. Jack saw only a few pieces of the home scattered across the area. Given the nine a.m. hour, Jack wondered if Mackinaw had left for work before the explosion.

Its lights and sirens blaring, a Fairfax cruiser arrived carrying Dorrian and Peters. Peters bolted toward them, Dorrian following closely behind. Jack's former boss didn't attempt to shake hands, his gaze piercing the Defalco siblings. "You two witness this?"

Jack shook his head. "Just the aftermath. Any word on whether Janet was inside?"

Dorrian pointed at the burned remains of a car in the collapsed garage. "That's her Jag, or what's left of it. Not a good sign. We've been calling her cell. Her secretary says she hasn't come in yet."

Phoebe picked up the useless bag of medical supplies and turned away. Jack let her go, assuming Janet's apparent death saddened her. He, on the other hand, didn't much care. Janet Mackinaw had screwed with his wife and Kayla, not to mention what she'd done to his reputation in the legal community.

Dorrian fell into a coughing fit, interrupting Jack's vengeful musings. Another handkerchief.

More blood.

Jack didn't think any human could look paler than Kevin. He patted the man's back, then rubbed it until the spasms subsided. "Kev, you should quit, you know? Go home, be with your family."

Nodding, Dorrian agreed. He looked at Rick Peters then at Jack. "I hate to give up this investigation, but—" Intense hacking, his lungs sucking for air. "I'm guessing I'm down to a few days. I feel like shit. All I want, once I say goodbye to Meg and my kids, is a ton of drugs to put me out."

Jack swallowed the lump creeping up the back of his throat. "You know, we're here," he looked at Rick Peters. "If your family needs anything. I mean it. You tell Meg to call me, alright?" He couldn't help it. Tears pooled in his eyes as he acknowledged this meant goodbye—the last time he'd ever see Kevin Dorrian. They hugged tightly, giving each other a man-pat on the back.

Jack managed an "I love you, bro," and Kevin a "Back at you, buddy."

Peters, too, grabbed Kevin into a bear hug, tears streaking his cheeks. He yelled at a nearby sheriff's deputy to drive Kevin home.

In the passenger's seat of the squad car, Kevin rolled down the window, pointing his finger at Rick Peters, the elected District Attorney of Fairfax County, and Jack, former prosecutor turned defense attorney. "You find the motherfucker who's doing this. And then you put a bullet between his eyes…for me." Holding their gaze, he rapped his knuckles on the outside of the door. "Promise?"

At their nods, he put on his sunglasses. "Later."

* * *

In Montana, Paige muted the television, leaving the CNN talking heads to report their drivel in silence. Kayla's head rested on her lap, the girl asleep and home from school, sick from flu or stress. Paige quietly answered Chief Bill's call. "Good news?"

"It is," the chief acknowledged. "They traced the anonymous call made to CPS. It came from the California Supreme Court building, specifically from the private office of one Carin Cross."

Excited but unwilling to wake Kayla, Paige remained still. "Bill, that's fantastic! It doesn't prove absolutely that Cross made the call, or that Janet Mackinaw knew about it, but crap, with the circumstantial evidence we have, I can sure make their lives miserable. Maybe even trade that information for..." She stopped, remembering Bill didn't know about her troubles with the California State Bar.

"For a deal if they charge you in the Ong case?" he offered.

She realized he didn't know the Defalcos had been cleared of Ong's murder. Although she hated to withhold information from her friend, she felt too exhausted to explain the State Bar situation. "Yeah, something like that. Can you get me a certified copy of the phone records that show the call came from Cross' office?"

"Got 'em here. You can pick them up anytime."

"Thanks, Bill. I owe you."

"Nope. Just take care of our girl. Jo Ann and I need more of her smart-ass remarks to keep us sharp in our old age."

Disconnecting, Paige's smile flattened when the TV showed a disturbingly familiar hillside and a burning home. The news crawl along the bottom of the screen shouted, "California Supreme Court justice's home explodes in suspected bombing! Acting Chief Justice Janet Mackinaw's whereabouts unknown, feared dead!"

"Jesus, Mary, and Joseph!" Paige grabbed a pillow and cushioned it under Kayla's head before she stood. Kayla barely moved. Paige flipped on the sound as she speed-dialed Jack. The CNN reporter at the scene yammered about the explosion as the camera panned the area, giving Paige a view of Phoebe's home and shattered windows. Relief welled in her when the reporter stated no victims had been found, and surrounding neighborhood homes suffered only minor damage from the blast.

When first Jack's phone went to voicemail and then

Phoebe's, Paige swore. "Fuck a duck! You'd think one of them would call when a nearby home blows up, right? Let alone Janet Mackinaw's house?"

From the couch, Kayla sat up. "Poppy, I really don't feel so good." The girl's latest hairstyle, a rainbow-colored high-and-tight, sat a little lopsided. Her otherwise creamy brown complexion paled. "Uh oh." She pulled up her sweatshirt, forming a trough, and vomited into it.

Paige ran for a bowl as her young charge retched.

Perfect. Murder, bombs, and now barf. Why not?

She cleaned up Kayla, the mess, and started the laundry. When her cell rang, she answered, blurting, "About damned time, Jack! I'm up to my ass in vomit, I see on the news that Mackinaw's house blew up, and neither you nor Feebs bothers to answer my calls." After she made sure a large stainless bowl was within the girl's reach, she laid a wet washcloth on Kayla's forehead.

Jack sounded harried on the other end. "Are you sick?"

Hearing his voice, Paige wanted him home. "Kayla is. I think it's just a flu going around. So tell me what happened." She walked into the kitchen to let the dogs out the back door.

Jack briefly described the explosion, the damage, and Mackinaw's disappearance. Unless the justice showed up, firefighters would continue to comb through the ashes for her remains.

Then, Jack told her about Kevin. Paige slumped onto a kitchen chair within view of Kayla. "I love that guy. It's just so unfair, at his young age, with four kids who need him." Fresh tears scored her face.

"I know. I want to set up a fund for his family. I think most of the cops and DAs are in." Paige heard him shut a door before he cautioned, "Listen, until we figure this out, lock the doors, and make sure the forty-five is loaded and within reach. I can't shake the feeling that one person is responsible for all these deaths, but I can't make the connection."

Paige looked outside at the brown lawn covered with thin patches of snow, at the mountains, fields, and blue sky. Hard to imagine California bad guys hurting her family up here in the wilds of Montana. "I promise to make sure we're safe. And here's some good news." She told him about Carin Cross' number coming up as the originating location for the anonymous call to CPS. "With that, at least we might have a bargaining chip to get her to back off from the State Bar prosecution, right?"

Jack concurred. "It definitely gives us some ammo. Come to think of it, I wonder if anyone's heard from Carin Cross today. If she was in the house with Janet when—"

Silence.

"Jack? You still there?" Paige looked at her phone screen.

Nothing except "Call Ended." Nor did her beloved spouse answer when she called him back. Neither did Phoebe when Paige tried her number.

Odd.

She walked toward the couch just as Kayla grabbed the bowl and heaved.

So much for taking time to reflect, solve murders, or grieve. Instead, reality spewed forth, disguised as masticated pepperoni pizza.

CHAPTER THIRTY

El Cerrito, California
November 5, 2005

HOLDING A SMALL SEMI-AUTOMATIC POINTED DIRECTLY AT JACK'S HEART, Carin Cross entered Phoebe's living room through the blown-out sliding glass deck door.

"Disconnect, Jack. Now!"

Jack clicked the phone's off button, ending his call with Paige. As he raised both hands in surrender, he showed Carin the black screen. "Done."

His heart racing, he realized he'd left Phoebe's nine-millimeter in the guest room. *Fuck!*

Carin stepped further into the room followed by a much larger figure. Her salt and pepper hair tucked under a knit hat, Acting Chief Justice Janet Mackinaw loomed like a specter in the doorway, western sun blinding Jack to her features. Wind from the missing glass windows ruffled her plaid skirt. "Carin, give me the gun so you can pat him down. Defalco, you move an inch, and you're dead."

Janet stood, feet apart, ready to fire. Jack allowed Carin to search him thoroughly for a weapon. She backed away, advising, "He's clear."

Jack lowered his arms. "Janet, listen—"

"Shut up!" She pointed the gun at him, although he detected a slight tremor in her grip. "Listen to me, you little shit, somebody blew up my house today, trying to kill me. Thank God, I spent the night at Carin's last night, or they would have succeeded." She sneered at him. "And I think that someone is you."

Jack's thoughts flew to Paige and the kids, thankful they were out of harms way, and praying this wouldn't be his final moment on Planet Earth. He glanced at Carin who stood near her lover, arms crossed, foot tapping. Rather than looking homicidal, the two women seemed terrified. That, he figured, was a good sign. Maybe they weren't the missing murderers after all.

"Ladies, Rick Peters will alibi me. I was here with Phoebe when the bomb went off. The killer is probably the same person who put the bomb under Peters' car, shot the AG, and maybe took out the gang bangers. In fact, Peters thinks the same person killed Stephen Ong."

Janet's eyebrows narrowed above her hooked nose. "How do I know you're telling the truth? And don't tell me to call Peters because I don't even trust him. He could be the killer, for all I know."

Now fairly confident Janet wouldn't shoot him, Jack rolled his eyes. "C'mon, Mackinaw! You were a better DA than that. Why would Peters whack all these people, especially Ong and the AG? Or you, for that matter? You guys have been friends for twenty years." He ran his fingers through the top of his hair. "Besides, Bobby was right. Peters is a turtle-necked wimp. He'd never have the balls to kill somebody." He sat on Phoebe's butter leather couch. "And neither do you."

Janet's face crumpled as she lowered the gun. "Okay, you're right. I just had to be sure we were safe here. We've been hiding since we heard about the explosion. Figured it was better if the killer thought he'd succeeded."

Jack gestured to the other couch, inviting both women to sit. "You guys want a drink?"

At their nod, he walked toward them, hand outstretched. "Hand it over."

Janet gave him the pistol, and he immediately unloaded it, placing the bullets on Phoebe's fireplace mantle, the gun in his back pocket.

He went to the kitchen to grab a bottle of something— wine, scotch—it didn't much matter. This had turned into such a mess. He just wanted to go back to Montana, killer be damned. He opened some merlot, took three glasses, and started back to the living room. Then, remembering the loaded nine-millimeter in his bedroom, he stopped, setting the bottle and glasses on the counter. "I've got to take a leak. I'll be right back."

He noticed the door to Phoebe's room was closed and briefly wondered if she was home. He'd been so busy fending off Cross and Mackinaw, he'd lost track of his own sister. Come to think of it, he hadn't even noticed whether her Beemer was in the garage.

Entering the guest room, he dumped Cross' empty gun on the bed, and stuck Phoebe's loaded one in the back waist of his jeans. He threw on his hoodie to cover the bulge and returned to Janet and Carin.

After pouring a round of wine, Jack sat forward in his chair, braced for either woman to flip out and maybe try to shoot him again with a gun he'd overlooked. Trust only went so far, and his faith in the integrity of the Lesbian Lovelies wouldn't fill a shot glass.

He set his wine on the coffee table, settled his elbows on his knees, and stared at them. "Here's the working theory according to Peters, Dorrian, and me. One killer, who drives a black Cadillac SUV with stolen plates, has access to this house, the potassium used to kill Ong, and a black raincoat from my sister's closet, which he or she wore at the hospital. This same killer might be terminally ill or suicidal. He, or she, wants to take out a variety of people on his bucket list because he has nothing to lose. We're on that list, along with Phoebe, Paige, Peters, the AG on the *Seavers* case, and three gang bangers. There's probably more. He's smart, cocky, and doesn't give a rat's ass if he's caught because he's going to die anyway."

Both women's eyes grew large, but they were staring over Jack's shoulder. A racking cough behind him caused Jack to turn around. Kevin Dorrian stood in the kitchen, his left hand covering his mouth with a handkerchief.

No, Kevin. Not you. Disbelief, mingled with fear, propelled Jack to stand. "Hey, buddy. I thought we said goodbye earlier today."

Kevin nodded, but couldn't seem to catch his breath. His right hand remained in his jacket pocket. As Jack walked toward him, Kevin stopped coughing long enough to wheeze, "The killer, Jack…his…Uzi."

"Okay, Kev, what about the Uzi?"

Unsure whether or not Kevin was there to help him or hurt him, Jack slid his right hand toward his lower back. As he touched his gun, Jack heard rapid pops blast from his left. He watched in disbelief as a spray of bullets shattered Kevin's head, blowing pieces of flesh and skull across Phoebe's meticulous kitchen. When the detective's body hit the tile floor, his service revolver flew from his jacket pocket.

Jack heard screams behind him, but ignored them. He couldn't tear his eyes away from his sister's bedroom doorway, where Phoebe stood, but barely. The only thing really holding her up was Bobby Erickson's strong left arm around her waist. His right hand held an Uzi.

Bobby grinned. "Hey, D-man. What you told the dykes," he indicated Janet and Carin by pointing the Uzi at them, "all true. Brain cancer. Doc said I had maybe ninety days to live, so I've decided to rid the planet of certain scumbags before I die." He dragged Phoebe into the kitchen, her small size simplifying that effort.

Jack quickly scanned his sister. No blood, but her wide blue eyes showed stark terror. Her hands held onto Bobby's left arm, gripping her like a vice. Her breath came in short huffs.

To Jack, Erickson's eyes held the unfocused gaze of a man living in his own, crazy head, barely connected to his surroundings, yet focused on his next victim. "Bobby, this is between us, right? Let Phoebe and these two go. They haven't done anything to you."

Bobby shoved Phoebe, causing her to fall near Kevin's body. Her hands landed in his blood. She whimpered, wiped them on her jeans, and crawled toward the living room.

Jack remained still, knowing Bobby could shoot them in a matter of seconds.

"That's right, sweetheart," the big man laughed. "Crawl away like the pitiful bitch you are." He looked at Jack. "You know, your sister's a pretty good fuck, but she's got a big mouth." He pointed the Uzi at Phoebe's retreating back. "You just had to tell my wife about us. Couldn't keep your fucking pie hole shut, could you?"

Phoebe froze in her tracks as Jack eased between his sister and the Uzi. She turned toward Bobby and curled the floor. "Screw you, you cheating asshole! I'd have dumped you anyway because you are a terrible fuck."

Bobby's face reddened with rage. "Shut up, cunt!"

Jack grabbed that nanosecond of distraction. "Bobby, why Ong? Or Peters and the AG? Even the gang leaders?" He needed to keep the man talking, sidetracked, and less focused on his belligerent sister.

Erickson switched his gaze, and the Uzi, to Jack. "I always hated that little Jap, D-man, you know that. Same for that prick, Rick Peters, motherfucker that he is for not promoting me. And the AG?" Bobby shook his head. "He fucked up so badly during the *Seavers* hearing, you got off with nothing, not even a reprimand from the State Bar!" Hatred strangled his shout. "You broke rank! You ratted us out, you cocksucker, and I will never forgive you for that!"

Jack heard a crash from the living room. Bobby glanced toward the women just before he fired wild shots into the ceiling. "Sit down, you goddamned clitlickers!" He pointed the Uzi at Janet Mackinaw. "You miserable snatch. I've hated you for twenty years. And to think you got appointed to the Supreme Court."

"No!" Carin Cross jumped in front of her lover just before Bobby fired. Bullets sliced across her abdomen. Janet screamed but managed to jump sideways, avoiding a hit.

Jack pulled out the nine-millimeter and quietly murmured, "Bobby?"

As Erickson switched his glance from Mackinaw to him, Jack took a breath.

Then he drilled two holes in Bobby's forehead.

Double tap.

Right between the eyes.

For Kevin.

CHAPTER THIRTY-ONE

Beartooth, Montana
Thanksgiving, 2005

JACK SWIRLED HIS COGNAC, STARING AT THE FIRE through his snifter. Sitting in his favorite chair comforted him, but not like the quiet presence of his wife and sister. Thanksgiving dishes sat in the china hutch, cleaned, stacked, and ready for next year. The harvest-colored candles no longer flamed on the table, backlighting his family's laughing banter. Claire, Sean, and Kayla argued upstairs over who'd won the latest foosball match. Fred and Molly, their aging and ever-faithful chocolate labs, snored at his feet.

He sighed at Paige and Phoebe. "So in the end, what good came from me testifying for Tom Seavers? Bobby Erickson killed Kevin Dorrian and the Chief Justice of the Supreme Court, along with a bunch of innocent people. I killed Bobby Erickson. You two were accused of murder. And my legal reputation is smeared from San Francisco to Mumbai." He shook his head before swallowing more amber liquid.

The women looked at each other before Phoebe ventured, "You did the right thing, Jack. You stood up for a guy who got screwed by Solomon P. Green, a judge who was supposed to be impartial. You had the balls to take on a corrupt justice system, and you took responsibility for your own ethical lapse."

Paige set her tea on a side table. "Just like here in Montana. If we don't speak out, nothing changes." She patted his thigh. "There's a downside for every witness who tells the truth. But it's the guy who acts anyway—knowing the risks—who changes the world."

"Bullshit, Paige." At his wife's wince, Jack softened his tone. "Tom Seavers is still sitting on death row, Janet Mackinaw's still on the California Supreme Court, and Rick Peters just started another term as the elected DA of Fairfax County. My testimony did nothing but cause this family a lot of pain and suffering."

"Wrong," his wife urged. "You shined a spotlight on the downside to death penalty prosecutions, not just in California, but nationwide. And Tom Seavers is a long way from execution. He still has to finish his federal appeal and a likely review by the U.S. Supreme Court. You don't know what they'll do with your testimony."

Jack smiled at the woman who'd stood by him through so many ordeals over so many years. He'd nearly lost her because of his folly with Maggie Tornow. Never again would he risk his marriage and family—for anyone.

Or anything.

Especially not for some dumbass, bleeding-heart cause, like saving America's condemned on death row. Screw Tom Seavers and his legal team.

Phoebe stood. "I am weary to my bones." She leaned over and kissed Jack on his forehead. "I'm sorry for my part in this mess. If I'd never screwed around with Bobby Erickson, Stephen Ong might still be alive, and we'd never have faced prosecution for his murder. And I should have told you about Bobby's old Uzi the minute you mentioned it. He used to keep it camouflaged in a potted palm next to his bed in case prison gangs blasted into his house." As she walked toward the guest room, Jack heard her mutter, "No fool like an old fool."

Paige finished a last swallow of tea before she tossed out, "Poor Feebs. She's way too hard on herself." She paused. "I'm sorry to hear about Maggie Tornow's son having cancer. Sounds like she's been through hell and back." She shook her head. "And that doesn't make me happy, by the way."

Jack took her hand. "I never thought you'd take satisfaction in that kind of tragedy, sweet pea." His eyes twinkled. "Although I bet if she'd grown warts and added a few hundred pounds, you might feel a tiny bit of glee."

She laughed. "Maybe." Then her brow furrowed. "I still have to figure out how to fight the State Bar."

"That's tomorrow's problem. Tonight, let's just enjoy the fact that we're together with our kids and Phoebe, nobody's in custody, and everyone seems healthy and safe." He grabbed Paige's hand as he set his snifter next to her teacup. "Feel like celebrating?"

She squeezed his hand. "Yep."

* * *

Two months later, in January 2006, Paige sat across from the Honorable Donald Snow, chief judge for the State Bar of California. The prosecutor sat to the judge's left. A high-end mahogany conference table separated the accused—Paige— from her accusers. She'd selected Los Angeles for her trial venue, rather than San Francisco, figuring the geographical distance from Janet Mackinaw and the now-recovered Carin Cross would work to her advantage.

She'd miscalculated.

"Mrs. Defalco," the judge emphasized, "by accusing Justices Ong and Mackinaw of bias and prejudice against you and your law firm, you threw a grave insult at the Supreme Court that they are not willing to forgive. They want blood. Your head on a platter, so to speak."

The prosecutor nodded his head, but refused to make eye contact with her.

Judge Snow had demanded a final mediation session before a different trial judge listened to the prosecutor's evidence against her. That evidence had grown thinner with every discovery request Paige made. At this point, all the guy had was a weak charge of failing to respond fast enough to the Supreme Court's request for an explanation about her pay checks.

The prosecutor had abandoned his claim that she hadn't earned the money and conceded that she had. He also couldn't prosecute her for alleging the Court was biased, because they were, and in filing her motion to withdraw as counsel, she'd only fulfilled her professional duty as demanded by the canon of ethics.

So now, after two months of haggling, trial preparation, stress, and taxpayer dollars, the entire case boiled down to whether or not she'd sent in her explanation on time.

"Your Honor, I understand, but the fact remains that I'm not guilty of any offense punishable by the State Bar. I did what I had to do, what I, and many colleagues, believed was in the best interests of my clients. I can't be prosecuted and disbarred for that."

The prosecutor doodled on his yellow pad, but Paige couldn't decipher his markings. She felt like she was the lead character in a Kafka novel—facing the end of her career without ever being told her crime. She'd opted to represent herself after the attorney she hired failed to prepare for trial, instead urging Paige to accept the loss of her license to practice.

Screw that. I fight for my clients. I can fight for myself.

Jack had offered to represent her, but she'd believed she could persuade the lawyer to drop her case.

Clearly not. He had no intention of letting her off.

Judge Snow pressed her. "I keep telling you, Mrs. Defalco, you only have one choice. Agree to give up your license to practice in California or face trial."

Paige stood. "Trial it is. If I lose my license here, I'll lose it in Montana, and that will be the end of my otherwise unblemished legal career." She scooped her yellow legal pad into her briefcase and headed toward the door to the courtroom.

Her hand on the doorknob, Paige turned back to the men seated at the table. As the prosecutor stood, she lobbed, "By the way, I have a witness here from Montana to impeach Carin Cross when she testifies. The police chief from Beartooth. He's the one who traced the false referral to Child Protective Services regarding my ward. He discovered it came from Ms. Cross' office. The Montana Attorney General has the matter under investigation."

Paige opened the door. "You know, of course, that filing a false report under oath is perjury? We've also referred Ms. Cross to this very agency for violating her ethical duties. I assume you'll follow through with your own investigation. And if our Montana AG connects Justice Mackinaw to the false report, the press will have a field day with that news."

The men looked at each other before Judge Snow cleared his throat. "May we have a moment alone?"

"Of course."

The men left the conference room but returned moments later. The prosecutor spoke for the first time. "Ninety days,

Mrs. Defalco. My final offer. Accept a ninety-day suspension, avoid the cost of a trial, and we're done."

Paige tapped her fingernail on the table. "Suspended on what charge?"

Judge Snow scratched his chin. "Failure to respond to the court in a timely manner. No mention of anything else. Standard fine of $3,000 payable over the next two years." He leaned toward her, his hands on the table. "If you go in there and put the state to the test, I guarantee you that judge will rule against you, even if you put on Jesus Christ as your witness. And after you lose, you can appeal. But the Supreme Court appoints our appellate judges, just as they appoint me, along with the prosecutors." Straightening, he finished with the obvious. "It's a closed box, Mrs. Defalco. Surely you see that?"

Inhaling her outrage, Paige stared at the men before her. "What I see is more corruption piled onto a cesspool of dirty tricks and cronyism." She set her briefcase on a nearby chair. "But you've got me by the proverbial short hairs on this. Even though I haven't done anything wrong, other than taking too long to send in my reply to the Court, you guys get to do whatever you want. No due process, no impartial tribunal, just another good old boy system with you and your buddies running the show. Is that about right?"

A moment of silence before the prosecutor slumped in his chair, imploring, "Take the deal, Paige. Call MJ O'Malley if you think I'm screwing you on this." He held up his palm as she started to object. "Forget it. I know she's been coaching you and, no, she's not losing her job. But she'll tell you that the Court, especially Janet Mackinaw, has *us* by the short curls. If we don't get something from you, our jobs will be history. So take it. Ninety days is a walk in the park compared to getting disbarred in two states."

Calling their bluff, Paige nodded. "Give me a couple of minutes to call her. I'm sure the trial judge won't care." At their nod, she stepped outside with her cell phone.

Moments later Paige had her answer.

"Ninety days, that's it?" MJ shrieked into the phone. "Shit, take it Paige and run like hell back to Montana. Nobody ever, in my entire time in this shitty job, got an offer like that. Mackinaw may want your head, but she'll have to take this or risk getting reamed by the Montana AG."

After thanking MJ for her wisdom, Paige headed to the ladies' room where she commandeered the special needs stall—more area to pace while she phoned Jack. She explained the offer and MJ's advice then waited for him to say, "Fuck 'em. Go to trial."

Instead she heard, "Take the deal, Paige. You can handle the career hit. You save yourself the stress of trial and getting screwed by those assholes afterward." He sighed. "This whole thing is because of me, because I testified against Mackinaw, made her look like a lying bitch, and besmirched the reputation of our old office. I'm so sorry, babe."

She couldn't handle more of Jack's guilt. "No. I'm the one who wrote the words that lit her up like a Roman candle." After listening to a quick Kayla update, Paige swallowed her pride, along with a hefty dose of bile, and disconnected.

She walked back into the conference and faced her nemeses.

She took the deal.

Then she hopped the next flight to Montana, ordered two Bombay martinis on the rocks, two olives each, and drowned her bitterness in gin. She hadn't tasted booze in a decade, but oh, did it hit the spot. When she walked off the plane in Kootenai County, she saw Jack smiling at her on the other side of security. She teetered to him, definitely hammered, and kissed him.

"By the way," she grinned, "I quit."

He cocked his head, likely smelling alcohol. "Uh, quit what?"

Paige linked her arm through his. "The law. Hate it. Done with it." She burped. "Fuck it."

Jack guided her toward the parking lot. "Sweet pea, I think you're shit-faced. Besides, you're more of a trial junkie than I am. What'll you do if you quit?"

Opening her car door, Paige paused. "I'm gonna write a book." Sitting next to Jack, she fastened her seatbelt. "Yep. A book about America's justice system and a couple of lawyers who fought back."

She closed her eyes against rare winter sun glaring off fresh snow and conjured an opening line:

Like my car keys or reading glasses, I've misplaced my soul somewhere between the Catholic Church and the courtroom.

EPILOGUE

IN EARLY FEBRUARY 2006, JACK DEFALCO SHOOK HANDS with Scott Kelly and Harry Bowers. The three defense attorneys stood in line, waiting to walk through the metal detector on San Quentin's death row. They removed their suit jackets, emptied their pockets, and slipped off their shoes. Each man passed inspection.

A guard escorted them across the grounds to the newly built execution chamber. Less than a year had passed since Jack testified at Tom Seavers' hearing to reverse his death conviction for the murder of Cowboy Jeffers.

So much could happen in a year.

Paige had begun her ninety-day suspension the previous month. During her enforced sabbatical, she'd grown excessively fond of Bombay Sapphire martinis, shaken not stirred, but had, as promised, outlined the plot for a novel. She'd even joined a group of women writers who met weekly to critique one another's work.

Also in the last month, the less-than-Honorable Janet Mackinaw and her lover Carin Cross had resigned their jobs on the California Supreme Court. Each had been investigated by the Montana Attorney General, who sought indictments against the pair before a Missoula grand jury. The grand jury agreed the women had conspired to file a false report with the Kootenai County Child Protective Services Office, alleging abuse against Kayla Defalco, as the young girl now called herself.

Not surprisingly, before the AG formalized charges against the justice and capital appeals coordinator, the two retired from the legal profession in exchange for private reprimands by the judicial commission and California State Bar.

When the Beartooth police chief informed Jack of their fall from grace, he'd let out a war whoop.

He wasn't smiling today, however.

Tom Seavers, old, deaf, and sick with cancer, had waived his federal appellate rights after failing to reverse his death sentence, and instead demanded that the State of California execute him without further delay. Those with bloodlust couldn't wait to accommodate his wishes.

Thus, true to his promise in 1988, renewed two months earlier in response to old Tom's written invitation, Jack found himself approaching the lethal injection chamber at San Quentin, about to witness Tom's death. Ditto for Scott Kelly and Harry Bowers. First, though, a guard escorted the three attorneys into a private room where they found Tom strapped to a table.

Seavers smiled when they entered. "You came, Mr. Defalco. Thank you, sir."

Jack approached Seavers, figuring the old man couldn't hear any better now than he had at his trial nearly twenty years earlier. He spoke slowly, so Seavers could read his lips. "Hey, Tom. I wish you weren't going through with this, but I understand your thinking."

Seavers nodded. "So tired, you know? What's the point? I'm gonna die anyway. Lung cancer. Might as well give the victim's family what they want. Sure hope it makes them feel better." He coughed, red-tinged sputum catching on his lower lip. He licked it off. "Sorry. They're here, aren't they? Cowboy's family?"

Jack looked to Bowers and Kelly, who nodded. "Yeah, Tom. They're here. Everyone's ready out there. I guess you are, too, huh?"

"I'm ready." Seavers looked at the chaplain standing nearby. "Let's do this, Father."

The priest anointed Seavers with oil, making the sign of the cross on the condemned man's forehead as he murmured a prayer. Jack followed Kelly and Bowers into the chamber to await the opening of the curtain once the executioner inserted the needle into Tom's arm.

For all his seminary training teaching him never to get attached to another human being, despite decades in criminal law that had inured him to death and human decimation, Jack Defalco fought back the urge to vomit. He didn't want to be here, loathed the idea of watching another person die, even a guilty killer like Tom Seavers. Still, he'd promised the man his presence and intended to keep that promise. Besides, Seavers had rotted on death row for nearly twenty years. Time to put an end to his suffering.

He looked at Kelly and Bowers, oddly stoic in the face of Seavers' pending execution. Neither showed any emotion other than exchanging a few quiet words, nor did they appear nervous.

Maybe they're Buddhists and figure old Tom's just moving to another phase of existence.

Several minutes passed. Cowboy's surviving family members fidgeted. A couple of prosecutors representing the Fairfax County District Attorney's Office stood nearby trying to look solemn as they glanced sideways at Jack. He didn't recognize either of them. Their expressions seemed to say, "That's the disloyal ass wipe who ratted out our office."

A guard entered, beckoning to the warden who stood talking to members of the press. The two held a whispered conversation, during which the warden's face shifted from smug to stunned. He left the room, but Jack could see him speaking into a cell phone.

The warden returned looking like Iran had just fired a nuclear weapon at Israel. "Ladies and gentlemen, if I could have your attention please." Silence. "Judge Jeremy D. Fogel, a U. S. District Court judge, has blocked the execution of Thomas Seavers."

Gasps erupted from some in the witness room, while the press furiously sent emails to their editors over their Blackberries.

Sighing, the warden pressed on. "It is the judge's opinion that if the three-drug lethal injection procedure is administered incorrectly, it could lead to suffering for the condemned that could amount to cruel and unusual punishment." He held up a palm to quiet the crowd's grumbling. "Therefore, an execution can only be carried out by a medical technician legally authorized to administer IV medications."

Many of the witnesses looked perplexed, as if this news signaled to them a big "So what?"

The warden glanced around the room. "The point is, folks, no such person exists. Anyone who meets the judge's qualifications has taken a Hippocratic oath to do no harm. We can't find anyone willing to administer the drugs." He rolled his eyes. "So, it's Mr. Seavers' lucky day. You can go on home."

Jack watched Scott Kelly and Harry Bowers high five each other before hugging. Their jubilance contrasted the mournful expressions on the faces of the other witnesses. He approached the pair. "You knew this was happening, didn't you? That's why you were so calm around Tom."

Kelly laughed. "Not only knew about it, we did it! We were the ones who took the writ to Judge Fogel. We weren't positive he'd sign it, but we figured he would."

Bowers piped in. "Shit, he cut it a little close. I was afraid we were too late."

Shaking his head, Jack spit out, "Did either of you bother to ask Tom Seavers what he wanted to happen?"

The other two lawyers frowned at him. "C'mon, Jack. This isn't about Tom Seavers. It never was. Everything we've done—your testimony, the hearing—it's always been for the cause. To end the death penalty in this state."

Jack felt his face redden as anger crept up his spine. "Really? That's news to me, and I bet it's news to that deaf old man in there suffering from cancer." He pointed to the preparation room where he presumed Tom Seavers waited. "You just fuck with people's lives like that, for a goddamn cause?" He slapped the wall next to Scott Kelly with his palm, causing the other man to flinch. "How does that make you any different from the bad guys, Scott?"

Before either defense attorney could speak, Jack left the viewing room. As he passed the preparation area, he saw a guard help Seavers off the gurney to which he'd been strapped. Seavers wiped tears from his eyes, then looked at Jack. "They fucked me again, didn't they, Mr. Defalco? Took away my chance for peace. That family's chance for justice."

The guard held up his hand, warning Jack not to approach the condemned prisoner. Still Jack said slowly, "I'm sorry, Tom. I had no idea they'd gone to court to stop this."

Seavers merely nodded before he placed his hands behind his back, letting the guard cuff him before leading him back toward his cell.

Two weeks later, that same guard found Tom Seavers dead in his bunk, serenity evident from the relaxed, but blue-hued smile on his face. The autopsy showed he'd died from a drug overdose. No one ever discovered how, on death row, he'd secured the multitude of sedatives he used to carry out the suicide.

Then again, no one really cared.

One less man on death row.

One less prisoner costing the taxpayers precious dollars.

THE END

256 P. A. Moore

ABOUT THE AUTHOR

P.A. Moore (her maiden name), wife, mom, author, and lawyer, lives in a small town in Montana, having fled there with her family from Big City, California in the late 90s. Her goal to achieve a peaceful, quiet life never materialized (does it for any parent?), but she's learned to embrace the chaos that comes with loving her incredible family, her work, and her ongoing effort to provide a voice for those who cannot speak for themselves.

Look for her next novel in Fall 2014.

Contact Ms. Moore at **p.a.moore@gmail.com,** follow her on Facebook at **P.A.Moore**, check out her website and blog at **www.pamoore-author.com** where, with her law partner, Ms. Moore offers every day law for every day people.

BONUS PREVIEW

COURTHOUSE COWBOYS

A Modern Tale of Murder in Montana

PROLOGUE

The Growth of Cynicism

Norton, California – November 1996

LIKE MY CAR KEYS OR READING GLASSES, I've misplaced my soul somewhere between the Catholic Church and the courtroom.

Today a navy blue suit, matching pumps with three-inch heels, and a string of pearls decorate my tall, 43-year-old figure. Precisely shaped red fingernails tuck back a strand of russet hair into a coiffed bun centered on the back of my neck. My green eyes glare down a slightly crooked nose at the defense attorney rising from his chair.

"I'm glad your husband lost the election yesterday," the fat toad wheezes. "He doesn't have the integrity to be a judge."

A flush of fury creeps up my spine, its venom spewing out the crown of my head. I want to grab his tie, twisting it until his brown eyes pop from his smug face. I, Paige Sheehan Defalco, am unraveling. I take a calming breath. It doesn't help so I throw my yellow legal pad onto the prosecution table as I square off with this huge bloated lawyer who carries his arrogance on his sneer.

"Fuck you, Palmer!" I hurl the epithet toward him.

The fat attorney rears back, as if scorched by an oven blast. "What did you just say to me, Mrs. Defalco?"

I sense the court reporter scurry toward the door leading to the judge's chamber, seeking safety from my wrath. The judge has yet to take the bench. A few people mill around in the audience but now they, too, rush for an exit.

Rage radiates from my perfumed pores. My next words erupt over my glossed lips. "I told you to go screw yourself, Palmer. You're a piece of shit, and so is that ugly ass client of yours." I nod toward the blond-haired, tattooed little man sitting at the defense table, handcuffed and smiling at the unfolding drama.

Palmer, for once speechless, huffs an indignant breath. I open my suit jacket, spreading it back as I place my hands on my hips. I shift toward Palmer, crowding the pointy tips of my polished shoes against the toes of his scuffed brown wingtips. The corpulent slug towers over me.

I glare up at his pockmarked cheeks, but lean away from his distended belly. "Your law practice is a joke, and as far as *integrity,* Palmer? You don't have the balls to carry my husband's jock, let alone fill it. Jack has more integrity in his ear lobe than you have in your entire bulbous body."

The lawyer's skin glows magenta, but before he can respond, the bailiff enters, announcing the judge's arrival. I back off as the bailiff and I smirk at each other, united in our disdain for defense attorneys and the criminals they represent.

"Good morning, Counsel," Her Honor intones. "We are on the record in the case of People versus Harvey Junior--"

Palmer, the jerk, interrupts. "Judge, before we begin, I want to put on the record that Mrs. Defalco just told me to go fuck myself, right here in your courtroom." His sniveling whine grates through the silence.

Oh, for crapsake.

This son of a bitch just *tattled* on me. I roll my eyes as I sit down, not deigning to respond to such a childish display. I'm ready to call my first witness in the tattooed guy's preliminary hearing.

The judge pauses before replying, "Counsel, I am aware that Mrs. Defalco's husband lost a hard fought campaign yesterday in his bid for a judgeship. Now let's move on." Nodding at me, a hint of sympathy in her soft brown eyes, she continues, "Mrs. Defalco, please call your first witness."

Whether from last night's multiple martinis, a lack of sleep, the shock of Jack's election loss, or a combination of all three, I feel too weary to stand. Instead, I mumble, "The People call the victim, your Honor, the defendant's wife, who is in custody herself for refusing to respond to my subpoena." I tap my manicured nails on the table as the bailiff brings out the prisoner/witness.

This battered wife glares at me, her hatred for me second only to her terror of her ogre of a husband. He's tortured her for years. The day she tried to leave him, he heated up a butter knife on the gas stove. He held her down, laid the red-hot blade across the tattoo on her right breast that read 'Junior' - surrounded by a heart and arrow - and burned her. Then he ripped that tattoo off, sizzling skin and all.

I return her glare, ignoring the tiny speck of conscience that demands I let her go, that I forget about forcing her to testify against her will. But I hate her husband too much to let him walk free. If I don't plunge ahead, the judge will have to release him, and I cannot let that happen. Demonic crimes require drastic measures. I will do whatever it takes to win a conviction against this Hell's Angels-loving, methamphet-amine-dealing, sadistic scumbag.

The victim has been safe in custody, more or less, but after today, she's on her own. Once she testifies, no one will protect her from her maniac husband. She'll have to hide again, begin again, find a new job in another community under yet a different name, all on her own.

Even if the ogre murders this woman after the hearing, I can still send him to prison forever, so long as I extract the truth from her today, under oath. The smarmy bastard already has a contract out on her life, knowing that if I succeed, he's toast. As a deputy district attorney for Norton County, I've sworn to protect and defend those who fall victim to the bad guys. Yet today I'm just another overzealous prosecutor causing more pain and suffering for the maimed citizens I am supposed to help.

My life, like life for most prosecutors, breaks down to black and white. I am a good guy, along with everyone else in law enforcement. The criminals are the bad guys, along with their lawyers and the idiots at the ACLU. Nothing complicates this equation.

Whereas I once spent my college weekends at U.C. Berkeley releasing the downtrodden from jail on their own recognizance, I now savor the wreckage wrung from criminals I thrash in court. Bad guys sit handcuffed before me, faceless and nameless, their humanity reduced to their prison-issued, personal file numbers.

In mid-life, I struggle to recall my days as a liberal, protesting the Vietnam War, fighting against the injustice of race, gender, and class discrimination. Instead, I detest every one of these rule-breaking, society-destroying creeps. I know nothing of their personal life histories, nor do I care. My scorn extends to their friends and fellow gang members, sometimes even to their parents and siblings.

White, Black, Asian, Hispanic - they all look the same to me. I mock their ghetto homes, their jungle-cruiser cars, their gaudy jewelry, their oversized jeans hanging off their saggy butts, and their lice-encrusted, greasy hair. I laugh at the cops' snide observations of their arrests, and smirk at these prisoners in their orange jail jumpsuits. I snicker at their feeble attempts to explain to the judge why they committed their vile crimes.

They smell, these criminals - of incarceration, of poverty, of hopelessness. Often I hold my breath as I walk past the jail vent that vomits fetid air to the outside parking lot. I won't release it until I reach my brand new Suburban, where I can inhale the aroma of clean leather and air conditioning.

The Great Unwashed, one of my colleagues calls them, these toothless, acne-faced kids who awaken every morning with nothing to do, nowhere to go, little to eat, and a world of crime opportunities spread before them.

With their families fractured, often before they're born, the children of the streets cling to each other, their loyalty to one another the constant source of gang-related murders. Drugs and sex numb their fear of a future predicted to last only into their teenage years, when they're cut down by another's bullet.

Yet here I sit in court, inured to their tragic lives. The sooner they kill each other off, the fewer psychopaths I have to prosecute. I closely follow the obituaries in our local paper, waiting to celebrate the deaths of those against whom I've filed criminal charges. The younger they die, the less time they have to injure or kill the innocents.

"Mrs. Defalco?" I look up at the judge. She tilts her head. "Are you finished? Do the People rest their case?"

I blink, amazed that I've completed my questions, that I've rebutted Palmer's cross-examination, all in a near state of unconsciousness. Like driving long distances, I blank out in court these days, wondering occasionally how I arrive at my destination, to the conviction of one more evildoer.

My prisoner/witness sits on the stand, now finished testifying, still stabbing me with her eyes. "Yes, Your Honor. And the People ask the Court to release this victim from custody."

Turning to the defense attorney, the judge inquires, "Counsel? Any evidence at this time?" The porcine piece of crap shakes his head. "Not at this time, Your Honor."

I've won. The heinous little tattooed torturer now faces trial and the rest of his life in prison. And his rat bastard defense lawyer will have to explain his client's conduct to a jury.

Perfect.

After the judge vacates the bench, I level one last malevolent look at Palmer as I leave the courtroom, heels clicking a brisk pace over the ancient linoleum floors. I'm weary of criminals and their obsequious lawyers. I've heard enough condolences about the election.

Inside my burgundy Suburban, I kick off my pumps as I debate whether to ditch out and spend the rest of the day at home, or drive across county to the office where I head up the Domestic Violence Unit. My fatigue reflects back at me from the rear view mirror. I convince myself the dark bags under my eyes result from smudged mascara.

I am a master of self-deceit.

* * *

As mindlessly as I perform in court, I drive toward my office rather than home. Not *my* office, I realize, after I've parked my land yacht in the employee parking space. Instead, I've driven to the Big House, the main office of the District Attorney wherein resides the man with all the power.

This man, however, is not the elected official. Rather, he holds the position of Chief Assistant. We mere deputies, his minions, refer to him as Lucifer. He seems to have dirt on everyone in the county and wields that knowledge with the flair of a Chicago politician. We suspect he even has dirt on God.

I greet the receptionists, skirt yet another brewing fistfight between two senior deputies, ignore my colleagues in the lunchroom, and beeline toward Lucifer's corner office. I knock, and he motions me to a chair as he gives the bum's rush to the person on the other end of the phone.

"Hello, Paige," he smiles, leaning back in his leather chair. "Tough break for Jack in that election. *The Year of the Woman*, my ass." He shakes his head in disgust.

I nod. If I open my mouth I might scream. If Lucifer shows kindness to me, I'll cry.

"So." He hesitates, likely sensing an emotional torrent lurks just under my pearl necklace. "How are things in the Domestic Violence Unit? I hear you could use some more help down there. We're a little short, but after the first of the year--"

I stand up, close his office door, and perch on the edge of my chair. "Joe, I'm done. I'm losing it. I told Palmer to go fuck himself in court this morning." I wait for his reaction.

He laughs then sobers. "Was the judge present?"

"No, of course not. I'm not *that* far gone." I run a finger along my pearls. "But it shows me that I can't do this job one more hour. Not with the kids at home, not if I want my marriage to last." Tears moisten my eyes so I look out Joe's window.

Joe isn't the kingmaker because he's stupid or insensitive. He surmises in a second that I'm lethally serious about dumping a promising legal career. "Paige, we've been close friends for nearly 20 years. We're like family. I've known Jack even longer, and we've all been through some tough times together." He sighs as a single tear escapes down my cheek.

Joe hates it when women cry. In the massive San Francisco earthquake in 1989, he and I stood together outside my law school as the city shook and buildings collapsed. Together we ran to his car and fled toward home. Nine hours later we arrived, but never once did I cry while he drove. I swallowed my terror, just as he did, because to do otherwise might have weakened his own resolve to get us safely to our families.

Indeed, I'm one of the few people in the office who knows the real man behind the myth. While he is Machiavellian in his ability to outwit most of us, he loves his wife and children with the same passion I feel for mine and possesses more compassion than he'll ever express.

"In all these years, I've never asked for a favor. I've worked my ass off for you and mostly succeeded at my assignments." I suck in a shaky breath. "If you won't transfer me out of the unit *today,* to a desk job filing cases or some other mindless endeavor, I'm walking out that door and never coming back."

My demand is fortified by the fact that Joe's wife recently did just that - quit her career, packed up the kids, and moved the family to their condo in Colorado. She did this to escape the stress from contemporaneously parenting, working, homemaking, and volunteering. Joe now commutes to and from Colorado while he waits out the months to his retirement. Not a great set up, but three months earlier, when I'd taken my own kids to visit them, I realized how the peace in Colorado had rescued them from chaos.

Joe gazes out the window, his fingers steepled in front of him, calculating my mental state. Minutes pass before he returns my gaze. His frown eases into head-shaking resignation. "Go home. I'll move you tomorrow. I'll let you know where to report later today."

I sniff, grabbing a tissue from his side table. "Thanks." I head for the closed door but turn back. "I can't promise you I won't quit, even with the transfer. I just can't seem to keep it all together, you know? All the carnage by day and the perfect mom expectations at night rip me apart. You and Jack can separate work from home. But no matter what I do, these people haunt me. The battered victims, the bad guys, even my own kids."

Silence.

I open the door, glance one last time at the exalted offices on the ninth floor of the Big House, and sneak down the back stairway to freedom.

Within the safety of the Suburban, I exhale. I shed the old grease and body odor smell from the jail, kick off my shoes, remove my suit jacket, and rest my head on the steering wheel. A knock on the window makes me jump. Heart pounding, I see the concerned face of a public defender I both respect and dislike merely because he's on the side of the criminals. I push the button to lower the window, no smile welcoming his intrusion into my misery.

"Hey, Paige." The older man frowns as he gently touches my arm. "Are you okay? Can I buy you some coffee, maybe? I heard what happened with Palmer this morning." He shakes his head, chuckles. "Don't let it get to you. We all lose it from time to time."

When he smiles, his kindness further unravels me.

I swipe at an unwanted tear streaking past my nose. "Thanks. I'll be okay. I'm just tired from the election."

The lie rolls out, but the public defender is too polite to call me on it. He pats my arm and walks away. I drive toward home to avoid anyone else's compassion.

Passing the mall I wonder what the hell I am doing. When Jack learns that I quit the unit to assume a lowly desk job, and that I'm contemplating following Joe's wife to the sanity of some hinterland, he'll go ballistic. As it sits, our 17-year marriage nears divorce at least once a month. If I leave my career, move the kids from California to parts unknown, will Jack come with us, or throw in the towel? Worse, given the ever-shifting state of our relationship, does it matter?

I exit the freeway to the suburbs and wend my way through the back roads to home. This beautiful neighborhood boasts great schools, elite thinkers, demure politics, sophisticated restaurants, and hordes of money. For most people, life here spells success. It suffocates me, especially today, when I have to face Jack and my children with the news that Mom careens close to a nervous breakdown. Fight or flight? The fight in me wanes while the urge to flee expands with every panicked breath. As I pull into the driveway, my kids jump from the branches of our plum tree, delighted that I've arrived early, ahead of my usual late homecomings.

"Mom!" My son, Sean, only seven, streaks to me. He grabs me around my waist so tightly I teeter on my heels. My daughter, Claire, twelve, hugs me higher. I cling to them, the only beings on earth who matter to me at this moment. Eyes closed, I know I must protect them from the bad guys. I must keep our family together no matter the cost. Sane kids might come from crazy parents, and I suppose mine exemplify that theory, but they deserve better.

They deserve a mom who focuses on them first, whose smile doesn't mask fear and loathing, whose laughter erupts from joy instead of cynicism. I owe them a change of heart and a new playground where they can ride their bikes without fear of kidnapping.

As they run off to chase Bob, their new puppy, I grab my briefcase, say goodbye to the babysitter, and stand paralyzed in my recently remodeled kitchen.

One place beckons to me for reasons contrary to logic.

Montana.

* * *

"*Montana!* You want to move our family to Montana? Are you *fucking nuts*?" Jack Defalco explodes these words as spittle flies from his lips.

In the privacy of our bedroom, away from our children who sit glued to the television, I try to stay calm in the face of his wrath.

I'm desperate. "Yesterday our son said, 'Mom, you always tell us what a great childhood you had growing up in Colorado because you could ride your bike all over with no fear of kidnappers. We can't even go in the front yard of our house without a grownup.'" I pause before delivering the punch line. "Then he said, 'Mom, what kind of childhood memories will I have?'"

Jack runs his fingers through the top of his thick brown hair. "Oh for chrissake! We live in a great neighborhood, we make decent money, I'll be able to retire in six years on my full salary from the D.A.'s office, and you're on a high-speed career track at yours. The kids go to excellent schools, they play sports, they have friends here, and so do we. I don't see the problem."

Sitting on the edge of the bed, I clutch the duvet cover. "The problem is this: One of us sits at the bus stop every morning with a loaded gun between the seats to thwart any pedophile who might snatch the kids. Both kids are imprisoned in this palace of ours because we know where every sex offender lives within a 50 mile radius, and there are tons of them."

I stand, gaining a superior position in the argument through my much taller height.

"And look at our jobs," I march on. "Last week I nearly got shot running through the ghetto chasing a victim who I needed to testify in court. I'm trying to help this crazy crack addict by putting her boyfriend behind bars, and she's *running away* from me. We spend all day hanging around killers and child molesters, reading about macerated eyeballs and blood spatter patterns, and then come home at night and try to act normal - whatever the hell that is."

Jack glares at me, his hands fisted on his hips.

But I'm on a roll. "You and I barely speak anymore because we're so busy at work or running from one kid event to the next. Our friends are grossed out by our dinner conversation because neither one of us can stop talking about our cases. Like you the other night talking about that burned corpse in the dumpster or me discussing how much digital penetration into a vagina is required before it's a rape."

Jack stalks closer to my inferno, his voice lowers, and he half-kiddingly threatens, "If I had a tranquilizer gun right now, I'd dart you full of valium. You're crazier than a bedbug if you think this family will move to Bumfuck, Montana."

I sit back on the bed. "I know I'm screwed up, but it's nothing a shrink can fix. Don't you see that I've lost my conscience, my soul? I'm numb. I don't give a shit about humanity anymore - me, the Berkeley protester, the defender of the downtrodden, the voice for those who couldn't speak up for themselves. What happened to that woman who cared about people - not just crime victims, but *all* people?"

My hands shake as I reach for a glass of water near the headboard. Jack sits beside me. His left hand reaches for mine, both of our ring fingers sporting fat gold bands that declare our long ago commitment to stick together through the hard times.

"Here's the worst part," I let him weave his fingers through mine but can't meet his gaze. "In religious education, I was the teacher in charge of creating a Christmas project for the first grade. I bought little trees for them to decorate, complete with little ornaments and presents."

"Okay," my spouse responds, "now I'm really confused."

I stare into his intense silver-blue eyes. "The other teacher, when she saw my *trees,* raced to the store to buy little baby dolls we could wrap in swaddling cloth and put into cradles made from popsicle sticks. She looked at me like I was a heathen and said, 'Don't you think we should keep Christ in Christmas?'"

I rest my head on his shoulder as he puts his right arm around me, both of us struggling with my weird metaphor.

Moments later I sit up. "You know that scene in Puccini's opera when the bad guy cries out, 'Tosca, Tosca, you make me forget God?'"

Jack, never an opera fan, shakes his head. "What's your point?"

"My point is that too many years living on the dark side, in the bowels of criminal law, have made me forget God. I hardly go to Mass because it interferes with my one morning off a week when I can drink coffee and read the *New York Times.* Seventeen years since I joined the Catholic Church, and I can't recall why I bothered. That's why I'm so lost and *that,*" I stand and pace to the dresser before I turn back to him, "is why we're moving to Montana."

Resolved, I drop my shoulders, easing the tension embedded in those muscles.

"Because when I remember God, I'll find my soul again."

PART ONE

CHAPTER ONE

Soul Sister

Eight months later
Beartooth, Montana – August 1997

THE AMAZON STUD WOMAN, aka my new neighbor, Anne, poured us each another shot of vodka and clinked her glass to mine. "To soul mates finding each other in the wilderness."

Anne's nearly six-foot frame - lithe, athletic, and tan - swam through my vision. I raised my own toast. "To you, Anne, for accepting me for who I am."

Clink.

A week earlier Anne had introduced herself, arriving at my door clad in shorts and an exercise bra. "Gotta soak in the rays while the sun shines in Beartooth, which isn't for very long." Her blonde hair, bronzed skin, makeup-free blue eyes, and wide grin sang out serenity and inner peace. "I'm a Buddhist Unitarian, a physical therapist at the grade school, a recent and ecstatic ex-wife, a mom, and a sinner if you believe the old guy who plows the sidewalks."

The sinner part hooked me, so we'd met several times since. Anne excelled at every outdoor activity. An extreme skier, biker, hiker, kayaker, whitewater rafter, rock climber, ice caver, and horsewoman, Anne enjoyed every activity I abhorred, to wit, exercise.

She'd only moved to the neighborhood a few weeks before us and believed, as I did, that no other residents consumed alcohol or cursed. Tonight she'd slipped between our homes, glanced around for spies, crept in the side door, through my garage, and set the backpack-concealed booze on the table. The next hour of sipping freed us to share our virtues and vices, as only women can do, whether drunk or merely standing in line at the grocery store.

Anne leaned toward me. "So is your husband dumping you, or do you think he'll move up here some day?"

In early July, after driving with us 2,000 miles to Montana, Jack helped me unpack some household goods, kissed us all adios, and returned to California. To the safety of 'The Known.' He promised to commute every few weeks but made no commitment to move to Beartooth. He'd arranged to housesit at his cousin's mansion in a gated community near our old suburb. His new office location, across from the home of the Fairfax As, provided him with all the baseball and polish dogs he desired. His latest job assignment threatened death from boredom but no trials or stress, so life for Jack Defalco brooked no hardship.

I added more tonic to my cocktail. "Debatable. He misses the kids. He thinks I'm crazy, so who knows if he'll cave in to my latest effort at sanity. He hates Montana, loathes the idea of starting over in a community where he knows no one, and shudders at opening a private law firm where he's off the government dole." I closed my eyes, perhaps to shut out Jack's angry image or simply to stop the spinning of the room.

"Don't you wonder why you're here? I mean, of all the places on the planet, why Beartooth, next door to me? I don't believe in coincidence. We've met for a reason." Anne grabbed the tonic bottle. "The change for you must be incredible. From big city prosecutor to housewife folding laundry. From constant crime to safety and calm. From black-tie dinners to blue jeans and boots." Anne swilled her drink. "And not knowing a soul in Montana when you moved? I couldn't do it."

From a nice fat salary to unemployment.

I opened my eyes as I paused to consider my life's monumental course correction. "Tough to explain, but it's as if I *had* to leave. Something bigger pushed me. I had to let go and let whatever it was move me to where I needed to be." I shook my head. "I must be hammered. That makes no sense."

Anne's greater size metabolized liquor far more efficiently. "Of course it makes sense. Look, we both have eight-year-old sons who instantly became best friends. We both have black labs the same age that play together constantly. We're Democrats, feminists, and spiritual. Just go with it." She finished her last sip of vodka. "And open some wine while you're at it. We need to remember this moment, even if it's by the size of the hangover."

I uncorked a cabernet, grabbed wine glasses since I still believed drinking wine from a cocktail glass showed the height of poor manners, and poured us each a finger of red. "You know I'm the soccer mom for our boys' team, right?"

Anne nodded.

"The coach? Your ex? He's a little tightly wrapped."

At this Anne coughed, spewing her wine. "A little? He's a narcissistic ass. I don't know how we lasted as long as we did. On the other hand, he's a good dad and a great lawyer. If you ever decide to practice up here, you should talk to him."

"I'm not practicing law again if I can help it. I want to live life as a normal person for a change. Except," I swirled my wine, watching it dribble down the inside of my glass. "I'm an addict, Anne. A trial junkie. Once that adrenaline flows, I'm out of control, you know? I'm not sure I can give up that rush."

Anne hesitated. "I don't know if you're meant to retire." She placed her wine glass on the table and used her napkin to dab up the scattered droplets. "There's something about you that exudes ... I don't know. Competence? Like you're the one people turn to with problems because you're smart enough and tough enough to fix them."

Ouch.

That hit too close to home. Mom, the fixer of all problems. Ms. Defalco, the one to win the tough cases. Paige, the wife who could do it all, all at the same time. Anne just described the woman from whom I'd fled. How had that same woman trailed me all the way to Montana?

Refilling our wine glasses, I tossed back two gulps with new resolve. I would *not* let that competent, crazy, possessed female take over my body again. I *would* spend my days watching soaps, folding laundry, and making homemade pizza crust. I would not practice law, I would never defend a criminal, and I would suppress my craving for the courtroom.

As my eyes glazed over, Annie slipped out the way she'd come in. Since the boys were at a sleepover and my daughter long ago asleep, I maneuvered to bed where I held one thought.

This hangover's gonna be a bitch.

* * *

With Halloween just weeks away, Anne and I stared at the cornfield skirting the pumpkin patch. Our boys screamed at each other as they wove their way through the tall stalks. Within moments only silence marked their paths.

I ran toward the yawning quiet, yelling my son's name, the name he'd inherited from his grandfather. "Sean! Where are you? Sean!" I turned around seeking Anne. "Jesus! I should have known better than to let him go in there." My breath caught as Anne ambled toward me.

She wrapped a flannel-shirted arm around my shoulders and smiled at me. "Paige, what do you think is going to happen to them in a little corn field in the middle of Kootenai County? Seriously, do you think your son will get kidnapped in there?" She shook her head and squeezed me closer. "You need to get a grip, girlfriend. You're not in California anymore."

No shit.

I eased out a little carbon dioxide, sucked in a bit of oxygen, and let my hyper-vigilance lapse to my normal paranoia. "Okay, I'm an idiot. Except I can't shake it, this incessant terror that evil will befall my kids if I don't pay constant attention."

Anne wandered around the pumpkins to select one for carving. "You mean unless you constantly worry. When are you going to get the message that you're not in charge of the world? All you can do is live each day, in the moment, and let whoever's choreographing the universe work out the rest?"

I huffed as I attempted to lift one of the heavier orange orbs. "Don't get all Zen on me, Annie. That touchy feely crap works for you, but I'm Catholic for God's sake. That means I excel at worry and guilt. Besides, I'm in the middle of a spiritual crisis, so turning to a higher power doesn't help."

I didn't mention that the priest at our new parish also seemed to be in crisis, evidenced by his hellfire and damnation ramblings. The kids and I sat at Mass each weekend transfixed by the old guy's dire warnings that we were all doomed, a foreign philosophy in the liberal parish we'd left behind in California.

As Anne and I paid for our pumpkins, the boys careened from the cornstalks, laughing, dusty, and carefree. I froze as I studied Sean, watching the smile that creased his small, pale face. Hay stuck out of his blond hair, his blue eyes glinted back at the afternoon sun, and his thin arms and legs pin-wheeled around his torso as he played the wild child.

My son.

Carefree.

Able to leap tall squashes in a single bound.

For the first time in his young life, free to ride his bike anywhere around town.

Free to be a kid.

I glanced east at snow-dusted mountains, north toward Beartooth, west toward the sun lowering over the hills, and knew for the first time that I'd made the right decision. We'd arrived where our family needed to be. More importantly, I believed that Montana held my memories of God. If I could let go of the fear that pervaded every cell in my body, I could tap into that mine of spiritual salvation.

First, however, I needed to carve a pumpkin, finish sewing costumes, put dinner on the table, fold the laundry, help with homework, and prepare for another visit from my beloved but recalcitrant spouse.

* * *

Anne volunteered her ex, Tim, to accompany Jack as they took the boys around on Halloween, while she and I stayed behind to feed the sugar frenzy of other kids coming to our doors.

Hours later, we grownups toasted the holiday. "Here's to making it through another Halloween without hidden razor blades or poison in the candy," I offered. Jack clinked his glass to mine. Anne and Tim stared at us, their faces expressing the same dismay on those of our friends in California.

"What I mean is—"

Anne held up her palm. "Don't even try to explain." She turned to Tim. "Paige and Jack are recovering crime junkies. Paige actually allows her kids out of the house now, unescorted, so they can walk to school with their friends. It's a major step."

Tim's brows rose, a bemused look in his eyes. "Are you two going into private practice up here?"

Jack's "Yes" slid out a nanosecond before my "No!"

Damn it.

I wanted to *appear* normal. "That is, Jack might open a practice, but I've retired from law to be a full-time mom." I looked to Jack for affirmation. Instead, he scowled. I stumbled on. "Of course it depends on money and whether or not Jack ever really moves to Montana." This last part I bit out somewhat harshly.

Tim, ever smooth, smiled. "More wine?"

I noticed Anne had retired to the couch. I excused myself to sit beside her. "What's up? Too much ex-husband for one night?"

Anne leaned her head back. "I don't know. I think I'm just old. Did I mention that when I biked over Malta Pass last week, I had to stop half way?"

I shook my head. "Geez, Annie, I couldn't make it a tenth of the way up that road, so you only biking half a million miles instead of the full ride doesn't sound like you're aging. Besides, you're only 47."

She chuckled. "Yeah, we're still sweet young things, you and I. In any event, I have my annual checkup tomorrow. Can you handle the boys at your house?"

"No problem. You're probably anemic from that brown rice and vegetable diet you're on. Cheeseburgers and garlic fries from The Bulldog. That'll fix anything that ails you."

* * *

Well, almost anything.

But not cancer.

The next afternoon, Anne relayed to me her diagnosis, advanced breast cancer. At the news I felt a hole burrow into my heart. My mother died of advanced breast cancer when she was 53 and I only 14, before chemotherapy existed.

Anne's wan face turned to me, tears streaming down her pallid cheeks. "So, Paige," she whispered. We held hands as we sat on her couch. "I guess now we know why you were sent to Montana, to drive me to chemo and watch over my boy while I fight this thing."

I placed my arm around her shoulders. Did I imagine that they'd grown thinner? "We're going to beat this, Annie. Between your friends, your doctors, my faith, our prayers, and a little luck, you're going to be fine." I swiped at my own runny nose with a tissue. "Just fine."

My confidence belied the terror that flooded every cell in my body, forcing me back on high alert.

CHAPTER TWO

A Christmas Murder

Kootenai County, Montana
December 25, 1997

FOR RICH TRUMAN'S FAMILY, Christmas 1997 shattered any belief they'd held in divine justice.

After celebrating the holiday with their children and grandchildren, Rich and Nina Truman hosted a party for their employees at the Swan River Inn in Shelton, Montana. Rich Truman was a popular Kootenai County businessman who had done well for himself and his family. Nina and he owned a lovely home set on wooded acreage near the small town of Whitehall, just a few miles south of the Shelton motel.

The couple began their life together as high school sweethearts, and recently marked 40 years of marriage. Best friends, compatible business partners, dedicated parents, and close confidants, they appeared inseparable to those who knew them well.

That night they took separate cars to the party so that Nina, exhausted from preparing for the day's festivities, could leave early. Nearly 60, the couple no longer had as much energy as they did when they were younger. After sharing a goodnight kiss with the love of her life, Nina left the party around 10:00 p.m. and retired for a well-deserved rest as soon as she arrived home. She expected Rich to return soon.

Rich left the party an hour later after wishing his employees a Merry Christmas one last time. The temperature hovered at 14 degrees, leaving the night air dry and crisp. It had snowed earlier, covering the ground with a picturesque layer of fresh powder. Weary but content, Rich thanked God his Christmas had been so full of treasure for his family and friends. Indeed, his family and friends *were* his treasure in life.

As he turned down the private road leading to his house, and to the home he took care of for his neighbor, Dr. Sam Jaffee, Rich noticed a car's headlights in the Jaffee driveway.

The birch and tamarack trees, devoid of summer foliage, revealed a partial glimpse of the house from the road. Driving closer, he also spotted Jaffee's open gate, the lock and chain that normally secured it now lying in the snow.

Suspecting vandals, Rich pulled out his cell phone as he drove up the winding route to Jaffee's home. He noted fresh tire tracks in the snow and followed them to a small Ford Tempo parked near Jaffee's shed. The shed door stood ajar. Rich saw someone in the driver's seat of the Ford and thought he glimpsed another figure dart into the forest adjacent to the property.

As he pulled his pickup in front of the car, Rich's eyes caught 11:45 on the dashboard clock. He called 911, but when the call didn't connect, he realized he was out of cell range. Irritated, he left his phone on the seat of the truck, cautiously stepped out, and approached the driver's side of the car. He saw the driver raise both hands in surrender, but remained wary lest the driver pull out a weapon. This was, after all, Montana, where nearly everyone packed all manner of pistols, rifles, and knives.

Rich knew no one should be at Jaffee's house, especially late on Christmas night. The driver squinted from the truck's brighter headlights, a temporary blindness Rich counted on when he parked directly in front of the Ford. He fervently hoped to prevent the driver from aiming accurately if he had a gun, enabling Rich to disarm him before the fool really did something dangerous.

Rich assumed he'd interrupted a teenage prank, played by typical teenage knuckleheads, looking for something to do on yet another boring night in Whitehall. The county's crime rate was one of the lowest in the U.S. and mostly involved DUIs, neighbor disputes, and domestic violence. Certainly, few residents risked becoming a homicide victim. After all, that's why so many Californians moved to Kootenai County. It was such a safe place to live.

The driver, a teenager, took off his gloves, still with his hands raised, and said, "It's okay. I'm safe, sir."

"You have any guns on you?"

"No, sir," the young man replied politely.

"Do you understand you're trespassing on private property?"

"Yes, sir."

"What are you guys doing here?" Rich inquired, in part to see if the kid was alone, or if, as Rich suspected, an accomplice had run into the bushes.

"Just fooling around, sir," answered the driver.

"What's your name?"

"Joe Smith, sir."

Rich nearly laughed out loud. "Where's the other guy?" he queried instead.

"He's out by the gate where you came in," the teen responded, now looking nervous, but confirming Rich's suspicions.

"Looks to me like you boys are burglars and I caught you in the act. Give me the key to your ignition."

The kid handed over the key.

Rich asked for the kid's driver's license, while he looked through the back window of the car. He spotted a revolver lying on the passenger side of the back seat. Rich opened the rear door, climbed in the back, and grabbed the gun, all in one swift motion. He pointed the gun at the driver and asked him if it was loaded, to which the driver, now angry, replied tightly, "Yes, sir."

Rich, growing angrier himself, told the driver to hand over his wallet. The teen complied. Rich felt tired, cranky, and cold. He hadn't planned on standing in the snow with some snot-nosed, little burglar. His wool plaid shirt, jeans, and cowboy boots were insufficient protection against this kind of cold. He wanted to go home, crawl in bed next to Nina, and sleep.

Still holding the gun, although no longer aiming it at the kid in case it accidentally discharged, he looked at the driver's license in the wallet. He quickly realized he knew this young man, or at least knew about him. The driver was a local hero, winning race after race in various wheelchair competitions. This would-be burglar was the same kid who had overcome personal tragedy and turned his paralysis, at the age of 11, into a talent and inspiration for other disabled kids.

Before Rich could ask the many questions that crowded his exhausted brain, the local hero pulled out a blued-steel .22 revolver from its hidden spot between the front seats. He aimed it at Rich's heart and fired four rounds at point blank range, all before Rich ever hit the ground. As Rich fell, the other revolver he'd taken from the Ford's back seat bounced to the ground. The car's ignition key flew into the air as the contents of the driver's wallet spilled onto the snow.

Rich looked at his own chest, at the blood pouring forth, and heard his breath coming in gasps. The echo of his own screams reverberated through the silence of that clear, winter night, as he desperately tried to move away from the car. But the driver, hands steady, leaned out his window and shot Rich two more times, emptying his gun. Still Rich crawled, away from the Ford, away from his killer, away from his imminent death.

He made it four feet before he sensed the presence of another person. Whoever it was, Rich could hear the newcomer crying, then scream at the driver, "Nick, oh my God! What have you done? What have you done? We need to get help! Call an ambulance! Oh, my God, Nick!" Rich heard more sobbing and then heard the driver order his cohort to finish him off. The kid who was crying refused and begged the driver, "Just go! Let's just go and get help!"

Rich Truman felt cold seep through his Pendleton shirt. He remembered when he'd put it on earlier in the evening, wondering if it was 'dressy' enough for the Christmas party. He thought of Nina sleeping peacefully across the way, and of his children and grandchildren, safe and sound in their own homes. He felt blessed they weren't with him, that he and Nina had taken separate cars. He wondered how she would cope without him.

Rich looked up at the Ford Tempo as the driver pulled the car forward. The wheelchair racer slowly and deliberately drew yet another gun, sighted down the barrel, and shot Rich one last time, even as Rich put his hand in front of his chest in a feeble effort to stop the bullet.

* * *

A few hours later, Nina awoke to an empty place in the bed where Rich should have lain. And then she sensed, as only wives can sense after decades of marriage, that something was terribly wrong. She called their son-in-law, Paul, who jumped in his own truck and headed toward the Truman's house.

As Paul approached, he, too, saw headlights at the Jaffee place, but they shone from Rich's truck. He cautiously drove up the long driveway, unaware that a terrified youth watched from the forest just beside the road. When he reached Rich's truck, the first thing he saw was his father-in-law's body, covered in blood, laying in a pool of blood-soaked snow. Paul called 911, and his call, unlike Rich's, connected.

As Paul waited for the sheriffs and an ambulance, still unable to comprehend why Rich died, Nina approached from her home across the way. He tried to stop her, to protect her, but she knew, somehow she already knew, that Rich was dead. She sobbed as she knelt beside her husband and kissed him. She held his lifeless body and repeatedly shook her head, denying the obvious.

The love of her life had been murdered.

* * *

The slaying confounded local law enforcement. Deputies at the crime scene puzzled over two sets of footprints left in the snow, one large and one small, both running in circular, incongruous patterns throughout the area. The prints trailed as far as a mile away, where they abruptly ended at the road. The investigators matched the tire marks left in Dr. Jaffee's driveway to tracks left at numerous, unsolved, storage unit break-ins around the county.

Yet even after chasing down multiple leads, even after accusing Nina and her son of killing Rich for the insurance policy he left, the cops failed to identity Rich's killer. So, for the first time in recent memory, the people of Kootenai County were afraid of something other than grizzly bears.

They were afraid of each other.

Made in the USA
Monee, IL
16 June 2020